Every Chance AFTER

JESSICA SHERRY

Published by Jessica Sherry
Copyright © 2025 by Jessica Sherry

ISBN: 979-8-9887254-7-3 (ebook)
ISBN: 979-8-9887254-8-0 (paperback)
Printed/Published in the United States of America

Cover Design by Ink and Laurel

To all those who defy expectations.
Be who you are, not who they tell you to be.

And to Joe, my perfect nest.

Author's Note

Dear Reader,

Though the story you're about to read is a feel-good contemporary romance, it features realistic, wounded characters and sensitive subject matter that may upset some readers. If you'd rather not know any spoilers, ignore the next paragraph and skip to chapter one with my thanks for reading.

For those who prefer to know, this book deals with the following difficult topics: on page descriptions of a car accident (no deaths) and injuries as a direct result; on page descriptions of emergency medical procedures; discussions of infertility (directly related to main character); discussions about pregnancy, pregnancy loss, grief, abandonment, an absentee parent, manic-depressive/bipolar disorder, and mental health representation. There are mentions of divorce. There is profanity and moderate sexual content.

Please know that I did my best to handle these topics with respect and sensitivity. Thank you for reading.

CHAPTER ONE

Grady

MY TRUCK HUGS the curves along Lakeview Avenue, bringing me closer to the sanctity of my log cabin, where I'll spend the next forty-eight hours sleeping, fishing, and talking to no one but my dogs. I long for the quiet and feel it penetrating me already. The light between the trees hits my eyes like tiny starbursts, its heat collecting through the windshield. The snake-like road surrounding Seagrove Lake is usually fun to drive, especially under clear skies and a playful sun.

Not today. I need to get home.

It's Friday, early afternoon, and the roads are subdued, with most people at work. I *should* be at work. But the compromise I reached with my aunt and office manager, Elena, after our staff complained about our long days is every other Friday off.

"When you overwork, we all overwork," she argued. "Every other Friday is the least you can do."

My phone alights on its dashboard perch.

> Can you pick up a bakery order from Sunny's Beach Market & deliver it to Zoe's class by 2:30? 24 Valentine's cupcakes. Please, Grady. It's an emergency.

I huff, watching the ellipsis wave under her text.

You're off today, right?

Reasons to refuse Mom's "emergency" bombard me, starting with the fact that I've been up for thirty-some hours and spent last night in a barn two counties over delivering a breech colt—a still-born colt—leaving me in no mood for family errands.

Not that I'm ever in the mood. Why can't my niece's life-or-death cupcakes be handled by her parents or grandparents? Or another Tripp sibling? Or hell, a delivery service? Why does my day off become a family free-for-all of tasks when they all know I'd rather be home, alone, with the dogs?

They mean well—it's a ploy to get me *involved.*

Mom's last "emergency" trapped me at my nephew's soccer match, with single moms fishing for dates at one ear and pet owners looking for free advice at the other. It creates an unwelcome preda-tor-versus-prey vibe, making me the helpless, irritated bunny in such situations. As I explained to Mom in a huff before finally leaving, "I prefer involvement at a distance."

Or not to get involved at all, if I'm honest. I love my family. I'm there for my family. But I need boundaries. If I'm the cupcake delivery boy today, what will that mean for tomorrow?

I groan, my grip on the steering wheel tightening as I imagine myself as Mom's substitute pickleball partner or Zach's soccer team's gator-costumed mascot. In a small town like Seagrove, horrifying annoyances are limitless.

Still, my valid arguments fade behind lazy resignation. It's easier not to argue.

I voice-answer with a terse

fine

But it'll be a drop-off situation, done *begrudgingly.* No getting suckered into conversations about Fluffy's mysterious drooling prob-lem. Or talks with single teachers over Seagrove's very absent nightlife. I'll limit myself to four words: *Here are Zoe's cupcakes.* And maybe a "Hey, Zoe," if she notices I'm there.

The afternoon sun heats the interior of my truck's cab, softening my irritation with quiet warmth, and my mind slips back to the colt.

Sometimes, nothing can be done. No matter how hard you try. No matter how much you hope, pray, bargain, work, or want a different outcome, certain things cannot be altered. Or made better. Hell, or even made sensical. Life is just shitty like that. It's a universal truth that exhausts and angers me.

But I was in a shit mood before the colt. I'm always in a mood, like general irritation is my default response to every situation this town and my family offer me. Even after two years, I can't shake it.

Afternoon light flickers through the trees, making me blink. The truck's warning system alerts me as I drift over the middle lines.

I correct myself, sitting more upright and fisting the steering wheel. I crack the window, letting in the crisp chill of February. I turn the radio up, and Chappell Roan's voice mixes with the wind. The upbeat melody of "Good Luck, Babe" fills the interior. *"You'd have to stop the world just to stop the feeling."*

I huff—there seems to be no stop to my world. I have thirty minutes to get home, let the dogs out, and complete Mom's errand. It'll get done, and then I'll retreat into a weekend-long solitary-confinement.

But damn, I'm tired. My thoughts drift to last weekend and my few hours fishing on the dock Sunday afternoon. I fell asleep in the Adirondack chair and woke to the sound of my rod slipping from my hands into the water. I spent the next hour debating whether to risk the lake's alligator population for the rod or lose it forever.

Gators are less active in winter, I remembered, diving into the icy lake. Besides, I'd dealt with far more difficult things since returning to my hometown.

Losses no one understands, not that I ever talk about them.

Then, nearly losing my father.

Losing myself.

That same drowning sensation envelopes me. The quiet. The dark. Sinking into it. I go deeper, trying to find that damn rod.

Disaster only takes a second. One stupid, ridiculous, devastating second. Disaster can happen with one mistake. The heavy droop of my eyelids, my arms going slack, and tension evaporating with the gentle sinking of my head as my body overrules me. *"Good luck, babe! Well, good luck, babe, you'll have to...."*

Have to get home... *Have to stop the world just to stop the feeling...* Whack! My head spins into a vicious pillow fight between my brothers and me. Colin's pillow side-swipes my face, followed by Gil's weaker attempt at my side and Luke's attack from the other. *Fucking assholes! Watch for Marigold!*

Is that her? Screaming?

The music vanishes discordantly behind a deafening collision. I choke awake, my head snapping forward and then back. Not pillows. Airbags. The truck's alarms blare under screeching tires as my boots slam against the brakes. I jerk the steering wheel behind the airbag, but it's too late. No control. *Sometimes, nothing can be done.* The truck careens, zigzagging across the road and twisting to a perpendicular end mid-road, facing the wrong direction.

The world stops.

Shoving the bags away from me, I blink repeatedly. *Fucking hell, what just happened?*

I move my extremities and check myself over. *I'm okay. I think I'm okay.* But my first relieved breath is cut off in a devastating glance up. Through the shattered windshield and the steam jettisoning from the bent hood, I barely make out another car, a blue orb, shoved off the road like a discarded matchbox toy in the tree-lined ditch.

I've hit someone. I've fucking hit someone!

Disoriented but functioning, I wrench my door open and emerge on wobbly legs. Glass crunches under my rubber boots as I stumble toward the other car. Dizziness threatens to overwhelm me, making me slow. But soon, I refocus as my brain processes the sight yards away from me—a mangled car cupped by trees like a fallen nest.

I did this. This is my fault.

I move toward the wreckage, boots dragging over glass and my vision clearing. An airbag deflates. A door screeches open. A red-haired woman stumbles out. Heels. White lace. Blood.

Is that a wedding dress? Is that a... knife?

A debilitating second passes as I close the distance between us.

It's a fucking nightmare. It *has* to be. Any second, Colin will whack me with a pillow again. Or the dogs will bark. Anything to shake me from the senselessness of what I'm seeing—a bride stepping from a car wreck with a pearl-handled knife jutting from her lower gut.

It can't be real.

She doesn't think so, either. Frightened and stunned, her eyes go from mine to the knife plunged almost sideways into her abdomen. In eerie disbelief, she seems to assess the situation, grabs the handle, and yanks the knife out, dropping it with a shaking hand. Now, a step away from her, it clinks against the concrete between us, joining her chilling moan at the fresh pain.

It's real.

Blood pours through her delicate fingers as she tries to stay upright. She wobbles on her white, blood-stained heels before they twist under her, and she falls.

I catch her, my arms reacting before I tell them to. We drift downward like feathers caught together in the wind.

Easing her against the glass-covered pavement, her red hair sprays fan-like behind her.

This is my fault. She's bleeding because of me.

Bleeding heavily *because of me.* The red inkblot around her midsection spreads over her white dress alarmingly fast.

"I... I'm sorry," I choke, head still spinning, "I'm sorry. What can I—"

"He forgot the cake knife. It kept sliding across the seat, so I put it..." Her voice trails into a pained grunt, and she gulps for air.

"Breathe. Just breathe." The words shuffle out from another memory—me calming Gil during a panic attack. "I'm here. I-I can help. I-I have to get my phone."

"Stay with her," a familiar voice orders gruffly behind me. "Ambulance is on its way."

"How long?"

A beat passes. "Twelve to fourteen minutes."

I spare a glance at the looming shadow—my fucking Uncle Wade. The universe is shitting all over me today. Even so, my head stops spinning, as if Wade's presence jerked the needle off the skipping record.

"Do what needs to be done," he barks, focusing me further.

"Okay. Get my med bag in the truck. Backseat. Paper towels. And stop blocking my light."

Sunlight breaks through when he moves.

I grip her soft wrist—it feels light, like a rose in my palm. Her pulse is weak and thready.

Fuck. The knife impaled her on impact, driven in by the force. What happened comes into focus, not that it makes it any better—it's still *my* fault.

"Tell us what you need, son." The second voice is familiar from my childhood—Wade's friend, Ed Christie, who always goes by Christie.

My brain resets. *Treat the patient.*

"Sanitizer or alcohol!" I say frantically.

"This do?" He hands me a flask from his pocket. "Vodka."

I snatch it and liberally pour it over my hands before pressing tightly against her stomach wound. Her blood feels hot and sticky, slightly steaming in the cold air and matching her strained breath clouds. She gulps under my strength, but I must slow her bleeding.

"Elevate her feet," I order Christie.

He stumbles over, plops to the pavement, and eases her legs into the lap of his stained jeans with surprising gentleness for a large man.

Finding the tear in her dress, I rip it open to eye the three-inch wound just below and to the side of her navel. Small, but gushing. She might go into hypovolemic shock and die from exsanguination.

Bottom line—she doesn't have twelve to fourteen minutes.

I try to think. Chimpanzees are the closest to human anatomy—not that I studied exotics much in vet school. But I did study pigs, and they're a close second. Judging from the bloody knife nearby, it penetrated a solid four inches, likely damaging her large and small intestines, at least. Her internal iliac artery must be punctured, perhaps uterine, too.

If I don't stop the bleeding, she'll die.

Right here. She'll die because of me.

In my frenzied deliberation over how best to help her, her delicate hand weakly grips mine, and the world seems to stop again.

"Don't look so glum, chum. You're doing your best."

For the first time, I *see* her, and her words, even her smile, feel like another devastating impact. She's young. Beautiful. Her too-long, natural red hair stands out, but so do her intense features—freckles, full pink lips, and a determined chin. Her sapphire eyes catch mine, holding me prisoner. *What the hell? Is she cheering me up?*

"What's your name?" I ask to get her talking.

"That's Marnie," Christie answers with a proud twang like this is a quiz he's hoping to score well on. *Idiot.* "She works at Sunny's."

"Shut up, I'm asking *her*," I bark. "Are you aware of what's happening?"

She sputters softly, "Car accident on my wedding day. Check."

"Marnie. What's that short for?"

"Marina." Her voice is faint like she's passing into another room.

"Full name?" I demand.

"Marina Ann Strange, age twenty-four. Nope, twenty-five. Today's my birthday," she manages between wincing. "I'm lucid."

"Aw, a Valentine's baby?" Christie coos.

She manages a weak smirk. "It's unlucky."

"Can't argue with that," he chuckles.

Though relieved at her lucidity, I know it won't last. "Allergies? Medical conditions?"

"Nope. Neither."

"Good," I say as her eyelids flutter. "Don't fall asleep. Keep your eyes on me. Um, I'm Tripp. Grady Tripp."

"Can't walk down the street around here without tripping over a Tripp," she chuckles raggedly.

"My parents were... prolific."

Uncle Wade groans with irritation as my leather satchel drops beside me, and he unwraps a new roll of paper towels salvaged from my truck.

Her lips edge into a wan smile. *How is she smiling?* She must be in shock. Time is getting away from me. Blood pools around her. I feel her weakening as if she's liquifying and sinking into the earth, soon to be lost. A beached jellyfish, evaporating. My mind races. I've been in life-or-death situations like this thousands of times with animals, even once with a person. But my confidence puddles on the concrete with her blood. She'd already be sutured and in recovery if she were a dog.

Same rules apply. You're a doctor. Stabilize the patient.

I apply pressure to the wound with wadded paper towels. *I let this happen. Let myself get this tired.*

Being the only farm vet for fifty miles in a rural area means I'm always on call. It's not like I can turn down breech colts to have me-time. Mom's said it for months. *You're working yourself to death, Grady.*

But what else can I do?

"Marina, look at me," I order. Her eyes peel open wide, and she nods.

"I won't make it." A slight divot between her furrowed brows for the first time reveals her distress.

I feel it, too. Fear for this woman, this stranger, multiplies with each passing second that help isn't here, leaden weights against my chest. "Shut up. You'll make it."

"To the wedding," she mumbles.

"Oh, hell no. You're not making that. Sorry, darling." *Darling?* There's a word I never say.

"I'll miss the wedding," she breathes like she's reporting the news back to herself.

"Stay with me, Marina. You're all that matters now... Um, who's the lucky guy, huh?"

"Ashe."

"Sullivan?" The first thing that comes to mind is *mama's boy*, but it's unfair. I don't know Ashe well. We weren't in school together, but he probably shared a grade with one of my siblings. Even so, everyone knows Sunny's Beach Market and the close-knit family that owns it, especially his intimidating mother, Cora, who heads the family and the business. "Well, I'd say you dodged a bullet, but it doesn't exactly fit."

Pain tarnishes her small laugh. She grimaces before tears slip from her eyes and run into her hair.

Wade extracts gloves from the bag beside me.

"Put these on," he orders, taking over and applying pressure to the paper towel mound.

I do as he says, first sanitizing my hands and further assessing her.

The bleeding isn't slowing enough. She goes ghost-pale, her eyelids fluttering. Her pulse grows weaker with each passing second.

I push the towels away and pour water over her wound. Then, taking a breath, I ease my fingers inside as gently as possible. She cries out, writhing but trying to stay still. I feel along her inner cavity, through skin and muscle, pushing through the damage until I source the main bleed. I pinch the wiry artery between my thumb and forefinger.

"Eyes open," I snap when I see her slipping.

"Sorry," she startles. "I'm trying."

"I know. It'll be okay," I say, knowing she must be in incredible pain.

Her lips curl again slightly. "Really? I'll be okay? Or is that just something people say?" She catches my eyes in hers, her brow creasing like she has experience with deceitful pleasantries. "Please, only the truth."

"Truth only, huh?"

"Nothing but. That's our policy," she huffs out, tears slipping.

"Truth is, he doesn't know," Wade blurts in a strange show of familial support.

Christie shifts against Marina's feet, gently adjusting her. "You're just a young thing. Pretty, too. You'll be fine."

She stares at me, waiting for my answer, as if the other two aren't there. Or she doesn't see them. And it's just us living this nightmare together.

"Fine. You have a nicked artery. I'm holding the bleed... but, truth is, I don't know if you'll be okay. Your life will teeter on ifs for the near future. *If* this is the only bleed. *If* the ambulance arrives in time. *If* we get to the hospital. *If* treatment is quick and successful... *if* there's no infection, no adverse effects of medication or anesthesia, no traumatic brain injury. It's all in the ifs."

She snickers weakly. "Sounds like every day."

"No. Worse than every day. We're in trouble here. How long?" I shout at Wade.

He repeats my question with the phone still perched against his scruffy face. "Five minutes."

A sigh pushes from me, taking hope with it. *Fuck. Fuck. Fuck.*

Her hand falls weakly on my upper arm, and through labored breathing, she says, "Tripp. Grady Tripp. It's okay. *Truthfully.*"

"No. It isn't." With her blood pumping, barely, through my fingertips, I shake my head, alarmed with fear and other feelings I haven't dared entertain for the longest time. I'm nearly over-whelmed with them, like a stampede takes a run at my heart, led strongly by guilt. "I fucked up, Marina. No matter what we do, every chance after this could go either way. But I promise I'll be here as long as you need me, doing everything possible for you."

With a shuddering breath, she says, "Okay, Grady."

I clear my throat to fight my emotional surge and try to bring levity to our dire situation. "The dress is a goner, but it can't be a white wedding with another man inside you, anyway."

"Eep," she blurts out in a pained laugh. "A dirty joke?"

Her sweet, bubbly laugh shocks me almost as much as the *eep*. Is that what the kids say these days? Twenty-somethings like her feel like an entirely different culture to me at thirty-six.

"Whatever gets you smiling."

Her chest rises and falls in a sigh, and she smiles again at my words.

Putting her at ease clashes with my usual bedside manner. I don't spout jokes (even bad ones) or offer comfort. I do my job, check off my obligations, and leave, desperate not to get involved. Aunt Elena calls me off-putting. My little sister Marigold fictionalized me as Shadow Man in her graphic novels.

But there's truth in it. Two years ago, I left my life and have been living an out-of-body experience since. I work, deal with my family, and go home. The only things I look forward to are my dogs and my bed. Animals are much easier to tolerate than people.

But here, now, I don't matter. There's *her*. She *needs* me.

"You're funny," she breathes, her voice strained.

"No, I'm not." Eyeing the blood still streaming through my fingers, I turn to Wade. "Find me a hemostat clamp—um, small scissors with flat tips that lock into place. I think there's a second bleed."

"You seem to know what you're doing," she mutters.

"Not really. I'm a vet."

She smirks. "That explains the smell."

I grimace, nose-blind to it. Still, in my overalls and t-shirt, it's no wonder she notices I stink of horses. "Sorry. Long night."

"No apologies. I like it. It's gentle, earthy," she whimpers. "I'm glad you're here."

The guy who ran you off the road and ruined your wedding day? The man who maybe killed you?

"Yeah, um, me, too," I say because, weirdly, it's true.

"Triscuit's been scratching her ears lately," she sputters faintly.

"What's Triscuit... besides a cracker?"

"A cat. I have three." Pain etches her face, and her eyes flicker again.

"Marina! Stay awake for me, and I'll do a house call," I say as if I can bribe her into staying alive. I don't know what else to do.

"Keep talking to her, Tripp," Christie says, still holding her legs in his lap.

"Here." Wade slaps the clamp into my hand.

"Douse it in the vodka," I order.

He spills what's left of Christie's flask onto the device and hands it over.

I say, "Marina, tell me more about your cats."

Her mouth opens, but she doesn't speak.

Hovering over her, her blood pumping lightly against my fingertips, I apply the clamp, wedging it tightly inside her as she yelps in agony. There's no way I'll be able to source the second bleed—not without causing her unbearable pain and probably more damage.

Fuck. Fuck. Fuck.

"I'm sorry, Marina. So sorry," I cry out the words, though I know they don't matter. With the clamp holding the bleed, I shift around to her head, easing her into my lap. "Wade, keep applying pressure."

He does as instructed, gently pressing more paper towels against the area around the clamp.

Her eyes blink slowly as she watches me. She looks eerily peaceful, lying against my thigh—desperately peaceful—and I hate it.

"Stay with me, Marina." I hold her against my chest and find her hand. It's disturbingly clammy as I search for her pulse. Her skin drains of color. Even her freckles go pale. Her hand curls into mine, soft and cold. I hold it gently. "Please," I beg. "Don't leave me."

"Tripp. Grady Tripp." She smiles, blue eyes glassy and drooping like flower petals weighed down with rain. "You always seem so sad. Don't be sad. It's like you have a million thoughts but no one to tell them to."

My throat closes like her words are allergens. "Um, not true." My voice cracks with fear and sadness. If I lose her, I'll lose me, too, even if I'm still here. "Um, my dogs are excellent listeners."

She laughs, but it comes out garbled. I expect blood to trickle from her lips. *She's dying. She's dying, and I killed her.*

"Hang on for me," I beg, as police cars position around the accident and the ambulance finally appears. "Marina, please."

She gives me a look like she wants to stay, but her fingers go limp inside mine, and her eyes close, shutting me out.

CHAPTER TWO

Marnie

"MARINA, STAY WITH ME."

His words snap me awake again.

The sky behind him is the color of a Morpho butterfly—bright blue, cloudless, beautiful. It's the perfect day. *Why did it have to be so perfect?* I've never seen a Morpho butterfly in person, but Wren Christie, my cashier protégé at Sunny's Beach Market, has a tattoo of one on her left calf. Their blue wings are scaled in real life, making them iridescent. They shimmer at different angles, depending on how you look at them.

Tattoos adorn the arms of the man hovering over me, but he moves so quickly that it's hard to make them out. A thick, dark line of pine trees on his right forearm is all I can decipher. It matches the tree-tops overhead, like a black-and-white comic book version of the real thing. Sun glimmers through their spiky branches like a disco ball, flickering softly in my eyes with an easy breeze.

It's so incredibly peaceful here. I slip into the peacefulness, wanting so badly to stay there. Let it take me.

"Marina!"

I gasp, and my breath clouds over my face. *Why am I so cold?* A warm blanket settles on my belly. It's blood, I realize achingly.

Oh, it hurts. I feel hole-punched. Gutted. Sliced.

I shouldn't be here. Unlucky. Cursed. Fated to be alone. Mom was right.

No, Marnie. Positive thoughts only.

Don't think about the pain.

Look for something good.

His eyes match the sky, the butterfly.

"I like your eyes." My voice doesn't sound like mine. There's no energy or cheer behind my words—two things I'm rarely without. I've been compared to Buddy the Elf, only every day is *my* Christmas, and my workshop is Sunny's Beach Market.

"I like your hair," he says, moving with me toward the ambulance.

I get that a lot—less than two percent of people have naturally red hair.

"It's a mutation," I sputter, but I don't think he hears me. That was the second fact Mom taught me about redheads. After a particularly rough day in kindergarten, she followed, "You're special, honey," with, "You have a gene mutation," and I remember being unable to sleep that night over fears that my classmates would google that tease-worthy tidbit. The world doesn't go easy on differences—an irony since we all have them.

I can't imagine what it looks like now. Mel worked so hard on it.

My mind drifts from the chaos around me to hours ago when I found Mel Moore on my porch carrying her 80s-style makeup Caboodle and an oversized bright red purse with a hair straightener peeking out. Seeing her was, for once, a relief. On her wedding day, a bride should have an entourage of old friends and family fussing over her, but I didn't. This only made my small house feel quiet and empty. So, in the throes of my lonely morning, I reminded myself—it will never be like this again after today.

After today, I'll have a family.

After today, I'll *belong* to someone.

Mel interrupted my hopeful mutterings and a long-winded game of pretend in front of my full-length mirror.

"This is my husband, Ashe."

"This is Marnie, my partner, my lover, my best friend, my wife," said in my deep-man-voice.

I giggled over my game, remembering the sweet satisfaction I felt when he first introduced me as his girlfriend at a ritzy charity event —that's how I knew I *was* his girlfriend. I couldn't wait to hear him call me his *wife.*

When I opened the door to Mel, I was blushing. Gawking, too— seeing Mel was a surprise. We aren't exactly friends.

"Mel, hi. What're you doing here?"

"What's it look like?" she bit back, eyes rolling like two bowling balls released down the lane at the same time. If she were a dog, she'd be a bulldog, gruff but warm under all those layers—not that I've ever gotten close to the warm parts. But she was good to my mother and let me sweep up around her salon for extra money some- times when I was a teen. "It's your wedding day, Marnie. Your mom would haunt me if I let you DIY it."

My heart palpitated and sped up, hearing those words. "This isn't your terrible way of telling me she's dead, right?"

"No, but I see your curse ideas are alive and well," she scoffed. "Why agree to a wedding on your birthday if you think you're cursed?"

"Because... it's what Ashe wanted."

"Marina," Grady's voice stirs me awake again—no one ever calls me by my full first name. It's always Marnie. But I like hearing him say it. It makes me feel important. We're in the ambulance now, and it bounces down the road. It's weird being in a vehicle without seeing the outside. I crave a window. My plants. My cats. "Marina."

I fixate on his crystal eyes to redirect my brain away from the pain. He's handsome, in a rough and rugged way, like he was once a kid who climbed trees rather than played video games. His heavy five o'clock shadow covers strong cheekbones and a dimpled chin— Tripp family traits—and matches his buzz-cut hairstyle—short, dark, but patchy with dirt and salted with grays. He's older, mid- thirties at least. Worry creases his forehead, but small starbursts around his eyes tell me he's no stranger to laughter.

He's not laughing now. He looks serious, even distraught. He listens to the paramedic, calling out numbers and words that don't make sense. Grady's worry lines deepen with the information, and this predicament is scary enough without knowing my heartbeat is *thready*, whatever that means.

Thready like threadbare? Tattered? Coming undone? Falling apart? I suddenly feel like a torn sweater, stringy and discarded, left forgotten on a heap in the back of the closet.

No, Marnie, no. Good thoughts only. No frowns, no fears, no tears.

Grady's hand is no longer hooked to my insides, thank goodness —that felt so embarrassing. A cold metal thing sticks out from my belly instead, pinning me together. Best not to think about that. He holds my free hand in both of his beside me, warming me like a glove, and our hands stick together from the blood residue. My French manicure, white with light gold sparkles, curls around Grady's sun-browned, dirty hands, making my skin look paler than usual. It's a ghost hand holding onto a live one.

"This'll pinch a bit," says the paramedic.

Grady grips my hand tighter, fixing my attention. "So, there's Triscuit. Tell me about your other cats."

"Hershey," I whisper against the oxygen mask, holding back a whimper as a needle punctures my arm.

"It's just the IV. You'll feel better with fluids and meds." He leans closer, nearly to my ear. "Let me guess. Black cat?"

"Long-haired. And my tabby, Sunkist. Rescues. From the dumpster behind Sunny's."

"Triscuit, Sunkist, and Hershey—sweet." His lips edge into a side-smile. "Surprised we haven't met before."

I use a Wilmington vet who offers free shots, spaying, and neutering for newly homed stray cats, but I keep that a secret to avoid offending him.

Even so, I've seen Grady Tripp before. Everyone knows the Tripps. But Grady gets the most attention in gossip circles, first for being the eldest, most handsome, and most mysterious brother, but a close second for his unfriendliness. He's known as Grouchy Tripp. He left Seagrove and his father's generous offer to take over Tripp Family Farm while working as the town's only vet for a wife and swanky practice in Charlotte, but returned two years ago with neither and has all but taken over his dad's farm, anyway.

Sirens echo, muffled by the oxygen hissing and the ambulance rattling. My abdomen rips with pain, like I'm an acupuncturist's practice dummy, and he's getting it very, *very* wrong. Lightheadedness brings bile rising in my throat.

"I'm sorry," I blurt, "but I might be sick."

The paramedic raises my mask and holds a plastic tub to my face as I roll gingerly to my side. *God, it hurts.*

Nothing comes out, but fresh agony surges across my midsection for the effort. "Sorry," I manage again.

"No apologies. It's like I tell my brothers," he says. "A body must what a body must."

Grady's voice pulls me from my dry-heaving, and I picture his close-knit family—him with his four brothers, hocking loogies or farting or whatever gross things boys do when they're together. I've never had that. Even Ashe and I still keep those things private—proper decorum, Cora calls it.

Now, with my guts open and stomach churning, I wonder what she'd think of me. Or if you can really claim to belong to someone without being privy to their farts and vomit and whatever else.

Oh, my God! Why am I thinking about that right now? Is this delirium?

He eases me back on the gurney, dabs my face with a towel, and replaces the oxygen mask. "Just breathe, okay? You're safe. You're in good hands. Everything's okay. Breathe."

"Truth?"

"Truth. That's our deal."

He's surprisingly gentle and comforting for someone so gruff—something I once experienced firsthand, though he clearly doesn't remember. I do as he says. *Relax, Marnie. What's done can't be undone.* But at the mercy of my circumstances, it's impossible to calm down. I'm reminded of times with Mom, when I felt helpless and desperate. The more I think about it...

Missing my wedding.

Upsetting Ashe and his family.

Disappointing our guests.

The money lost on food and flowers.

My dress. Oh, my dress.

The honeymoon. We're supposed to leave Sunday morning.

... the worse I feel, like the knife hit my heart, too, cutting it into pieces. Tears slip from my eyes—I *never* cry. *Never.* It's the life code I adopted at fifteen—*no frowns, no fears, no tears.* But aches and a sharp gnawing burn my midsection. Excruciating pain is the one understandable exception to my no-tears rule.

I got stabbed. I could die.

I crumble a little more, imagining leaving this earth with a stranger holding my hand. The pastel card I left unopened on my kitchen table haunts me now. I knew it was from her—her curvy handwriting gave it away. She never does anything without drama. Should I have opened it? Somehow, I imagined that tearing open that envelope would set off her Marnie-spidey senses, and she'd show up in one of her classic states (she called them her upsies and downsies) and ruin everything. Now, the day's ruined anyway, and I wish she were here, freaking out and making a fuss.

Sometimes, it feels good to be fussed over.

Grady barks at the paramedic to do something—I don't understand what. She shakes her head and rattles off numbers as they watch the monitor beside me. Best not to know. His fear tells me everything, anyway.

His sad eyes fall back to me, and his voice cracks when he says, "Marina, I'm so sorry. What can I do?"

I've never seen someone more distressed or vulnerable, not with me. His dirty face looks shadowed with guilt. *Was it his fault?*

In the same breath, I know it doesn't matter. Unlucky. Cursed. Alone. Life changes as easily as the wind blows, and no one can stop it.

"No apologies. I mean it. Life must what life must."

He manages a pained chuckle, and a tear falls down his scruffy cheek.

My grip tightens on his. "No matter what. It's okay. Thanks for holding my hand."

"Anytime." He chokes up, almost surprised by it, like he's unaccustomed to feeling. We're probably both in shock—I know I am. He's not the hand-holding type, and, until now, I've never been one to need it.

But today, everything's different.

Bad feelings swirl again. "I feel woozy."

"That's normal. It's the pain meds," he says.

"We're five minutes out," the paramedic says. "They're prepping for surgery."

"Surgery?" I gasp. "I've never had surgery before."

"It'll be quick and painless. When you wake up, you'll be patched up, and Ashe and your family will be there. Can I call anyone for you?"

I shake my head. "Just Ashe. There's no one else."

In my agony, worries swarm me. I don't know what to expect from Ashe. Will he be angry over our failed wedding? Cora will be. Will he be disappointed in me? Upset? Or will he step up like the gallant knight I know he can be?

Or at least, I *think* he can be. It's difficult to say; we've never had hard times before. The most upset I've ever seen him was when the local newspaper, *The Seagrove Groove*, misspelled his name in our engagement announcement. *Ash* instead of *Ashe*. A misspelled name ranks pretty low on life's list of inevitable challenges.

Chances for chivalry and swoon-worthy heroism are sorely lacking these days. But maybe that's a good thing.

Sometimes, it amazes me—Ashe's life. He's never known poverty, grief, or illness. He's never had to find a job or question whether he'd go to college. He's got more stamps in his passport than anyone I know (our honeymoon will be my first). Even in high school, good grades and popularity came easily to him. It's one of the things I love about him—his pristine life. It's shiny and hopeful like the sun peeking out from behind rain clouds. Ashe has never known a truly bad day.

Until now.

The ambulance blares its sirens again, and the vehicle shifts to the right. My body starts to relax, as if it's forgotten the word *surgery* or the clamp poking my gut. The numbing effect overtakes me—I don't like how out-of-control this feels.

The ambulance slides to a squeaking stop, and chaos ensues. Doors swing open. The gurney is pulled out, and a team meets us. Hurried words are exchanged—I can't keep up. But Grady hops out with me and doesn't let go of my hand, as if crashing into each other has affixed us permanently.

What a funny thought—but true, regardless. He and I will always share this memory and our unique before-and-afters of the crash. We may be strangers. We may never speak again. But we will always have this.

I hear Mr. Frisk's monotone voice over the PA system, reporting that ferns are buy one, get one this week at Sunny's, but I know I'm not there. My thoughts drift to strange places, strange, even for me.

Playing *The Game of Life* by candlelight, Mom telling me that the power company messed up, *again,* (it took over ten years for me to learn that electric companies don't make mistakes), and her joyfully choosing the life path over the family path. She'd also complained about being forced to get married. Though I agree with her now, her statement felt bitter when I was twelve.

"Don't you want a bigger family?" I asked her.

"That just means more people to disappoint you."

Fluorescent lights flicker overhead, bringing me back to Grady as he hovers over me, and I sputter, "I thought I'd get a family today."

"Eh, they're overrated. Trust me," he quips with a weak shrug.

His words mesh with Mom's, and my internal light blinks before going dark.

CHAPTER THREE

Grady

THE NURSE STOPS me from entering through the wide double doors leading to the surgical department. Marina's hand slips from mine like warm water.

"Are you family?" the nurse asks, drawing my eyes away from the glass slits in the doors as Marina's red hair vanishes around a corner. The nurse wears a headband with extended springing hearts—an annoying nod to Valentine's Day.

"Yes," I lie, knowing how this works.

The petite brunette reaches out in a consoling gesture, but seeing my dirty, blood-covered arm, rethinks it. "Come with me. You should clean up and start her paperwork."

She leads me through nondescript corridors and stations, all typical of hospital decor, bland and sterile. But flashes of red from Valentine's gifts catch my attention everywhere. Roses. Carnations. Balloons. It's weird, mixing celebratory tokens with sick and injured people. But it *is* a workplace.

It reminds me of how awkward it feels to lead clients into the clinic's cheery waiting room after losing a pet. But Aunt Elena always smiles and offers consoling words for them, a kind distraction.

The nurse pushes me into a unisex bathroom. "You'll want to look presentable when she wakes up," she says, closing the door.

I hold my bloody hands out in front of me. They're shaking... fucking shaking as adrenaline pulses through me. I move in front of the mirror and turn the water on. Running my hands and arms through the stream makes pink swirls in the drain. *Her* blood.

As it washes off me, tears run down my cheeks that I caused this, that I hurt her. Dealing with life's inevitable agonies is one thing. *Sometimes nothing can be done.* But *I* did this. She could die because of me. Two other times in my life, I've felt this scared about losing someone, but I've never felt this overwhelming misery over what I've done.

God, please let her be okay.

Please, save her. I'll do anything.

Marina, please be okay.

I've only prayed a handful of times—I don't know what good it does. But I have to do something. The last time I prayed was a week after I returned home when I found my father having a heart attack in the barn. He survived, barely.

That was bad. This is worse.

With Marina on a stainless steel table, undergoing surgery, it's like my heart's being ripped from my chest. I'm open, exposed, gutted. I don't even know this woman. And yet, her life suddenly matters more to me than anything.

I can't lose her. Not because of my Godzilla-sized guilt, wreaking its havoc over my mental city—that'll exist regardless. But simply because she doesn't deserve to be lost. Not to my stupidity. Not to some twist of fate or unconscionable bad luck. And certainly not on a day when all her dreams were meant to come true.

Goddamnit!

Hot steam rising and dancing across the mirror, I lean against the porcelain sink, staring at my reflection. I look like shit. My eyes are shaded from lack of sleep, cheeks drawn in, like old, weather-beaten skin stretched tightly over my skull with nothing in between. Grime from horse stalls wedges under my fingernails, and dark blood stains my coveralls, mostly hers. My forehead and neck are smeared with muck, and my hair looks darker from embedded field dust.

With trembling hands, I wash my face, neck, head, everything.

The nurse with the ridiculous headgear is right—I don't want her to see me like this when she wakes.

If she wakes.

If she wants to see me.

If I'll have the courage to see her.

All these ifs.

A stern knock breaks my thoughts. "Occupied," I bark.

"I have some clean clothes, if you want them."

A glance at my grungy, blood-stained coveralls confirms this is a good idea. Though ideal for tending to livestock on a farm, my dark blue and thick, mechanics-style work garb doesn't fit here, and the smell radiates from me in this small room—a pungent mix of horse sweat, hay, and manure.

I open the door and accept her generous offering with a calmer "Thanks."

The teal scrubs clash with my black-rubber paddock boots, not that it matters. I meet the nurse in the hall, and she leads me to a private waiting room.

She equips me with a clipboard and pen. "Fill this out as best you can. I'll be back with updates."

"Thank you," I mutter, regretting how I snapped at her.

I stare at the forms, surprised when I start filling in the blanks with what I learned at the accident.

Full name of patient... *Marina Ann Strange.*

Age and birthdate... *25, February 14, 2000.*

Allergies... *None.*

Medical conditions... *None.*

Employment... *Sunny's Beach Market.*

My handwriting is jagged, with my hands still trembling. I drop the clipboard into the empty seat next to me and bury my face in my hands.

Marina, please be okay.

I don't know how long I sit there. Maybe I drift off, repeating the same prayer. But I don't look up until I feel a firm hand grip my shoulder.

"Son?" My father's deep but gentle voice, his worn but friendly face, his large, sturdy frame all call to me at once.

I stand, falling into his outstretched arms. "Dad."

"Wade called. Got here as soon as I could. It's okay. It's all okay."

"No, it isn't." What's left of my strength melts into him, like I can't grip it any longer, and he's all that's holding me up.

He pats my back, hanging on while I confess, "I fell asleep, hit her, she's... she's hurt, Dad."

"It was an accident, Grady. Nothing more."

"No, it's my fault. She was supposed to get married today..."

My voice trails off. I haven't cried like this in years, not since losing... *I can't think about that now.* I feel small and devastated, wishing I could take her place, wishing I could rewind time and make better choices, go a different route, anything to have spared her this. Wearing comfortable scrubs against my father's nearly invincible shoulder, I feel like a child in pajamas, being consoled after a nightmare.

Only the bad dream is real.

"It's okay, Tripp," another voice cuts through, splintering my moment with Dad. "Wade and I are here for you, too."

"No, we're not." Wade shoves a paper bag at me. "Here's what we could salvage from your truck."

I eye the contents—a hoodie, my medical bag, odds and ends, and my phone. The screen is cracked, but it works.

"We brought Marnie's things," Christie chimes in. "Her phone. Her veil, though it's... how is she?"

"She's... I don't know."

"Cops'll be here soon," Wade says. "They'll have questions."

"They can wait," my father insists as I plop back into the nearest chair and run my hands over my fuzzy head. I plant my elbows on my knees, staving off a rising panic. *She has to be okay.*

"They don't take kindly to assholes who leave the scene of an accident," Wade says gruffly.

"What are you implying?" Dad returns, hands going hip-side.

"Stating facts, Mack. That's all."

"Yeah, you'd know all about cops and accidents."

"Look, I don't need this," Wade huffs.

"Stop fucking talking," I order. "No bullshit today. Please."

Dad glares at his wiry, unkempt brother like he wants to challenge him. His jaw twitches in a forced sigh. Then, he extends his hand. "Your help is appreciated, Wade."

"Just doing my civic fucking duty," he grunts, refusing the handshake. "Christie, let's get out of here."

"But, Wade, you promised we'd see how she is," Christie whines.

Harsh heel-clicks storm through the corridor. Cora Sullivan appears in the waiting room's large glass window, looking one way, then another, in privileged frustration as if the entire hospital should stop for her.

"Can someone tell us where to find Marnie Strange?" she calls out to no one in particular.

The nurse with the heart headband appears and directs her and the two tuxedoed men behind her into the waiting room. *Our* waiting room.

Cora enters wearing a long, dramatically sequined red evening gown that swishes and tinkles when she walks. Her husband, Wes, follows, head lowered and hands crossed at his waist. His red rose boutonnière hangs crookedly on his lapel. He looks bored like he'd rather be home with a crossword.

Finally, Ashe bumbles in. His hair has been shellacked into an immovable brick on his head, but otherwise, he looks like I'd expect —distraught, frustrated, worried.

He's no longer the scrawny third baseman I vaguely remember from my brother, Marty's, high school team. He's still thin, lanky, like his Dad, but broader in the shoulders and his chin more defined. He flicks his hands at his wrists, anxious with energy he doesn't know what to do with.

"When can I see her?" He bounds around the nurse like a kid, trying to get an adult's attention.

"Soon. I'll check on her status and return with an update." She disappears down the hall.

Cora locks eyes on our group, narrowing her heavily made-up gaze. "Mack Tripp? What's your family doing here?"

"Grady was involved in the accident," my father answers.

I stand, cutting between the men around me. "I hit her. I fell asleep around a curve, and... I hit her."

Ashe's face goes from anxious to angry in a heartbeat. He looks unsurely at his mom before lunging in my direction. He bangs his knee against a chair, clearly hurting himself, but continues to his target.

I don't react. I deserve whatever this kid throws at me.

Only Wade steps in, catching Ashe's fist in his palm like a baseball. "You're upset. I get it. The Tripps are notorious for pissing people off. But, son, this isn't the time or place for that."

"Ashe, calm down," his mother chides. "Let the police handle him."

"I'm sorry," I offer weakly. "I didn't mean to... I'm sorry."

"If I might interject," Christie cuts in, moving between the two groups. Cora eyes his long, stringy gray hair and purple-painted fingernails like she might hiss at his gender nonconformity. "Grady hit her, but also saved her life. If not for his quick thinking, she would've bled out on Lakeview Avenue."

This news only makes Ashe more agitated. "Seriously? Bled out?"

"From the fancy knife in her lap. The impact drove it right into her. She almost died," Christie reports softly.

Ashe crumbles against his mom's bare shoulder in a fit of tears.

"Perhaps it's best to remain silent as we await news about *our* dear Marnie," Cora suggests.

"Christie, we're leaving. This place reeks of entitlement," Wade says, but neither moves.

I offer the Sullivans the clipboard and pen. "I didn't get very far with this."

Cora's head snaps toward her husband, already seated. "Wes, make yourself useful. Fill out Marnie's paperwork."

Her tone tenses my shoulders, but Wes doesn't seem bothered. He accepts the task and almost looks glad for the distraction.

A uniformed police officer enters the room, with Detective Jim

Watson behind. He's my uncle, married to my Aunt Elena. Jim's all-business demeanor silences the room.

"Make him take a breathalyzer," Ashe orders. "And a drug test. He should be arrested."

"Ashe's day is ruined. Do you have any idea what this wedding cost? Treat him the same as any other menace," Cora adds, wagging her red-tipped nails at me. "You cannot show him favoritism because he's your nephew."

Though confident that Uncle Jim will be fair, if not tougher on me, Cora's hypocrisy fills the room like a bad smell. She doesn't even try to hide her nepotism at Sunny's Beach Market—her husband handles the books, her son runs the store, and he's engaged to an employee working under him. It all feels wrong.

Or maybe I'm looking for somewhere to shift the blame.

With his typical blank-faced stoicism, Uncle Jim bypasses their requests with a simple, "I'm sorry for your distress. Any news on Marnie?"

"Not yet," Cora says, her voice cracking.

"She's in everyone's thoughts and prayers." He lays a gentle hand on Ashe's back before moving toward us.

He eyes Wade and Dad with a cocked brow, probably surprised to see they haven't come to blows yet. It's the first time they've been in the same room together in years.

"Wade. Mack. Christie," he lists, nodding to each before landing on me. "Grady, we need to talk."

"Whatever you need."

"Let's talk down the hall," he says, motioning toward the door.

Cora and Ashe watch from the window while the officer gives me a breathalyzer test. It's negative. A nurse takes my blood, and I answer his questions until the nurse from earlier reappears, her bobbing heart headband gone. She goes to the waiting room doorway, clearing her throat for the room's attention.

"Miss Strange is out of surgery," she says, her voice monotone. "We're moving her from recovery into a private room now. The doctor—"

"She's okay?" Ashe cuts in, relief sweeping over his face.

"She's still recovering but lucid," she says quickly, and the room lets out a collective sigh as if that's an affirmative. All it means is that she survived surgery—a definite relief, but not a complete answer. My uneasy gut twists with more discomfort, especially when she says, "The doctor is speaking to her now, and she's asking for Ashe?"

"That's me," Ashe says, like he's surprised. "I want to see her."

Cora lines up behind him, as if that means her, too. Then, Wes, looking unsure, rises from his chair, hugging the clipboard, and joins his wife, which I imagine is his usual modus operandi.

The nurse glances between the three faces. "You're her family?"

"Yes, we're her family," Cora says with certainty, "and we need to see her."

She motions for the threesome to follow.

"I need a bathroom," I tell Jim, who nods before re-entering the waiting room.

Having navigated these corridors once before, when Dad had his emergency surgery after his heart attack, it comes back to me as I follow them at a distance. I'd gone with him in the ambulance, so I'd been there when he woke up, groggy and confused. But when his world made sense again, he gave me his widest smile, gripping my hand with his thick, calloused fingers.

"Son, I'm sorry I put you through that, but I'm glad you were there. You saved my life," he said, tears budding in the corners of his heavy-lidded eyes. "It's good having you home."

Home. The word felt strange when he said it. Sure, Seagrove is where I grew up, and Tripp Family Farm is like a member of the family. But returning to it after my life blew up didn't feel like coming home at all. It felt like a penance.

Then.

Now.

The nurse escorts them into a room with the word *Strange* scribbled on an exterior whiteboard. Wes enters last and doesn't bother closing the door. I hover against the wall, just outside, desperate to see her and know she's okay.

Please, let her be okay.

I peek through the opening, over their shoulders, and between their bodies.

I remember the crowded hospital room Dad was in after his surgery. Despite the traumatic circumstances that landed him there, the room was filled with laughter, love, and relief, and everyone felt happy seeing his smile and hearing him crack jokes.

There's none of that here. There's only tension and anxiety.

Another sickening feeling sweeps me when I see her—copper hair against the white pillow, her face pale, her arm and chest wired with tubes and monitors. Her wedding dress is gone, surely filling a biohazard bag by now, and the usual hospital garb swallows her like a fallen tent. Her make-up has been washed away, revealing a dusting of freckles under her eyes. She looks young, weak, and pained, but Ashe's arrival brings a wide smile, lighting her up.

"Marnie," he cries out, going to her side. "Are you okay?"

"Getting there. Sorry about the wedding."

"It's okay. We'll figure it out."

Then, he must kiss or embrace her because she says, "Easy, Ashe."

"Oh, sorry, babe."

"Doctor, this is my fiancé, Ashe." Her voice sounds tired but still cheery somehow. "And his parents, Cora and Wes."

"Miss Strange—"

"Oh, call me Marnie, please."

"Marnie, I want to review your surgery and the extent of your injuries—*private* medical information. It might be best for everyone to wait outside."

"It's fine. They're the only family I've got," she responds with forced cheer.

I peek around the corner to see the white-coated doctor sitting on a rolling stool beside her, tablet in hand. In my experience, doctors don't hang out with patients after surgeries. They check in, read charts, and disappear.

Hell, that's what I do.

Unless there's a problem.

I practically plaster myself to the wall, listening by the door. It's wrong, *I know.* But I must know she's alright to minimize the agony over what I've done. If she's fine, it's a wrecked car and a wedding to reschedule—we all move on.

If she isn't... well, I have to know that, too.

With a gentle breath, the doctor says, "Surgery went well. You suffered damage to your large and small intestines, but we patched those easily. Your iliac artery was nearly severed. The paramedic said that someone at the scene applied a clamp?"

"Um, yeah. Tripp. Grady Tripp."

A pained smirk travels across my lips, and a tear slips down my cheek, hearing her say my name again, especially like that.

"He saved your life," the doctor reports.

I hate hearing that—I'm the villain here.

"He's also the asshole who hit her," Ashe scoffs, reading my mind. "So, she'll be okay?"

"The uterine artery was also damaged," the doctor continues, "and your uterus. We repaired the arteries, of course, but there was too much damage to the uterus. Irreparable damage, unfortunately. A hysterectomy was our only viable option."

No, no, no. My back slides against the wall until I crouch over the floor. My guilt compounds into a boulder on my shoulders, an imaginary world, heavy and untouchable—an existence that could've been hers and now never will be. *I did this to her.* I took away her choice. Her children, if she wanted them. Her family. The weight feels unbearable.

"I don't get it," Ashe says.

"Recovery from surgery will take several weeks. You have a nasty hip bruise to contend with. Barring any infection or complication, Marnie will make a full recovery. However—"

"I can't have kids," she says in a wildly unemotional tone. "No uterus means no kids."

"Oh, Ashe." Cora's voice trembles.

"What?" Ashe demands loudly. "Is this a sick joke? She comes in here for a car accident, and you're telling me she can't—"

"I shouldn't have had the knife in my lap," she says. "It slid around the passenger seat on the curves, and I wanted to keep it from falling into the cracks or on the floor. It was a dumb mistake. An accident. It's my fault."

"No, it's that asshole's fault for hitting you," Ashe corrects rightly.

"The hospital provides counseling services," the doctor offers, "or a Chaplain, if needed. The important thing is that she's going to be okay."

"Okay? She's not okay," Ashe argues. "She's…"

His voice trails like he can't finish his sentence. I wonder, briefly, what he would've said. *Broken. Defective. Unfixable.*

I peer around the door's edge to see him on his mother's shoulder again. Even worse, I see Marina. She isn't crying; she doesn't even seem sad. With her delicate fingers looped together at her stomach, twisting her engagement ring, she looks strangely content as she stares up at Ashe and his mom, consoling each other. Her face hints at an almost wanton expression—I think. I don't know this woman. Sure as hell don't understand why she isn't balling her eyes out or, at least, cursing, yelling, throwing shit across the room.

If this isn't a life-is-shit-moment, I don't know what it is.

But watching her watching them, I wonder if she feels left out of her own tragedy. *She* should be the one being consoled right now.

Not that I can offer her that. Or anything. I'm nothing but the man who did this to her.

Somehow, I find my legs and return to my father, nearly collapsing into his arms again. Wade and Christie are gone. Jim and his officer await their turn with Marina, dutifully holding the bag with her salvaged things—the shattered and torn remains of the devastation I caused.

Regret and guilt swirl in my head, making me dizzy. I don't deserve to take comfort in my father while Marina lies there, no one holding her. *Why is no one holding her?*

Into Dad's shoulder, I whisper, "She can't have kids, Dad. She'll recover, but she can't have kids. Because of me."

"It was an accident, son. Plain and simple," he breathes against my head. "An accident."

His words don't ease my grief.

"There's nothing more you can do here," he says, an echoing reminder of last night's stillborn colt—it seems like a lifetime ago. *Nothing can be done.*

"Let me take you home."

The word sounds strange, like I don't know where that is. "Not yet. I need... not yet."

CHAPTER FOUR

Marnie

THE ROOM IS QUIET, aside from Ashe's sobs and the faint beeping of the monitors. My heart breaks for him and our lost plans. *His* plans. *Our* plans. We were so close to our dreams, so achingly close. Watching Ashe crumble against his mom solidifies the harsh reality of what's happened and pulls my remaining hopes through my fingers, unraveling the strings that hold us together. No hope-reconstruction project can salvage them. Those hopes are gone. Forever.

Poof.

A dark side of me, the part that lives in my previous abandonment like an inescapable shadow, fears that's not all I've lost.

I know I have to be strong for them, but a black hole forms in my emptiness, sucking me into it. I'm here, lying in a hospital bed, but I'm not here at all. I'm lost in a new reality. *I can't have children.* My *Game of Life* car has suddenly downshifted, backtracked, and off-roaded from the board, forced to sail over the table's edge. Game over.

"We'll keep you here for a few days as you recover," the doctor continues.

"Wait, what about Jamaica?" Ashe's sudden return to the conversation makes my shoulders jolt. And then, ache. "We leave Sunday morning."

The doctor shakes her head. "Marnie can't travel. Recovery will take six weeks or so."

"That's what they said when I had my hysterectomy," Cora says, "and I was back to work in three."

The doctor is nonplussed. "This wasn't a routine surgery. Marnie's injuries are substantial. The hip bruise alone will make it difficult for her to get around. She'll need care."

Ashe rushes to my side, grabbing my hand like it's his cue. "We'll take care of her."

"Of course, we will," Cora says, hand going to her son's back. "Your family is here for you."

Her words spin in my head, and I think *'you'll be good as new in no time'* just as she says the same words aloud.

I'm not psychic. I've heard her spiel at Sunny's Beach Market when employees have asked for leave over illnesses, broken bones, or sick kids. *Your family is here for you. You* (or your daughter, son, husband, grandmother, insert relative) *will be good as new in no time.*

She means it. Just because she says it a lot doesn't mean it's insincere.

And yet.

That's just something people say. Isn't it? I long to demand a truth policy with them as I so easily did with Grady Tripp. But it's too late. If not established early, it might as well not be done at all.

Besides, being family is understood, not something that *needs* saying. If one has to say, "We're family," is it really true?

Not that I know much about family.

"Thanks," I manage, warmed by Ashe's comfort, at least. His fingers intertwine with mine, fitting just right.

"Marnie, what's your house number again?" Wes asks once the doctor leaves, and the room slips into silence. I eye the clipboard he's holding, not surprised that he was tasked with filling it out.

"I'll take care of that, Wes. Thank you," I say, patting the movable table beside me. He sets it down, smiles weakly, and shoves his hands into his pockets. "How're you feeling?"

I'm a conversational ringleader most days, but the question baffles me. I feel like I'm on mute and set to black and white—an old fifties-style tube television on the blink. Is this how Mom used to feel?

Can't think about that now.

"Um, tired." My head falls to the pillow behind me. "Sad. This isn't... It's hard to... I'm so sorry about the wedding."

"We'll reschedule," Ashe says quickly. "As soon as you're better... the honeymoon, too."

Not only do his words bring relief but they remind me how much I love his excitement. Ashe is like a handsome version of the Energizer Bunny, always pushing forward.

Cora smiles admirably at her son. Seeing her softer side is a privilege I don't take lightly. They call her Cora the Conquerer at work for her tough negotiations with vendors, employees, and distributors and her stealthy, ninja-like apprehension of shoplifters. Many people find strong women intimidating. I find them inspiring, especially her.

"What about the guests? The arrangements? Should I make some calls?" I offer, considering all of the must-haves for this wedding. Cora wanted a grand affair "the likes of which this town has never seen." Thinking of the gourmet food, uneaten. The gorgeous flowers, unseen. The expensive wines, uncorked. And the string quartet's music, unheard. It makes my head swim, and my stomach turn.

Of course, that could be the meds, too.

"Don't worry your pretty, little head about any of that," Cora says. "It's being handled. Focus on healing, Marnie. We know this wasn't your fault."

I swallow a lump in my throat, suspecting her words say otherwise. I wasn't blaming myself, though my god-awful birthday bad luck could be the real culprit. *Is this my fault?*

"Ashe, honey, how about we take you home and let Marnie rest?" Cora suggests.

"I don't want to leave her, Mom." He looks almost defiant as he reaches for the remote control strapped to the bed.

"You can change, fetch her things, and come back. Huh?"

"Mom, I want to stay."

"You haven't eaten," she protests. "You're no good for Marnie on an empty stomach."

She gives me a look, prompting me to say, "Ashe, she's right. I'll need my things, and you should get out of that suit. Besides, the drugs are kicking in. I'll be snoozing in no time."

A gentle knock on the open door sidelines our discussion. I recognize Detective Watson from Sunny's. He buys his wife Elena a chocolate chip birthday cake from the bakery every year, which is so sweet in more ways than one.

"Miss Strange? Sorry to interrupt. I have a few questions if you're up for it."

"Of course, Detective Watson."

His appearance convinces the Sullivans to leave; they line up at my bedside, Cora's extravagant dress shimmering as she moves in for a quick kiss on the cheek.

Cora says, "Feel better, Marnie. That's an order."

"Yes, um, feel better," Wes says, following her lead, his beard tickling my cheek.

Ashe goes for my lips, soft and sweet—the kiss that should've come at the altar. I linger there, holding him with my hand on his cheek.

"I'll be back," he promises softly. "Love you."

"Love you," I breathe out weakly.

The room empties, leaving me with Detective Watson. He sets a paper bag on the table. "The gentlemen at the scene took the liberty of salvaging items from your vehicle."

"How thoughtful." I smile softly. "Is Grady Tripp still here?"

"Um, I don't know. He probably left."

Of course, he left—why would he stay? "Oh, I wanted to thank him."

"Thank him?"

"He saved my life." My light shrug hurts; everything hurts.

"He also says he caused the accident. Do you remember what happened?"

My eyes pinch. "Um, Ashe forgot the cake knife for the wedding and asked if I could run by their house. Cora wanted her mother's pearl brooch, too. They were already at the venue—the Lakeview

Club. I'm the go-to girl, you see. I couldn't find the dang pin, but she texted that she had it after all."

I stop for a breath. "Anyway, I was in a hurry by that time, worried I'd be late for my own wedding. I wasn't speeding, though. Promise. It's a curvy road; the knife kept shifting in the passenger seat, so I grabbed it. Held it here," I explain, gesturing to my lap. "The next thing I remember is him. Grady. And the sky—it was the perfect shade of blue today."

"Um, yes. It was."

"It was an accident, Detective Watson." I chuckle weakly. "You have the perfect name for a detective."

"Well, Holmes would've been better," he says.

"True. Watson should've gotten more credit. The accident was an accident, though. I don't want to press charges."

"The investigation will determine charges. At least he'll be cited for traffic violations; this protects you and the insurance process."

"Um, okay. How is he? Is he okay?"

"He didn't sustain any injuries in the accident," he reports.

"No, I know. I mean... is he okay?" I say the question slowly, hoping he understands me.

For the first time, Detective Watson shows concern. "He's upset. Like I've never seen him."

I nod, understanding, though my heart breaks a little for this grouchy stranger. I remember how distraught he was over me, his sad eyes, and unsaid thoughts—he shouldn't suffer lasting effects over this, even if I will. *Can't think about that now.* "He has to know it was an accident."

"He'll see that," he says. "Eventually. He's my nephew, you know."

"Oh, no, I didn't put that together."

"I married his Aunt Elena."

"Right, of course... chocolate chip cake on her birthday."

His lips upturn in a distinct smile. "You remember?"

"How could I forget something so sweet?" I gush weakly.

Slight blushing appears just below the dark rims of his reading glasses. "You're kind, Marnie. To remember."

"I love my job." I pull the blankets over my hospital gown. "That makes it easy to remember things like that."

"Kind to ask about Grady, too."

"Tell him I'm okay. *Truly.*"

"Will do. You're tired. I'll let you get some rest. If there's anything else…"

"You know where to find me," I smile.

"Feel better, Miss Strange."

He exits the room, closing the door gently behind him. I curl my body, the best I can, toward the window, locking eyes with headlights passing on the busy street across the parking lot. The sun has set, leaving orange and gold bands across the darkening blue sky.

We'd be married by now and feasting on filet mignon at the reception. I try envisioning our first dance, the champagne toasts, pressing cake into his lips, tossing the bouquet, but what was so delightfully imminent yesterday, even a few hours ago, feels weirdly impossible now.

I've missed my chance.

My no-tears rule takes a needed reprieve as they slip, sliding over my nose and dampening the pillow.

Mom's voice echoes, *"Don't cry, Marnie. It doesn't do you or anyone else any good. No one likes a crybaby."*

Still, I let them come, bargaining that I won't allow them again, no matter what happens. But for now, they're a must-do before getting onto the next steps of my recovery.

Only there is no recovery. Not really.

Mom sweeps into my thoughts again. *"Life isn't fair, sweetie, and it ain't changing the rules for you."*

Until Ashe, I rarely thought about kids. Why should I? I'm twenty-five, a career woman, and happy to bypass family talk until later. *Much* later. Or never.

Besides, love and necessity have kept me career-focused. The only family I've known for the last ten years has been through work. And though Ashe and Cora talk about us having kids often, I thought it was just something people say. Something for later. Great, if it happens. No big deal, if not.

Yet.

Lying there, it hits me. The sore ache around my midsection travels upward, permeating my heart and head with a gnawing hollowness. Whether I want them or not, I can't.

I can't.

I'll never know the feeling of life growing inside me. Never feel a baby's tiny kicks and punches wriggling in my belly. Never say, *"Ashe, put your hand here. The baby's kicking,"* like I've seen moms-to-be do with their spouses. Never have pickle and ice cream cravings, like Cora had with Ashe. Never carry that glorious basketball paunch that tells the world something beautiful and adorable is arriving soon. Never know the beauty of loving someone made from me. Would she have had my red hair? My freckles? Would he have had my eyes or my crooked smile? Would they have had the same raspberry birthmark at the base of their neck, as I do?

Now, I'm sobbing—something I haven't done in over a decade. Sobbing for a dream that I never had the chance to grasp and hold on to and watch grow as Ashe and I framed our lives around it. Sobbing for children I can't fully see, that I'll never meet, who don't exist.

My heart breaks in grief for their eyes that'll never open, the words they'll never say, their little fingers never gripping mine, and for the people they'll never be. I cry over ghosts. Not even ghosts, but hints of souls in my imagination.

How can I hurt so much over what never was?

A gentle voice whispers, "I'm sorry, Marina," behind me. I don't turn around to see the man shadowing my bed—I know who it is. I'm crying like I've never cried before; I can't face him. No one has ever seen me like this.

Broken.

Vulnerable.

Hurting.

But on second thought, that's not true because *he's* seen me at my worst. He was there, going through it with me. Accepting his comfort felt natural and necessary—I had no choice. Besides, it was easy. He's not in my life. There are no expectations. He requires nothing of me except, perhaps, to heal. What he thinks of me doesn't matter.

Once again, he's here. There's no one else. And I want to comfort him, now, too.

My hand drops to the bed behind me, reaching for him. His hand slips into mine, wrapping my fingers in his, and bringing some sweet relief. *I'm okay. He's okay.*

"I'm sorry," he whispers again.

My tears fall freely, vanishing into my damp pillow, as my grip on him tightens. He says nothing else, and it's a relief. I can't be smiling, cheerful, go-to Marnie with the words everyone needs to hear. All I can be is this.

The bed dips behind me like he's sitting on the edge, but still, I don't turn around. He caresses my fingers, warming and relaxing me. I don't care if he's a stranger. I soak up his comfort like a dry sponge, cracked and broken and desperate. Why didn't I feel this relief when Ashe was here? Is that why I pushed him away? For the comfort that should have been?

Grady's hand is rough and calloused, but I like it. In the inconceivable string of absurd events today, this grounds me. His hand feels... real. Consequential. It's here for *me*.

I can count on one hand the number of times I've made something completely about me.

When I contracted the awful norovirus after a field trip in second grade.

At home after *The Sound of Music* in high school.

The next day, my birthday, when Mom left.

Now, this. This is about *me*. And I need someone holding me, even just my hand.

The tears spit from my eyes like they're making up for lost time, and, for once, I don't care about being a crybaby. I've earned it. Right? And if nobody likes a crybaby, then that's okay. He doesn't know me, let alone need to like me. A terrible day binds us—nothing else.

His breath hits my fingers. "I'm sorry," he whispers again. I hear the tears in his voice, feel them on my fingertips. We ache in different ways, but it's a relief to ache together. And the sad, pathetic, hurting part of me wants to lock him there forever.

But I don't get a lifetime-hand-holder. Even *with* Ashe. *Cursed to be alone.*

Soon, my tears slow. And the ache I feel lessens. *It's okay. Everything's okay.*

Stubble grazes my fingers as his second hand joins the first. He clasps my fingertips with one and my palm with the other, gently caressing. Soon, unexpectedly, tiredness overrules my agony. The lights moving by outside the large window, the world going on regardless of me, glisten through my blurry eyes, hypnotic. With the soft press of lips against my fingers, his breath warming them, I drift into a fitful but necessary sleep.

CHAPTER FIVE

Grady

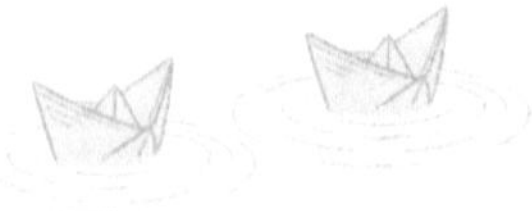

SCRATCHING WAKES ME, soft and faint. My eyelids feel heavy as I force them open, like they're not ready to take in the world yet. I know I'm not.

Yesterday's nightmare replays, kicking up my heart rate and making my head spin.

Then, I remember holding her hand, and the anxiety whirlwind stops. It centered me, made me feel needed, and allowed me to do *something* for her.

I scrub a hand over my face, wanting to be there for her again, but knowing I'm not that guy.

My sister Marigold sits beside me with her sketch pad open, working a charcoal pencil against the thick paper. Her fingers are black from smudging, and a charcoal mark wisps across her cheek.

"What are you doing?" I grumble.

"Drawing."

"Why?"

"The Shadow Man has bad dreams," she says, matter-of-factly, like reading a thought bubble over one of her comics. "I wanted to capture it."

I groan. "Let me see."

She twists the sketchbook, revealing a hard-lined, gray and black version of me. Not a bad likeness except for the pinched and wrinkled brow and my wiry fingers tucked in at my chin.

"Damn, Marigold. I'm thirty-six. Not eighty." I sit up, rubbing my head.

"It's an accurate depiction," she says, returning to her work.

With a breath, I scan the room for clothes, finding an old pair of jeans and a t-shirt draped on the bed's end. Resurrected from some box of my left-behinds and freshly laundered. Mom's in full force today. I even smell bacon frying.

She gets like this when something's happened.

"It's inconsiderate to draw people while they're sleeping. Remember?"

Now, her brow pinches as she considers the question. "Yes, but I thought you meant *other* people."

"Other people?"

"Mom. Dad. Gil. Overnight guests. Children I babysit." As she delivers her list, she grows frustrated, probably because she misunderstood my meaning. Marigold's biggest personal hang-up is anxiety over getting things wrong. Facial expressions. Social cues. The *rules*. I often tell her that no one is better at being genuine than she is, and the only thing *wrong* would be not being herself.

Well, except when it comes across as creepy. She's scared the hell out of everyone in the house at one time or another over her sleep drawings. Once, she penned Gil in the dark, sending him into a full-blown panic attack when he startled awake and saw her hovering over him, scratching away.

"Thanks for not lumping me in with *other* people," I smirk, refraining from giving her a consoling pat on her leg. She doesn't like touching. "You're right. I'll be the *one* exception."

She continues her sketch. I check my watch. "It's 11:30? Fuck."

"Mom says not to cuss."

"She means *other* people."

I stretch, getting out of bed, my joints cracking enough to make me groan again. I roll my shoulders, sore from the accident and the weight of yesterday resettling against them.

"Mom said you needed to sleep," Marigold mentions, failing to connect that remark with her need to draw me. "She said someone almost died."

"Did you bring the dogs over?" I ask, redirecting.

She nods, not looking up. "They are fed, watered, and walked."

"Thanks. What would I do without you?"

"Hire a professional dog sitter," she answers dryly.

"What's everyone up to today? Give me the 4-1-1."

"No one says that anymore," she says.

"Will you please update me on our family's activities this morning?"

"Dad's out on the farm. Gil's gaming downstairs. Mom's in the kitchen, baking bread. The dogs are with her, waiting for scraps. We *should* be at Zach and Zoe's soccer game. Everyone else is, but Mom said we needed to stay home. For you. So, thanks."

"You're welcome. What's the general vibe, you think?"

She lifts the pencil to her chin, tapping. It's a question I try to ask often, my small effort to help her notice such things. "Um, busy and tense, I'd say. Mom's been on the phone all morning."

"No doubt," I sigh, grabbing the clothes. "Alright, time's up on the portrait. Show me the final product."

She turns the sketch toward me with slight amusement as I take in the exaggerated lines now etched into the image's face.

"Fucking hell, Marigold! You made me look older?"

"It's a joke," she giggles.

"That's pretty good," I admit, "as long as you burn that sketch."

Her face grows serious again. "Can I just throw it away?"

"Fine."

I exit the guest bedroom, once the room I shared with Colin, and sneak into the bathroom across the hall.

Leaning against the sink, I vaguely remember Dad finding me in Marina's room once she'd fallen asleep, driving me *home*—my childhood home, it turns out—and pushing me into a shower. Trying to eat, but failing. Crawling into bed, sopping up tears with my pillow like she did.

I can't remember the last time I cried like that. I don't cry, generally. Not that I have some idiotic machoism about it—men can, should, and do cry—but I prefer not to. When you're a doctor, it's best to be as emotionless as possible. It's oddly comforting.

Staring into the bathroom mirror, I look older than yesterday. Marigold's drawing wasn't that far off. Baggy red eyes. Matted lines from sleep and worry. Rough stubble, grays mixing with the browns. I look almost as bad as I feel.

Is she okay? Should I call? What would I say?

Hey, Marina. It's me, the asshole who wrecked your wedding day and nearly ended your life. Can you please alleviate my guilt and tell me that you're okay? Can I hold your hand again so I'll feel better?

Goddamnit.

Splashing my face with ice-cold water, I know I must leave her alone. She doesn't need me around, reminding her of what she's lost.

She's suffered enough.

Nothing can be done.

In the kitchen, the dogs yap and yowl when I appear. Harley Quinn, my chocolate lab with a stubbed tail, reaches me first, wiggling her ass and drooling on the hardwoods. I rub behind her ears with one hand and along Hannibal's back with the other. A Bassett Hound, he howls his appreciation, perking his ears, one of them only halfway, as it was nearly ripped off as a puppy. Finally, my three-legged German Shepherd, Blackbeard, moseys between them, politely waiting his turn, which I often tell him is very un-pirate-like.

Fighting the soreness, I wrestle them to the floor, letting them get their fill of my overdue attention.

A shadow moves over us. Mom stands there, hands on hips and looking exasperated, watching us with a mix of delight and criticism.

"Grady, don't get them wound up. They just settled. They've been underfoot all morning like they know something's wrong."

"Yeah, they want to go home," I say, standing up.

She pushes a sandwich plate at me. "Here. Have a BLAT."

"What's a BLAT?"

"A bacon, lettuce, avocado, and tomato sandwich. You need lycopene for antioxidants and vitamin C in the tomatoes, and avocado is a superfood, rich in vitamins C, K, and E. You need the energy. The bacon makes it taste good," she explains. "Right, doggies?"

Blackbeard grunts an affirmative, speaking for the group.

Mom, a.k.a. Carmela Tripp, is the town's pharmacist and a staunch believer that the right vitamin, mineral, medication, or meal will cure anything from a sour stomach to a bad mood—she's yet to convince me.

"Are you okay?" she asks, her voice pitching higher.

"Fine." I take the plate and sit at the elongated island next to Marigold.

"I could call Dr. Hinky." She reaches for her phone.

"Gil's shrink? Why?"

"You need someone to talk to, Grady," she sighs. "What happened yesterday—"

"Not now, Mom. Please."

"It's traumatic," she continues, "and not just for... them."

Them. The word sounds so separatist. Maybe "them" fits the Sullivans—*they*, with their luxury cars, mani-pedis, and housemaids, aren't like *us*, with our grimy boots and fingernails, family BBQs, and economy everything.

Still, as different as we are, Marina doesn't seem so. She wants to be a *them*, but is she? She's more an *us*. Her words swirl in my head. *I thought today I'd get a family.*

A dark thought passes through me, remembering Ashe crying into his mom's shoulder rather than consoling Marina, and, later, finding her alone. It seemed *off*. But everything about the Sullivans and most people generally feels off to me.

Sighing, I peer across at Mom. Her critical stare reminds me of a strict teacher, evaluating me for errors.

"Grady, please. Dr. Hinky's worked wonders with Gil's anxiety," she says.

If I had the energy to argue, I would. My nerdy, twenty-eight-year-old brother contracted COVID-19 in the early days of the pandemic, rendering him quarantined for nearly a month. His difficult bout with the illness, combined with the solitude, instigated a crippling anxiety disorder. He's lived in our parents' basement ever since. He rarely leaves the house and only for pre-approved places. He doesn't drive. Or date. Or have a life outside of family and online gaming. Hardly a testament to Dr. Hinky's skills as a therapist.

"He's better off now than last year," she points out.

True. Gil isn't depressed. Resigned would be a better word.

"Just talking to a professional will help you feel better. I wish you'd done it sooner, when you came back—"

"Mom, I love you. I can't do this now," I say, as gently as possible. She's as sensitive as she is pushy, like most moms, I think. "But I'll keep it in mind."

She nods, looking somewhat victorious, and returns to her stress baking.

"I see Dr. Hinky sometimes," Marigold says.

"Ah, snap! Is she Shrinky Hink in your Shadow series?" I whisper, wide-eyed and impressed with myself for making the connection. Marigold's homemade comic books are sometimes way over my head. Since returning home, she's designated me as her alpha reader —one familial assignment I don't mind.

My insight earns me a rare smirk from my sister. "Taking over the world one shrunken brain at a time."

"So, she's a villain, huh?"

"You should still see her. She makes my head feel tighter from thinking too much, but it's less cluttered at the end."

"Hm, maybe."

"Grady, don't say *snap* anymore."

"My bad, Marigold."

She gives me a funny look, debating whether to correct me on that, too. Sometimes, I use more old-school slang around her than usual, inspiring her to correct me. It's one of life's few joys, getting her to communicate. She hardly spoke at all during the first half of her life.

Even that joy feels muted today. Every smile, laugh, or warm feeling gets snuffed out by the travesty I caused yesterday.

I stare at the sandwich, unable to muster the strength to pick it up.

The backdoor opens with my father's booming voice. "Do I smell bacon?"

Mom whips a second plate at him. "Low-sodium turkey bacon for you, love."

"That'll do," he says, kissing her.

Marigold and I roll our eyes at each other. Our parents' unreserved affection has been a source of many groans. Nearly four decades of marriage haven't diminished their attraction—a fact that's beautiful in theory as long as you're not one of their six children playing witness to it.

He hangs his coat on a hook by the door and moves to the island. "Grady."

"Dad."

"Sleep okay?"

"Okay," I repeat, though it's a lie. At my body's insistence, I slept hard, but not comfortably. The accident kept repeating in my dreams in weird variations. Always me *hurting* Marina, but with the details altered. A black sky. A red dress. One car instead of two. The whole town watching. In one version, I rammed my truck into their wedding. In another, I took her home with me to hide what I'd done. In another, she died. In another, I kissed her.

My hand rolls over my stubbled head. "Mom, can I get this to go?"

Before she answers, Gil strolls in, his headset slightly askew over his ears. He nods toward me and heads to the fridge.

"You should stay here for a few days," Mom says. "It'd be good for you to be with family."

"Oooh, *Call of Duty*?" Gil says, lighting up as he flicks open a soda.

"No, I'm spent."

"You've been asleep for twelve hours," he says.

He's right, but I still feel exhausted. "The body must what the body must, Gil."

He shrugs and disappears down the hall.

Mom's phone rings, and glancing at the caller on her screen, her smile fails her, and she hesitates. It's probably someone angling for details about yesterday from her book club, her pickleball team, or the Women's Club. Mom has her hand in nearly every organization in this town, as awful as that sounds.

Seagrove's gossip game is Olympic-level—the town is full of bored busybodies who've trained their whole lives for news like this, not that I can blame them. The prince of Sunny's Beach Market left at the altar because his sweetheart bride was stabbed in a car accident caused by the town's asshole vet with zero bedside manner? TMZ has wet dreams about headlines like that. Or, at least, *The Seagrove Groove* does.

"Let it go to voicemail," I breathe out. "That's what it's for."

Her cheeks puff in a sigh before she answers. "Hey... oh, yes... he's fine, thanks for—oh, I don't know the details. I wasn't there." She moves her call into the living room.

I glance at Dad, suddenly worried that Mom knows the extent of Marina's injuries through Dad and my weepy confession yesterday. "Did you tell her about the, um... the whole story?"

"No, son. That's between us, and it's Marnie's business, anyway."

"Thanks."

"Anytime."

Marigold doesn't bother questioning us. She doesn't enjoy intrigue.

"Sorry, I didn't help this morning," I tell him.

"Glad you didn't. I'm hiring more farmhands. You're doing too much, Grady. It stops. Now."

"I appreciate that, but *now*, I need to work. To think of anything else. Tell me about that colicky baby calf."

Dad launches into his morning activities, tidbits about the calf and diarrhea-stricken chickens, news that sends Marigold to her room. I advise him accordingly, grateful for the distraction. I almost wish it were Monday with a waiting room full of patients to keep me occupied.

The back door opens after a light knock, and Uncle Jim enters, looking official in his suit, tie, and the gold badge hooked to his belt.

"Mack. Grady." He nods.

"Jim," Dad says, motioning to another barstool. "Have a seat. Want a BLAT?"

"Um, no thanks. I'm on duty." His stone-like expression turns to me. "Grady, I've spoken with everyone, and we've concluded our investigation. You're being cited for reckless driving. You'll be fined and—"

"What? That's it? Reckless fucking driving?"

"Grady, calm—"

"I *hurt* that woman, Jim. She's... she'll never be the same again."

He looks confused but continues, "Grady, yes, she's hurt, but not in a way that justifies criminal charges. Miss Strange didn't want charges brought against you at all. Everyone agrees—this was an accident. Wrong place, wrong time. You should accept that, too."

"He's right, son. Accidents happen."

"No. That's not good enough."

"Even charging reckless was a stretch," Jim continues. "Improper driving would've been more accurate. You'll probably talk the judge down at trial."

"So, I fucked up, but she's the one fucked."

Jim's shoulders fall in a deep breath. "Take heart, Grady. You're still financially responsible for the damages and her medical bills. Your insurance companies will hash it all out. With the Sullivans involved, there's hope for a civil suit. So, cheer up."

Dad chuckles, but I shake my head, steaming. "I don't care about the Sullivans. What about Marina? She *should* sue me."

"She might. But, given our chat last night, it's unlikely. She wanted a chance to thank you—"

"Thank me?"

"For saving her life. She wanted me to tell you she's okay. Truly. Her words."

My eyes close tightly with the word, thinking of our promise. *She remembers our truth policy.* Only she's not okay. Not the way I found her.

I lean against the counter next to Dad, lightheaded and uneasy. "She should hate me. Is she... what is she? Foolish? Naive? Insane?"

"No. None of that. She's *kind*, Grady." He moves toward the door. "I gave Donny the go-ahead to fix your truck. It's salvageable. Hers isn't. Talk later."

He leaves, and Dad groans. "It's best to let this go, son. Focus on taking better care of yourself. Get your fishing pole and put this behind you. Yeah?"

"Yeah," I breathe out, wanting exactly that. She's a stranger, yesterday's over, and, surely, her family, such as it is, is caring for her by now. Even so, remembering her words, my fists tighten against the granite countertop. *I thought today I'd get a family.*

Like he's reading my mind, Dad says, "There's nothing you can do."

"I know." *Sometimes nothing can be done.* "Dad, I gotta go. Can I borrow The Beast?"

"Keys are on the peg," he says.

I grab them, my bag of effects, and whistle for the dogs. We load up in my grandfather's old Ford, nicknamed The Beast for its size, heavy rumble, and few modern conveniences. It's a beast to drive. But it works. Once it groans to life, me and the dogs do what I've wanted to do for the last two days.

We go home.

CHAPTER SIX

Marnie

I DREAM IN ASHE-VISION, a jumbled version of our greatest hits.

All the times I worked the cash register at Sunny's Beach Market as a teenager, hoping he'd notice me. The summer before his senior year in college, he finally did.

"Marnie, you have the sunniest smile at Sunny's," he said. "Mom should give you a raise just for that."

Laughing in the break room over Mountain Dews and guessing what flavor they'll think of next.

His first day as our store manager after he graduated, brandishing his degree like a scepter. He went to the booth overlooking the registers, and his voice came across the PA system, like a seasoned deejay.

"Good morning, folks. It's another bright and beautiful day at Sunny's Beach Market," he said then, and every day he's worked since.

I still love that.

When we built cases of Coke and Sprite into a Christmas tree in the store's iconic gazebo and, the following year, a fireplace with Santa peeking through. That was the same year he danced with me at our Christmas party, and I went home still smelling his faint cologne in my hair.

"It's my New Year's Resolution, Marnie," he said the following week as we worked on a Valentine's display.

"What is?"

"Taking you out on a date. If you don't say yes, the entire year will be a huge letdown," he grinned.

Of course, I said yes. We spent the evening at a fancy restaurant, and he actually listened to my ideas for Sunny's—many he advocated for with his mom. Self-checkouts. Expanding our catering services. More local products. And finally, expansion plans. That led to me becoming the youngest customer service manager in Sunny's history.

I'm one of those lucky ducks who genuinely loves her job. Falling in love with Ashe seemed like a natural extension of what was already a perfect fit.

He surprised me by proposing at the store, surrounded by customers and our work family.

After learning about my disappointing birthdays in the past, he wanted to get married on Valentine's Day to break my bad luck.

Funny.

I remember lying in bed at his condo, him strumming his fingers along my bare side, tickling me, as he gushed about what he wanted for us. "A house close to the beach. A dog—Mom never let me have one. Kids, too. Lots of kids."

"*Lots* of kids?" I asked with a laugh, endeared by his excitement for us. No one had ever *wanted* things with me before, let alone a lifetime together. Hearing Ashe say these things felt impossible yet gorgeously uncomplicated like my loneliness finally reached its expiration date.

"Well, at least two. I hated being an only child. Mom smothered me. She'll be even worse with grandkids. She talks about it all the time—drives me crazy. It's best to spread her attention between a few, right?"

"Um, right."

He eyed me suspiciously. "You *want* kids, don't you?"

Fears swarmed me then. I didn't know if I wanted kids. *Love, marriage, baby carriage*—I understood the expectation, even the inclination. But me as a mom? I couldn't see it. Perhaps my rocky childhood blurred what should've been a clear vision—me taking the family path over the life path. Then, I didn't know if that's what I wanted. But Ashe always knew.

"I want what you want," I told him.

Ashe-vision crackles and fuzzes out.

"Marina, stay with me." I'm there again, the road under me and the devastatingly blue skies waving their treetops overhead. My fingers twitch, and I close my hand, surprised to find it empty.

I blink awake slowly. Through my drug-laced exhaustion, I hear a rolling suitcase stop at the foot of the bed. Then, he crawls into the small space beside me.

"I'm here," Ashe whispers. He snuggles gently into the back of me, kissing my shoulder. "Everything will be okay, Marnie. We'll adopt. Or get a surrogate. Mom says..."

He goes on, but I can't listen. Hearing "solutions," with the agony so sharp and fresh, only makes me feel like a problem, desperate to be solved.

Is it selfish? This need to wallow in my pain a little while longer? To give it the respect it deserves?

For once, I don't engage him, answer, or even offer a *hmm* to let him know I'm listening. I'm not ready to be *that* Marnie yet.

"I'll stay until you fall asleep," he says, eventually. So, that's what I do.

Ashe leaves sometime during the night but returns the next morning, oozing with handsome positivity but carrying Starbucks coffees. We've discussed supporting locals over big corporations before, but he forgets to listen. Today, I'm too pained to remind him.

"How's my beautiful girl this morning, eh?" he asks, meeting me bedside, where I sit sideways, my feet grazing the cold floor.

"I'm okay," I say, slightly winded and agonizingly sore. It's been a busy morning. I glance at the whiteboard posted near the TV, where the morning nurse scribbled today's goals.

Shower Power (full-body cleanse with anti-bacterial soap, done)
Power Walk (the hall to the nurse's station and back, done)
Eat Like You Mean It (Eat something)

Get Things Moving (making sure my bowels function properly)

Ease off the Good Stuff (lessen my narcotics)

The nurse, Ivy, has a cute sense of humor, and who doesn't love a chipper bedside manner, especially considering the overall misery of a hospital stay? I've never been so poked, prodded, or explored. Ivy didn't hide her fascination with my hip bruise when she assisted me in the shower. It *is* massive, a ginormous red blotch with blueish twinges covering my left side from kidney to thigh. It resembles a giant jellyfish with a big head and many stringy tentacles. *Giant Jelly* —that's what everyone calls it now. Our power walk felt the opposite—I could hardly do it. My insides feel like they've been extracted, shuffled, like a deck of cards, and stuffed back in me like I'm a Thanksgiving turkey.

Ivy might be the first person in history to wear me out.

And I'm still not hungry.

Ashe settles into the visitor's chair after a short kiss. "Brought you coffee."

"I see. Thanks."

"You okay?"

"Getting there," I smile. I edge the rolling IV aside, staving off nausea with measured breaths. Ivy and I have only just returned from our power (no power) walk. The movement mixed with the meds has turned my stomach.

"Here you go, hon." Ivy bounds into the room with an icy ginger ale.

I take a small sip through the crooked straw that immediately disappoints her.

"Come on. You can do better than that. You got this."

My head spins with the hundreds of times I've said that to Sunny's employees, always with the same encouraging smile and upbeat tenor. Though it's my job to inspire excellent customer service, I see now, with Ivy's persistence, how it may come across as annoying.

No, she's not annoying. She's motivating.

I take another small sip. "Thanks, Ivy. This is Ashe, my fiancé."

"Nice to see you. Marnie could use the company," she says, checking my IV and updating her tablet.

"Ashe, could you get my cardigan and fuzzy socks from the suitcase?" I ask, my voice weak. I'm the textbook definition of miserable—chilly, in agony, nauseous, and wondering how I'll feel better when it hurts so badly now. I'm not my usual Marnie self and need my little comforts.

"Sure thing." He goes to my secondhand, honeymoon-ready suitcase and opens it on another chair. He brought it last night—my entire ten-day supply of beach clothes and sexy lingerie for Jamaica—and though, yes, technically, it has everything I need, it has most things I don't. He sifts through my neat packing, pulling out my long, pink cardigan and fuzzy sleep socks.

"And my brush and a scrunchie," I tack on, twiddling my damp hair between deep breaths.

In his efforts, he knocks the suitcase over, spilling everything onto the floor. Then, he fumbles, putting it all together again, picking up armloads of jumbled clothes and piling them on top.

He almost looks nervous.

My stomach shifts, and my head swims—a headache pecks at my temple. I reach for the plastic container on my cluttered rolling table and spit up the fizzy ginger ale in a sickening gag.

"It's because you haven't eaten," Ivy decides, hand going to my back in soft circles like I'm a baby. "Try to relax."

My abdomen clenches with the effort, forcing tears into my eyes. I cough and spit up again. It hurts so sharply that I fear my stitches will burst open. *Could that happen?*

Hot tears slip down my cold cheeks—pained tears are acceptable. *A body must what a body must.* Still, I feel embarrassed as the spell passes. I glance up to gauge Ashe's reaction.

He's not there.

Ivy shrugs beside me. "He said something about the vending machine."

She goes to the abandoned pile of clothes, unabashedly searching for my requests, and finds them quickly. She drapes the sweater over my shoulders and helps me into the sleeves. Then, she kneels, pulling on my socks.

"He's handsome," she smirks. "I bet the wedding would've been gorgeous."

"Red, white, and pink," I mutter, "for Valentine's Day."

"It's not unusual for people to feel distressed, watching a loved one in pain," she offers in Ashe's defense.

"He means well, but he's no carer. He's not used to it."

She nods, gently easing my legs under the covers and tucking me in. "Breakfast will be here soon. We'll try something easy on the stomach. Toast, grits, and maybe some eggs."

"Okay."

"Later, we'll try walking again. It's good for you, and the sooner you can do things like eat, poop, and walk, the sooner you'll get out of here."

"I can't wait."

She hands me the brush and scrunchie from my suitcase and flips on the *Today Show*. "Here, let's see what's happening today."

Then, she leaves, and I breathe out a grateful sigh.

I miss Mom. I think of her as I weakly brush my hair. I loved when she brushed and braided my hair, and not just because she did hair for a living and was amazingly good at it. There was something sweet, comforting, and intimate about her caring for me that way.

I sweep my long hair to the side and limply manage a loose braid, Mom's words about family emerging in my thoughts, unwanted. *That's just more people to disappoint you.*

That won't be Ashe.

He returns, peering into the room, unsurely. My smile brings him in.

He holds up Doritos. "Had a craving for chips. Feeling better?"

I take a breath. "A little."

Returning to his chair, he bypasses the mess he's made of my suitcase. He tosses the Doritos on the table, grabs his coffee, and pulls out his phone. "Everyone's been chill about the wedding, and your IG's been lighting up. I helped Mom make a post this morning."

"Aw, let me see."

He scrolls to the notifications under my handle, ♡ *MarnieLoves-Sunny's* .

"Everyone's so sweet," I coo, reading the comments on my last post, a Happy Valentine's Day edit featuring our deals on heart-shaped cakes, cookies, and bouquets. In the caption, I added a winky face with the message: *Wishing you a happily-ever-after as Ashe and I begin ours.*

It hits me as bittersweet now.

Ashe and Cora's post yesterday afternoon was a muted beige background with fancy lettering thanking Seagrove for its support during this difficult time and asking for their prayers for "our sweet Marnie's quick recovery."

Nothing about the wedding, not that I expected it.

My account has nearly 3,000 followers, practically the entirety of Seagrove, the ones on social media anyway. The hundreds of messages wishing me well make me tear up. Seeing our town so invested in us is wonderful—it's a far cry from my nomadic child-hood, when I never stayed in one place long enough to make friends.

"My phone's in the paper bag," I say. "Can you see if it works? It probably needs charging."

"Sure thing."

Miraculously, the screen looks workable, minus a crack along the top. He prompts it with no luck, and then digs through my exploded suitcase for a charging cable.

"Oh, I may've left it on my nightstand," I say.

"No problem," he says, perking up. "I'll run to Best Buy for a new one."

He's nearly out the door before I call out, "Wait, Ashe. Don't worry about the phone right now."

"It's just around the corner. I'll be fifteen minutes. Tops."

Then, he's gone.

His antsy behavior isn't new. Ashe rarely sits still. Our dating life has been filled with mini-adventures. Weekend getaways. Surfing. Kayaking. Arcades and mini-golf. Clubbing. Boating. Jet skis. His contagious energy has no end, and I love being his playmate.

Yet, a sinking feeling shades me in my empty room. The chill in the air makes me shudder in my sweater.

He's not just antsy but nervous, like he doesn't know how to be around me.

His fifteen-minute errand takes an hour, but he seems happy on his return, unwrapping the cord and setting my phone to charge. He tells me about traffic congestion and admits getting distracted by the security section; he's keen to upgrade Sunny's motion-sensor lights and backdoor access points.

I nibble a dry piece of toast, fearful of my stomach again.

Finally, Ashe settles into the side chair, sipping his cold coffee.

"Are you okay?" I ask.

He leans his elbows against his knees, catching my gaze. "Yeah, sorry. I'm not good at this kind of thing."

"It's okay," I breathe out, relieved by his honesty. "I know this is hard on you, too."

"It's... so unfair."

I risk my stomach for a long gulp of the watered-down ginger ale. "I'm sorry. I know how much you wanted..."

"So, did you."

A lump forms in my throat, making it hard to breathe. "If this changes anything... better to tell me now. I'd understand."

"God, no, Marnie. I love you," he insists, grabbing my hand. "We'll work through it, figure it out. We're good at that, right?"

I nod, his words stirring memories of us brainstorming ways to create the complicated displays I envisioned at the market. Fishing hooks, superglue, sponges, duct tape, and stacks of pennies are only a few of the quick-fix solutions we've devised to make our creations happen.

I smile and say, "Yes, you're right."

His lips graze my fingers as he holds my hand close. "Tell me what you need."

A little gasp escapes in a chuckle. Hearing him say that warms those frigid temps previously circulating in my room. *This* is the Ashe I love and need. So, I go for absolute honesty—lying in a hospital bed, it's hard to do otherwise.

"I know this is hard. I always take care of us, take care of everything. I love that. But now, I need you to take care of me for a little while. Please." My voice cracks in tired desperation; I rarely ask anyone for anything, even Ashe. It almost hurts being this vulnerable, like standing naked in a blizzard. "I don't need you to be the perfect caretaker or wait on me hand and foot. But I need you. I just need you here. With me. Holding my hand."

"I'm here. I'll be here. Promise."

He fiddles with my side braid, smiling, and I sigh against the pillows, relieved.

CHAPTER SEVEN

Marnie

OUR TALK DOES us both good. Ashe makes me laugh through many episodes of *Midsomer Murders*. He fields phone calls, flower deliveries, and social media. He stays with me until well after dinner, and we're dozing off. I encourage him to go home and get some rest, and with a lovely kiss, he promises to return early in the morning.

Cora shows up instead, arms full of gifts and in her Sunday best, like she plans to drop in at church after her visit.

I've always admired Cora, from her tough business tactics and management style to her mama-bear love and commitment to her family, especially to Ashe, her only child. She is the *whole* package.

Her heeled booties click against the floor and echo in the small room as she awkwardly unloads her gifts. She places a luscious fern at my bedside, bright green and bursting from its blue mosaic pot.

"You've been to see Mr. Frisk," I chuckle, thinking of our stoic but expert floral department manager.

"He insisted on a plant, something alive rather than cut."

"He knows I love my green family," I say, considering where I might find room for it. But it's a silly thought—I'm moving in with Ashe soon. His condo has a full-sized balcony with an ocean view and plenty of room for plants.

"I also brought magazines." She angles open a reusable tote from

Sunny's (one of my brilliant ideas) to reveal issues of *Vogue* and *Coastal Living*, though I'm more of a *People* and *Woman's Day* girl myself.

"Thanks. How sweet."

"Blueberry muffins, fresh baked, and your favorite—Reese's Peanut Butter Cups," she coos.

"Wow, you've outdone yourself. I will gobble this all up. Well, except the fern—Frilly Willie will come home with me in a few days."

Cora beams. "Oh, Marnie, you are handling everything so well. I love your glowing optimism."

No choice. "Thanks, Cora."

She settles into Ashe's chair, but not before unbuttoning the jacket to her striped, black pantsuit and setting her Louis Vuitton bag at the end of my bed. "Ashe tells us you made great progress yesterday."

I automatically eye the whiteboard Ivy updated this morning.

More Moving & Grooving (Walking)

Clean Your Plate (eat a full meal)

Bye Bye IV (self-explanatory)

Tame Your Cane (practice using a cane)

Snooze-Fest (get good sleep)

"Yes, everything's functioning properly and healing well. It's just a matter of mobility and energy now."

"Excellent. You've never been one to be down for long," she says. "Women like us can't let that happen, huh?"

"Right." *Women like us?* I almost do a giddy clap and an exuberant *woot-woot* over her lumping us together into a strong-capable-women sandwich, as equal and important as meat and cheese. But I keep my cool. A light shrug makes my shoulders ache. "Um, where's Ashe? Sleeping in?"

Her red-lipped smile takes a sudden detour. She straightens the wrinkles in her pants with a brisk swipe. "No, Marnie. There's no easy way to explain this, but you love Ashe, so I know you'll understand."

My heart drops like an untethered elevator crashing to the bottom floor. "Understand what?"

"I put him on the plane to Jamaica an hour ago, he and Tyler," she says, locking eyes with me in that painfully direct way she does that reads: *I'm Cora the Conquerer. Never question me or my power.*

"I don't understand."

"He's put up a good front for you, Marnie, but he's a mess. He needs to get away, clear his head. He didn't want to go, but I insisted. So, if you're upset, it should be with *me*. Not *him*."

"I'm not upset." And I'm not. I twiddle my engagement ring around my finger, feeling sad, disappointed, not surprised. *More people to disappoint you.* "Nonrefundable tickets. I get it."

"Yes, but that's not why. It's for his mental health, Marnie. That's why I told him to go."

"He seemed fine yesterday," I argue lightly, offended by how quickly she plays the mental health card. It's not that I don't buy it— mental health is as important, if not *more* important, than physical health, and anyone can be struck by such difficulties at any time, like bold and debilitating lightning bolts. I know that better than most people.

But Ashe has never been to therapy, never known the throes of a panic attack or agonized over getting out of bed. He's never known a bad day. And I was once privy to a discussion between him and his mom over "acceptable uses" of paid time off, and they both agreed that mental health "didn't count."

I argued until we reached a rare compromise, calling all leave personal time off, no matter the reason. And, whatever the case, the employee should not be required to explain.

"*For you*, he's fine. But he isn't. At home, he's different. You understand how much he wanted this."

Her words hang there like dangling hooks, baiting me. Latching on would mean pointing out that he's not the only one grieving, asking why he isn't *himself* with me, and debating the obvious cruelty of his leaving. How could he abandon me like this, barely able to walk or eat or even breathe? After he promised?

But that's what people close to me do. They abandon.

And getting upset isn't a reaction I can afford.

"Yes, I know." It feels like the moment I came out of surgery, trapped by cords and bedding, confused and hurting. So, I react in a way Cora understands. "You surprise me, putting him on a plane with me here. Aren't you concerned about... what was the word you used when we discussed putting Wren on the floor? *Optics?*"

Her red lips widen. "You always think about the family. I love that about you."

"I don't want anyone thinking badly of Ashe for leaving."

"They won't, not after all the wonderful pics and positive updates he posted yesterday. For all anyone knows, you *encouraged* him to go."

I nod. As usual, Cora thought of everything.

Ivy bounds into the room as if she senses my distress. "Sorry to interrupt. Ready for more moving and grooving soon, Marnie?"

"Yes!" I answer a little too loudly. "If that's okay, Cora."

"Of course!" She glances at her fancy watch. "If I leave now, I'll make it to Saint Francis's before the choir starts. I'm lighting a candle for you, Marnie."

"Thanks."

She gathers her bag at the bed's end and rests her hand on my covered foot. "Your family is here for you. When you get out, come home with me for your recovery—no arguments. I'll have a room prepared. I'll check in later."

Then, in a brisk wind of expensive perfume, she clicks into the hall.

"Oomph." Ivy tugs my blankets back. "She's a force to be reckoned with."

"I once saw her drop kick a shoplifter and put him in a choke hold until the police arrived," I say. "She didn't even wrinkle her suit."

"Impressive."

I lift myself from the bed, refusing Ivy's extended hand. I fight through the soreness with quick, determined steps.

"Look at you!" she beams. "You'll be running marathons in no time."

"Is the doctor here? I'd like to see her if she has time."

She checks her watch. "She should be in shortly for rounds. Why? Is something wrong?"

"No, not at all. I need to talk to her about getting out of here. Early."

CHAPTER EIGHT

Grady

THE LINE for coffee at Moon Beans & Books is atrocious. Six customers await service ahead of me. I fold my arms over my chest, hugging my thermos, and stare at my boots, hoping my cap and general bad attitude prevent anyone from talking to me—usually, people know better.

I shouldn't be here.

It's Sunday morning. A more tolerable fifty-two degrees and sunny. I woke to the usual cacophony of dog shuffling, licking, and barking, not that I slept much. My sleep marathon must've confused my internal clock and made it think I've met my quota for the week. Real rest proved impossible with guilt keeping me awake and bad dreams circulating whenever I managed to circumvent it. I spent most of the day trying to lose myself in chores, dog care, and Marigold's comics. Nothing worked to distract me, though I have enough firewood chopped to last three winters, and my dogs have never been so clean and groomed. Even with small accomplishments, it's hard not to hate myself.

While filling my coffee pot with water at the sink this morning, I flashed back to Marina's face, wincing in agony, and her words. *There's no one else... I'm glad you're here... You always seem so sad... You look like a man with a million thoughts but no one to tell them to. That* she thought of me at all dredged up more anger over what I stole from her. I smashed the carafe into the sink, shattering it into a thousand pieces.

After destroying my coffee pot, I latched on to a tiny shred of clarity. If Marina is *truly* okay, I should move on, call it what it was—an accident—and do nothing, beyond paying her expenses.

It's best for everyone if I don't get involved. So, that's the plan.

Once I fill my thermos, I'll spend the day on the lake, catching tonight's dinner and drinking many beers. Alone.

The line inches up, but the spandex and ponytailed women in front of me hardly notice outside their engrossing conversation.

"I bet Cora tampered with her brakes," one whispers to her friend.

She looks aghast and scoffs. "Why would she?"

"Are you kidding? Marnie lives in a shed, drives a crap car, and works in a grocery store. She's not Cora's first pick for Ashe. Everyone in the Women's Club says so."

The friend nods. "Yeah, my book club says the same thing. I heard Marnie got her wedding dress from a thrift store, even though Cora offered to buy her one."

"Gross."

"Yeah, gross. Think they'll still get married?"

"Don't know. I heard Cora canceled everything yesterday afternoon—not postponed. *Canceled.*"

"Marnie's been canceled? She's so sweet. She helped me find the perfect gift for my granny last year, and that woman doesn't like anything. She still talks about those handmade soaps—"

"She's Sunny's sweetheart, for sure. But is she still Ashe's? *That's* the question."

"Maybe Marnie drove herself into that tree, you know? To get out of it? I don't think I could handle Cora being my mother-in-law."

"Me, neither."

Don't get involved. They keep yapping over what would've been at the wedding and theories about a more suitable woman for Ashe. That they speak so disparagingly of Marina and completely disregard the true culprit in all this—me—makes me want to jump in and defend her. Somehow.

Someone bumps me from behind, nudging me into one of their messy buns.

"Watch it," she says.

"Shut up and move up," I bark.

"Rude," she gasps before obeying. "I swear, the oafs around here!"

"Yeah, we're almost as bad as the fucking busybodies."

Finally reaching the counter, I hand the barista my thermos to fill with overpriced coffee. Rushing to The Beast parked outside, I glimpse *The Seagrove Groove* on a table, its headline larger than usual —*The Wrecked Bride.*

I hate this town.

Driving home, I go slowly around the same curve where I hit her. The road is scarred with brake marks on her side and the gray ashes of flares, burnt out. And the guilt crashes over me again.

Her red hair flayed on the gray concrete.

Her labored breathing.

Holding her delicate hand.

I still feel it. Feel her.

At home, I enact my plan, anxious to melt into one of my few pleasures. Within ten minutes, I cast my first line into the glassy lake. The dogs whimper at my feet, so I throw a ball from their toy basket. Harley gets there first, or maybe the boys let her have it—hard to tell sometimes. Blackbeard's as good on three legs as most dogs on four, and Hannibal doesn't let his shorter legs hold him back. Harley prances in her win, racing through them to return the prize to me.

My phone pings with a text from Mom.

Want half of a Valentine's Day cake? It's delicious. I could bring it over.

No.

Grady, I'm worried about you.

I'm fine. Fishing. With the dogs.

As much as I know you love one-sided conversations, the dogs may not be the best therapists right now. Would it hurt to have some company?

Yes. Conversation scares the fish.

Marnie's doing well. Father Andrews offered prayers for her at church today. Cora gave an update—good as new in no time.

No. She'll never be the same again, not that I dare explain that to Mom or anyone else. I wonder how she's handling it. If she's talked to someone. If she needs anything.

My phone buzzes in my hand again. It's Colin, asking me to dinner at their house tonight.

A minute later, a text from Luke, inviting me to the bar later for half-price beers.

Mom must've sent out the family Bat-Signal.

I toss another ball for the dogs. Hannibal gets it first this time, promptly rolling around in a patch of grass as his victory lap.

It could've happened to anyone. There's nothing to feel bad about.

I groan over Mom's text while yet another comes in. Marty—my only sibling not in town. He joined the Peace Corps, currently doing humanitarian work in Haiti.

Hey, you okay? Mom sent an all-caps text for me to reach out. What's going on?

A turtle prowls around my line, ready to steal my bait. Not that anything's biting. I reel in an empty hook, debating whether to cast it again, and consider my family's onslaught.

They mean well, and asking them to back off wouldn't do any good. And maybe they shouldn't. If one of my siblings had caused the accident, I'd be by their side, ensuring they were okay. I don't let family down. Not like I used to.

Are you family? The nurse's voice replays in my head along with my lie. *Yes.*

"Shit," I mutter, getting up and calling for the dogs. Distraction is only temporary, and what's the point?

I return all their texts, politely refusing their offers while reassuring them that I'm okay.

But I'm not. How can I stop thinking about her? And what kind of shithead would I be if I did?

Besides, I made a promise.

It's midafternoon when I arrive at the hospital and snake my way to her room. The Valentine's Day balloons and bouquets are gone, and the place is quiet. I steel my nerves with a deep breath, expecting the worst. The Sullivans will probably kick me out within five minutes, and part of me wants them to. If she or they don't want me around, staying away will be easy. I promise myself to avoid confrontations, if possible. All I need is to see that she's okay.

Finding Marina dressed and standing over an open suitcase on the hospital bed surprises me almost as much as finding her alone. Sunlight streams through the window behind her, dancing through the thin sundress she wears and delicately revealing her soft curves. Her long hair is pulled to the side, waving lightly down her chest. She looks... lovely.

It's a relief, seeing her this way. It's the first time I've seen her look normal—not lying on the ground or in a bed or bleeding or in pain.

But the pain is there. She winces with her movements, struggling to haphazardly fold the messy clothes pile with one hand while balancing a cane with the other. She closes her eyes to the pain, almost like she's shutting it in.

A light knuckle rap against the open door brings her attention to me. A warm smile miraculously replaces her obvious discomfort.

"Tripp Grady Tripp." She drops what looks like a bikini into her suitcase and waves me in. "I'm glad you're here."

"Um, really?" I say.

"The guy who saved me and made me laugh while doing it? Of course." She smirks. "Aren't you happy to see me? Standing and everything?"

I nod. "Very happy."

She smiles wide, her brow pointing with suspicion. "You don't *look* happy."

"This is how I always look," I defend awkwardly, not for the first time. Once, Aunt Elena secretly organized an office pool where everyone took bets on their attempts to make me smile. She handed me the winnings at the end of the day because I never did. "I'd do a happy dance, but I don't want to make you jealous."

"That *would* make me jealous," she laughs, "but don't worry. I'll be dancing in no time. Promise."

I stand on the other side of the bed, unsure what to do or say. I remember Dad in a room like this after his heart surgery, how full and alive it was with laughter and chatting. Gil was near-panicking over the crowded space. Circling his bed that day felt like healing for us all. He'd be okay, and we, his cheerleaders, would be there to ensure it.

There's no cheer here except from her. Marina's quiet room is weirdly devastating.

"Where is everyone?" I ask.

She shrugs lightly—a move that makes her wince. "It's just me."

It's not exactly an answer, but I don't press. I hold out my shopping bag, and she takes it one-handed.

Her amused suspicion makes a return. "A present? Ah, you didn't have to get me anything."

"I, um, wanted to, only not flowers or shit you can't use." I motion to the many bouquets across the room—it looks like half of Seagrove sent her flowers, funny since no one's here. It looks and smells like a florist's shop. Or a funeral.

"Aw, cat treats and toys! They'll love these." She shakes a toy mouse, making it jingle. "That's very thoughtful. Thank you, Grady."

Her delight eases my nerves.

"How do you feel?"

Her smile widens. "Like I got hit by a truck."

My mouth drops in sudden horror.

She laughs, her wry smile cocking up her left cheek. "Relax, Grady. If we can't laugh…"

She shrugs rather than finishing her sentence. Her lightheartedness warms me more than the sunlight pouring into her room. People rarely surprise me, but she does. My guilt appreciates her good mood, but I know she's making it easy on me.

Problem is, I don't want easy.

"I'm doing well, thanks," she says. "Sore, but healing properly. Oh, the bruise on my side where I whacked my hip looks like a giant jellyfish. We nicknamed it Giant Jelly. Everyone on the ward talks about it."

"Marnie, are you talking up your bruise again?" a nurse booms, entering the room.

"Oh, Ivy. This is Grady Tripp."

"Hi, Grady Tripp. Marnie, here's the biggest ice pack I could find. Apply it at least three times a day to keep the swelling down," she says, handing over a thick, blue patch.

"Thanks." Marina drops it in her suitcase.

Ivy looks at me, hands on her hips. "I feel slightly better about this since you're here. I was starting to worry that no one would show."

"Still waiting on those papers, Ivy," Marina says. "I know I'm your favorite, but seriously. I've got it covered."

"Okay, okay. But I don't like it." Ivy bounces from the room.

"What doesn't she like?" I ask.

"That I'm leaving."

"Isn't that… good?"

Marnie shrugs, winces, and then eases herself onto the side of the bed. I meet her there, anxious to help.

"I'm fine, Grady. I need breaks, that's all." She manages a weak smile, but I don't trust it.

"Why doesn't she like that you're leaving?" I try again.

"The doctor wants me to stay another day or two, but we *eventually* agreed it wasn't necessary."

"What the hell, Marina?" I demand, my abated frustration

making a quick return. "That's ridiculous. You should stay. Why argue with the doctor?"

She winces at my abruptness but doesn't lose her friendliness. "Thanks for your concern, but I know what I'm doing."

"No, you don't. This was a major surgery, not a damn oil change."

Her bright, denim-blue eyes narrow, but her smile stretches at my harshness. "This is why they call you Grouchy Tripp, you know."

"I'm serious. Wait... Do they?"

She nods, her left brow cocked high on her forehead.

I take a deep breath, not surprised. "Call me whatever you want, but going against a doctor's advice is risky, even dangerous. If the doctor says stay, you should stay."

Her head tilts as she peers up at me, seeming to evaluate my frustration. I rake my fingers over my head before perching both hands on my hips.

"I need you to relax, Grady," she says, almost breathless but still managing a weak smile. "The rest of Seagrove might tolerate Grouchy Tripp, but here, now, I don't have the energy. So, either *he* goes or *you* do."

Her words stun and disarm me. *Was I being harsh?* I rethink our conversation and realize, alarmingly, yes. I don't notice how I come across to people anymore—I often don't care.

But with her, I do. She doesn't deserve my harshness. She doesn't deserve any of this.

"I'm sorry," I say, dropping my hands from my hips and taking a breath.

She smiles. "Good, now that the grouch is gone, I'm happy to explain." She motions to the chair in front of her. "Sit down."

I obey, feeling bad for challenging her, even though I'm right, slightly weirded out by her good mood, and unnerved by how easily she put me in my place—this woman bewilders me.

"I'm off the IV and the serious pain meds. My mobility is good. I'm eating, drinking, and bathroom-ing exactly as I should be and without help. I'm showing zero signs of infection, and my wounds are, and I quote, 'healing perfectly.' Another day or two won't matter to anyone but me. Besides, being here is all the cost of a mega-luxury hotel without any juicy amenities—"

"If it's about money, I'll cover it."

"No, Grady, it's not that. Not entirely. Trust me, okay? The doctor said that though she prefers keeping me, I'll be okay as long as I don't overexert myself. She went over all the red flags. I've already made appointments for follow-ups with my general doctor and my, um, all the necessary doctors. And Ivy's giving me phone numbers in case I have questions."

Her speech makes her breathless, like she can't deliver it with her usual speed, and pains her to try. "So, see? I'm fine."

My hands claw across my head as I consider her—she's not fine. "It's not that simple. The pain alone will be difficult to handle."

"Look, I've been fully adulting since fifteen. I know how to take care of myself."

"I didn't mean to suggest otherwise," I say, feeling even more like an ass, if that's possible. "I just need you to be okay."

Her smile alights in the sunshine through the window, making me wonder which one is brighter. "Keeping to our policy, I see."

"Truth. No sense in going back on it now."

"Then, I have another motivation for leaving early. A selfish one, I'm afraid." Her face scrunches with reluctance.

"Tell me."

She groans in a weak slump. "Have you ever been desperate for home?"

"All the fucking time."

A light smirk edges her lips. "That's what I want, Grady. Waiting until tomorrow means going home with Cora, in *her* care. Or her maid's care. I love Cora, but I don't want that. I want my bed, my cats, my plants, my things. If I sneak home now, she'll see I'm fine and don't need anyone taking care of me."

"But you *do* need care. What about Ashe?" A sinking feeling rushes over me—the same feeling I had when Ashe failed to comfort her and later when I watched them leave and found Marina alone. *Crying.* Where was he then? Where is he now?

Her smile falls, but only for a second before she takes a breath and slowly returns to her feet. My hands go to her arms, bracing her. "Thanks."

"If you're leaving, where's Ashe? Why isn't he here to—"

"Here you go, Marnie, dear." Ivy pushes a wheeled cart into the room and waves a stack of papers. "Aftercare instructions. I wrote the phone number for the nurse's station on page one. Your prescriptions have been sent to Seagrove Pharmacy." She loads flower arrangements onto the cart.

"Thanks, Ivy. Please, take the flowers for you and the other nurses. Let them brighten up your kitchen tables. All I want is Frilly Willie."

"Only if you're sure," Ivy says. "These peonies are gorgeous."

"Gorgeous until the cats nibble on them and throw up everywhere. Please, help yourself and share with the other patients, too."

"You're so dang sweet, Marnie," Ivy says. "I'll roll them around the floor and see if there are any takers. I'll be back with a wheelchair to wheel you outta here."

"I'll be ready."

She disappears again.

Marina's eyes circle up to mine, her smile faltering. "Ivy's dad studies carnivorous plants. Her sister, Vee, hasn't been home to visit in over a year. She's somewhere exotic, doing environmental research. Can you imagine? Gosh, what an adventure, huh?"

"I don't care about any of that. Where's Ashe?" I try again.

She takes a deep breath, firming her smile. "Jamaica. He and his best man are enjoying our honeymoon. I *encouraged* it. I'm doing so well and didn't want him missing out."

Anger rages inside me, but I try holding it back. I take a deep breath, and with my gentlest voice, I say, "He left you here, like this, in pain, in the care of his tyrannical mother so that he could have his fucking me-time?"

"I wouldn't call her tyrannical. Don't be hard on Ashe. He's... he needs time."

Her big, round eyes circumvent mine, dropping to the suitcase, the floor, the window. She doesn't want to discuss what he needs time for, and shouldn't have to defend him anyway. Not to me. He needs time to mourn what I've stolen, their chance to have children together.

Only I'm not supposed to know that.

"Time," I repeat. "It's generous of you to be okay with that."

Her shoulders bounce softly. "All I'm going to do is lounge on my couch with my cats and watch British TV all day. There's a *Downton Abbey* marathon waiting for me. I don't need Ashe or Cora for that. Leaving today is easier on everyone."

Marina is either the most foolish and naive woman I've ever met or the most stubbornly pragmatic, solving a problem before it becomes one. I wouldn't want Cora's icy brand of mothering or Ashe's moping, either. Could she be a clone of Cora—fiercely independent and happy to keep her man in the background of her life like an accessory she wears on occasion? Not that my opinion matters.

"Fine. How can I help?" I say.

"You aren't responsible for me, either. I don't need any help, but thanks for—"

"How are you getting home?"

She waves her phone. "Lyft. I'll request a ride as soon as I'm on the elevator. We'll pitstop for my prescriptions. I'll have dinner delivered. I've thought of everything."

Her lips edge upwards in a triumphant smirk.

"Not everything. You forgot one important detail about our irritating small town."

"What?"

"It's Sunday. Seagrove Pharmacy is closed."

Her entire demeanor shifts with an anguished expression that still comes off as mildly adorable. "Oh, no, dang it! You're right. I'll have Ivy—"

"Stop. I'll get your meds if you let me drive you home."

Her thin brows cock in a challenge. "If you think I'm letting you drag your mom into work on a Sunday—"

"It's that or Cora, unless you want to spend your evening in unbearable pain."

Her lips pout in a sigh.

"Mom sends me on a hundred errands a week. She'll jump at the chance for me to send her on one. Besides, you're going to need more help than you think. Please, Marina. Let me do this."

Her arms fold in dramatic protest, pressing against her stomach and causing her to grimace. She hesitates to answer, as if debating whether she can trust me.

"Marina, you'll be safe with me. I promise. I'll even be... nice."

She smirks. "Okay, Grady."

CHAPTER NINE

Marnie

IVY ROLLS me to the entrance, where Grady drives up in a classic, red and white Ford truck with honking big tires and a loud rumble like the purr of a very happy cat. It squeaks to a stop, and I chuckle—this isn't what I expected.

Lifting and bending from the chair to the truck steals my amusement. It's downright excruciating. Sharp, angry pains race across my belly. Grady's right—I'll need more help than I expect.

Getting an early release from the hospital may not be one of my winning ideas.

Unless the game is pain. I'd win and get an award for best sportsmanlike conduct.

Not that I want to tell him about my pain. This man has wiggled around in my insides *and* witnessed me at my absolute neediest—I refuse to give him another show. I can't let myself be so vulnerable— not with the people who claim to love me and certainly not with a stranger.

Even a stranger with an uncanny knack for showing up when I need him and superior hand-holding skills.

I ease into the truck. Grady refrains from throwing any I-told-you-so's at me, even as I wince, moan, and otherwise fail to smile through it. He's gracious rather than grouchy, for now, anyway.

I try for quickness, nerves heightened over relying on a stranger's help.

But he braces me gently, our arms snaked together, and says, "Go slow," not like an order but like permission. The same way holding my hand felt like permission to cry.

I breathe and obey, resting my weight against him because I have no choice. Relying on my muscles hurts too much. Once seated, he eases my legs inside the cab. He perches on the running board, leaning over to buckle me in. He smells like a fresh shower and pine.

Though he's a smidge older than me... well, more than a smidge—a decade older—I can't deny that those extra years have done him a favor. He's not just hot but ruggedly handsome. Classic. Time-tested. It's a shame his attractiveness is usually hidden behind his grouchy demeanor. It's like he wears a sign that says, *"Leave me alone."*

He closes the door with a soft click beside me, loads my things in the back, and comes to the driver's side, carrying Frilly Willie. He places that between us, belting it to keep it from sliding. Once behind the wheel, he glances my way. "Okay?"

"Okay."

The engine revs with an impressive growl. The old truck has a long bench front seat, a stick shift rising from the floor, and nothing digital.

"Um, is this yours?"

"No, my Dad's. It was my grandfather's. We call it The Beast."

I smirk. "Aw, a nickname? Cute. It's sweet that you're keeping it in the family."

"I would've brought something more comfortable if I'd known I'd be taking you home. You'll feel every bump. If you need me to slow down, say so."

"I'll be fine," I assure him, just as a small dip in the road makes my insides twinge. In my stationary bed at the hospital, I had no clue that movement would hurt like this. Every time he shifts or brakes, my body takes offense.

"Breathe easy," he says after a few miles. "It's normal to feel pain like that."

"Is it?" I say, breathless and unsure how I'll endure the half-hour out of the city toward Seagrove.

"Yes. Your injury and surgical sites are tender. Your skin, muscles, tendons, arteries, and organs have experienced trauma, and although that soreness is required for healing, jostling worsens it. It's your body telling you to stay still and give it time."

"I'm getting the message," I moan.

"What can I do?"

"I don't know. Keep talking? What's it like being a vet?"

The question irritates him. His rough hands clench the steering wheel while he navigates typical Wilmington traffic, which always seems congested no matter what day it is. He goes slow, double-checking his mirrors whenever he merges. I wonder if the accident made him nervous about driving or if he's nervous about driving *me*.

"What's it like being a cashier?" he redirects, either too distracted by traffic or unwilling to talk about himself. Most likely, it's the latter.

"I'm not a cashier." I wince at the rough road, suddenly jiggling my guts like cranberry sauce during an earthquake. "I'm the customer service manager, the youngest Sunny's has ever had, and I *absolutely love* my job."

He smirks, cutting a glance at me like I've told a joke. "Seriously?"

"As serious as a stab wound," I giggle weakly, but he's not amused. "Don't you love yours?"

His broad shoulders shrug. "I like the animals well enough. Could do without the people."

I laugh. "Somehow, I thought you'd say something like that. My job *is* people. Hiring them. Scheduling them. Making sure the front end runs smoothly so customers feel welcome and can get in and out. And handling all customer needs—"

"Sounds horrible," he breathes, looking anxious as he drives well below the posted speed limit.

"I love making customers feel like family at Sunny's. Not everyone has a family, you know?"

"I've never felt like family in Sunny's."

I give him a curious stare. "How *do* you feel there?"

He groans, his knuckles twisting on the wheel. "Like a victim, assaulted by pretentiousness and high prices."

"Oomph, you're one tough cookie, Tripp Grady Tripp."

"A box of mac-n-cheese shouldn't cost five bucks, and no one in Seagrove needs a ten-dollar box of macaroons or a fifty-dollar jar of saffron."

"It's *organic* mac-n-cheese. Some people buy those items all the time. What's wrong with a grocery store with pizazz?"

"Right, pizazz that pads the Sullivans' pockets. It's a tourist trap that pretends to be a grocery store. No locals would shop there if the nearest Food Lion weren't twenty miles away."

I nod. "Being the only game in town does work to Sunny's advantage. But it's a happy place that people enjoy, too. *Most* people."

"If you say so."

Another laugh escapes me. "You're what I call a customer service challenge, but one I welcome. I almost won you over. Don't you remember?"

His brow pinches until a light flickers in his memory. "Shit, right. I remember."

I smile. "Tell the truth. You still have your complimentary Sunny's keychain, don't you?"

He groans. "Only because the sun is a bottle opener."

I laugh. "I knew you'd keep it. You're practical and willing to fight for a bargain. I appreciate that."

His fingers relax on the steering wheel, like he needs his hands to talk. "If you're going to advertise a buy one, get one, then buying only one steak should mean it's half price."

"Except when the sign says you *must* buy two to get the deal." A shiver runs through me, remembering his angry words through gritted teeth when I made the same argument. *That's bullshit. I want a manager.* And then, the disbelieving look he gave me when I said that was me. In his defense, I present young with my freckles and pale skin, especially at work when sporting a ponytail.

"Sorry if I was... gruff," he says.

It's a surprise to hear him apologize and admit it. *Nice* isn't his go-to behavior. Once, I passed him on the street while he gruffly told a man with a poodle to *"Make an appointment."* Another time, at the pharmacy, I overheard him arguing with his mom, Carmela, over dropping off something to his brother. *"Mom, I'm not the Tripp family delivery boy,"* he said before taking the bag anyway and storming down the aisle.

"You were a little lamb," I chuckle, not wanting to make him feel worse. "And not the first or last to complain. I was happy to give you the deal... Between us, I don't like that sale either. It puts me on defense. It's hard delivering my excellent customer service when the customer's already pissed off."

He cuts me a surprised look. "Hm, Marina cusses?"

A light shrug makes me wince. We climb the bridge over the Cape Fear River, the gentle thumps underneath us creating a constant ache in my belly. Tears pool in my eyes, anxious for the bridge to be over despite how much I love ogling the battleship, the choppy waves, and the quaint downtown.

"Need a break?" he asks, his voice surprisingly gentle. "We could stop on the other side. Get something to eat if you're hungry."

My head shakes before he finishes talking. "I just want to get home... Sorry if that sounds weepy."

"No apologies, remember?"

A relieved sigh calms me, especially hearing him say my words from *that* day. I didn't need his apologies then, and I'm glad he doesn't want mine now. It's like he's giving me permission to be whatever I need.

"Um, did you tell the Sullivans that the deal was bullshit?" he asks, drawing my focus.

"I voiced my concerns, but it's a numbers game for them. Most people buy multiple steaks. Some see a buy one, get one, and decide to stock up their freezers. Little do they know, the Sullivans raised the price per pound days before the sale. So, really, the savings are pretty negligible, and the Sullivans get to move a lot of steaks, even with lone dissenters like you."

"They're crooks."

"They're smart business people. Besides, it's best to pick my battles for something that matters to more people. You know, the ones not buying steaks."

"Like?"

"A grocery rewards program for locals," I say, perking up. "Something that'll save them money across the board, and keep them from driving to Food Lion. Once Ashe takes the new store and I'm Seagrove's manager, I think Cora will let me try it."

"Don't you feel weird? Marrying your boss?"

A chuckling scoff erupts. "I did at first. But it happened so naturally over time that it seemed almost inevitable. Sunny's *is* my family, so it makes sense—Ashe and me."

"And Ashe taking off on you... is that another example of you picking your battles with the Sullivans? Anyone else would be furious."

I fiddle with the hem of my sundress, feeling suddenly uncomfortable. *Should I be mad?*

I hate being twenty-five and still not knowing what I should be. Navigating hard emotions, especially regarding Ashe or family in general, feels like standing on the wrong side of a raging river and not knowing which rock to jump on to get me across. Will the angry rock get me to the other side of this? Or the sad one? Resigned has space. So, does the disappointed rock. Or should I simply stay put and avoid rocky emotions altogether?

That seems the safest choice.

"I love him and wouldn't deny him anything," I say. "Why would I deny him this?"

"Why would he deny you his love and care when you need it most?"

His question hangs there like a bad smell, lingering and making me grimace. Though I'm cold, the truck suddenly feels stifling. I use the crank to lower the window, wincing with each tug and pull. The cool air hits my face, drying my eyes, and makes my hair dance in crazy waves. The last thing I want to admit right now is that a stranger's comfort has been kinder than that of my fiancé.

I've been alone since fifteen, paying my bills on time and caring for myself. I operate on a budget, get routine oil changes, pay taxes that I do myself, and worry about things like affordable health care and rising food costs. I was an adult before my time and am certainly one now.

But sometimes, I feel an awkward, child-like uncertainty over the basics like love and family. I didn't grow up with it, so how can I know the roles, rules, and expectations? Even TV versions feel fake, existing in this untouchable universe like "normal family life" is my Mars. I don't know how to survive here.

Except to smile, chat, and make everything okay for everyone else.

My work family takes me in stride, but I see my awkwardness reflected back on me whenever I ask about their children's birthday parties or ailing grandparents. I feel as if I'm not supposed to know or care about these things, even if they share tidbits of information with me in passing. Sometimes, I feel like people chat to fill time, not realizing someone's actually listening.

I listen. That's what having a work family means. Right?

It's the same with customers. If I'm told about your husband's upcoming surgery during a chat in the cereal aisle, I'm going to ask about it next time I see you. Still, I catch people off guard.

"Ah, you remembered," they say, glancing quickly at my name tag. "He's doing well, Marnie. Thanks."

Rarely does anyone ask about me, let alone question my relationship, and maybe I'm not close enough to anyone for that. But it bothers me that *he* cares to ask—this stranger with a ginormous, beautiful family and slews of Seagrovians desperate to know more about him, though afraid to approach Grouchy Tripp themselves. He makes it clear that he couldn't care less about getting to know any of them.

The day he confronted me about the meat, no less than seven customers and employees asked me about the interaction.

So, he's definitely not a vegetarian?

What else did you find out about him?

What's he like?

Did you see his smolder?

Do you think he's single?

Did his heart seem dead from euthanizing so many animals?

That came from my reluctant protege, Wren Christie, whose pitch-black hair, piercings, and witch vibe provide an unusual challenge in customer service, not that I don't rise to meet it. I don't care how black your eyeliner is or how many piercings you have, a smile works wonders.

The point is, Grady Tripp's existence doesn't match mine. Not by a mile. And the distance between us is full of thick forests, rocky terrain, bodies of water, and booby traps.

Anyone with the *luxury* of being a grouch doesn't have a clue what Marnie-land is like.

Knowing this, his question shouldn't bother me. But it does. It's niggling away at my insides like his words are toothy termites.

Why *would* Ashe deny me his love and care?

Why *wouldn't* he choose me over himself just *this once*?

Or choose his mom's advice over *his promise*?

The more I think about it, the more it hurts.

But Grady does me a favor and says nothing else until we reach Seagrove.

CHAPTER TEN

HER HOUSE ISN'T A SHED, as those idiots in the coffee shop said, but close. It's a small cottage, maybe five hundred square feet, oozing with forced homeyness, like it's convincing itself it's a house with plants all over the tiny porch and a front window that's too big for a place this size. A sprawling brick rancher with an enormous attached garage and workshop overshadows it from thirty yards back and they share a driveway, like the tiny house was an afterthought. Or a lawn decoration.

Her place is within walking distance of Seagrove's downtown and a half-mile from Sunny's, making convenience its best amenity. She directs me to the gravel lot between her front door and the road, and The Beast comes to a squeaking stop.

"Thanks for the ride," she says, not sounding as chipper as usual. She works the handle, barely pushing the heavy door open and wincing with each movement.

"Wait. I'll come around." I rush to meet her there before her stubbornness puts her in more pain with a move that's too quick.

She looks unsure when I lean into the cab beside her.

"Where are your keys?"

She motions to the bag at her feet. I maneuver around her, finding the keys and putting them in her left hand.

"Let's do this easier than we did at the hospital," I say, locking eyes with her. "What's your pain level, one to ten?"

"Six."

"Let's not let it get any higher. I'll carry you."

"Um, no. That's unnecessary. It's just to the door—"

"It's getting out, walking, stepping up. You feel the most pain when your body is straight. I can keep you bent like you're sitting."

Her brow pinches into a worried V. "I could hobble."

"You could, but the trip was hard enough. I only want to make it easier for you."

When she hesitates again, I slip my hand over hers, taking a chance that she'll remember my comfort, not just the pain I've caused. "I look rough, but I promise I'll be gentle."

Her soft smile widens like she's almost breathless. "You are gentle. I know that already. It's just..."

"Weird," I finish for her. "I get it. But I'm here and happy to help. Or not. Whatever you'd like."

"You, happy?" She gives me a challenging grin.

A smirk rises on my cheek as I lean against the doorjamb. "It happens from time to time. I know it's hard to trust me since this is my fault in the first place."

"No, it's because you're practically a stranger." Her brow pinches as she fiddles with her gauzy dress. "I'm fully aware that it shouldn't be you taking me home and carrying me through the door."

My empathy for her reaches a new level. Not only is she hurt and in pain, but she's reliant on me because her so-called family couldn't bother to step up. This must absolutely suck for her. I vow then and there to ditch my grouchy side, at least with her, and be whatever she needs me to be. Whatever it takes to get her through this.

"You're right—it shouldn't be me. But I'm glad it is. I like being here, doing this for you."

She perks up slightly. "Really?"

"Truly."

She smiles at this. "Thanks, Grady."

"Could be worse. A Lyft driver would've been more awkward, right?"

She allows a short smirk and hesitantly rests her right arm on my shoulder.

I move closer, ready to scoop her into my arms. "I can flip a sheep into a catatonic state. I can handle you. If that helps…"

"Oh, Grady, sheep flipping? I bet you say that to all the girls," she snickers.

I chuckle despite myself. "Sheep flipping. Parasite control. Dehorning calves. I've got all the best lines. That's why you see me with so many women."

Her laughter rumbles and fills me with rare delight—I'm glad she knows I'm joking. No one in Seagrove has seen me with a woman, regardless of how many have tried. She slips her hand tentatively around my neck. One arm against her back and the other under her knees, I slowly and easily cradle her to me. The initial jolt of going airborne causes a pained gulp, but then, resting her head on my chest, she sighs.

"Okay?"

She manages a smile. "Yes, that's good."

I shift her against me, momentarily struck by how much I like her weight in my arms, her long hair dangling over my shoulder, and her inexplicable softness. I take one careful step around The Beast at a time, gauging her expression as a pain indicator.

"My father had a heart attack two years ago," I say, hoping to distract her. "After heart bypass surgery and six days in the hospital, I drove him home. He had to put a pillow between his chest and the seatbelt."

"Dang, that would've been a good idea," she winces.

"Here's what I learned going through that with him," I continue, taking one step at a time up to her porch. "First, the next forty-eight hours will be the toughest."

She watches me as I talk, and I like her rapt attention so much that it unnerves me. I stub my foot against the top step, distracted by her. "Um, overexertion makes it worse," I say quickly. "If it's not an absolute necessity, leave it. Understood?"

"Yes, doc."

"Unlock the door."

She fumbles with the keys but gets the door open.

"Couch or bed?"

"Couch, thanks."

Cats meow and circle my legs, but I shift through them to a plush, red couch. It's not full-size; I doubt anything full-size can exist here, but it's large enough to seem comfortable for her. With careful precision, I lay her down. She looks surprised not to be writhing in pain. I go slow, releasing my grip underneath her, allowing myself to linger close.

Then, I realize I'm hovering, too close and too much touching, too many thoughts I shouldn't be having. "Um, I like your freckles."

She laughs. "That's better than the sheep flipping line."

I stand up straight, letting go. "Not a line. Truth."

"Thanks, that's sweet. Next thing I know, you'll be calling me Carrots."

"Ah, no. I won't do that."

"Never seen *Anne of Green Gables*?" she asks.

"Hmm, it sounds like something I'd watch, but I must've missed it between *John Wick* and *Die Hard* marathons."

Her laughter makes me smile. *Wait, am I... bantering?* Secondary to that phenomenon, *am I enjoying it?* It's been so long, I can't remember the last time I willingly engaged in pleasant conversation with someone outside my family. More surprising is how easily it's happening with her.

Her laughs end with an uncomfortable wince. "You're funnier than I thought you'd be."

"No, I'm not. You bring it out of me."

"Then, good. It looks nice on you." Her eyes dance with mine. "But I can't handle any more giggles. They hurt, you know?"

"Well, if you aren't laughing, then..." I tease.

Her cats jump onto the couch beside her, and she laughs at the purring welcome party.

"So, learn anything else from your Dad?" she asks, mid-pets.

"Oh, one last thing. It takes as long as it takes."

She repeats my words, as if memorizing them.

"Yep, healing, walking, getting back to normal, everything," I say. "So, no rushing it."

"Got it. How is he? Your dad?"

My eyes narrow, taken aback by the question. "Good, thanks. As bull-headed as ever."

"So, it runs in the family, then?"

"Absolutely."

Her side smirk stretches up her cheek, puffing it in an obnoxiously friendly, adorable way. I could elaborate on Dad's health, and she'd soak up the tedious information regardless of how boring it'd be to her. So, I don't wait for more questions but leave to bring in her things.

I don't ask permission to take her suitcase into her bedroom. I set it atop an old chest at the foot of her bed so she doesn't have to pick it up, and even open it for her, putting her things at arm's reach. I glance around and spot things I wouldn't expect in a twenty-five-year-old's bedroom, not that I've been in many.

A puffy, antique quilt in a rainbow of colors monopolizes her bed —something Mom would buy at a craft show.

Oddball art covers her walls. An almost-bad painting of a cat wearing a crown. Random British-looking landscapes with chunky frames.

An old CD player and two short CD towers.

I round the double bed to eye her music. One tower is labeled AM, and the other PM. Upbeat music falls under her morning listens. Early Taylor Swift. Mac Miller. Mozart. Bach. Beyonce. Pharrell Williams. The Beach Boys. Katrina and the Waves. Under PM, she prefers Juice WRLD, Post Malone, Chance the Rapper, Jay-Z, Ruth B, and Norah Jones.

I smile, flipping through the stack of old-school CDs and her eclectic collection. She has everything from jazz to classical to rap.

"Everything okay back there?"

I answer by popping in a CD and hitting play. The sultry sounds of Norah Jones and the delicate taps of a piano fill the small house. The notes appear in my head, making my fingers twitch.

"Nosey Nelly!" She exclaims, laughing.

I travel through the short hallway, passing a large bathroom with a stackable washer and dryer. A closed door across the hall makes me curious, but I don't go in.

"Thought you might like a little music," I tell her.

"I'm always down for music." She smiles at me from the couch, still petting the cats, snuggling at her sides.

"Nice CD collection. I thought I was the old one here. Ever heard of streaming?"

She gapes over my joke. "Yes! But I get ten CDs for a dollar at any thrift store! That's way better than paying monthly for a service. Plus, it's nice, rescuing things."

I nod, looking around at her rehomed cats and thrifted furniture. That's what she does. She rescues things.

Her place is tidy and interestingly put together. It's all warm beiges, pops of red, and earthy greens, but not like Christmas. The red couch matches her red hair and the red tulips on the curtains. The greens in her lampshades and knick-knacks match her enormous plant collection—they're everywhere, somehow livening the place up without looking cluttered. The beige carpet, throw pillows, and blankets match her mismatched wood furniture, adding warmth and golden hues. It's a home constructed via yard sales that somehow works.

But for what it has in oddities, it lacks in personable items. Nearly every blank wall space is filled with shelves and frames, but only one picture—a framed selfie of her and Ashe at the beach—sits on the table beside her.

The best feature of her living room and kitchenette is the natural light from the oversized window in the front and a smaller version in the back. Cat towers take up most of the real estate there, what space isn't monopolized by plants hanging from the ceiling or shelved against the walls. There's a small TV and console opposite the couch, a two-seater dining area shoved against the back window, and a kitchen so small it's a wonder there's room for an oven.

Between jazzy Norah Jones ballads, I bring in a tote of magazines and snacks and Frilly Willie. She instructs me to put him on the dining table. I set the magazines on her coffee table—she doesn't seem the type to read *Vogue*.

In the kitchen, I put the muffins and Reese's cups on the counter near the coffee maker. While there, I check her nearly empty fridge and cabinets.

Watching my every move, she says, "I'll have someone bring me supplies from Sunny's. No biggie."

"Who'd you have watching the cats?"

"Oh, my landlord and neighbor, Peter Pike. And Wren Christie from work."

"Ed Christie's kid?"

Marina grins. "Gosh, was that her father? I didn't make the connection. I've already told them I'm home, but they'll still check in. They won't mind picking up some groceries for me. I've got it covered, Grady."

I prop her cane beside her. "Need help to the bathroom or anything?"

"No, thanks. I can do that."

"More music or TV?"

"Um, TV," she says.

In her bedroom, I turn off the CD player. Then, I hand her the remote control from the table and kneel before her since the small couch is overrun with cats. The orange tabby, presumably Sunkist, stands and arches next to me, flicking her tail along my cheek.

A laugh rumbles out of me as I pet her velvety fur, and she meows her approval.

"She likes you," Marina whispers, like this is a secret. "Hershey's unsure yet. He's not used to another guy around."

A glance at the narrow-eyed cat at her feet confirms his suspicious glare. "Not even Ashe?"

"He doesn't like my place. Triscuit scratched at him once," she shrugs, and then winces. "Um, thanks for all you've done."

"I'm not done yet. Here's what's going to happen, and it'll be quicker if you don't argue. I'll get your prescriptions so you can have them before you start hurting. When I come back, I'll take care of Triscuit's ears."

"Ah, you remembered!"

"Course. Anything else you need?"

She shakes her head, making her long, copper locks dance on her shoulders.

"I'm taking your keys to lock the door, so you won't have to get up when I get back." I tug the crocheted blanket on the back of the couch over her and around the cats.

"There's cash in my purse," she says, "for the prescriptions."

I stand, ignoring her money offer, and grab the keys on the coffee table. "Get some rest."

I leave, locking the door behind me.

After a Food Lion haul, I meet Mom at Seagrove Pharmacy, where she lets me in the darkened store with the bells chiming overhead.

"Just printing out the labels." She waves me through the quiet aisles to the pharmacy in the back. She wears her white lab coat, though the store is closed.

"How's Marnie?"

"Home and hurting."

She flashes a concerned look. "Grady, it's not your fault."

"Stop saying that. It *is* my fault."

"It was an accident. The more times you hear it, the quicker you'll believe it," she says, her reading glasses perched on her nose. She taps her computer keys and moves around the small space. "I'm glad you're helping her, but I'm surprised, too."

"There's no one else to do it. Cora's too much to deal with and Ashe's gone on their honeymoon without her."

Mom's the textbook definition of appalled. "No! Did they break up? Over a car accident?"

"No, not that it's any of our business. Almost done? I want to get back."

She folds the paperwork, checks the pill vials, and puts everything into a small paper bag. "I don't know Marnie well, but she deserves better."

"Anyone deserves better."

"She used to come in here, haggling for her mom's pills," Mom muses.

"Haggling?"

"She'd try and get her mom extras to hold her over until her prescription was renewed. Her mom struggled to make her doctor's appointments. She'd go off her meds. Then, get back on them. It was hard on Marnie."

"Again, not our business."

She hands the bag over. "Grady, take a heating pad from aisle three. I'll put it on my account. Marnie might need it. Oh, and a box of chocolates. They'll all go on clearance tomorrow anyway, and the antioxidants will give her a healing boost."

I grab the electric heating pad and pass the long table up front with Valentine's Day leftovers. It seems like a dumb idea, bringing her Valentine's Day chocolates—another reminder of the day I ruined for her.

But she'd probably appreciate the gesture.

I tuck the biggest box under my arm.

"Atta boy!" Mom says.

"Thanks, Mom."

"Anything to help, Grady. I mean that. All you have to do is ask."

I nod, knowing that's true and feeling grateful for once.

CHAPTER ELEVEN

Marnie

PAIN WAKES ME, sharp and unforgiving, like electric shocks ripping over my midsection. It's a wonder I fell asleep at all. Sunkist meows near my feet, like she can sense my distress. It feels like I've been run over by a motorcycle, and the driver keeps spinning the wheels on top of me. I groan, trying to sit up.

After he left, I initiated all my comforts. I carefully changed out of my ridiculous sundress and flip-flops to warm pajamas and slippers. I managed the bathroom, washed my face, and brushed my teeth. A mug of chamomile tea sits mostly gone on the coffee table. At the time, it felt good to move around and be here, where I'm most comfortable.

Now, I regret leaving, the hurt so debilitating that my eyes water, and I fully expect to spend the night moaning and wincing. I've never known pain like this. Not even close. Not even on *that* day, as if the trauma and shock subdued my nerve sensors.

When the doorknob jiggles, announcing Grady's return, I nearly call out, "Go away!"

My cats' scrutinizing glares are bad enough. Their perked ears and rapt big eyes prove their heightened anxieties, and add tension to my pain. I don't need other witnesses, especially if I break down crying.

I *hate* crying.

But I can't find my voice or the nerve to be so mean. I refuse to let my pain become someone else's. Grady overflows with regret as it is.

With a breathless groan, I sit up, gripping my cane like a stress ball.

He pushes inside, arms loaded with reusable totes from Food Lion, the tags still hanging from their handles. Food Lion has the *best* reusable totes, and he splurged on the heavy-duty ones.

Elbowing the door shut, his bright blue eyes run over me. "Pain level?"

"Um, rising."

"Give me a number."

"Eight."

He drops the bags at the door and digs through them. Within a minute, he's beside me, handing over pills and water. I sling them into my throat and guzzle the water to push them down.

But queasiness soon joins the pain, making me think they'll come back up.

His hand rests softly on my back. "Deep breaths."

"Hurts," I mutter, unable to hold it in.

"I know."

"Please, go. I'll be fine. I want to be alone."

"I know, but indulge me. Please," he says softly. "You should eat. Soup, salad, sandwich, or junk food?"

I want to argue. He's done enough and surely has better things to do with his time than babysit me. But I don't have the energy. "Um, soup."

"Good. Keep breathing."

He leaves me for the discarded bags, hefting them into the kitchen. Wincing with pain, I grab the remote and turn up the volume on *Antiques Roadshow UK*, if only to distract me from the intense pain and the man in my kitchen.

But it's hard not to watch him.

Oh, the gossipers at Sunny's would have bug eyes and dropped jaws at this sight—hot and mysterious, Grady Tripp in my kitchen. He's top-tier good-looking. If Seagrove sold a sexy calendar for a Christmas fundraiser, Grady Tripp would be every month; only the cute animal he was holding would vary. He's not very tall, but he's solid, like a bookend or brick wall, especially with his arms folded, his signature move. It's not just his overall ruggedness that makes him so nice to look at, either. It's his age, too. Men are so dang lucky that way. There's a mature rigidness to his features, hammered out by years of heavy lifting and farm work. But a gentleness, too. His fine lines and spotty grays make him look approachable when he isn't scowling. And his smile, when he dares share it, warms me with delight.

It's almost a surprise to learn that he's kind, too. The way he helped me, saved me, held my hand.

From the looks of his bounty, he cleared out Food Lion's premade sandwiches, salads, and soups. He pops one into the microwave before filling my fridge with the rest. He stocked up on staples: eggs, milk, cheese, yogurt, butter. He places Cheerios, chicken noodle soup cans, and mac-n-cheese boxes in my cabinet. A loaf of bread, peanut butter, and a package of deli meat appear next. Frozen entrees go into the freezer along with a tub of Neapolitan ice cream.

It's more food than I usually have. Or need.

But his kindness keeps showing up in unexpected places.

"You're turning me into a traitor." My joke comes across as weak and half-hearted with my increasing pain.

He smirks lightly, holding up Food Lion brand tuna from deep inside my cabinet. "Seems like you're already converted."

"Yeah, I can't afford Sunny's, either," I breathe, wincing. "I wear hats, sunglasses, and baggy clothes when I go to Food Lion in case I run into a local. Don't tell anyone."

This earns a slight chuckle and that dazzling half-smile. "Your secret's safe with me."

He brings me steaming hot potato and corn chowder with crackers on the side, which he sets on the coffee table. I scoot up, wincing as I do.

"The pain pills will kick in soon," he says. "Don't take them without food. Okay?"

"Okay."

He grabs a notepad and pen from the coffee table and jots something down. Then, he holds it up to show me that he's logged the date, time, and medication I just took. "It's good to keep track to prevent under- or overdosing."

He makes me think of Mom. "Um, that's smart. Thanks."

"Another thing I learned from Dad." He nods toward the soup. "Eat."

Though my stomach revolts, I gulp several spoonfuls.

"Grady, take some money from my purse. For the groceries."

He grunts. "Not a chance. Stop offering."

When the cats circle him in the kitchen, he asks about my feeding routine. He follows my instructions, even separating their bowls without me having to say anything. Hershey gets greedy.

When they finish, he hand-washes their bowls and sets them on the rack to dry. Then, he retrieves his medical bag from The Beast and gently examines Triscuit's ears.

"Wax build-up," he says after ten seconds. He scratches under her chin, and she purrs loudly. "No wonder she's bothered. I'll irrigate them."

"Aw, thanks. You're a lifesaver," I say with a short giggle.

His blue eyes cut to mine. Not amused.

Triscuit's ears get cleaned in less than five minutes. He frees her with a gentle, "Good girl." Then, he snaps off his gloves and washes his hands in the kitchen sink. He sorts his things, rearranges some of the groceries, and, looking somewhat sheepish, sets a large heart-shaped box of chocolates on the coffee table. "Mom said you'd want something sweet, and chocolate's good for the, um, antioxidants."

"Ah, Carmela's always been so good to me," I say, thinking back on all the times I asked her for help with Mom's medications as a teenager. "Thanks, Grady. I don't know what I would've done without your help today."

He runs his hand over his cropped head, looking agitated, like a propeller plane, unsure where to land. He returns to the kitchen, folding the bags and tucking them behind my bread box.

"If you want to stay, the rule is you have to relax."

"Do you want me to stay?" He catches my eyes in his. "Truth."

"You aren't obligated to me, Grady."

"Leaving you alone worries me. What if you need help? Do you have someone to call?" he asks gently.

My mind goes blank. I shake my head, feeling weaker than seems possible. The pain in my midsection, a headache nipping at my temples, and my swirling pit of a stomach beg me for solitude. I predict a long night of sobbing and whining to my cats. These are private things I should handle alone, as I've done with every uncomfortable moment I've ever had. But Grady's crystalline eyes fix on mine, intense and desperate. Regret shadows the lines on his face like scars he'll never get over. I understand the feeling.

"I'll be fine, but you're welcome to stay if it helps."

"I only want to help *you*," he groans.

"You have. All I want to do is sleep," I admit, sounding weepy.

He nods, takes a breath, and crosses the room. He grabs my phone from the side table and hands it to me. "Open it."

I do as I'm told. He snaps a stern picture of himself with my phone and swipes his fingers across it in a flurry. As he types, a message pings, causing his brow to quirk and his eyes to roll slightly.

He returns the phone, showing me that he's added himself as a contact under Tripp Grady Tripp, using the stern pic as his avatar. I chuckle lightly. Under a new text from Ashe, Grady texted himself one word.

Marina.

"It doesn't matter the hour. It doesn't matter the reason. I'm here if you need anything. Promise me, you won't hesitate to reach out."

"I promise."

He looks skeptical, sizing me up with those electric eyes of his. Once again, it looks like he has a million thoughts damned up behind his intense stare. I reach out, and his hand drifts easily into mine. His rough gentleness takes me back to my first night in the hospital when his hands around mine felt like a lifeline in a dark place. He kneels before me, enclosing my hand in both of his.

"Marina," he says finally, "You might be the nicest, sweetest person I've ever met..."

I'm about to coo and gush thanks, but his stern look cuts me off.

"...But now is not the time for *nice*. Whatever you want or need takes priority. Understood?"

My eyes narrow while my lips curl into a smirk I can't contain. "Go home, Grady."

He laughs. "That's my girl."

Then, looking sheepish again, he diverts to the cats, giving them each a pet before heading to the door.

I close my eyes, breathing in the cold wave from him opening the door. My phone pings again—reminding me of Ashe's text.

> Are you mad?

I don't know how I'm supposed to be. Not *nice*, I suppose. I push the soup away, my appetite gone. My side aches.

I lean against the back of the couch, closing my eyes and willing the pain pills to do their thing. *Come on, little buddies. You can do it. Kick that pain's butt.*

My phone pings again.

> I'll book a flight home. I shouldn't have listened
> to her.

But, you did listen to her, Ashe. You left. Wrangling my inner not-niceness, I type words I know I should say.

But then I can't hit send and delete them.

Instead, I give him the words he wants. I always know what he wants me to say, like I'm a Magic 8 Ball of acceptable responses designed to appease him.

> It's okay, Ashe. I'm doing so well, I came home early.
> If you need time away, then you should take it.

I hit send quickly, wanting him to argue. Needing him to do the right thing on his own. Hoping he books that flight anyway, just because he misses me and knows I'm hurting. Clearly, he regrets taking his mom's advice—maybe it took a plane ride for him to come to his senses.

I'll see how I feel tomorrow. I'm exhausted. Glad
you're home. Is Mom taking good care of you?

I close my eyes, letting more disappointment settle atop the high stack like a wobbly game of *Jenga*. When will it become too much, making me fall over?

Another text pings, this time from Grady. My eyes roll that he uses my full name.

Marina

This is entirely fucked up.

My fault.

I only want to make this easier for you.

Tell me to back the hell off if I'm ever too much.

Grady.

I groan and whimper from the pain it causes. All these needy men!

Even worse, I can't help but compare this stranger who wrecked everything to my almost-husband, who's not even here.

Grady, I understand.

It's like that time I dropped a jar of pickles, and green pickle juice splashed all over Mrs. Johanson's summer white capris. She was on her way to karaoke with her girlfriends. I felt horrible. I tried to clean them for her. On my hands and knees, I tried to Tide-pen the green out. Finally, I offered her my pants so she wouldn't be late. We're roughly the same size. She treated me graciously, said a little pickle juice never killed anyone, and went on her merry way. But that didn't stop me from feeling bad about it. I offered to pay for her dry cleaning the next time I saw her. She didn't accept, and, to this day, I feel I didn't do enough.

That's how Grady feels on a much deeper and meaningful scale.

He pickle-juiced my day, and feels horrible about it. I believe he'd do anything I need to make it better—he'll even be nice about it. That's how I'd be if the situation were reversed.

But what can make it better?

Ashe could. He's the one I don't get. My almost-husband now feels more like a stranger than ever, as if not meeting him at the church meant we expired like sour milk. Never to be the same again.

We aren't the same. We've never been *the same*.

The drugs work their numbing magic. They do nothing to numb my sadness, though. *Don't think about it now. Good thoughts, Marnie. No frowns, no fears, no tears.*

I text Grady back, smirking as I use his format.

Grady.

Okay.

Marina.

Good.

He answers a moment later.

Ice packs are in the freezer. There's a heating pad on the kitchen table if you need it. I forgot to tell you.

I thumbs up his message, grateful. Ten agonizing minutes later, I have the icepack resting on my giant jellyfish-sized bruise and the heating pad against my sore shoulders.

I stare at Ashe's words, again disappointed that he's let me down.

Still, I answer him.

She doesn't know I'm home yet. I want to recover here with the cats. I'll call her in the morning. I'm tired, too.

The ellipsis bubbles.

I'll explain to Mom. Get some rest.

"Well, that's something."

Like my words are an invitation, Triscuit jumps into the space beside me, and the other cats follow, taking their usual spots—an orange, black, and Calico bundle.

My phone pings again.

Pills kicking in yet?

Yes. Relax, Grady.

Good night, Marina.

I fall asleep during *Antiques Roadshow UK* and dream about pine trees, concrete, and Grady's solid chest, his heartbeat rumbling under my ear.

CHAPTER TWELVE

Grady

MARINA LOOKS GENUINELY SURPRISED to see me at her door at 7:30 the next morning. It *is* early, but I wanted to check in before the clinic opens at 8:00.

"Tripp Grady Tripp," she says, her voice weak and her eyes squinting. "Aren't you an early bird?"

"What's wrong?"

Her delicate fingers wave me off as she leans against the doorjamb. "Headache. That's all. Didn't sleep much."

"Pain level?"

She sighs, rubbing her temples. "With the headache, I'd say eight. I've taken my pills."

"Did you eat?"

She shakes her head, but the action pains her. "Too nauseous to eat."

"When did the headache start?"

"I don't know. Around midnight. It's been worse than the rest, if you can believe it."

"This is an example of you being too nice. You should've called me."

She blanches at my tone. "Why? What would you have done? It's a headache."

I edge by her, bringing us both inside. I rest my palm against her forehead, but my hands are too cold to tell if she has a fever.

"I checked. It's normal," she says.

Of course, she's checked, Grady. She's an adult with common sense. Try not to be condescending.

I take her wrist between my fingers and eye my watch. Her heart rate is elevated but not racing.

"Any unusual swelling or heat around your wound sites?"

"I think it looks normal."

"Want me to look? I'm a doctor."

She hesitates in a mental debate that ends with a simple nod. She lifts her pajama top, but unable to see her wounds clearly, I drop to my knees and slowly tug her loose-fitting pants down to her hip line just over her panties. Goosebumps appear under my fingers as I touch her.

"Cold hands. Sorry."

She smirks, her eyes squinted. "It's okay."

Her pale, freckled skin is patched by internal stitches, pinching her skin together. Scabs reveal typical healing—no redness or inflammation.

The bruise on her side brings a "Fucking hell" out of me. I edge to her left, ogling the enormous contusion.

"Giant Jelly," she breathes out. "Told you."

It looks as if she received a terrible tattoo—all blacks and blues, stringing down her hip from a large round knob that starts under her left arm. Touching it causes more goosebumps, but I run my fingers over it anyway to test the temperature and swelling. Again, nothing stands out except how painful it looks.

Her hands fall to my shoulders, bracing herself like she can't stand this long. I hold her at her hips for extra support, and she doesn't mind my grip, the way she presses into me.

"Have you been icing this?"

"Yep, every three hours or so."

I ease her clothes back to their appropriate places as tenderly as I can.

"Thanks, doc. But sometimes a headache is just a headache," she says, looking woozy.

In her dizziness, she leans toward me. I gently scoop her into my arms as I stand.

She gasps, wrapping her arms weakly around my shoulders and muttering, "Grady."

"Everything's okay, but here's what's going to happen," I say, edging her through the hallway. "I'm going to take care of you. You're going to let me. We'll get through this together. No arguments."

Her head falls to my chest, forgoing any further discussion.

I lay her gently onto her unmade bed, careful of her left side. Her red hair flays out behind her against the white pillowcase, reminding me of *that* day when her head was against the concrete. All her pain is my fault. My responsibility. My doing. And just like that day, I can't leave her.

I wouldn't want to, anyway. Even if I hadn't caused this. Something about her shatters my rule about not getting involved. I *want* to be here.

After tucking her in, I return to the living room and do what I *never* do. I call in sick to the clinic—baffling Aunt Elena.

My second call is to the hospital unit, and luckily, Ivy answers the phone. Once I have the necessary information, I check Marina's medicine log—she's up-to-date on everything. Then, I grab the ice pack and return to Marina.

She's in the same pained heap that I left her in. I draw the curtains to make the room darker, kick off my shoes, and climb into bed beside her. I wrestle her pillow into my lap with her on it and gently apply the ice pack.

She gasps at the cold shock but soon smiles and sighs as the numbing relief hits her.

"It's a migraine," I say softly. "It may be a side effect of the anesthesia. It happens. Ivy will speak to your surgeon and ask her to prescribe a migraine medication for you. Once it's called in and ready, Mom will drop it off. Then, we'll balance that with your pain pills."

"Oh, never had a migraine before."

"Yeah, they suck." I slip my fingers under the cold icepack, gently massaging her temples.

Her crinkled brow releases immediately, and the tension in her shoulders deflates.

"Grady, thank you."

Her genuineness catches me off guard. I hear thank you's all the time, quick responses to me taking care of a pet or solving a cattle problem. Mom rattles off thank you's as often as please's, especially when her tasks get done. Even Marigold says it easily now—a social expectation she's learned well. Thank you's drop into my don't-care file along with a dictionary of words that are nice, but don't mean much.

Marina is a thank-you-type person, but I feel warmed by her gratitude for such simple things as a phone call and an ice pack—warmed by her generally.

There's a delicate strength to her that shines through her beauty. It makes me think of my grandmother's heavy crystal dishes that Mom pulls out for Thanksgiving. How the cut glass reflects the candlelight. Soft and strong together.

Mom's words come to mind, how Marnie would haggle for her mom's pills at fifteen. There's no mom here now, fussing over her like mine would, no buzz of her phone, asking if she's okay, no nothing. Hell, she couldn't even reach out to one person to pick her up from the hospital.

She's lived in this town since she was a teenager. Where the fuck are her friends, at least?

Marina, how the hell are you so alone?

If she were a recluse or an asshole, I'd get it. I'm the asshole who tries to be a recluse, and it doesn't work out most of the time; avoiding people is hard work. But she's friendly, outgoing, beautiful, even interesting. She's the type who'd befriend anyone. But no one's here for her.

Marina's existence comes into focus as I rub her head. She's a fucking golden retriever, friendly and happy-go-lucky, almost to a fault, always smiling. But without a family. Close connections aren't inherent for her. She exists in the background of other people's lives at Sunny's. She might as well be a mascot—everyone's happy to see her, but no one takes her home.

I don't get why. She is beautifully easy to be with, even for me. Or maybe the easiness is just us. We're trauma-bonded. Connected. She must feel it, too—I wouldn't be in her bed otherwise. She falls asleep, her rhythmic breathing lulling me.

I didn't sleep much last night either, plagued by Marina-nightmares. They were just a manifestation of my anxiety over her healing, but those dreams rattled me. In the worst one, pieces of her were scattered all over the road, and I tried desperately to put her back together again. A finger here. A freckle there. I remember finding her smile and thinking, how can she still smile? I gathered all the pieces but couldn't hold them together.

Relax, Grady. A deep breath centers me as I lean against her headboard.

The world will slow down if you let it. If you stop setting the pace. Aunt Elena's words circle with Marina's, loosening my tension.

She's here. She's sleeping. She's okay. I run my hand over her forehead and through her hair. The world gets quiet.

A dreamless sleep swallows me up.

Knocking wakes me. Soft, at first. Then, harder.

Marina sleeps soundly, nestled to me, her arms locked around my midsection like I'm a body pillow.

I'm strangely okay with that.

The knocking persists. It must be Mom with the migraine medications. Gently, I shift out from under her, untangling us, though I don't want to. She doesn't wake.

I swing the front door open mid-loud pounding.

Cora Sullivan. In full business-formal. Carrying an absurdly large gift basket wrapped in cellophane.

Her practiced smile drops at the sight of me. She practically seethes. "Why are you here? Where's Marnie?"

"In bed. Asleep," I whisper. "I'd like to keep it that way. She's had a rough night."

She scoffs, pushing the basket into my arms and bulldozing her way inside. "You've been here *all night*?"

"No."

"You shouldn't be here at all," she barks, not even trying to be quiet.

"Someone had to be," I say.

"And she called *you*?"

"No. My involvement is purely coincidental. Not that it matters. She needed help, and I offered. She's in a lot of pain, she barely slept, and she's suffering from a migraine because of the anesthesia. So, please, keep your voice down."

Her eyes narrow, but her furrowed brow softens somewhat. "Well, I'm here now. You can go."

"Not a chance."

She gawks—she's not used to being told no, but I'm happy to do it, for Marina's sake.

Though it's my first clash with Cora Sullivan, she's never liked the Tripps. She grossly overcharges for Dad's dairy products, something they debate often. She bickers with Mom over charity fundraisers at church. At one of Marigold's art shows, I heard Cora call her work "pedestrian." A deep-seated hate or general snobbiness? I don't know. All I know is that it comes out around *certain* people.

People she doesn't need or want things from. Like us Tripps.

For the rest of Seagrove's population, her sophistication and determination draw people in like flies to a bug zapper. She's an anomaly for a town like this. Many people in Seagrove have money, but Cora wears her wealth in her attitude, clothes, everything, and she's always snubbed her nose at our blue-jeans and dirty-boots family.

I take her basket of gourmet cheeses, crackers, and fully cooked snacking meats to the kitchen. The gift might as well be a salt lick— fine for horses, but not okay for someone recovering from surgery. The salt content alone would kick natural anxiety into a panicked frenzy—another thing I learned from Dad after his surgery. Not that I'll bother explaining that to Cora.

She drops her expensive bag and keys on the coffee table, eyeing me. "Inserting yourself into her life won't spare you a lawsuit."

"I don't care about that. Just her." My arms fold over my chest, and her brow cocks over the sight of my tattoos. "How's Ashe? Did he land in Jamaica okay?"

"He's distraught over Marnie. He wouldn't be too happy about this intrusion, that's for sure."

Her words almost sound like a threat. "Anyone who loves Marina would want her to feel better. That's all I'm trying to do. If Ashe has a problem with that, then he should bring his ass home."

Her eyes narrow. "There's that Tripp family arrogance. You've got some nerve, lecturing me. Marnie wouldn't be in this condition if not for you. Haven't you done enough damage?"

Her voice catches with emotion, hooking my guilt and reeling it in. The pain I've caused Marina affects her, too—maybe it is arrogant, engaging her like this when I'm the one at fault.

"I'm sorry about what happened and the pain I've caused your family," I say, clearing my throat, "but that's why I need to be here for her."

Another pound rattles the door just as Marina edges around the hallway corner. "What's going on?"

She carries the lukewarm ice pack in one hand and her cane in the other. Her pajamas practically swallow her up, and her pained expression and pallid color tell me that her migraine is still there.

Cora goes to her, cooing and gushing with, "Aw, Marnie" and "You poor thing."

I get the door, where I'm greeted by a flower bouquet that completely blocks the delivery person behind it. A heavy floral scent hits me. I sign for the flowers and move them inside.

Marina lets a weak, "Aw" escape while Cora grabs the card.

"They're from Ashe," she beams. "*Thinking about you every second. All my love, Ashe.*"

I roll my eyes. The oversized bouquet is incredibly fragrant and takes up most of the kitchen table, except there's enough room for Hershey to perch and nibble at the leaves. White lilies feature in the arrangement, which are highly toxic to cats. I rush in, gently easing him off the table and debating putting Ashe's gift on the porch.

"That's sweet," Marina manages with watery eyes. She brings a trembling hand to her mouth like she might be sick.

"Marnie, honey, it's inappropriate for him to be here." Cora flicks a red fingernail at me. "Is he the reason you left the hospital early?"

"No. Grady showed up to visit and gave me a ride home," Marina explains. "Perfect timing."

Cora's arms fold over her olive green suit jacket and silky blouse. "It's the least he can do, considering the damage he's done."

"Grady's protective," Marina says in a strained defense—a word that catches me off guard. "He saved me, remember?"

Cora's hard-nosed expression melts. Slightly. "You're right, Marnie. Forgive me for any undue stress. I'm also feeling protective of you, sweet girl."

Marina smiles weakly, still rubbing her head.

A light knock brings my attention to the door again. It's Mom and Elena, arms loaded with things and faces donning sly smiles.

"Prescription delivery!" Mom coos.

"And homemade chicken soup," Elena chimes in.

"Aren't you supposed to be at work?" I ask.

She smirks. "Aren't *you* supposed to be at work? It's the first time you've ever called in. I had to come. I *had* to."

Her full cheeks widen into a very auntish grin, like she knows a secret. Aunt Elena is a fifty-five-year-old powerhouse—a happy side effect of growing up in a household with my grandfather, Dad, and Uncle Wade in a constant battle. Now, she runs my vet practice with a beloved ringmaster's personality and a neurosurgeon's precision.

She's also a good person who refuses to let bullshit get her down —a feature I respect and wish I had myself. When Granddad died, he left Tripp Family Farm to Dad, the eldest. To Wade, he left half ownership of a twenty-home mobile home park called The Marshes and a convenience store, The G&G. Grandpa left my brothers and me equal shares of fifty percent of the property to keep Wade responsible. The property borders a swamp, vastly different from the rest of the Tripp land, though it's all beautiful. Sharing ownership with us solidified the endless family feud between the brothers.

Wade believes Dad talked their father into the division. Dad denies it. That's the bullshit history.

But Aunt Elena doesn't let that history get to her, though she has the best reason—Granddad left her out of the will completely. "She's married, and she's got brothers to take care of her," is how he explained it, going old-school misogynistic. I've since given her shares of the vet clinic to counter my grandfather and prove *that* shit isn't tolerated anymore.

My aunt stares me down with urging eyes. "Going to invite us in, Grady?"

They push inside before I can answer. It's suddenly turned into a chaotic and overwhelming madhouse in here.

Mom goes directly to Marina, relieving her of the warm ice pack. "Oh, honey. You look wretched. That migraine must be hitting you hard, huh?"

Elena goes to the kitchen, delivering her food offerings to the cluttered counter. "Cora, a pleasure to see you. Ah, what gorgeous flowers. Boy, do they smell."

"They're from Ashe," Cora says, looking rather bamboozled by the Tripp invasion.

Hershey jumps up on the table again, going for the leaves. Elena coaxes him away.

"How's Ashe?" Mom asks in her sweetest, softest voice.

"Thanks for coming," Marina says weakly, her hand going to her mouth again. "Please, make yourselves at home."

"No. Don't. This isn't a good time for a social call." I grab the bouquet and haul it through the living room. "These flowers are toxic to cats."

"Oh, I'm sure they're fine," Cora huffs.

I dump them onto a rocking chair on the front porch.

Returning inside, I notice Marina gripping the wall and her cane like they're the only things holding her up. I get a glass and fill it with water. Then, I find the migraine meds amid their offerings. I read the instructions.

"Um, it's so nice to see you all," Marina tries again. Her cane falls as her hand goes to her mouth. "I'm sorry."

She rushes, as best she can, toward the bathroom.

"Migraines are the worst," Elena chirps.

"So debilitating," Mom agrees.

"I've got her." I step through the group, determined to help Marina. But as I pass through Cora's heavy perfume, I stop, remembering what she said about how I shouldn't be here.

I offer her the glass of water, and the pill pinched between my fingers. "Unless you'd prefer to go to her, Cora."

She hesitates, her dark eyes narrowing. "I'm needed at the store."

"Some fucking *family* you are." Shaking my head, I push by her. "Thanks, Mom and Elena, but you can all see yourselves out."

CHAPTER THIRTEEN

Marnie

MARNIE STRANGE—THE most horrible hostess in history! My head splits as if acid eats away at my brain. The flowers mixed with Cora's perfume, making it worse. And now, I'm hugging a toilet, dry heaving, while more guests than I've ever had at once congregate in my living room. My eyes water and spill over under the strain of it all—the aches across my abdomen, the soreness of Giant Jelly, and the devastation of unattended guests, now left in the care of Grouchy Tripp.

Oh, and Cora looked about ready to commit murder. The last time I saw her this upset was when a disgruntled bagger egged her BMW. When she gets back in that swanky BMW of hers, I expect she'll call Ashe to tell him that the man who destroyed our wedding day is taking care of me. *This isn't good.*

I gag over the toilet again, just in time for Grady to slip into the bathroom. He sets something on the counter and rushes to my side. He angles himself on the tub's edge, supporting me between his legs as I moan. Coughing and gagging cause serious pain in my midsection.

"You're okay," he tells me, pressing his cold hands against my head. "Try to relax."

"I can't," I whimper. "I have guests."

"They're leaving. What did I tell you about being nice?"

My shoulders sink. He wets a washcloth with cold water and drapes it over my forehead. I lean into him, desperate to feel better.

"Just breathe," he says. "There's nothing in your stomach to throw up. When you've calmed down, I have your migraine medicine. Then, you have to eat something."

The idea of keeping anything down feels agonizing. I choke back another gag with a deep breath.

Grady's hands move gently through my hair as I lean against his knee.

"Thanks for moving the flowers," I manage, knowing Hershey would find them hard to resist.

"You're welcome. Saves us both, right?"

"Yeah." I hover over the toilet again, an acidic surge playing in my throat.

"It's okay," he whispers, sweeping my hair off my face. "In and out. Just breathe."

I do as he says, focusing on the rise and fall of my shoulders rather than the dizzying feeling in my head. But, soon, a surprising but familiar tug and pull on my hair relaxes me most. I don't even realize he's doing it at first—braiding my hair. It's gentle and comforting, reminding me of Mom.

"What's it going to be today, sweetheart?" she'd ask before school. *"Feeling up? Or down? Or somewhere in the middle?"* She'd laugh, listing off the hundreds of styles she could do. I liked high ponytails or long braids best. *"Easy peasy,"* she'd say.

"You braid hair?" I mutter weakly.

"Yeah, usually just on horses," he chuckles, "but I thought it'd be nice to get it out of your way. Is that okay?"

"Yes, thanks, but Grady Tripp being *nice*?" I mumble through heavy breaths.

"Desperate times and all." He moves away from me and grabs a scrunchie from the counter to tie the end.

I lean against the tub's edge and close my eyes. "Mom used to do that."

"Braid your hair?" he asks.

"For school. On good days."

"What do you mean? On good days?"

My eyes open, but barely, enough to see him leaning against the back of the door, hands in the pockets of his scrubs. My temples pound with pressure, and I feel flushed and embarrassed, on the floor against the toilet and babbling about Mom.

I brace myself against the tub's edge to get up, and he quickly assists me.

"Easy," he says.

"I think I can move to the couch now."

"Good."

We navigate the narrow hallway slowly and with little contact as if braiding hair and mom-talk cross an invisible line between us, and we need to pull back.

He retrieves the water and pill, and soon, I feel good enough to keep it down. He opens a window to air out the floral smell and warms up Elena's chicken soup, assuring me "from experience" that it's easy on the stomach.

It's delicious, teaming with chunky vegetables in a creamy broth. The cliché is true—homemade is always better. It's a shame I rarely get it since I don't cook. I enjoy it slowly. And soon, my head isn't spinning. After an hour, Grady gives me a second dose of the migraine medicine, and belly-full and headache numbed, I comfortably drift off to old British mysteries on PBS with my cats curled beside me.

When I wake, the room is dark except for the glare of the TV. My head is sore but not hurting. The same with the rest of me. I spy a note on the coffee table.

Marina,

Anytime for anything. I mean it.

Grady.

I'm glad he's gone, not because I don't want him here. There's something extremely comforting about him. But he has a life, a career, and a busy family to contend with, and he shouldn't feel guilty over me. Besides, I don't want Ashe or Cora to get any wrong ideas.

Cora visits the next morning and seems almost surprised that Grady isn't here. We've texted a few times—he likes checking in—but I haven't needed anything except time to recover.

"Keep your distance from him, Marnie," Cora says. "He's liable for everything. More if we file a civil suit. The pain and suffering alone—"

"I don't want that. Please, Cora. I don't want this to be any worse than it already is."

"*He's* making it worse," she counters, voice shrill. "Inserting himself into your life, taking advantage of Ashe not being here, doing all these favors, he's buttering you up."

"He feels bad," I say weakly. "He's trying to make up for it. Besides, the help has been nice."

"He's only being *nice* to protect his wallet. He doesn't care about you. *That one* doesn't care about anyone except himself."

I don't know what she means by *that one*. That Tripp. That man. That human. Not *that* it matters. His reputation makes it hard to argue.

"I don't know him well, but that's not what I think."

"Exactly! He's putting on a caring show for you, appealing to your good nature so that you won't sue the pants off of him." She shimmies to the edge of her chair, leaning closer like a TV news reporter in a tense interview. "You don't see the lasting implications yet. You're young and still recovering. But as someone who struggled to get pregnant, who battled the shame and disappointment of infertility for years before our miracle happened, let me tell you... this is only the beginning of the devastation that man has caused. You will feel this loss every day for the rest of your life."

She's right—the impacts haven't hit me yet. Physical pain has taken priority over long-term effects, and I'm almost grateful for it. Considering every day for the rest of my life is an overwhelming prospect.

Cora smiles weakly, like she knows her words have gotten through to me. "Enough of that. Now, Marnie. What can I do for you, huh? I took the afternoon off, so give me one of your famous to-do lists."

A chuckle emerges, thinking of my infamous list-taking at Sunny's. I have a notebook for it—a repurposed Trapper Keeper filled with every concept, idea, display creation, and, yes, many lists, I've had since starting. I call it Marnie's Market Manual, and it's become a running joke at work. I'm rarely seen without it. Right now, it's safely locked in my desk at work.

Giving my boss and future mother-in-law a to-do list seems like a bad move, so I do what I always do. Tell her I'm fine, but ask, gently, for her to bring my notebook next time she visits.

"If I'm couch-ridden, I might as well get some work done," I tell her.

She claps her hands, beaming with pride that Sunny's is on my mind, and promises to bring it.

Only she doesn't.

Not at her next visit, days later.

Or at her final one.

CHAPTER FOURTEEN

Marnie

THE DAYS BLUR together in a mix of sleep, pain, and boredom. Cora calls and texts, but doesn't show up until the following Sunday, three days before Ashe's return, with more gifts I don't need—face masks and bath bombs this time. She doesn't stay long but says something that lingers and haunts me like a ruthless ghost. I expect that was her intention.

"He wants to marry you, Marnie. But if you love him, should you let him?"

I spend the days before Ashe's return yo-yo-ing between the unfairness of her remark and the truth in it.

It's a dreary Wednesday, a week and a half after the accident.

Ashe should be here any minute.

Yesterday, I was excited about his return. I decided to forget Cora and her not-so-subtle push to let Ashe go. I am the same person I was before the accident, the same woman he fell in love with, who loves him and wants to spend my life with him.

So what if we can't have biological children? That was never guaranteed, anyway. We didn't start dating and fall in love based on breeding expectations. We just liked each other. Loved each other. Wanted to be together. That still holds true.

This isn't the Dark Ages when having babies decided a woman's life success. Nor is it an age when suitable matches are made based on marginalized nonsense like wealth, class, ethnicity, or what someone brings to the marriage.

This is Seagrove, North Carolina, 2025. Not 15th century England.

Besides that, my aspirations have never been child-centered. Why should they be? If I had a Marnie Manual with all my best ideas for my life—things *I* want—it'd be filled with career milestones and what would set me apart as a store manager, Sunny's Expansion Coordinator, and perhaps even Cora's job, someday. It'd be a scrap-book of travel destinations—I want to see real castles, go on a murder mystery cruise, and visit every national park. That notebook would feature all the adorable cats I could rescue, organizations I'd love to support and give time to, owning a beautiful house with a catio, investments I'd make, and properties I'd buy. Children are wonderful, but do they have to be *everything*?

That this *one thing* has been taken away from us doesn't mean there's no longer an *us*. It shouldn't, anyway.

I am still Marnie Strange. Independent, smart, and strong. Good person. Friend to all. Queen of Customer Service and Unique Product Displays. Ashe's fiancée, his love. His best friend, lover, playmate, and teammate. I'm still worthy.

Aren't I?

My thoughts go back and forth mercilessly as I slowly tidy the place. Though my mobility has improved over the last week, the soreness still keeps me at a tiresome pace. Whenever I push my limits, my body revolts with sharp pains and lingering aches. It's a test of patience, surely. But I keep thinking of Grady's advice. *It takes as long as it takes.*

Regardless, my excitement to see Ashe builds, battling back my nerves. I've missed him. The fun of him. The way he always makes me laugh. How he rolls his eyes over his mom's antics. We'll laugh over Cora's words—one day.

Seeing him will put everything back in its proper place.

Only it's not him who shows up. It's Cora, just like that morning at the hospital. She pushes inside my place, mentioning something about the dreadful weather. I don't bother with pleasantries.

"Where's Ashe?"

"He's not coming, Marnie." Her tone is soft but direct. She bypasses me and drags an upright chair from the kitchen table into the living room—her usual seat. "Best sit down. I don't want you to hurt yourself when you've been doing so well."

The anxious knot in my stomach spreads throughout my entire body. I wobble to the couch, easing Sunkist aside for space. I sit as uprightly as possible, bracing myself for what I know is coming—what I should've seen coming. It doesn't matter what I want with Ashe. It's no wonder he left. He knew he wasn't coming home to me.

Voices circle through my mind, crystallizing my fears.

Mom: *Men can't be trusted. They never do what they say they'll do.*

Cora: *You will feel this loss every day for the rest of your life.*

I swallow hard, waiting.

"Ashe has had a change of heart." Her face fixes on fake sympathy —a look I've seen a thousand times but never before directed at me. "He no longer wants to get married."

It sounds so innocent and normal like one might change clothes or cars.

"Ashe *said* that?"

She leans forward. "I know that's difficult to hear, but you must've felt it, too. It'd be such a sacrifice for him now."

Marrying me would be a sacrifice.

"He was having second thoughts before the accident," she tacks on as if that makes it better. "He loves his independence. He's about to take on the new store. He loves you *despite* this, but you want different things now."

"We *want* to be together," I manage, nearly tripping over her use of the word *despite*. "That shouldn't have changed just because... *one* thing did."

She scoffs slightly. "That's not how the world works, and you know it."

Life isn't fair, sweetie, and it ain't changing the rules for you. I want Mom here, now, with Cora so I can demand them both to explain why life seems fair to everyone else *but* me.

"Why isn't he here to do this himself?" I ask bluntly.

"Men are cowards, Marnie. He didn't want to hurt you."

But he *is* hurting me. Suddenly desperate for the bathroom, I rise weakly from my chair. My no frowns, no fears, no tears policy slips as my eyes water and the horror of my situation compounds. I excuse myself and speed-hobble down the hall, not getting there fast enough. *It takes as long as it takes.*

Inside the bathroom, I turn on the cold water, splashing my face with it. Three days ago, Ashe texted all day with a series of can't-waits.

> Can't wait to see you.

> Hold you.

> Kiss you.

> Tell you about my trip.

> Talk about a new wedding.

How could he change his mind so fast, like I'm a broken fever or a stomach virus that's finally been purged? What happened to him loving me *forever* and wanting me *always*? This doesn't sound like Ashe. In our early days, he fought for us with Cora. She thought he should focus on the store, not the staff. She had other ideas for him than someone like me.

Then, I wonder if this *is* her, not him, and a tiny ray of hope emerges.

I slip my phone out of my pocket, staring at his last messages. I text him.

> Cora's here. She says you want to break up. Is this true?

The ellipsis appears. Disappears. And finally appears again.

> Sorry.

Everything inside me crumbles and turns to dust. I'm no longer

Marnie Strange. I'm her dried bones, withering and lifeless. He's drained all the love and cheer right out of me. It's a small mercy that he responded at all. At least, he didn't leave me wondering by ghosting me altogether.

I return to Cora, head held high and eyes dry. They need me to be the usual Marnie—strong, steady, and forgiving. And though Grady's probably right about my tendency to be too nice, it's the only way I'll get through this. I need *that* Marnie, too.

"Are you alright?" she asks.

"Yes, sorry. The medications don't play nice with my stomach."

"You poor thing," she coos, her voice like sandpaper.

I pull the engagement ring off my finger and set it on the table between us. She takes it, dropping it carelessly into her Louis Vuitton.

"Was there anything else?" I ask, even-toned.

Her fake sympathy flashes in a weak smile. "Under the circumstances, we think it's best that you don't return to Sunny's."

The air in my lungs solidifies into something hard and lifeless as cold reality strangles me. I barely get words out, but they come clipped and bitter. "I no longer meet *expectations.*"

I've heard her say that repeatedly to unsatisfactory employees, always with the same coldness. Cora was never one for second chances and almost enjoyed what she called "getting rid of dead weight."

She bypasses my accusation by tugging an envelope out of her bag and sliding it onto the coffee table.

"What's this?" I ask, not touching it.

"Severance," she answers dryly.

My brain skips to what that means, fumbling a bit. As the store's human resources department, I know *severance* isn't in our vocabulary. People are let go, move on, or get fired, of course, but we've never offered anything to facilitate their exit. It's a grocery store, not a Fortune 500 company.

"You're firing me?" I choke out, trying my best to hide my shock behind my stoic barriers.

"We're overdue for restructuring with the new store about to open. You understand. We're dissolving your position with a generous thank you for your time with us."

She nods to the envelope again, practically ordering me to look inside. I don't.

"So, you're firing me but calling it a layoff for the optics," I summarize, swallowing my baseball-sized anger, nearly choking.

Her snide grin makes my skin crawl.

"I won't accept it."

"Oh, yes, you will." She leans forward with a chilling smile. "You'll cash that check and tell anyone who asks that, as much as it breaks your heart to leave Sunny's, you're ready for a new start, preferably in a new town."

"So, now I'm moving, too?"

She shrugs. "I can't *make* you, of course, but there's enough money for such a change, and I highly recommend it."

"I'm not moving. This is my home."

Her shoulders droop in a sigh. "I thought you might say something like that. You're still family, and we want to make this easy on you."

I cringe at the word. *Family.* She reaches into her bag again and sets a business card on the table.

"Wes's brother, Liam, is looking for an office manager."

"At the funeral home?" I gape.

"He's already agreed to take you on. It's the best you'll get around here, especially without a degree."

Take me on? Like a project? Like an orphan?

"I realize that nothing's gone as planned, Marnie. I regret that. I also know that you could sully the Sullivan name around here with stories about unfairness regarding your... *condition* as a result of the accident if you wanted—"

"My condition?" I sputter, scoffing. "My only *condition* is this blatant discrimination. You can't do this. I love Sunny's."

"I'm doing you a favor, Marnie. The accident wasn't Ashe's fault. Or mine. But it's unfair to all of us to be constantly reminded of what could have been. Don't you think?"

My shoulders slump. It's a point I cannot argue. Even so, Ashe gets to go on with his perfect life while Cora writes the narrative for mine. This is what loving her son cost me?

"I'm being generous here." She pushes the envelope and the business card to the very edge of the table.

Many things happen at once: my hackles rising, my hands fisting under my thighs, her belittlement stinging, and the full reality of my situation setting in. My anger kickstarts my brain into a tornado frenzy, whipped up by her condescension and kept quiet only by my keen survivalist instincts.

I have been reduced to whatever's in that envelope.

Amid the intense stare-down between us, I tally up *The Things Marnie Lost in the Accident.*

A car.

A wedding.

A uterus.

Ashe.

My career at Sunny's.

My work family.

My almost-family.

My love and respect for the Sullivans.

But I haven't lost *me.*

If anything, my identity solidifies through this series of unfair events. In my anger, a brilliant vision of the future forms. Me, taking my non-degreed self somewhere else, becoming a tremendous success, and making them regret this day. Somehow.

It's a pipe dream, a fantasy. But it's what I need to believe in now.

I decide *this* is my defining moment. Not the accident. Not becoming barren. Not losing Ashe. Not getting fired. But *this.* This beautiful clarity and confidence she's inspired. Me taking back control of my life rather than being someone else's puppet or plaything or *breeder.*

They won't see me break. I *don't* break. I bend. I have built my life from nothing. I'll rebuild it even stronger. They have not seen the last of me.

A survivalist never refuses a check. But I won't give her the satisfaction of seeing me open it. No matter how much it is, it's not enough.

Taking the check means agreeing to keep my silence—I know that, too.

"I have one condition," I say. "Promise me, no lawsuits against Grady."

She guffaws. "Why not? Do you realize how much he's cost us? What he's cost *you*? He's ruined your life."

"No, he saved me from a *weak* husband and a *fake* family that could *never* love me the way I deserve—unconditionally," I bite back. "I *owe* him. Promise me no lawsuits against Grady Tripp, or I'll take this severance to the nearest lawyer as a retainer and file one against you, your family, and Sunny's for wrongful termination and discrimination."

Her eyes narrow, and her lips press together, sizing me up as if wondering if I could pull off such an enterprise. I almost hope she challenges me so I can prove it to her.

Her hands rise submissively. "Fine. From that perspective, I suppose he saved Ashe, too—half his assets. You two never would've lasted."

"It's time for you to leave." I hobble to the door and hold it open for her. Smiling, always smiling. Steaming on the inside, though. I slam and lock the door behind her.

Deep breaths calm me as I mourn my decade-long career coming to such an unexpected end. I have lived and breathed Sunny's for so long that I never would've imagined this outcome, that it could all be destroyed to rubble over *my* personal trauma. *My* body and what it can and can't do. My love and worth shattered over this. An accident. An absence. A future never guaranteed anyway.

But here I am. Once again. Family gone. Abandoned.

CHAPTER FIFTEEN

Grady

"THAT'S BULLSHIT!" I blurt.

All eyes in the Seagrove Public Library magnetize to me, standing with Marigold in the checkout line. The two women in front of me, whose conversation I've just butted into, stare over their shoulders with their gossiping, hate-spewing eyes.

"You heard me," I tell them. "And you're jerks for talking like that."

"Um, mind your own business," one says ironically.

"Watch your filthy mouth, Grouchy Tripp, or I'll have a word with Carmela," says the other.

"You're going to tattle on me?" I spit back. "Grow up."

"Sir, quiet, please," says the librarian at the counter.

"Grady, rules," Marigold whispers, cowering with embarrassment beside me.

Another checkout opens, and the irritating gossipers flee to it. I scrub a hand over my face as if I can wipe their words away. But I only get angrier the more I think about it.

No one should talk about Marina that way.

It's been two weeks since I've been by her place. Once her migraine subsided and after the awkward encounter with Cora, I reinstated my policy to limit my involvement. The last thing I want to do is make things harder for her with the Sullivans.

But we text often.

This morning, when asking for my usual update on her healing, she answered with an adorable picture of her cats, staring up wantonly at the camera.

> We're cat-tastic!

Her response, as cheesy as it was, made me laugh. I texted back with a similar picture of my three dogs begging for breakfast.

> We're dog-gone happy for you.

Not one of my best jokes, but she still responded with three laughing-with-tears emojis. Swapping pet pics has become a daily trend for us.

Two nights ago, I sent her a picture of an orangey sunset over the lake. The golds and reds mixed so beautifully that it reminded me of her hair. She has sunset hair—I decided. But I didn't include words. Didn't know what to say with it, anyway.

Still, she texted back: *Oh, Grady. How lovely. I needed that.*

Our short communication bursts are nothing compared to our delightful back-and-forths over the dumbest things. Recovering from surgery, stuck in bed or on the couch, I suspect she's bored.

But I like the engagement. And it's something I can do for her. Without getting in the way or upsetting Ashe the Ass. He's home by now, hopefully groveling. I don't know. I don't ask.

Instead, she talks about her preference for British TV.

> They're real people, Grady. Not air-brushed or boob-jobbed to please American eyes. Plus, I love the accent. Can you do a British accent?

> No. Can you?

> Oh, yes. Cockney and the Queen's English. I practice with the cats.

Of course, she does, I think, grinning. This prompted a phone call so I could hear her attempts. Between laughing my ass off, I assured her they were "passable." They weren't. Not even close.

When we returned to texting, I confessed my TV habits.

> I watch National Geographic and Discovery. Nature shows. They put me to sleep like a grandfather in a recliner, but it's how I relax.

> If only your dogs could take pics of that, I'd bribe them for copies.

> I'm not ashamed of my old-man-ness. I own it.

> You're not an old man. You're a good man. You should own that, too.

Whenever our long conversations wane, I ask:

> Need anything?

Often, the text ellipsis lingers and disappears and starts again, like she doesn't know how to answer. Then, she comes up with something like:

> Only world peace.

> Only world domination.

> Only for the cats to finally take over and win world domination.

> A good night's sleep (to dominate the world tomorrow).

I always end our talks with the same message:

> Anytime for any reason still stands.

Now, in the library with Marigold, I'm livid that people are still talking about her. For my part, I've forbidden talk of Marina Strange at the clinic and family gatherings—I don't want to hear it and don't want it spread in my vicinity.

So, I've resumed what Mom calls my "full but empty life." Dad's farm and work keep me busy, though Luke and Gil have been helping out more since the accident. To lessen my workload at the clinic, I've tasked Aunt Elena with hiring more vet techs and securing an intern from NC State's vet school over the summer.

But for now, I welcome the work. Otherwise, I'd have too much time to think. And those thoughts would inevitably be about her.

Is it weird to miss taking care of her when all I wanted was for her to recover and no longer need help?

We reach the counter. I set Marigold's books down and nod to her. "Go on. Like we practiced."

Her shoulders rise with a deep breath. But instead of saying the words we practiced, she slides the librarian a note like it's a goddamn bank robbery.

He opens the full-page note and smiles warmly at Marigold. "Aw, what a gorgeous sketch of the library."

"Read the fine print," I huff, motioning to the asterisk at the bottom.

He leans into the page, squinting. Then, he laughs. "Ah, I see. This is my first late fee apology sketch."

"It won't happen again," she says quietly.

"No worries." He takes her card and eyes the computer. "Are you able to pay the... thirty-five cents?"

She nods, setting the prearranged coins on the counter.

He scans her new finds—books on cathedrals and castles to use as inspiration for her next comic book.

A brief smile makes it to her lips—the first I've seen since last week when she told me about her overdue books and admitted she couldn't handle it alone. If not for me agreeing to take care of it with her, I think she never would've gone to the library again out of shame. Social interactions are excruciating for her.

For me, too, these days.

The bullshit-shoveling women pass behind us, eyeing me as they go. "Poor Carmela. The Wines and Spines girls'll be astounded to hear about this."

"Hey, tell 'em I said to go fuck themselves," I call after them.

"Grady, *rules*," Marigold tries again.

"Sorry," I mutter to the librarian.

He shrugs, amused. "Maybe I should institute a swear jar, hmm?" Marigold chuckles.

Marina's voice rushes into my thoughts. *Relax, Grady.*

I've tried locking her out, but lately, she breaks in anyway. Sometimes, late in the day, if I've been called out for a farm emergency, I hear her. *Relax, Grady.* I respect those moments like she's become my inner voice, telling me when to slow down. Set a new pace. Take a breath. Think of what I've done.

I drive Marigold to Rebellion, where she's meeting Mom and Elena for lunch. This would normally be a drop-and-go situation. It's the clinic's Friday off, and taking care of Marigold's library fees was the only family task I agreed to do. I have an afternoon of fishing and beer drinking at home planned. Hanging out with my easygoing bartending brother Luke wouldn't be bad—he's tied with Marty for requiring the least from me. But spending time with Mom and Elena doesn't fit with my quest for relaxation.

Still, Marigold and I are both surprised when I park, shut off the engine, and follow her inside.

I hear them before I see them, their laughter filling the slow restaurant. Luke gives me a nod from behind the bar. We head toward the back corner booth. Rebellion's rustic woods and high ceilings remind me of my cabin—dark, low-lighting, and currently untouched instruments in a nook near the back. Of course, those instruments get played most nights. My baby grand piano at home doesn't.

"Grady?" Elena gapes. "Are you joining us?"

"Oh, say yes. We'd love to have you. You must stay," Mom says.

"Calm down. Only for a minute." I take the lone chair while Marigold slides into the arched booth next to Mom. "Are people saying that Marina's relationship with Ashe was about money? Seriously? And what's with the 'was'?"

"Oh, so talking about Marnie Strange is back on the table?" Mom asks.

I huff.

"People are saying all sorts of things about Marnie," Elena says. "You'd know if you hadn't forbidden all mentions of Marnie or the Sullivans at the clinic."

Mom's eyes meet mine over her perched phone. "You haven't embarrassed me, have you? The Wines and Spines group chat is lighting up suddenly."

"Those women embarrassed themselves," I correct. "Right, Marigold?"

"No comment," she says, staring into her water glass.

I grunt and roll my eyes. So much for sisterly loyalty. "You shouldn't associate with them, Mom. They're small-minded, big-mouthed busybodies with no right to talk disparagingly of Marina."

Mom and Elena share a glance and take simultaneous sips from their wine glasses like they're engrossed in a tantalizing reality show.

"So, you thought it'd be a good idea to give them something else to talk about?" Mom questions, motioning to her phone.

"Better me than her. I said a few choice words. That's all," I say, running a hand over my head.

"I don't like you cussing," Mom says. "The rule is that adults shouldn't cuss."

"That rule is for *other* people," Marigold corrects, pulling her sketchbook out of her bag.

I smirk while Mom cocks her head and brow at me. "Mom, spreading lies about people is worse than dropping the f-bomb."

She gasps, hand to chest. "You dropped the f-bomb?"

"Let's focus on what's important here," Elena says. "Grady, it's a small town. People talk. And the drama between Marnie and the Sullivans is better than a soap opera."

"What fu—freaking drama?"

Luke moseys over with Marigold's usual lemonade and a beer for me. He folds his tatted arms over his broad chest, looking tough, like a club bouncer. "Everything alright over here?"

"Your brother is astounded to learn that this town gossips," Elena chuckles.

Luke scoffs. "They call you a hermit for good reason. Maybe you should come out of hiding every once in a while?"

"Look, I don't care that people gossip, just that they're lying about Marina. She doesn't deserve it," I say.

"Town sweetheart to Seagrove's worst gold-digger in a month's time," Luke says with authority. "I agree. People are being harsh. Willow saw her at Seagrove Funeral Home—she was there for her grandfather's arrangements."

Mom and Elena simultaneously go, "How's she doing?"

"She's fine, thanks. The arrangements are made. She saw Marnie and told me she's never seen a darker aura."

"Why was Marina at the funeral home?" I gawk, my confusion thick.

Mom rolls her eyes. "She works there now."

"Do you *really* not know anything that's been going on?" Elena gawks.

"I text Marina every day. She hasn't told me anything," I say. But even as the words come out, I know she's not the type to complain, and certainly not to me. My respect for Marina grows. Keeping troubles private is something I completely understand and admire— more people should do it.

But it also reminds me that she and I are still strangers. Holding her hand when there was no one else to do it is one thing. Letting me into her life is another. I get it. But I don't like it.

Mom and Elena share a look before Mom explains, "Ashe and Marnie broke up. Rumor has it, Cora did it. Can you believe it? Marnie no longer works at Sunny's. People say she was fired, but the Sullivans claim it was an amicable restructuring. Now, Marnie works for Liam, Wes's brother, over at the funeral home."

"Wait, she's back at work? It's too soon." Everyone looks at me like I've just woken up from a coma. "The doctor said *six* weeks."

"Marnie didn't listen," Mom says. "She hasn't asked for any refills on her pain meds, either."

"So, the rumor about her pill-popping addiction can be ruled out," Elena notes.

I hate this. Everything about it makes me groan.

"Wait, did you say a *funeral* home?" I grunt. "Marina?"

"I know, right?" Elena grimaces. "Doesn't suit Marnie."

Damn right, it doesn't. Not only that, it's a fucking insult.

Luke takes their orders. Mom and Elena scrutinize me over their refilled wine glasses.

"Grady, what's happened isn't your fault," Mom says, pointlessly.

"The Sullivans are awful," Elena adds. "We already know that. Now, Marnie knows it, too."

"She's lost *everything* because of me." Pissed, sad, and guilty, I push up from the table.

"No, Grady, don't go yet," Mom says. "Hang out with us. It's your day off."

"I have to go."

"Well, be at the house tomorrow for game night, at least," she presses, "and bring some chips."

"I don't do game night," I say.

In the truck, I grip the steering wheel and twist the leather. *No, Grady. Don't do it. Don't. Don't get involved.* She doesn't want or need me. Otherwise, she would've mentioned her life turning into absolute shit.

I start the engine, determined to go home and enact my afternoon plans. Me. The dogs. Fishing.

But then, I hear, *"Come away with me, and I'll never stop loving you,"* filling the cab of my truck, the haunting music of Norah Jones —sweet, buttery, soft, and mesmerizing.

And I think of Marina—sweet, buttery, soft, mesmerizing.

Goddamnit!

CHAPTER SIXTEEN

Marnie

MY NEW JOB IS GREAT. Really, *really* great. I have a sweet little office with a window to the parking lot—not much of a view, but the breezes are nice. I'm thinking of hanging a bird feeder outside for some cheerful, wing-flapping action, if Liam, the funeral director, lets me. He's a bit of a stickler about things. I'm allowed one plant, for instance. But one is better than none.

The benefits surely outweigh the small sacrifices. It's a cushy job, much easier than Sunny's. I get to wear whatever nice clothes I want as long as they're "subdued." Liam says I need to practice smiling less—that's a challenge I'm working on. I practice my 'sympathy smile' at home with the cats.

Owen, the mortician, is a quirky fellow obsessed with reality TV. We've had interesting talks about turning a funeral home into a reality show. He wants to call it *Died, Sealed, and Delivered*, which I argue might be insensitive. We're working on other ideas. Regardless, I love getting to know people.

So, I'm sure it'll be *great*.

Marnie Strange—Office Manager for the Dearly Departed. It has a ring to it, I think.

Not that I manage much. The phone. Data entry. Files. Appointments. The front door—it's visible from my office. Being on light duty has been easy since there's so little to do. People don't die very often in rural areas. Not that I'm complaining.

This work meets a definite need for Seagrove. That's important.

Ridding me of my sudden aversion to heavy floral scents is another perk. My migraine days have made me sensitive. Checking in the floral delivery for Mrs. Johanson's wake—not pickle-juice Johanson but her grandmother—I take a deep breath and only gag a little.

It takes as long as it takes.

A smile crosses my lips—just a little one—thinking about Grady. The other night, we got into a music discussion that lifted my spirits more than all my AM CDs put together. He's a music lover, and when I got a little sheepish about loving old-school Phil Collins, he was quick to alleviate my embarrassment.

Never apologize for loving what you love, Marina.

There's a teeny-tiny part of me that knows I *should* be angry. When navigating the rocks across my emotional river, I picture Grady on the other side, arms folded and looking intense. I could hop onto the angry rock and stay there, blaming and hating him for what he's cost me.

But how can I hate the man who held my hair back when I heaved? Or held my hand when I cried? Or held me together when I was dying? *Stay with me, Marina.*

Hate simply isn't in my vocabulary, not for Grady Tripp. Besides, he takes in wounded pets and doesn't mind getting down and dirty with farm animals—what decent person could hate a man like that?

I finish checking off the floral delivery, resisting the urge to move the arrangements into their proper places. I can't lift anything heavy yet. The other morning, I picked up Hershey as he tried stealing Sunkist's food and nearly fell over. I hobble through the small chapel, aching from being on my feet too long.

Returning to work early was probably foolish, but survival wins over aches and pains. Securing the job and a steady paycheck topped my priorities, even with Cora's vile, *keep-your-mouth-shut* money. I still haven't cashed her $25,000 severance check. I will, of course. That's more money than I've ever had at one time, more than I've ever seen. But I'm waiting until I need it.

That'll be soon.

I step and click through the wide hallway, with its pseudo-soothing landscapes and cushy chairs. Even the lighting is dimmed to set the correct mood. A low hum of conversation comes from the casket room where Liam meets with clients—I know not to disturb them under any circumstances. I made that mistake on my first day. He said I was too friendly, as if happy they were there.

But I'm always happy to be around people, even if they're sad. Oh, well. Another thing to work on.

It'll be *great*—I know it.

The wide double doors at the main entrance scrape and swing open as I approach them, screeching through the quiet hall. A formidable force barrels through the doors.

My heart pitter-patters seeing him, but then it registers that he's upset and I sink with worry.

"Grady? What's wrong? Is everyone okay?" I demand too loudly.

Liam pokes his head out of the casket room with irritation. "Marnie, shhh."

"Sorry, Liam," I whisper back. My attention returns to Grady, and my arms lift to meet his, even though I have my cane. He braces me, hooking my cane to his forearm like I don't need it if he's around. "Has something happened? You look distraught."

"You frustrate me—that's what happened. You shouldn't be here."

His tone is curt, borderline angry, but that's how his intensity comes out. I sigh with relief, tapping my chest to calm my heart. "Oh, that's all? You had me worried."

"Worried?" he blanches.

"It's a funeral home, Grady."

His brow pinches. "Oh, right. Everyone's fine. I'm worried about you."

I grab Grady's hand and pull him gently into my office. I'm

embarrassed at how drab it is—it *really* needs more plants. I lean against the desk and offer him the chair. He doesn't take it but stands front and center, arms folded and eyes fixed on me.

"So, I frustrate you?" I ask, smiling like always. "Was it my obsessive PBS watching or taste in music that finally did it, huh?"

His brow quirks, but his shoulders soften. Slightly.

"Marina, what are you doing here?"

"I work here now. It's really... great," I say, desperately holding onto my upbeat tone.

He huffs, runs a hand over his shorn head, and tries again. "You aren't supposed to work anywhere for at least three more weeks. The doctor said—"

"I'm on light duty, short shifts," I chime in quickly. "I had cabin fever. Besides, I'm taking it easy. I spend most of the day sitting and wanted to get acclimated at my new job ASAP."

His eyes narrow, analyzing me.

"I'm *okay*, Grady."

"You've lost your fiancé, the job you loved, and you're working at a fucking funeral home. You can't possibly be okay."

My smile retreats with his bluntness, and suddenly, our truth policy feels difficult to manage.

"We talk every day. Why didn't you tell me?"

I manage a smile. "Tripp Grady Tripp, those shoulders are impressive but can't carry everything."

"When it comes to you, I'm a packhorse." He edges closer. "Tell me what happened."

I've wanted to tell him. To pepper our innocent convos with *oh-by-the-way* drama bombs. To latch onto the *one* person forced to care and gobble up the comfort in those packhorse arms of his. Whenever he asked if I needed anything, I hesitated between wanting more from him and knowing how inconvenient and unfair it would be to ask. Still, my pesky longing grows with every word we manage to share and aches now that he's here. *I've missed him.*

But allowing feelings for Grady is an unstable rock I can't afford to jump to in my emotional rapids. It's not right—exploiting his guilt for my comfort. It'll only make him feel worse about *that* day. How could I do that to him?

"Marina, truth," he urges when I hesitate.

"Sounds like you're caught up." My arms fold over my chest. "What's left to tell?"

He hooks my cane to the edge of the desk beside me, but refuses to break eye contact. "Ashe is no loss, but how could you lose your job over this?"

"I no longer met *expectations*." The words tumble out—me forgetting to use my top-notch, finely-meshed filter.

A fire sparks in his eyes. "Those motherfuckers said that?"

"Not exactly. What does it matter? Ashe and I are history, and Sunny's didn't feel so sunny for me anymore. Cora arranged this opportunity."

"This isn't an opportunity, Marina. This is a fucking joke. You don't belong here any more than I belong in customer service."

I chuckle, trying to imagine Grady forced to smile and chit-chat. "I understand your point, but I'm lucky to have this job."

"How is this lucky?" He groans.

"I'm making nearly what I made at Sunny's—that's pretty good for someone without a degree," I say, hating myself a little for it. "Other grocery stores and retailers like to hire managers from within, so getting another job like that would mean starting at minimum wage again. I can't do that, Grady."

"So, your years at Sunny's mean nothing?" he asks like he doesn't believe me.

"Not *nothing*. My experience matters. I took Sunny's from mediocre to magnificent during my career there, and everyone knows it. But retail employers don't equate experience monetarily when hiring someone new. That's all. Until I find just the right opportunity, this is *great*."

"There's nothing *great* about this. You deserve better."

I smile at his kindness. "Better will come along. Eventually."

"It's not just the job, Marina." He edges onto the armrest of the office chair, his features softening. "You've suffered loss. I know something about that. Carrying on business as usual isn't healthy."

His voice catches like his words are difficult, caught in his throat, especially about loss.

"Tell the truth," he urges. "This bothers you, right? You must be... hurt."

All my instincts tell me to smile wide and lie, to bank my emotions rather than spend them and engage my superior filters.

But this is *Grady.* How can I lie to the *one* person who's been there for me through all this?

"I am devastated," I admit finally, "but I can't let them break me."

His lips curve into an approving smile. "Good. How can I help?"

A little laugh bubbles from me at his genuine intensity—having someone on my side feels good. "More cute dog pics would be nice."

He still looks annoyed but more concerned, like he doesn't know what to do with me. A beat passes, and I long to engage him in silly conversation like we so easily do over text. But I fear asking him about his workplace plant preferences or telling him about Owen's tacky reality show idea will only annoy him more, given how upset he is. And I *need* a friend right now.

"You don't belong here, Marina," he says, raking a hand through his hair.

Not here. Not anywhere. "Well, until I get to good ol' England, it'll have to do," I say with my British accent.

He's not amused. He looks as though his million thoughts are hitting him at once. And I don't know what to do.

A step brings him into my bubble, pinning me to the edge of the desk. He's close enough to grab and hold on to. Not that I would. Or should.

He looms over me, his annoyance slipping behind what looks like a gentle mix of worry and affection. But that could be me projecting. Truth is, I very much like Tripp Grady Tripp.

His *laser-through-my-soul* stare makes my breath hitch, and my heartbeat quicken.

"Pretending to be okay won't make it true. Don't pretend with me. It goes against our truth policy," he says, his eyes circling my face like he's mapping my freckles.

A quiet moment passes between us—I don't know what to say. Truth is, I like his attention.

But he's not expecting me to say anything. He smirks lightly before backstepping toward the door. "Don't get too comfortable here, Marina. I'll talk to you later." He doesn't wait for pleasantries but offers a short wave before leaving.

CHAPTER SEVENTEEN

THE SCREEN DOOR on Uncle Wade's double-wide trailer shakes when I pound on it. I know he's home. His pickup sits crooked in the dirt lane, and the store isn't open. Still, it takes four knocking sessions before I hear movement inside. The inner door swings open.

"What?" he demands, looking as scraggily as ever.

"It's the afternoon," I say. "What're you still doing in bed?"

"Sleeping, jackass."

He sweeps his long gray hair back, picks a cigarette from the pack in his pocket, and lights up. "What do you want, Grady?"

Stubborn defiance, a Tripp family trait, rises within me. I don't want to be here. My father would be pissed. Every family has a black sheep. The Tripps have Wade.

Asking him for a favor goes against everything I know, my very DNA, and all logic.

But I don't know where else to turn.

He steps out of his trailer—the first in a long string at The Marshes—and blows smoke in my face. "Well? Are you lost, or is someone dead?"

"I need something," I say, pushing the words out in a breath.

His scruffy, horseshoe mustache bends up in satisfaction. "Hell must've frozen over."

"Feels like it."

"What do you want?" he asks again, with more irritation.

"A job. For a friend. For Marina. The girl from the—"

His laughter cuts me off. "Christie! Roy! Get out here! You won't believe this."

Shit, I think, as his buddies emerge from their neighboring trailers.

Even so, long-forgotten memories of them kick off in my head. They've been fixtures in Wade's life for as long as I can remember. At the store, Roy used to challenge me and my brothers in hot dog eating contests. He always won—we couldn't stop laughing at him long enough to eat. Christie taught me to bait a hook on the dock overlooking the swamp, and we'd fish while he carried his young daughter, Wren, around in a pouch against his chest. Once, when things were difficult between Wade and my dad, Christie acted as a calming presence between them and assured me that my uncle was "rough around the edges but soft in the middle." I only hope there's still truth in it.

"Oh, hey, Grady," Christie greets, flashing his hot pink fingernails and pulling the ends of a pink terrycloth robe together.

"Somebody dead?" Roy asks, his basketball belly reaching us before he does. He scratches what little hair he has left and scrubs a hand over his gray stubble.

"No one's dead," I try again now that Wade's advisors have arrived. "But this concerns the G&G—"

"They help me run the store," Wade defends.

"*All* of you work there now?" I ask. I only remember them hanging out there, not working.

"We're part-timers. I was a lineman for Duke Power for over twenty-five years, till I fell off a pole. I'm retired. Disability," Roy says, looking offended.

"My job is life," Christie says whimsically. "Want to come in for tea or a cocktail?"

"Nope—he's not staying. Roy, go get a six-pack." Wade's gray eyes burrow into me. "As you can see, I'm fully staffed. You've got a business. Your dad's got a farm. Why don't y'all hire her?"

I wave my hand toward his forgotten business. "This is more her... vibe. I think."

"Who's vibe?" Roy asks, his trailer door swinging shut behind him.

"Marina's."

"Aw, Valentine's baby? How is she?" Christie coos. "She wants a job? Here?"

"Are we talking about the chick Grady nearly killed in that car wreck?" Roy clarifies, handing each of them a Miller Lite. They crack the cans open and take long gulps in unison.

"That's the one," Wade burps. "We don't need help, and why would you even bother asking me?"

"Forget it," I say, heading toward my truck. "This place is a lost cause. And so are you."

"Grady! Get back here." Wade's stern voice sounds like Dad's, freezing me in place. "You dragged me from bed. At least explain yourself."

He flicks his cigarette into a puddle.

Christie ushers me into the huddle with an encouraging smile on his long face.

"Give us the full story. What've you got to lose?" Christie says encouragingly. Behind him, his daughter Wren exits the trailer and sits on the front steps, holding a book.

"Fine. The car accident not only hurt her but cost her a car, her wedding day, her fiancé, and her job. Now, she's stuck working at the funeral home, all because of me."

"Marnie's at the funeral home?" Wren winces. "That must hurt her positive energy."

"Definitely," I say.

"Oh, Marnie's too cheerful and friendly for that," Christie agrees. "And too creative. I loved her displays in Sunny's gazebo."

"She's wasting away in a dead-end job because she has no better option. I believe the G&G could give her purpose and hope again."

"Despite appearances, I ain't running a rehabilitation center here," Wade argues. "Take your stray dog somewhere else."

"Ah, Wade. She's not a dog," Christie argues in a hurt tone. "She's a *lioness*."

I don't know what to say to that. "Um, there is nowhere else. I've called every grocery store, retailer, and market within twenty miles. They're either not hiring or only filling managerial positions from within. She'd have to start at minimum wage, a heinous joke. She needs more and deserves better for the ten years she's put in."

"She won't find better here," Wade counters, motioning to the G&G down the lane.

The large convenience store looks so rundown that it might as well be abandoned. The outside is littered with nonsensical junk. The large gravel parking lot butts up against the swamp, where a short dock looks more likely to hold sunbathing alligators than people. Since no one's working there at noon on a Saturday, the only sign of life is a blinking neon sign in the window that says PEN as the O has burnt out.

"Make her manager, and she'll turn this heap into a profitable business again," I say, hoping it's true.

"How intriguing," Christie beams, turning toward his daughter. "Wren tells me Marnie practically ran Sunny's. All the beautiful displays were her ideas. Plus, she's done wonders for Wren's social skills, though no one should be forced to smile so much."

"It hurts my face," Wren says.

"I know, honey," Christie returns.

"I can't afford a manager," Wade snaps after a long belch.

"I'll fund her salary. She should've sued me. At least this way, she'll get *something* back for what I've taken from her. All you have to do is let her be the manager, put her on your payroll, and give her freedom to change this place."

"I don't like changes," he huffs.

"We like things just the way they are," Roy tacks on. "We don't want any lassie coming in here with her curtains, flowers, and girly things."

"Hey!" Wren groans, glancing up from her book.

"Pretty things aren't *girly*, Roy, just like trucks aren't *manly*. We talked about this," Christie pipes in. "Did you see her Father's Day grill display? It was stunning."

"Marina turns the mediocre into the magnificent," I say, using her words. "It'll be like the old days when—"

Wade's finger shoots up, nearly ramming me in the nose. "Don't you dare say her name."

I step back, immediately regretting it. I haven't stepped foot in the G&G in over a decade, but before then, we always visited when Maureen was here. Wade would let us pick one treat from the candy bar aisle after playing hide-and-seek with him, using the store's round shoplifting prevention mirrors perched in corners to guide us. She'd have pop music playing over the speakers, and we'd perch on the barstools, where she'd feed us hot dogs from the store's canteen. It was never a bright and shiny place like Sunny's, but it was rustic, charming, and part of us, like the farm.

Those memories—memories of *our* family—led me here. To a possible solution that Marina might go for, and that won't seem entirely like a handout. This place needs help, and she's the perfect person to turn it around.

But Wade's old wounds run very deep. Too deep, maybe, to find hope anywhere.

Christie's soft voice breaks through my uncle's harsh, angry stare down. "What harm would it do for the place to get a makeover? Huh?" His pink fingernails land on Wade's forearm, gently lowering it.

"Might help business," Roy says, his lanky frame bouncing on his dirty slippers. "Be nice to have a new customer every once in a while. Especially the *ladies*..."

"It's not my job to ease your guilt, Grady," Wade snaps.

"No, but if anyone understands guilt, it's you, right?" I pause as he glares. "I need to help her. It wouldn't hurt you to help, too."

"She'll be like a breath of fresh air," Christie coos. "Come on, Wade."

"Give her a chance," I beg, eyes locked on Wade's. "And I'll give you my shares of the place."

Christie gasps, hand going to mouth. Roy gapes, burps, and goes eyes-wide toward Wade.

Wade keeps his poker face, but his mustache twitches encouragingly.

"You'll have majority ownership," I say, "like you should've had when Grandpa died."

"Damn straight, I should've."

"Deal?" I extend my hand.

He grunts, rolling his eyes like he might throw a punch rather than accept it. "One more thing. I want help around here. You're always doing this or that for my brother—"

"My *father*, yeah."

"I got chores, and my back isn't—"

"Fine, whatever." I push my hand closer to his chest. "Deal?"

Slowly, he shakes it, smirking with devilish satisfaction.

"I'm proud of you two. Such growth." Christie claps. "When do we get Marnie? I'm going to wear my turquoise blouse."

"I'll bring her by later if she agrees. She has to say yes for it to work, so you better make it good," I warn, dropping my uncle's hand.

"Should I pick some flowers or something?" Roy scratches his head.

"It's not a fucking date. Just be..." I glance them over. "...clean and sober."

Wade grunts.

"Tipsy okay, Grady?" Christie clarifies. "It's Saturday."

"I'll grab the Lysol for the bathroom. And breath mints," Roy says, rushing to his trailer. "Maybe a candle or two."

Wade and I share a distressed glare. This is going to be a nightmare.

CHAPTER EIGHTEEN

WALKING home from a four-hour Saturday shift at the funeral home, I'm physically and emotionally exhausted. Liam wanted me there for Grandma Johanson's service, but when Seagrovians (all former customers) noticed me working there, attention unfortunately diverted from the deceased to me.

Liam sequestered me in my office after that.

But boring office work tires as much as being a busy bee. My hip aches. My giant jellyfish bruise is only a large yellow smudge now and only hurts after standing too long.

Walking home doesn't help. But I'm lucky that the funeral home is close enough—I haven't been able to buy a new/used car yet. Not because of money—I have the awful severance (still uncashed) and the insurance payout for my old car. It's just a matter of logistics— how do I go see cars when I don't have a car to get me there?

A problem for later.

It's a beautiful day, leaning toward spring. Daffodils peek through the mulch around the Pike's flower beds, and the grass will be long enough to mow soon. My subdued black pants and gray blouse absorb the sunshine. I'm ready for jeans and a t-shirt. Maybe a pain pill. And time with the cats.

Edging down the road to my house, I spot Grady's truck, tailgate down, and him with his sister sitting on the back. She has a sketchbook propped up, hands moving furiously. He leans against his hands, watching me approach from the tops of his eyes like I'm frustrating him again.

His intense stare warms and scares me at once—is that even possible?

"Marina, you're walking to and from work? That's too much," he sighs. "Didn't you get the insurance check?"

"Yes, but no car yet," I say, turning to his sister. "Hey, Marigold. It's so nice to see you. Come inside. Are you okay with cats?"

She glances up, blue eyes narrowing towards mine. "I like cats."

"Purr-fect," I giggle. "You can give them treats if you're comfortable."

She nods and scoots off the truck's tailgate.

I turn to Grady, "You can come, too, if you promise to relax."

"I'm relaxed. There's somewhere I want to take you. I have an idea."

"Oh, that sounds intriguing… slightly concerning. Does it involve much walking or any extreme sports?"

"No. Just assholes and gators," he answers with a hint of a smile. "Trust me?"

"Of course." I unlock the door to a cat chorus. Marigold looks overwhelmed at first, but seems to assess her surroundings and soon relaxes, petting Sunkist as she circles her Mary Janes.

"How's the art going, Marigold?" I ask, grabbing cat treats from the pantry.

She looks unsurely at Grady, who gives her an encouraging look, urging her to answer.

"Good."

"Marigold won every art show at Seagrove High when I was there, even when she was in middle school," I say. "My favorite was your Shadow Man Series."

Grady and Marigold share a familiar glance, and she says, as soft as a baby kitten, "Grady's Shadow Man."

A laugh rumbles out as I hand her the cat treats. "Oh, I see it! That makes sense."

"Marigold finds inspiration in the least artistic places," he says as she divvies treats to the meowing congregation.

"Oh, I don't know." I step closer and stare up at him. "All your gentle lines and hard edges could be inspiring."

Grady's eyes narrow with amusement, and his arms fold over his impressive chest. "Inspiring, huh? Never been called that before. Hope you feel the same after today."

"Will you be trying to inspire me, Tripp Grady Tripp?"

"Something like that."

His raspy voice taunts a grin that widens the longer I take him in. *Is he blushing?*

"Feeling inspired already." *Oh, wait, am I flirting?* "Um, do I have time to change?"

"Take your time." He breezes by me for the couch, and Triscuit promptly joins him like they're BFFs.

I scoot by Marigold in the hall, where she ogles a rough painting of a waterfall I picked up at a thrift store. "Make yourself at home."

"I like your art," she says.

"Thanks. Most of them are probably discarded school projects or family hand-me-downs that no one wanted, but I like rescuing things. Back in a jiffy."

I lean against the closed bedroom door, steadying my breaths. Whatever Grady's up to makes me nervous—I hate that he feels indebted to me.

But I like that he's here, and my curiosity builds into excitement over spending time with him and Marigold.

I dress in jeans, an off-the-shoulder white t-shirt, and comfortable slip-on shoes. I take down my high ponytail and wrestle my long hair into loose waves on my shoulders—a relaxed look that I hope will inspire Grady to relax, too. With a spritz of perfume and a touch of lip gloss, I leave the bedroom.

A gasp escapes, and nerves bubble at the sight of Marigold ogling my tiny workshop—the room I keep closed. She stands at my workbench, holding the clumsy stick figures I constructed for game pieces with an X-Acto knife and thick cardboard.

"Oh, hi. You found my little secret," I say, fighting insecurities over my homemade efforts.

She looks unsure. "You said make yourself at home."

"Yes, I did. It's perfectly okay."

Grady appears beside me. "Sorry, she wanders."

"No problem whatsoever."

"What is this?" she asks.

"It's my game room. Game-making is my hobby."

Grady glances from me to the menagerie of board games scattered on shelves and tables across the small space. "You *make* board games?"

"I tinker. I'm no artist like you, Marigold. That's why my pieces leave a bit to be desired. But I like strategy and solving puzzles. I buy old games second-hand and try to create something new out of them. That one's called *Milk & Eggs*. It's a grocery store game—go figure. The object is to avoid the distractions, obstacles, and pitfalls around the store to get the items you came there for and get out quicker than your opponents."

Grady looks confused, but Marigold says, "Fun. What about this one?"

"Oh, that's *Tickety-Boo*. I heard the expression once on an old British mystery. It stuck with me, though I'm sure it's not a phrase anyone uses these days. Tickety-boo is a funny way of saying everything's okay, like hunky-dory. The object is to handle embarrassing moments on the cards with as much grace and politeness as possible. Oh, and when you read the cards, you have to keep a straight face. It's always so funny when someone tells you not to laugh. What happens?"

Marigold laughs.

"Exactly. The game ends at a formal dinner party when the guests vote for the most well-mannered household member. That person must give a toast, mentioning the day's mishaps without cracking up to be deemed the winner."

"Sounds fun," she says.

"Yeah, thanks. I think they're fun. Um, they have yet to be tested by anyone but me and cats."

"You invent games, you don't play?" Grady asks, his narrow eyes and folded arms making me feel judged.

"I *want* to play them... It's just... Anyway, nothing says family like a board game. Mom and I used to play sometimes. Um, anyway, do you have any hobbies, Grady?"

"He fishes," Marigold answers, "and complains."

I chuckle while Grady grunts

"Can we play sometime?" Marigold asks.

I gasp. "You want to play them with me?"

Her brow stitches like she's unsure. She glances at Grady.

"Yes, she wants to play with you," Grady clarifies. "She gets nervous when you answer a question with a question."

"Oh, sorry, Marigold. I'd love to play games with you. Let's make a night of it soon. I'll let you decide if you want Grady to join us. Do you like popcorn?"

Marigold nods. Grady waves her out of the room, saying, "Are we ready to go?"

I grab a fuzzy, pink cardigan from the back of a chair, my purse, keys, and cane. "Ready. I think."

Grady ushers us out, takes my keys, and locks the door behind us. His hand grips my elbow as I move more slowly down the stairs. His hand is warm and rough, just like him. He opens the passenger door and hooks my cane to his forearm.

"No Beast today?" I ask, glancing over his much newer black F150.

"Nope. This is my truck. Just got it out of the shop."

He takes my hand to help me inside—help I don't need, but appreciate. Is it wrong that I like him having an excuse to touch me?

Geez, Marnie! Lonely much?

He gets in the truck and starts the engine, but hesitates, turning to me with a pinched brow. "All I ask is that you keep an open mind."

"Oomph, now you're making me nervous."

"Me, too," Marigold chimes in from the backseat.

His head tilts as he takes me in. "No need to be nervous. Or *nice*. You can always say no, Marina."

Then, he hits me with one of the top five sexiest side smiles I've ever seen—devious like he knows a secret and *admiring*, especially the way his eyes trail down my long hair like he wants his fingers to follow.

Now, I need to relax. I must be imagining it—Grady Tripp has zero interest in hair-fondling or general Marnie-fondling. *Right?*

Still, delightful twinges skitter through my nervous system whenever he looks my way, making me wonder.

Wherever he's taking me, whatever requires an open mind, saying no to him might be impossible.

CHAPTER NINETEEN

Grady

I'VE MOVED into forgotten territory—*wanting* to know someone better. I know Marina *differently* than anyone. In some ways, our bond is stronger than most. But I don't *know* her, not well. She doesn't tell me her problems, doesn't share her cool hobbies. These things bother me.

The afternoon sun through the passenger window hits her just right, highlighting her fiery hair, sapphire eyes, and the delicate spray of freckles over her rosy cheeks. She threw on the simplest outfit—jeans and a t-shirt—but there's nothing simple about how plain clothes make her seem bolder. Hair redder. Eyes brighter. Even her hope in me emanates across the cab when she flashes a smile. Everything about her is soft and lovely, from how her top hangs off one shoulder to the fuzzy sweater she carries.

It's hard not to cut glances at her.

To hang on her words and marvel at her incredible hobby. *She creates games? Who does that?*

To wonder what else I don't know about her.

To wonder what it'd be like to let my touches linger.

She didn't need my help down the stairs or into the truck, but my hands went to her anyway. To protect her, yes, but mostly from long-ing. I *miss* having a reason to touch her. When she stood in the doorway of her game room, nervously explaining her hobby, all I could think about was bringing my face into the crook of her neck to feel the softness of her hair and catch her perfume—something like vanilla and lavender. Supporting her down the steps provided an opportunity, but I regret it now. Touching her once has me craving to do it more.

Damn it. I can't have these thoughts, not about her. I'm too old for her, too surly, too gray against her vivid color.

I *need* that reality repeating through my head, but flipped—she's too young, too beautiful, too goddamn rosy for me—because the more I see her, the more I *want* to see her. And I have no business wanting more of her at all.

My eyes shift her way again. She angles sideways against the door with her leg propped, like she wants to engage in conversation but doesn't know where to start. She fidgets with the buttons on the sweater, looking apprehensive.

"This is nice, but I like The Beast better," she says.

"Really?"

"It's got character." She turns even more in her seat, wincing slightly but looking hopeful. "Do I get a hint, at least?"

Her hopes rattle my nerves. *What am I doing?* Suddenly, putting lovely Marina inside Wade's store feels like the worst idea in history. Like hanging the Mona Lisa in a dive bar and letting drunks throw darts at it. These things don't belong together.

But do they belong together more than Marina at a funeral home? I don't know.

I wrangle my anxiety and tell her the truth. "Do you know the G&G?"

Her brow cocks high on her forehead. "That sketchy place by the swamp?"

Shit. "Yeah, Uncle Wade owns it, and he needs help."

Her face scrunches with confused contemplation.

"Wade needs a manager to help him turn the place around and bring in business. I thought of you."

Her brow kinks, and she turns toward the window like she might be preparing a nicer version of, *"Fuck off, Grady. Take me home, you meddling bastard."*

"Dad calls the G&G an armpit," Marigold offers dryly.

"Not helping," I snap, catching her eyes in the rearview mirror.

A beat passes in awkward silence.

"Marina, you can say no," I tell her again. "But humor me first? Let's check the place out and hear what he has to say. Okay?"

She fiddles with her lap sweater again. "It's tickety-boo. Relax, Grady."

Marigold snorts behind me.

The dirt and gravel lot crunches beneath the truck's tires when we arrive at the G&G. The store sits on the outskirts of Seagrove, where the lake turns into swamps before disappearing into rural farms. It takes four turns and about six miles from the main highway to reach it—it's not an easy pitstop for anyone except those who live around here.

But those who live here generally don't stop into the G&G unless they're residents of The Marshes trailer park to the right and up a gravel hill. For them, it's the only thing within walking distance.

I park beside the building. Marina slides from the truck before I get a chance to come around and open the door for her.

She doesn't need your help, Grady.

With a slow circle, she scans the area: the three ancient gas tanks, the rickety overhang, and the Pepsi-Cola sign advertising the store's name. *Welcome to the G&G.* The cracked plastic has chipped away at the W, and the colors have faded over the years. I wonder if it still lights up.

Probably not.

Wade hasn't repaired or improved this place in a decade.

"What does G&G stand for?" she asks when I take her side.

"Grab and Go."

She chuckles. "That's not what I heard."

I huff. Grubby and Gross is the most popular variation when people talk about the G&G. Not that they do anymore.

"Shall we?" I motion to the storefront.

"What about Marigold?"

"She'll wait in the car. Sensory overload. I'm surprised she wanted to go inside your place."

"Well, I lured her with cats," she smiles. "Who can resist?"

"Who, indeed?" I smirk, meeting her eyes again.

I lean into the open window of the truck. "Please, don't wander."

"Tickety-boo," Marigold answers, not looking up from her sketchbook.

The long porch that stretches the length of the building feels narrow with all the junk lining the corridor. Crab traps, barrels, pallets, empty boxes, water jugs, antique Coke and milk crates—it's like a junkyard vomited out here. She peers inside the picture windows, which are too dingy and cluttered to see through.

"It needs work," I say, regretting this already.

She smiles but doesn't answer—probably preparing her hell-no speech, one I'll deserve.

The door rattles when I open it, and sets off hanging door chimes that lazily clink together like they're tired of the place.

Inexplicably, my fingers fall on her lower back, easing her inside, as if she doesn't know the way or I'm impatient.

Her eyes catch mine, offering a warm smile, but my hand drops, and I regret touching her again.

Inside, the smell hits us first—mothballs, cigarette smoke, and stale beer—with clutter covering every surface a close second.

"Fucking hell," I mumble. Insisting on a tour before agreeing to the deal would've been smart. It's a shit heap, barely recognizable from the G&G of my childhood.

Old metal shelves flank out like a fan around us. Products are sparsely arranged—candy here, chips there, canned goods over there —but nothing looks organized. Magazines and old newspapers tower in a corner. Random standalone displays of keychains, individual packs of medicines, and lighters occupy odd spaces. Lights flicker in the cold cases along the wall, and fluorescents buzz overhead. A case that once held ice cream sandwiches and Nutty Buddies now only has bait and ice-crusted frozen dinners. Fishing rods and nets line the wall, most crooked.

And like a cherry on top, a legs-up cockroach the size of my fist lies on the rough, paint-chipped floor at Marina's foot.

In her slow pan of the store, she sees the cockroach but says nothing. I steer her around it, and we walk deeper into the store from hell.

"Is that Marnie?" Christie's voice rises from the back corner of the L-shaped store.

Marnie's feet move somewhat quicker through the aisles to reach the source.

Seeing my uncle, his buddies, and what's become of the place makes me cringe. What Maureen once called "The Canteen," a short kitchen and bar with a few fixed metal stools where she'd serve us fountain drinks and hot dogs, has been overtaken by cigarette cartons and the insipid grunge of ashtrays.

Roy occupies one stool of the canteen to our right, legs stretched out to the register counter and belly protruding from his dirty t-shirt.

The counter is a large, battered wood monstrosity covered in ancient advertisement posters, mostly for beer and cigarettes. Overhead, a slotted shelf holds loose cigarette packs like an umbrella over Christie and Wade, who occupy high-top bar stools on the other side of the counter. They look like an oddball gang of old bikers, smoking and drinking in their corner, protecting themselves from customers.

Not that they get many. Or any.

Embarrassment makes my cheeks flush as I turn to Marina. It's so awful that I want to scoop her into my arms, make a run for it, and find a way to erase her memory of this. She should hate me for bringing her here, let alone suggesting she work here.

But she stifles my upcoming apology with a wide smile. "Yes, it's Marnie. Are you three heartbreakers my welcoming committee?"

Christie nearly falls over himself, coming from behind the counter to greet her—at a lumbering six-four, he tends to look clumsy. "It's so wonderful to have you here," he says, hand grazing his heart.

"I'm happy to be here." She shakes his extended hand. "What a lovely blouse—a very good color for you. Brings out your eyes."

Christie looks like he might tear up at the compliment. He fingers the collar of the silky shirt. "Told you, boys. She has exquisite taste. I still dream about your starry night display at Sunny's."

"Picnic Under the Stars? You remember?" Her cheeks redden

sweetly. "We sold out of beach blankets and picnic baskets over that one."

Christie raises his hand. "Guilty of buying both! Wren and I love going on nighttime adventures. Well, I call them adventures. She calls them evening spells and incantations. Do you know Roy?"

Christie motions to the idiot on the stool, who promptly stands, bows, and salutes, but does each clumsily. "Roy Fontaine. Retired Duke Power lineman. Glad you ain't dead."

"Um, thanks. Me, too."

He rubs his gray beard, scrutinizing her with his drunk eyes. "You're a lot prettier than Grady said."

Marina flashes a coy smile in my direction.

"I never said," I correct sternly. "Stop talking."

Roy fumbles back to his stool.

Christie motions to Wade, still sitting behind the counter. "You remember Wade?"

Wade nods and flicks his cigarette ashes into the dirty tray beside him.

For the first time since we entered, Marina's smile falters. "I remember. Nice to meet you under better circumstances. Thanks for being there, you and Christie, my heroes."

Christie gasps. "A terrible day, but not tragic, thanks to Grady and the universe. Glad to help."

"Just doing our civic duty," Wade huffs.

I give him a stern glare over Marina's shoulder. I should've known he wouldn't make this easy.

"Grady tells me you're looking for a manager," Marina says, scanning her surroundings. Her finger lands on an empty stool. Its wobbly spin makes her smile widen and stirs my memories. I wish she could've seen the place when Maureen was here.

"That's right," Wade says.

"Someone to revitalize the place and our sales," Christie chimes in. "We need a customer service makeover, Marnie, and you're just the person to do it."

"I'll match whatever you were making at Sunny's," Wade says, "and add ten percent." His gray eyes find mine, and he smirks under his unkempt horseshoe mustache. "Make that twenty percent. I hear so many good things about you."

He chuckles, making me irritated.

"That's wonderfully generous. But would you turn over control?" she asks, head tilted as she assesses the space. "Or would I just be a glorified cashier with good ideas that don't happen?"

Wade's hands fist as he glares at me. "You'll have control within reason. The place needs a good cleaning. You can start there."

"She's on light duty," I cut in sternly. "You three will have to step up and help."

"I'm getting better every day, but he's right. No heavy lifting or long hours for a few weeks yet. Is that alright?"

"I'm sure we can figure something out," Wade allows, "so long as Grady chips in, too. Call it a family project."

Christie claps. "It'll be fun—a Marnie-style makeover. Does that mean you'll say yes?"

She opens her mouth but hesitates. "It means... can I think about it? And look around some more?"

"Our G&G is your G&G," Christie says, bowing. "Make yourself at home."

"What's behind that black curtain?" She points to a thickly draped doorway with a scribbled sign that reads "Members Only."

Their eyes dart toward each other, unsure. "That's our adult film section."

"Goddamnit, Wade," I blurt.

"We're only meeting the demand of our customer demographic," Wade says snidely, holding his hands up.

Marina breaks into a full-blown laugh. "Your customer demographic is people who don't know how to use the internet? That's a very niche market."

"It meets a need," he argues. "Who am I to judge?"

"I don't watch them, Marnie." Christie looks sheepish.

"I do," Roy chimes in. "Wade has some of the best titles you can find. They don't make 'em like they used to. We do an employee's pick every month if you want to get in on that, Marnie. Be nice to have a lady's choice. You have a VCR?"

"Stop talking," I order him, finger pointed.

Meanwhile, Marina erupts with laughter again. "I *need* a VCR?"

"Let's not debase G&G's *vintage* collection," Wade says. "It's a customer favorite."

"And how many customers have you had today?" she asks.

The men exchange puzzled glances. Christie uses one hand to count while Roy helpfully reports, "Four. Five if y'all buy something."

"No offense, Wade, but are you sure you can afford me?" she questions.

"Look, sweetheart, I wouldn't make the offer if I couldn't," he snaps. "It's about time I give the ol' G&G some TLC... to honor the lost."

His beer can rises, and the other two meet it with theirs, a gentle clink and swish of beer.

"To the lost," they repeat before guzzling.

Marina appears moved by their drunken display. Her lips press together in an approving smile.

Then, she turns to me, her fingers lightly grazing my forearm. "I'm going to look around, okay?"

"Sure."

She drifts away, seeming to examine everything from the floor to the ceiling, and I want to warn her not to look too closely, but what does it matter?

Cockroaches, cigarettes, idiots, and porn? There's no way she'll go for this.

Not that I want her to—she deserves better.

I meet Marina at the short dock overlooking the swamp a half-hour later. She stands there, gazing at the scenery. I imagine she's upset. I would be. This isn't a career option. It's an insult. A death sentence. A cruel joke. Another funeral home.

The boards creak under me when I move beside her. The stagnant water swirls with green algae and lily pads. A lone car goes over the short bridge to our left, startling a long-legged heron into flight. Deeper into the swamp, the majestic, thick-bottomed bald cypress trees dripping with Spanish moss form an eerie tunnel. The dying sun reflects the trees onto the water's surface, doubling their mystery and beauty. Croaking frogs begin a nighttime chorus, and a hawk makes a forceful dive onto the weedy grasslands. Like the woman standing beside me, it's beautiful in the strangest way.

I'd forgotten how much I once loved it here.

My arms fold as I struggle to put together an apology.

She turns to me, eyes and smile wider than seems possible. "I'll do it."

"Seriously? You don't have to. You shouldn't. It's a mess. I never should've brought you here. We'll think of something else."

"*We* don't have to think of anything else. But since you took the initiative of finding me something I'd enjoy, I want to do it."

"Why?" I ask, breathless and confused. "You're so much better than this place."

Her bare shoulder bounces in a one-sided shrug. "There's potential here, and I love a good challenge. Lost causes and second chances are two of my many specialties. You'll see."

Her warm smile carries her optimism over to me. "I don't doubt it. If you're sure."

"I am, but I need you to promise me something." Her delicate hands fall on my folded forearms like she wants me to pay attention. "This pity train you're on stops here. I know you facilitated this job offer more than you let on. That man does not want a manager, does he?"

"He... warmed up to the idea."

"Well, he needs the help. You're right about that, and I'm perfect for the job," she says, pleasing me with her confidence. "But, Grady, you've done enough. Okay? I know you feel bad about the accident and the aftermath, but it's done. Nothing can change it."

Sometimes, nothing can be done. "I know, and I'm sorry, and I won't stop feeling sorry just because you want me to."

Her hands tighten on my forearm, and her eyes lock on mine. "You know, don't you? About *everything* I lost in the accident?"

Her question hits me so hard that I almost step back. Only I can't. Stepping back means leaving her touch, and I refuse to do that. Or outright lie to her. "Yes."

"I thought you might."

"I overheard. Outside your room, when the doctor... I shouldn't have listened."

She chuckles softly, still holding on with both hands like I might leave her. "It's okay. A relief, actually. That someone else knows. Someone who... doesn't hold it against me."

I swallow a growing lump in my throat. Her vulnerability with me, letting me into her pain like I'm not the cause of it, does something to the outer crust I've worked so hard to build around me since moving back home. It flakes away under her gaze, her words, her fingertips, like old paint off weather-beaten boards. I imagine if she snapped her fingers, it would disappear altogether. "I would *never* hold it against you. No one should. Still, Marina, I'm so—"

"Grady, please, listen to me. It's not your fault. *I* held the knife in my lap. Ashe was the dummy who couldn't remember the *one thing* he had to do besides get dressed and show up. Cora didn't even notice it sitting on the counter in their kitchen—it was *her* family heirloom. Don't you see? The blame game has us going around in useless circles. Still, nothing changes."

"I fucked up your life, Marina. I'm responsible."

Her eyes fix on mine, locking me in. "Remember what I said? Those impressive shoulders can't carry everything. And I don't want them to. I didn't deserve what happened, but you don't deserve a lifetime of guilt for it, either. I won't be defined by a freaking body part, and, you know what? I'm stronger without it and better off with a question mark for a future than one as the Sullivan's go-to girl. Please, Grady. Let this be the last thing."

"I can't promise that, Marina. Not until I know you're okay. Not just hearing you say it, but *knowing* it. I need to see you physically, mentally, and financially, okay. You almost died in my arms. Like it or not, that connected us, and I'd be a shit person if I didn't grab onto that connection and let it take us wherever you want it to go. Truth is, I'm not okay until you are. You're stuck with me until then. Understood?"

She sighs and nods. "Two castaways on the same boat, huh?"

"Yes, but it's not just a boat. It's a damn pirate ship reclaiming what's been taken from you. As much as we can, anyway. I want you to ram it into the Sullivan's cruise ship. Sink them, Marina."

She laughs at this like she's had similar ideas, her distress vanishing in her amusement.

"Make them regret the day they valued your body over you," I say more seriously. "Make them regret ever *pretending* to be your family."

Her hands slide to the crook of my elbows. At first, I think she's pulling away, but she tugs my arms loose instead. When she latches onto me, I'm stunned. I'm no hugger. Aside from Mom and Elena, people know better than to try.

Even so, I wrap around her, her head tucked under my chin, and my hand laced into the soft bands of her hair, holding her close to me. She grips my shoulders like she doesn't want me to let go. Not that I would.

For her, anything goes. I know this already. Whatever I have to give is hers to take.

 Marnie

MARNIE STRANGE, *what're you doing?* I nearly stumble, leaving Grady Tripp's impressive chest and strong, *melt-me-like-butter-on-a-hot-day* arms. I let go of the poor man, blushing from embarrassment and flushed with *something else*—I dare not speak it.

"Sorry, Grady. I'll refrain from taking advantage of you for free hugs. You're not the hugging type, are you?"

He looks confused. "No, but it's okay."

"Not okay," I argue, finger-wagging. "It's not every day that I score the protection and help of a pirate captain. I got carried away."

"First of all, *you're* the captain. And if I thought you were over-stepping, I would've told you. For you, hugs are allowed. Encouraged, even. Let's keep it between us, though. I can't let anything ruin my Grouchy Tripp reputation."

He makes me smile, and everything feels lighter. "Understood."

His hands perch on his hips as he takes in the oversized, rundown convenience store behind us. "Are you sure about this? I didn't know how bad it'd gotten. Trying to turn this place around seems like agreeing to take a nosedive into a pool of shit."

"Wow, what creative imagery," I chuckle. "I'm sure."

"Truth?"

"Truth." I don't mention that, yes, the place is overwhelmingly awful. The clean-up alone will take weeks of hard labor. Half of his products have expired. There's definitely a bug problem, perhaps rodents, too. And any rebranding attempt means getting Wade and company to change their ways—a feat in and of itself. Diving into a shit pit is an accurate assessment of the undertaking.

And yet, I can't think of anything else I'd want to do, partly because challenges and special projects are my jam. *Seriously.*

But more than that, I want to do it for Grady. He saved my life—he should have his back. If taking this job alleviates his guilt and restores his peace of mind, then, of course, I'll do it for him. He needs this as much as I do.

By the time we finish working out details with Wade, darkness falls, turning the swamp into black ink and gray shadows. Heading toward Grady's truck, I pull my sweater on to battle the chill in the air.

"Hungry?" Grady asks.

"Um, yeah."

"Marigold doesn't like eating out on the fly, but how about we take her home and raid Mom's kitchen?"

The question surprises me. "Are you sure she wouldn't mind?"

He smirks. "She'll be ecstatic. Trust me. Only let's not mention the Wade situation. Okay?"

"Okay, why not?"

"Did you hear that Marigold? We aren't discussing Wade or the G&G. That's off-limits." He peers at his sister through the rearview mirror.

"Off-limits," she repeats dully. "Yes, Grady."

His eyes cut to me. "Wade and Dad don't get along. They had a falling out over a decade ago. Dad prefers us to keep our distance, and Wade is perfectly fine with that arrangement."

I want to ask about the falling out, but it feels nosy.

"I apologize in advance for Wade. He might be difficult to deal with."

"Aw, honey, I'll turn him into a teddy bear in no time. You'll see."

He chuckles. "Darling, if anyone could do it, it'd be you."

A bit flushed by his faith in me and the word *darling*, I gaze out the window, focusing on passing lights instead of Grady. But it's hard. The tight veins in his forearms, tensing as he turns, nicks from old injuries, and the dark lines and smudges of his tattoos are all delicious little things that could keep me entertained for hours.

I must be lonely. Or hormonal—I still have those.

Soon, we pull through the gates and bump up the long driveway of Tripp Family Farm. Flanked by fields and pastures, their home guides us in like a lighthouse amid the seas. Light beams in every window, and twinkle lights adorn the wraparound porch. It's bigger than I expected, but it housed eight people at one time. Eight!

I can't imagine having siblings or being a part of any large household. The idea of someone always being there seems so cozy and comforting, and makes me sad. I spent so much time alone growing up. Maybe that's why I said yes to Ashe even though I never fully believed in us.

I realize that now, though maybe I could've lived blissfully unaware of my doubts for ages. Moving along in our marriage until something snapped—a promise broken or an expectation unfulfilled. Then, that undercurrent of unease would be clear in wretched hindsight, the dirty frenemy.

Everyone abandons me eventually.

Now, that loneliness returns and digs in, especially when Grady pulls in beside other cars, muttering a breathy, "What'd I forget, Marigold?"

"Game night," she says.

A full gasp erupts from me. *Game night? They have a game night?*

He turns to me apologetically. "Sorry. We don't have to stay."

"No, I want to. If it's alright," I pipe up quickly, "I mean, I don't want to intrude."

He groans. "It's no intrusion. I just don't want *you* to feel bombarded by *them*. They're a lot."

Nervous but desperate to see this family event, I take a deep breath and straighten my shoulders. "I can handle it."

Grady's light touch finds the small of my back when he ushers me inside, and a heat joins my unease. I *really* shouldn't enjoy his touches this much.

Marigold beelines through the chaotic room and disappears. It's not a living room but a great room with beamed arched ceilings, an open concept into the kitchen and dining room, and a blazing fireplace against the far wall. Card tables and chairs have been set up around the room, all boasting games. *Scrabble* at one, *Ticket to Ride* at another, *Sushi Go* around the coffee table, and *Farm-Opoly* at the dining room table. The room bursts with noise and laughter while the games are played simultaneously.

All of which stops when eyes land on me. Silence takes over as they glance from me to each other and back again like they're stunned and unsure what to do with me. Wild déjà vu takes over—the production of *The Sound of Music* in high school when I was the set designer, perfectly content to stay backstage and let my backdrops and props take the starring role until *she* showed up with other ideas. That red-faced humiliation returns now, making my skin hot and my fingers tremble.

"This tells you how often I show up with a woman," he whispers before his hand gently urges me forward. "Guys, you know Marina?"

"Marnie, welcome!" Carmela rises from the *Ticket to Ride* table. She maneuvers her way to me as the others break their silences with greetings and how-are-you's. Uncharacteristically uneasy, my answers are quick and automatic. *Fine, thank you. Nice to see you. How are you?*

They aren't exactly strangers, but they aren't friends, either. The story of my life.

I know them all in one way or another. Carmela from the pharmacy. Mack from delivering his eggs and dairy products to Sunny's —another idea of mine, local vendors—and his arguments with Cora over her inflating the prices. Colin's face is plastered all over Seagrove, being the town's only real estate agent. His wife, Tamsyn is a frequent customer at Sunny's and a keen produce selector. We once got into a lovely discussion over finding the perfect cantaloupe. Their kids, Zach and Zoe, love the candy bar at Sunny's. Luke practically runs Rebellion, the best restaurant in town. His wife, Willow, looks like a bohemian princess and frequents Sunny's section of natural beauty products. I don't see Elena often—she must shop at Food Lion—but I feel like I know her, considering Jim and his chocolate chip birthday cakes. I graduated from Seagrove High before Marigold, but after Gil—he's the one I know best since we both worked on *The Sound of Music* together; he was in charge of sound.

Carmela reaches me, going straight for a gentle hug and then grabbing my free hand to pull me into the house. "I'm so glad you're here."

She means it, though I feel like a spare card mixed into the wrong deck.

"Come to the kitchen. It's taco night. Hope you're hungry."

With me occupied, attention diverts to Grady—his father asking for his help with hay tomorrow, Colin reminding him about Zoe's bake sale, Gil asking about a trip to GameStop, and other requests that I don't hear as Carmela moves me into the kitchen.

"Hope you like tacos... I could warm up something if you don't... How're those headaches?"

I ramble off quick answers, dazed by her beautiful but intense attention. I see where Grady gets it from, though I imagine he wouldn't like that observation pointed out.

Mom's voice stirs in my head. *"Let's move south, find out if there's anything to Southern hospitality."* Her idea took us to Virginia briefly. Then, six towns in North Carolina, like we were having trouble finding the elusive cliché. Until Seagrove, where I found it, but she didn't. I wonder if Mom's still searching.

The grand kitchen island seats eight with bar stools around all sides but one, where Carmela moves to turn off a burner and fixes me a plate.

Games resume in the great room. Pop music plays on the large TV perched above the mantel, and a light show matches the beats on the screen. Elena follows us into the kitchen, grabbing an open bottle of red from the drink station.

"Wine, Marnie?" she asks. "Are you a red or a white?"

"Um, I don't know." I rarely drink wine unless at Cora's house for a dinner party or at the Seagrove Lake Club for one of the Sullivan's charity events, and then, I always take what they hand me. "Surprise me."

She smirks at the challenge and contemplates the bottles.

Carmela presents a plate with two meat-filled, crunchy tacos. "Help yourself to all the toppings, chips, and dips."

The island is crowded with condiments and dips: seven-layer, bean, queso, cheese, avocado, and fresh salsas of every variety, with little index cards indicating what they are and their spice level. Tiny splotches of tomatoes, chip crumbs, and cheese drizzles dot the granite surface between dishes, revealing that the family has already been through the line.

"So, um, how often do you guys have game night?" I ask, piling veggies on my tacos.

Grady helps himself, moving around his mother and sampling as he goes.

"Once a month," Carmela answers, her eyes darting to a huge wall calendar near the fridge. It's jam-packed with Sharpie-marked events. Zoe's horse shows. Zach's soccer matches. Trivia night at Rebellion. Birthdays. Anniversaries. Book clubs. Church events. I can't find one empty space.

"Wow, you're a busy family."

Elena hands me a long-stemmed wine glass. "I went with red. You *are* a red, after all."

"It's a mutation," I blurt before taking a gulp. Why am I so freaking nervous all of a sudden? "My hair. It's a genetic mutation."

Grady eyes me curiously, his lips twitching in a smirk.

"Oh, that's... I didn't know that," Carmela says.

"Um, thanks for the wine and dinner." I tip my glass toward them. Elena stands next to Carmela on the other side of the island, both seeming to scrutinize me.

Willow strolls in, smiling. "Your aura is lighter today, Marnie. That's nice to see."

"Oh, thanks."

Zoe and Zach race in, bumbling around Grady for more chips and gloating about how they just stomped their grandfather in *Farm-opoly*, an irony since he's the farmer.

I take another long sip of wine, wondering how long before the alcohol will mellow me out. It makes no sense to feel so anxious around these wonderful people.

But these aren't my people. And this isn't my stomping ground.

Colin weaves into the kitchen, shuffling around Grady and rounding up his kids. "Oh, Marnie, do you know if Ashe is still buying that house?"

I almost choke on tacos. "House?"

"The four-bedroom place near his parents?" Colin clarifies so matter-of-factly that I first think he's confused his clients. Ashe has a condo near the beach and no house plans, as far as I know. We discussed buying a house later, once we settled into our store manager positions and found a good middle ground between them.

"I've been trying to reach him," he goes on. "The owners are ready to keep his security deposit and move on if he doesn't finish that paperwork. Should've closed already. They accepted his offer nearly two months ago."

"Um, that's news to me. I don't know." I force a smile. "You should try calling him at the Carolina Beach store. That's where he's working now."

"Will do, thanks." He rushes from the room like he might make the call now.

Suddenly, everyone in the room stares at me—not helping my nerves. "These tacos are delicious."

Grady looks practically murderous, hovering at the bar's end, his teeth clenched and his muscles flexed like he might rip the granite off its foundation.

A beautiful lakeside house gets added to *The List of Things Marnie Lost in the Accident.* Is that what's transformed Relaxed Grady back into Grouchy Tripp? Or is he mad at his brother for dropping the bomb? Or both? I don't know, but I feel bad either way. Spending time with me might hurt Grady more than it helps.

I finish the wine and hold my glass out to Elena for a refill.

"I knew you were a red," she smirks.

"So, Marnie, do you like board games?" Carmela asks.

Do *I* like board games? It's like asking if a bank robber likes money or a race car driver likes going fast. I don't *like* board games; I adore them. Study them. Build them in my head. Sometimes, I wake up in the middle of the night with a killer concept for my next project and can't go back to sleep. That's how much I love board games.

And yet, my thoughts jumble and race. Instead of relaxing with the wine, I'm overrun with angst over one sharp, prevailing thought.

I don't belong here.

I'm just the woman with the ruined life, latching on to the man who pushed over the first domino.

"Bathroom?" I ask instead, the bar stool scraping the floor as I push out of it.

Seconds later, I'm behind a locked door of a guest bathroom. My hips ache as I shift to the counter and wobble against my cane. I've done too much today, and my body's retaliating.

Worse, so is my head.

Warmth from the wine spreads through my belly, but it's not giving me the jubilant feels I need for the occasion. It's a game night, for goodness' sake! It should be fun, witnessing a family at play.

Instead, it makes me wearily sad.

Sad for the house I never stepped foot in. That he never told me about. That he bought without me, knowing I'd go along with anything he wanted.

Sad for the home outside this door, the family game nights, kids running around, and big dinners that'll never happen for me.

No wonder I don't feel like I belong.

I don't.

The last time I felt this out of place was, weirdly, that one night in high school that changed my trajectory. Was that a mistake, too? *I miss Mom.*

But I can't think about that now. Deep, determined breaths firm my shoulders and help me resume my safe position on the riverbank of my rocky, emotional rapids.

No frowns, no fears, no tears.

When I leave the bathroom, my warmest, widest smile accompanies me.

CHAPTER TWENTY-ONE

Grady

MARINA DISAPPEARS down the hall for the bathroom, and I hope she's okay. Earlier at the G&G and the dock, she seemed confident, hopeful, and excited. But here, even before Colin's dick move, it's like we took a wrong turn, evident in her uncertainty and wine-guzzling. It's a family game night—she should enjoy this more than anyone.

As soon as I think it, the realization burns through me like wildfire—I'm a fucking idiot. This must be excruciating for her so soon after the accident. I destroy her chances for a family and then bash her over the head with mine to make sure she knows what she's missing. I must have an advanced degree in being an asshole for how expertly I'm accomplishing it.

Appetite gone, I dump my plate in the sink between Elena and Mom as they theorize how much money Ashe must've put down on the expensive home.

"Does that matter?" I ask. "The entitled prick made that decision without her. What does that tell you?"

I'm unsure what shocks them most—that I volunteered an opinion or what I said. I don't stay for more conversation, though I hear words like "controlling" and "awfully close to Cora" as I venture down the dimly lit hallway.

Marina's cane catches on the doorjamb when she exits the bath-room, making her tumble into my arms. Her cane falls, and so does her plastered-on smile.

I say, "You okay?" as she says, "I'm okay."

"Want to get out of here?" I blurt over her breathless, "I'm a little tired."

We both take a breath, chuckling at talking over each other. Her grip on my forearms tightens as my hands gently rest at her sides like middle schoolers about to slow dance for the first time.

She doesn't need my help, but she's not letting go. I'm close enough to catch the sweetness of the wine on her breath and wonder about the softness of her lips as she lightly nibbles her bottom one.

"There you go again, catching me," she says softly.

Her words yank me back to *that* day when she stumbled from her wrecked car, ripped the knife out of her body, and fell into my arms. Here we are again, two feathers caught in the wind.

"I'll always catch you."

My promise brings a smile to her face, but a pinch to her brow, too. She's sad, and my words only make it worse, somehow.

"I love your family," she says, "but can we go? I don't want to be rude or unsociable—"

"Why the hell not? I am all the time. They're used to it."

She laughs, hands slipping to my biceps. "They make allowances for you. I still *care* what they think. I care what you think, too."

She hesitantly says the last part, and her words hang there, mixing with the warmth collecting in the small space between us. The ends of her long hair dangle, tickling my forearm. Heat rises with my quickening heartbeat—it's been an age since I've been this close to a woman. It's been even longer since I remember goosebumps over someone's delicate touch. Or felt twinges of anticipation and hope, staring into someone's eyes. All those things are happening with her. She is sunlight, peeking slowly through the window, waking me from my self-induced coma, and begging me back to life.

She is too young for me, too beautiful, too goddamned nice. My guilt and her losses render our situation too fucked up for anything beyond friendship. *I know this.*

And yet, our proximity pushes me into thoughts beyond friendship. I want to say fuck it and dive into her like I did at the lake after losing my fishing rod. Go deep, searching her. Get lost in her. Let her have all of me. My rough hands massaging those sore hips. The aching pressure of my affection sending her against the wall just to feel all of her on me. Lips tangled with mine, hot, and breathy. Clothes off to make an exploration of every single freckle. I'd fucking worship her.

I doubt she's known real attention or release, full-bodied and mind-shattering—not because of her age but because of the selfish prick she almost married. Maybe he'd "let" her get hers, but never would've prioritized it. Not like I would. Not like she deserves.

Not that I deserve a chance with her.

Damn it, Grady. Focus.

Her breath hits my cheek, and I fixate on her eyes. Her widened pupils bring selfish satisfaction. "Who would dare call *The* Marnie Strange rude or unsociable?"

She laughs. "There's a first time for everything. Like you calling me Marnie. That might be a first... Not sure I like it as much, coming from you."

"I'll stick with Marina, then."

"Tell me, Grady. Are you trying to stand out, or do you see me differently than everyone else?"

"Both."

Her lips curve into a pleased smile, and I can't help but offer one, too.

"Are you a couple now?" Marigold's voice carries down the quiet hallway, forcing our hands away from each other.

"Damn, Marigold," I huff. "Don't sneak up."

"It looked like you were going to kiss," she points out, sounding confused.

"We weren't going to kiss. We're just friends, and I'm an old man, and it's none of your business."

Marina glances at her feet, looking almost disappointed. I pick up her cane and return it to her.

"The hallway belongs to everyone," Marigold explains weakly.

"You're right." I rake a hand over my head. "We were talking. Friends talk."

"It's just… you're less shadowy today."

I feel less shadowy today, not that I'll admit it aloud. Even to Marigold. My head droops, wondering how to end this line of questioning without confusing her or making her feel bad.

Marina gives me a curious look as if registering my shadow level. Then, she turns to my sister with a brimming smile. "That's because I'm his sunshiny nemesis, determined to get him to *lighten up*."

Marigold's lips twitch with a smirk. "He needs to lighten up."

"Exactly." Marina meets Marigold in the hall. "Grady's taking me home, but let's do a game night soon. Will you let me know when you're free?"

"Thursday."

"Thursday, then. Can you drop her off around seven?"

"She has a car," I report, "when she feels comfortable driving it."

"I'll drive. I've been to Marnie's place, so I know where I'm going."

"Purr-fect." Marina giggles, prompting Marigold to do the same.

Marina rounds the room, beaming with friendliness—a different woman than the one who scurried into the bathroom. She's even nice to Colin, though his sheepish look assures me that Mom and Elena had words with him in our absence.

She moves slowly to the car, her cane crunching against the driveway. "You aren't an old man, Grady."

Exhaustion laces her words like she's almost too worn out to say them.

Starting the engine, my shoulders slump. Before I can defend my statement, she speaks again.

"But, I understand why you might feel like one," she says. "You're the go-to guy for everything—I know what that's like. Do you ever just stop and hang out with them?"

"They want me to hang out. I don't have the time or patience for it." I pull out onto the main road and head to her place, which isn't far but feels a world away.

"Why are you their go-to guy for everything?"

"That's the curse of being the oldest, taking care of the others. But it's more than that... Dad wanted me to take over the farm when I left school, but my ex-wife, Emma, wanted the city. Emma didn't work out. Neither did the city. A week after I came back home, I found Dad in the barn in cardiac arrest. He would've died if I hadn't been there. So, now, I'm always there."

Her nod draws my eye, but she doesn't say anything for a moment.

"*There*, but not present," she decides. "That's a ginormous amount of pressure to put on yourself."

I turn onto Seagrove's Main Street, hands tightening on the steering wheel. "I fucked up my marriage. Nearly lost Dad. I refuse to let anything else slip through my fingers."

"So, you catch everyone. Who catches you?"

I don't have an answer.

"No wonder you're exhausted."

"I'm okay. I have nothing to complain about." My eyes cut to her, sitting sideways in the passenger seat. "You do, though. Want to vent? About the house?"

She groans. "I've nothing to complain about, either. What's the point?"

"Might feel good to tap into some rage, scream into the void, and exercise creative cursing."

She laughs. "How very pirate-like."

"Don't knock it until you try it. You can't be everybody's sweetheart all the time. *That* would be exhausting."

"Eh, I'm an endless fountain of energy... usually. You'll see."

"Can't wait," I say. "What're you doing tomorrow? Working?"

"No, but crafting my resignation letter is on my list."

"What? No dramatic take-this-job-and-shove-it thing?" I whine. "Come on, Marina. Pirates don't craft resignation letters."

"I'll make it snarky," she whines, making her cuter than usual.

"Snark is good. I have some time tomorrow. How about I help you with errands or whatever you need? The mall, grocery shopping, anything."

"Oh, Grady, you want to paint the town red with errands?" she teases as I turn onto her road. "Do you get a lot of dates like this?"

"Um, date?" I glance at her coy expression, surprised by the word. *She's just teasing, Grady.* "Not a date. Just friends, spending a Sunday together."

"Something tells me you wouldn't normally do errands on a Sunday."

"No, I'd usually fish on my dock with my dogs, and I'll still do that... after errands," I say, pulling up to her house.

She considers my offer, nibbling her bottom lip again. "Grady, want to know what makes me sadder than finding out about the house?"

"What?"

The porch light gleams in her eyes as she turns to me. "Becoming another chore for you."

"That's not what I meant," I quickly defend. "I wouldn't offer if I didn't want to."

"Whatever this is between us, I like it. I like *you*," she says, "but we shouldn't spend time together if I'm another item on your to-do list."

I shake my head, pissed for sounding that way and even angrier with myself that there's truth in it. I *have* turned her into another chore, though she means more than that. Uncomfortably more. I grip the steering wheel, twisting it in my hands. "You're right. I'm sorry."

A soft smile later, she reaches for the door. She's on the top step of the porch when I stop her.

"Wait, please," I call, jumping out of the truck.

She turns on the porch, planting her smile weakly, like she no longer has the energy to keep it up. At the bottom step, I take her in unsurely. I should be driving away with my Sunday open and my conscience somewhat cleared.

Instead, I say, "I like you, too."

Her tired smile widens. "Wow, Grouchy Tripp. Did that hurt?"

"A little," I chuckle. "I *want* to spend Sunday with you doing errands. *Truth.*"

"In that case," she says slowly, "errands sound nice."

"Ten too early?"

She scoffs. "Only for vampires. I'll be ready."

"Good night, Marina."

"Good night, Tripp Grady Tripp."

CHAPTER TWENTY-TWO

Marnie

GRADY SMILES coyly from the driver's side of The Beast when he pulls up to the house the next morning, and finds me waiting on the porch for him. My stomach erupts with little somersaults over his unabashed smile—I love that he's no longer stingy with them.

"Ah, Grady. The Beast? For me?" I coo, descending the stairs.

He slaps the side of the old truck, grinning. "Thought you'd prefer it."

Grady Tripp considered my preference? A bit tickled by the gesture, I feel my cheeks flush. I circle the classic truck and climb onto the leather bench seat.

"So, where to?"

I twist in my seat to see him clearly, but hesitate to deliver the mini-speech I prepared. He's more handsome than usual, which seems impossible. He's clean-shaven and a hair above casual in his dark jeans, long-sleeved blue and gray shirt, and white sneakers. Even the air collected in the cab around him screams classy. He's wearing cologne, a gentle mix of cedar and ginger that's incredibly pleasant.

Everything about Grady is pleasant—a surprise, given his whole Grouchy Tripp reputation.

A second passes, and he says, "You look nice," beating me to the words I want to say to him.

I *did* make an effort—my mission today required it. A sage green maxi dress that I bought for my honeymoon combined with a little jean jacket and white tennis shoes for a chic, casual vibe that hopefully says *I'm doing just fine*, even if it's not 100% true.

"Thanks. You, too. We *look* like we could be on a date," I tease.

He huffs. "I don't date, but if this were one, you'd know it. Now, where to?"

"Wait, you don't date? Ever? Why not?"

"Don't want to. Quit distracting me, and tell me where to go."

"It might sound weird."

"Marina, tell me."

"Sunny's Beach Market at Carolina Beach," I blurt, determined to get it out. "I know it's a haul. I'll pay for gas—"

"Why?"

"Ashe has something that belongs to me, and I want to get it back."

"What is it?"

"Marnie's Market Manual," I explain, hoping he doesn't think I'm steering our ship to a fool's quest.

He puts the truck in reverse, backs into the Pike's driveway, and turns left on the road.

"It's an old-school Trapper Keeper notebook I scored at a thrift store," I continue, "repurposed for all my best ideas. There are sketches and how-tos on every display I've created, plus sales ratings to show their efficacies, displays to try, design layouts for department floor plans, and how sales increased by putting things in one place over another, seasonal displays, promotions, marketing, everything I've pitched over the years, whether they agreed to it or not. It's all my future ideas, too, like starting a customer VIP program, pickup and delivery services, and lists of local vendors I've discovered. It's ten years' worth of brainstorms and light bulbs to make Sunny's the best it could be, over three hundred pages."

"Ashe took it?"

"I left it in my desk drawer at Sunny's. I asked Cora for it weeks ago. She sent a box with my stuff, but no notebook. I called all of Sunny's managers. No one's seen it. I even had Wren snoop in my old office for it—no luck. The only explanation is that Ashe took it to help him with the new store. He's used my ideas before to impress his parents, a few times in college for business projects."

"Of course he has," Grady huffs, rolling his eyes.

"I never minded helping him. It's just... I'll survive without the notebook, but why should I have to? They're *my* ideas. *My* research. *My* creativity. Asking Ashe in person is the best way to get it back. I checked. He's at work today, so I'm sure he has it. He'll do the right thing."

Grady doesn't look convinced, but he turns left onto the main highway, heading toward the beach. "Have you seen him since the breakup?"

I huff. "I haven't seen Ashe since the hospital."

His brow pinches. "Wait, how did you break up, then?"

A heavy sigh plummets from me. "Cora."

"Fucking figures," he fumes. "You think a guy like that will do the right thing?"

"There's always hope. I need to try, anyway. It's been over a month. I'm about to start a new endeavor. He's not the guy I thought he was, but I love him. Or I did. Seeing him will be like testing a battery to see if there's any charge left. Does that sound crazy?"

"Makes perfect sense. I felt that way seeing Emma after we filed for divorce."

"Any charge left?"

"No. Not for a long time."

My brow crinkles at the thought. I want a charge left between Ashe and me, not because I enjoy heartbreak, but because it might hurt worse knowing that our love could change to nothing so quickly. "It's sad how fast that can happen."

"Not all love stories are forever. It's good we're doing this together," he says, like he understands something I don't.

I don't argue. He probably does.

Sunny's Carolina Beach is my dream come to life. All the right words pop into my head when we walk in. Stunning. Pristine. Inviting. Friendly. Elegant. Supercool. Perfect.

He used my sunburst design for the store's layout (duh,

Sunny's). Aisles extend outward from the curved ball of the front end, allowing customers to see almost the entire store at first glance, with Sunny's signature gazebo pulling them to the middle. Beach murals adorn the free wall space, with a wide section at the front honoring the town itself and Sunny's owners and managers, with portraits next to their titles. My conceptualized displays adorn every end cap. The *What's for Dinner?* display boasts a rectangular assortment of gourmet taco kits, cheeses, and a rainbow of tomatoes, avocados, onions, and peppers. He even used my Oasis idea—palm trees and blankets to create a wall of books, sunglasses, sunblock, beach toys, and beach chairs. Everything needed for a day at the beach.

It's a heaven of a grocery store.

Grady breathes out beside me. "This is all you. Isn't it?"

"If you could walk through my brain, this is what you'd see," I gawk. "It's beautiful."

"There's the asshole now."

He motions to the store's left, where Ashe stands, arms folded around his checklist clipboard, talking with another employee in the dairy section. He looks as handsome as ever in his dark blue chinos, crisp white button-down, and fitted blue vest.

My nerves knot into tight balls, and my determination wavers into regret. This is the store I imagined, yet I don't belong here.

"How do you want to play this?" he asks.

"I'll talk to him alone," I say.

"Sure you don't want your cane? You might need a blunt object."

I scoff, glad I left it in the truck. "I'll be fine."

"Of course, you'll be fine," he smiles. "You're Marina fucking Strange." Then, he tucks his hands into the pockets of his jeans and wanders into the store.

I beeline toward Ashe. He doesn't see me coming, but the grocery manager standing with him does. "Can I help you find something, ma'am?"

Ashe turns, and his smile unravels like a pulled shoelace, falling apart and dangling limply at the sides.

"Hi, Ashe," I say, determined to keep my smile though he lost his.

Nothing disarms a person quicker than a smile and a kind word. "How are you?"

He looks annoyed. "Give me a minute, will you?"

"Sure thing, boss," the other manager says before heading to the front end.

I offer a wider smile when his eyes finally land on me again. "The store looks beautiful, Ashe. I'm blown away. You've worked so hard on it."

"Well, I had more time on my hands, so…" He shuffles his feet. "What're you doing here?"

"I wanted to see the store," I say, nerves rising as his eyes dart around me. "You talked Cora into the motion-censored freezers, I see. That's impressive."

This buys me a timid smirk. "And automatic lights in the bathrooms, loading docks, and an in-store recycling center. She gave me whatever I wanted after… well, after."

"Well, you deserve all the bells and whistles," I tell him, and I mean it. "And blue *really* is your color."

It was another thing we planned together—having a different color scheme at the beach store than the olive green at Sunny's in Seagrove. His hands go to his vest, straightening it out. "Yeah, I love it here. It's close to my condo. I surf or paddleboard every morning before work. It's been good for me."

"I'm glad. I only want what's best for you."

He releases the tension in his brow, allowing a short smile. He shifts on his feet, still holding his clipboard to his chest like a shield. "Yeah, um, you, too."

Memories tell me I should feel things, but I don't. Our battery is dead—a fact that saddens and unburdens me. I couldn't show up at the altar how he wanted; he didn't show up for me when I needed him. Over and over. He drained the love right out of me.

"Here to beg me to take you back?" His smile curls with cold arrogance.

"No. You don't want me back, Ashe. I don't want you either. Not after… Anyway, that's not why I'm here," I mutter, trying to keep my voice low.

"Then, what do you want, Marnie?"

"I want my notebook."

He hesitates. "What notebook?"

I scoff. "*My* notebook. The one you used to make *that* display." I motion to the nearest end cap. "And every other one in this store. The one that told you what layout to use and what lights to buy. *My* notebook. It belongs to me."

His hazel eyes narrow as he looks down on me. "What notebook?"

He says it slowly, assuring me I'll never see it again. A cheesy, handwritten, and sketched scrapbook of my time at Sunny's, the culmination of every conceivable effort over a decade to make his family's store the best it could be snatched away like I was never there. Like *I* didn't matter.

And him, bitterly keeping me from it. He could've made a copy, transferred the information to the cloud, and had it forever. He could've asked me for it in the first place, and I would've handed it over. I never minded him using my ideas or even taking credit for them. But under his intimidating glare, I know his refusal isn't about ownership of the ideas or worries that he can't survive without them.

It's about keeping me from what's mine—the one thing I have left to claim. A game of keep away with me, squirreling around after it while he holds it just out of reach. It's about hurting me.

As if I haven't hurt enough.

"You are such a child," I breathe, smiling through the simmering anger. "Thanks for assuring me I'm better off without you or Sunny's."

His jaw tightens as his lips clamp together. "Get out of my store."

"Your store? Doesn't look like it."

Practically seething, he points toward the entrance as if I don't know where it is in *his* store and stares me down as my feet inch backward.

I don't breathe again until escaping the final double doors. The cool March air hits me first, followed by sunlight, as I step wearily onto the pavement and search the parking lot for The Beast's distinctive red and white panels. I feel genuinely winded by my encounter with Ashe, angry at him and myself for thinking this could've turned out any other way. Even my fingers tremble with irritation as I chalk this excursion up to yet another foolhardy move by Marnie fucking Strange, and add my Trapper Keeper to the long list of things Marnie lost in the accident.

But then, my eyes land on the truck and zoom in on Grady Tripp. He leans against the passenger door, waiting for me with a devilish smile.

The sun catches on the plastic and flickers in my eyes, forcing a gasp as I realize what he's holding. Grady Tripp has commandeered my notebook.

CHAPTER TWENTY

Grady

THE LOOK on Marina's face when she sees me holding her notebook is something I'll remember forever. Her distress vanishes into surprise and then gasping relief and appreciation—she can't fucking believe it. I bet whatever he said to her, the stunted prick, convinced her that she'd never see it again, that it'd be his to steal forever, holding a piece of her captive.

That's what men like him do. They take.

She makes her way to me, barely looking both ways before crossing and slowed only by the pinch still in her hip. Then, like she's crossing a difficult finish line, she lunges forward, latching onto my neck and crushing the thick notebook between us.

"Thank you," she whispers against my neck. "Thank you."

I force down the uncomfortable lump in my throat and breathe her in—the softness of her, the way her hair tickles my cheek, her delicate strength—and, for the first time since the accident, the unbearable weight of guilt eases gently off my shoulders.

"My fucking pleasure, Captain," I manage finally.

She chuckles, pulling away and taking her notebook with her. She doesn't look at it, though. Only me. Her sweet, adoring smile becomes my new mission.

"You really are something, Tripp Grady Tripp."

"Yeah, but what? That's the question." I turn and open the door for her. "Ready?"

She climbs in, and I quickly follow on the driver's side, lest the idiot realize what's happened and chase us down in the parking lot. While I'd love a confrontation with Ashehole, I don't want Marina suffering anymore. She's had enough for one day.

We drive silently like she's digesting what just happened, hopefully finding peace about it. Closure, if there's such a thing. She's not upset like she was when she exited the building. Instead, she beams, watches the world pass by her window, and occasionally taps her fingers on the binder as if reminding herself that it's still there.

When we reach Monkey Junction, I pull into the Staples parking lot. The Beast rolls to a squeaking stop in the closest space I can get, and I switch off the purring engine.

"Short on office supplies?" she asks.

"We're not here for me." I turn toward her. "Here's what's going to happen. We're going to go in there. You'll find a new notebook, paper, pens, markers, stickers, whatever your organizing heart wants. My treat."

Her lips part like she wants to argue.

"Marina, please." I motion to her worn and rather overfull Trapper Keeper. "This belongs to you, and I'm glad you got it back. But Sunny's is over. A new store needs a new notebook. Don't you think?"

Her pink lips curve into a resigned grin as she takes a deep breath. "Sunny's is over," she repeats, wanting it to sink in.

She roams the aisles aimlessly at first, contemplating something and putting it back on repeat.

"How'd you get the notebook?" she asks, playing with pens.

"It's a grocery store. Not Fort Knox. I found his office. It was right there on his desk. His door wasn't even locked." She nods listlessly, still not dropping anything into the basket I'm carrying.

Watching her light up when we walked into the new Sunny's, her passion for her work became abundantly clear. It's not an act she puts on. She genuinely enjoys what she does. I even saw hints of it when we toured the G&G. That shit heap didn't turn her off; it fucking inspired her.

"Marina," I say, as she contemplates the fiftieth pen she's examined since we strolled down this aisle, "If you don't start filling this basket, I'll fill it for you."

She purses her lips. "I *do* love school supplies."

"Prove it."

She drops the multicolored pens into my basket.

"Fill it, Marina. Seriously. Get everything you need to start the G&G project."

A few steps later, she adds more, seemingly more unrestrained every time something drops in. Good. After Ashe, I want her to feel better. Or at least, distracted.

"Tell me more about Wade," she says, ogling measuring tapes. She chooses a pink one and tosses it in the basket. "Why exactly is he off-limits around the rest of the family? Or is that too personal? Just say it's none of my—"

"Nah, asking questions falls under our truth policy. Right? I didn't want to discuss it with Marigold in the car. Family drama stresses her out."

"Yeah, me too."

Thinking about Uncle Wade and where to begin, I'm overrun with memories. "Dad and Wade have always had a strained relationship. Dad was always the responsible one, Wade the partier. My grandfather died, leaving the farm to Dad and half of the G&G and the trailer park to Wade. He took that as a slight."

"Well, it *is* a swamp, but it's surprisingly beautiful there." She circles the notebook aisles, picking up binders and putting them back. It's a struggle, focusing on my story with her nibbling her bottom lip over every decision and smiling as ideas come to her. I swear, I could watch this woman all day without saying a word. Her eyes cut to mine, urging me to continue.

"Um, yeah. In Granddad's defense, Wade's never been good with money or responsibility... at least not until Maureen came into his life."

"Oh, tell me about Maureen." She perks up, finally deciding on a hardcover spiral notebook with tabbed sections, interior pockets, and a pen holder. She holds it up. "Green, like the lily pads around the swamp."

"Perfect." I smile as she drops it in. "Maureen was Wade's... everything. He was at a particularly bad place in his life, drinking a lot, pissing people off, until finally, one day, he took off on his motor-cycle for a cross-country adventure. Three months later, he came back with Maureen."

"A whirlwind romance." She tugs her jean jacket off and ties its arms around her waist, making me remember my hands there last night and wanting them there again. *Damn it, Grady.* "That's sweet."

I chuckle. "He says they met at a biker bar in Texas—not sure I'd call it sweet, exactly. But they were perfect for each other. She was loud, direct, and sassy, never took his crap, and we all loved her instantly. Maureen helped Wade run the store. I wish you could've seen it then. It was the perfect convenience store. Ice-cold sodas, all the best snacks and candy a kid could want, a chest full of ice cream treats, weird random shit like packs of cards and poker chips, maga-zines and comics, and The Canteen. That's what Maureen called the bar where she'd serve fountain drinks and hot dogs. I've never had a hot dog as good since then. We'd fight over the stools and spin on them until we got dizzy. Or fell off. The G&G was never new or fancy, but it had..."

"Character," she finishes.

"Exactly."

She adds Post-It Notes and a flexible ruler to the basket. "So, what changed?"

"Wade and Maureen went out on the lake on his boat, had a lot to drink, fell asleep, and when he woke up, she was gone."

"Gone?" She stops in her tracks.

"She was found the next day. She drowned. Wade has no idea what happened, only that the authorities concluded that she must've fallen overboard during the night. An accident precipitated by alcohol."

Marina's entire frame slumps as if she knew Maureen personally. "Grady, I'm so sorry."

"It was a huge blow to the family, especially Wade."

"He must've been devastated."

"Still is. Everything fell apart after that. Dad blamed him. Wade blamed himself. They fought about it. Dad said he wouldn't bring us around him anymore, that he couldn't be trusted with us. That pretty much ruined their relationship permanently. Sounds harsh, but Dad had a point. Wade buried himself in a bottle."

"Everyone has a story that defines what comes after and changes them forever."

"Yeah, like us."

"Mom used to say *I* was her story." Her soft smile hooks my attention. She curves around the aisle's end, offering slightly more explanation when she says, "She had me young. She wasn't ready. She'd tell me *I* was her story but never that it was the one she wanted."

She laughs lightly, though I don't know why. I remember her mentioning her mom during her migraine and how she would braid her hair *on good days.*

"What happened to her?" I ask.

"I don't know." She moves into the next aisle, leaving me with this rare insight into her.

I'm not sure what bothers me more—her not knowing where her mom is or her belief that she wasn't wanted.

I want to know more, but she gives me a pointed look. "I don't know much about how families are supposed to work. But I bet Maureen wouldn't want Wade or any of you holding on to guilt and anger over losing her. What good does that do? It only keeps you apart."

I can't argue. She sounds like Aunt Elena—the only one who still talks to Wade regularly—and I feel bad for the distance between us, especially when I think of all my good memories of him.

"Tell me about Roy and Christie," she urges, dropping felt-tip markers into my basket.

I share what little I know about them. They've been friends as long as I can remember. I chuckle, explaining Roy's hot dog eating contests, how he always made us laugh, and how he often advised me badly on how to pick up girls when I was a teenager. I share that Christie used to be an electrical engineer, but gave it up when he came to live at The Marshes after his marriage ended. Being a stay-at-home dad and staying close to his friends mattered more to Christie than a big house or lucrative career. I remember Wade, Roy, and Christie often fixing cars for people in the trailer park. And that they'd always drop whatever they were doing to hang out with me and my siblings when we stopped by. It was like we were *all* family—a feeling I forgot until now.

Marina doesn't say much as I ramble on about them and my memories of the place. But she smiles at my stories with the same wanton approval I remember from the hospital when she saw Ashe crying on his mom's shoulder.

After Staples, she asks to go to the G&G for what she calls "detailing." On the quiet drive there, I consider what she said about not knowing how families work. Her mom is gone, her 'work family' dissolved, and the family she thought she'd have with Ashe destroyed. For her, family must be an intangible fantasy that exists for everyone else but slips through her fingers like rain in a cupped hand. I can't imagine how lonely that must feel or how she smiles so easily despite everything.

And I feel bad for complaining.

When we arrive at the property, Christie tumbles out of a hammock in his front yard when he sees us. Then, he beams, waving at us with the book in his hand before racing inside his trailer.

Wade and Roy watch *Seinfeld* on an old tube TV behind the store's counter, smoking and drinking as usual.

"Don't let me interrupt," Marina says cheerfully. "I'm just here to take some notes."

Wade huffs. "Whatever floats your boat."

"*Friends* comes on after this," Roy reports. "Pull up a chair and have a beer or two."

"Too much to do, I'm afraid." Marina pats her notebook. "But y'all enjoy. You won't have many more lazy days like this once we start."

She bookends her remark with a shoulder bounce and a giggle, striking sudden fear into the two men as they exchange pained looks and twist in my direction. I return their gazes with irritation and a look that says *yes, you'll have to get off your asses*. They groan, taking in my meaning without needing words.

Marina takes in our cryptic exchange. "Don't worry, fellas. It'll be fun."

Then, she gazes across the store dreamily. She wanders through the aisles with her lily pad green notebook, pink measuring tape, ruler, and a handful of markers and pens sticking out of her dress pocket. She's abandoned her jean jacket and pulled her long hair into a ponytail that sways softly when she walks.

I repeat my new mantra that she's too young, too beautiful, too goddamned nice, but bittersweet imaginings erupt anyway. Combing my fingers through her sunset hair. My lips skirting across her moonlight skin. Breathing her in like oxygen. Just the thought of her makes my body hum. Hell, being this close to her feels like an honor.

What is it about this woman that makes me feel things again—things I sure as fuck don't want to feel?

"Oh, somebody's got it bad," Roy coos, snatching my attention away from her. "I've seen that look before."

Wade huffs. "Shit, Grady. Hope this isn't more about your dick than helping her out."

"Shut up," I yell-whisper across the counter. "I don't have a look."

Wade's lips sputter as he rolls his eyes. "Yeah, you keep telling—"

"I'm here, Marnie!" Christie bursts into the store, sending the door chimes into a discordant tangent. His shoulder-length gray hair hangs around his face, but he quickly sweeps it into an awkward ponytail. "I'm here, ready to help!"

"Jesus Christ," Wade mumbles while his cohort laughs, shaking his head. "Least someone's excited about the extra work."

Marina beams. "You put down your book *for me?*"

Christie nods and pulls a mass market paperback from the pocket of his housedress. "It's a good one, too. Amalie Howard is one of our favorite authors. The Duke and the ballerina finally kissed. Wren and I are buddy reading it."

"That looks saucy," Marina says. "Wren mentioned your father-daughter book club."

"We set reading goals every year. We're on track for thirty buddy reads by Halloween. Gives me something to do on a lazy Sunday or while waiting for the fish to bite," he grins before smoothing out his housedress. "Wore this for the dust."

"Smart. Would you help me with some measurements?" Marina hands him the pink tape measure. "And tell me all about this duke and ballerina? I *love* a first kiss."

"Me, too! It'd be my pleasure," Christie returns, bowing.

They embark on a detailed store tour and enthusiastic book talk for over an hour while I research cars for Marina and field family texts. This morning, I helped Dad move hay bales, which first meant changing the battery on his tractor. I barely had time to go home, shower, and change before meeting Marina. Even now, Mom asks me to pick up supplies for tonight's dinner—a dinner I haven't agreed to attend—and I feel weighted and exhausted over their demands. I'm pulled in a thousand places, but none are truly where I want to be.

Glancing up from my phone, I find Marina and Christie laughing over a page he's sharing from his worn book. She whispers something, and he grabs onto the shelf to steady himself as he laughs. They look like old friends sharing a hilarious secret.

All this change topped off with a rough encounter with her former fiancé, yet she remains unequivocally Marina. I can't help but admire how present and upbeat she is.

She catches my eye as she gushes over their private joke. Her smile widens, making my heartbeat thud harder, and my feet almost move in her direction. That smile was for me.

I don't just enjoy her. I *long* for her attention. With her, I don't need my grouchy, reclusive shields. They drop so I can be whatever she needs me to be. Protector. Helper. Fucking lapdog, if she wants. Weirder still, that's what *I want*—to be Marina's go-to guy, for her to pull me in a thousand places as long as it brings me closer to her.

My guilt has turned into a guilty pleasure. That's disturbing territory for a self-proclaimed loner hellbent on his solitude. And foolish considering she's too young, too beautiful, and too goddamned chipper for me.

Smoke fills the air, drawing my attention to Wade and Roy. They snicker, leering at me from behind the counter like idiot schoolboys about to share my crush with the rest of the class.

"Fuck off," I mouth, only making them laugh harder. Huffing, I return to my phone.

CHAPTER TWENTY-FOUR

Marnie

GRADY'S TEXT pings just as I slug through my front door after quitting the funeral home.

> Did you do it? How'd it go?

I collapse on the red couch, eyeing his words like they might give me profound insight into him. He keeps going above and beyond for me. Does he see me as another sibling he's obligated to care for, only instead of being born into the role, he crashed into it?

This makes me feel horrible.

More befuddling—the sparks I keep imagining between us. He sets off warming firecrackers through my core whenever he looks my way. He's so delightfully intense. *Whew.* Undressing me with his eyes feels like a gross understatement. It's more like undressing my soul, rendering me naked but safe, nested to him.

What *is* he thinking? Is he thinking the same thing *I'm* thinking? Well, probably not the whole naked bird Marnie in Grady's nest thing. *Geez.*

But something like it? Does he have *those* kinds of thoughts about *me?*

I remember his reaction when Marigold thought we were about to kiss, how absurd he made it seem, and how determined he was not to label our outing a date. He *doesn't* date. *Ever.* Reason tells me that Grouchy Tripp has no interest in sparks, undressing me with his eyes, or nesting me to him. Soul Penetrating Stare is probably just Grady's resting face.

I must go shields-up whenever I'm in his atmosphere. Or anyone's, for that matter. This thing with Grady, whatever it is, will end, just like every relationship I've ever had. I prompt my phone and start typing.

> Piece of cake.   Don't you have a cow's rectum to explore?

> No, but thanks for ruining cake for me forever.

A chuckle rumbles from me.

> I'm getting you a cow cake for your birthday.

> Yours will be a pirate ship.

The phone falls to the couch. I take a breath, thinking about my birthday. I never want to celebrate it again. Next year, I'll lock the doors, pull the curtains, turn off my phone, and spend the day in bed, hiding under the covers with the cats if they want to risk being that close to me on my unluckiest day.

Last night, he insisted on seeing me to my front door. It was dark when I finished detailing my notes for the G&G.

"You didn't get to fish," I noted with regret. "I'm sorry."

"Don't be. I enjoyed today."

I cast him a disbelieving look. "Really? Errands and light theft?"

"Truly," he said. "But, are you okay? The thing with Ashe must've been difficult."

I didn't want to lie and say I'm fine. I also didn't want to admit that *the thing* with Ashe felt like having my heart scraped out by a melon baller.

"It had to be done," I said with a light shrug.

Grady's hands tucked into his pockets, and his brow crinkled. "I wasn't always like this."

"Like what?"

"Difficult. Angry. Grouchy Tripp," he said. "Marigold has it right. After Emma, I defaulted to a shadow life. I thought it best to be numb, hoard my pain, and be what everyone needed me to be. But healing doesn't happen that way. It's a slow poisoning, holding the agony in. That's what happened to me. It'll affect you somehow, too. It's better to deal with it as it comes rather than letting it fester into something worse."

My head swam with questions, starting with *something worse?* But quickly circling back to him and wanting to know more about what he went through. Wanting to know more generally. What's Grady Tripp like in love? In sadness? In heartbreak? Why does a man so kind and with so much to offer shut himself off from the world?

I couldn't respond, but trapped by his signature soul-penetrating stare, I couldn't move either.

A soft smile played on his lips as he took me in and said, "I'm here, Marina. Whatever you are. Whatever you need. Whenever you're ready to fall apart."

Then, when my silence assured him that it wouldn't be tonight or ever, he left.

Now, similar misgivings swirl into a Marnie-thought-tornado. I don't know how to be *whatever* and certainly can't fall apart. No matter how much my edges curl under the heat of my general brokenness, I cannot and will not let myself become more vulnerable than I already am.

The best way to fight vulnerability and stay out of my emotional rapids is by staying busy.

I scoop up my phone again and go to my Instagram account. *My* Instagram account, not theirs, I remind myself, first changing the password.

I change my handle from *MarnieLovesSunny's* to *Marnie-SavestheG&G* . I share a tasteful post featuring a picture of the G&G and inviting everyone to follow my updates on its transformation.

Then, I gather my supplies and get to work.

Days pass in a blur of sketches, ideas, and research. I construct a strong reinvention plan for the G&G and schedule an all-hands meeting for Wade and company on Saturday morning.

A call to Alice Harvey of Lavender Fields Forever, a vendor I recruited for Sunny's and a growing friend with many contacts, solves my transportation issue. Within hours of asking Alice if she knew of a reliable used vehicle for a good price, she and her husband, Jack, deliver his 1977 Ford Bronco, a rusty, dulled mint green convertible truck with rips in the leather seats, no working radio or AC, and a sizable dent on the rear bumper.

"She purrs like a kitten, though," Jack assures me, starting her up. "And drives like a dream, especially on the beach."

The truck doesn't have the modern conveniences of my former car, but it oozes character.

We settle on an amount surely lower than its value, but Alice says they're pleased that his truck—nicknamed Beauty—is going to a good home.

Now, Beauty belongs to me.

I happily put my busyness aside when Marigold arrives on Thursday for our game night. She's alone, driving a cute yellow VW Bug with eyelashes on its headlights and daisy stickers plastered to its sides.

"No Shadow Man tonight?" I ask after gushing about her cute car.

"Working. Farm emergency," she replies dully.

"A girls' night, then. Just how I prefer it."

Before I invite her in, Peter Pike appears around the corner, carrying his knit hat and wringing it like a wet paper towel.

"Oh, Marnie, sorry," he says, noticing my guest. "Didn't think you'd have company."

I chuckle. "I usually don't. Want to come in? We're having a game night."

He glances awkwardly at his feet and then full-on stares at Marigold. He says nothing for two awkward beats and then, "Marigold, it's nice to see you again."

Her shoulders tense, and her lips push together. "Peter Pike."

My brow quirks over their obvious history. We shared the same high school—Marigold, two years younger than me, and Peter, between us. Perhaps they were friends. But, judging by the way Marigold's arms fold, I doubt they're friends now.

Peter seems disappointed. "I need to talk to you, but I'll come back."

"No need." I wave him to the porch. I push the front door open and tell Marigold to make herself at home. She's happy to disappear, closing the door quickly behind her. "What's up, Pete?"

He looks nervous. "Um, it's Mom. We thought you were moving out, and she promised this place to her sister, Aunt Charity."

The news rattles me, but I shouldn't be surprised. Mercy Pike, merciful in name only, has wanted me out since she moved in with her son. She spends her days on his front porch or at the picture window, grumbling over anything and everything her eyes partake, like a grumpy queen with no power. "Are you sure you can handle Mercy *and* Charity?" I joke.

His large shoulders bounce in a shrug, and he scratches his messy brown hair. "They're family."

The word cuts. And the dagger twists in my gut at the idea of losing this place—the only home I've ever really known. This house is so familiar to me. I know which floorboards of the steel-blue deck creak underfoot and exactly which siding pieces rattle when the wind hits them just right. I know the window over the kitchen sink is a tad off-kilter, making it hard to open, and the cats love how the shower drips into the tub long after I'm done. The bedroom's ceiling fan wobbles at high speed, and I'm probably the only human alive who can make use of the oddly shaped, nearly-tiny second 'bedroom.' This is *my* home.

Now, I don't belong here, either.

"I love this place. I don't know where I'd go." The words spill out in a stream of consciousness, no filter, and I immediately regret them. I have absolutely no business making him feel bad. He, and his grandfather before him, have made me feel welcome and safe here for a decade, even when I shouldn't have been here on my own. How can I ask for more?

"Sorry, Pete. You've been a terrific landlord."

"I'm sorry things didn't work out with Ashe," he says, still wringing his hat. "I didn't know you were friends with Marigold."

"It's new."

"She's... I, um, we were friends in high school." His eyes lock on his work boots as he shuffles his feet at the bottom of the stairs. "She's a nice person."

"Yes, and a talented artist. Like you."

His cheeks redden. Pete is a carpenter. He makes a living from craft shows and odd jobs. He built my porch and the rocking chair that sits on it. He's also surprised me with carpentry gifts over the years—a handmade cat tower, shelves, wooden planters, and once a hanging lamp that fits perfectly over my dining table.

"You know what, I bet she'd love seeing your trains."

Pete perks up. "Really? You think so?"

He's also a model train enthusiast. His workshop is larger than their ranch house, and only half is devoted to his carpentry projects.

"Absolutely. Maybe you should ask her to see them sometime."

He smiles weakly. "If you need longer than July, I can put Aunt Charity off until the fall. No later, though. Her arthritis gets worse in the cold."

"Far be it from me to keep your family apart. I'll figure something out. Thanks, Pete."

He lumbers away like a walking surfboard. I tuck his news behind my smile; that's a problem for another day.

"I think he likes you," I tell Marigold once inside.

She huffs. "He said my lines were too crooked at my first art show."

Her venomous words come quickly, and I'm taken aback. *Marigold has a venomous side?* I suppose we all do. "Well, he makes furniture, so he deals more with straight lines, you know?"

"Yes."

"Maybe your beautiful art threw him for a curve," I laugh, and she smirks. "Or maybe you made him nervous, and he didn't know what to say."

"Why would I make him nervous?"

"Because he likes you," I say slowly.

Her eyes widen before narrowing to angry slits. "He doesn't like anything except killing trees."

"Whoa, harsh. You have *very* big feelings about Peter Pike."

Her brow knits. "Yes, big feelings," she agrees with a small voice.

"Hmm, big feelings are valid, and maybe they're big for a reason."

"What reason?"

"You must care what he thinks. Since you still feel this way after all this time, your big feelings might push you toward a second chance. I love second chances. A lot of times, a second chance leads to something better than it was before."

"Like recycled art?"

"Exactly. And my secondhand board games."

"And your cats."

"Ha, yes, my sweet collection of beautiful strays. That's a perfect example. Pete's a nice guy, and he thinks you're nice—he told me so."

"He did?"

"Yes, so keep an open mind about a second chance. Okay?"

She nods, fidgeting with the hem of her crocheted sweater. "Mom says you're Grady's second chance."

Now, my nerves rise with big feelings. "Second chance for what?"

She shrugs. "I don't know. Can we play games now?"

We set up on my small dining table under the wooden globe lamp that Pete created (and I pointed out to her). I learn quickly not to bombard her with questions, that she doesn't like sharing dips, and that she loves rules, making gameplay second nature for her. What she lacks in conversation, she makes up for in being an excellent opponent. We play every finished game I've created: *Milk & Eggs, Tickety-Boo, Zombie Grocery Store*, and *Scaredy Cats.* She giggles incessantly over *Tickety-Boo*'s funny situation cards, making it a definite win, but *Milk & Eggs* is her favorite. We play it three times.

Returning it to my game room, she motions to another game spread across a folding table. "What about that one?"

"Oh, that's *Play Together, Stay Together.* It's about family dynamics and strengthening the ol' family tree, but, I don't know, it's giving me trouble. It's not right yet."

"A work in progress. Can we play when it's finished?"

"Absolutely," I return, though I wonder if the game is a lost cause. I started it the day after Ashe proposed, modeling it after the Sullivans and employees at Sunny's, but keep hitting obstacles to finishing it. Creating the game has become a game—a bad one that's more frustrating than rewarding.

We have fun testing my games, and it's a pleasant surprise to find them playable, even enjoyable, especially under Marigold's rule-abiding scrutiny.

She's quick to point out that they need artwork—actual game boards with colors, pictures, and pieces that aren't recycled from old games. When she asks if she could help, I jump at the chance.

"You know, Marigold, I could use an artist's eye at the G&G, too," I say as we clean up our snacks and drinks. "Would you be interested in helping redesign the store and creating marketing materials?"

"Yes." She fiddles with her long, blonde hair, struggling with words. "I take care of Grady's dogs when he's working. I'm responsible for the chickens at home. I babysit for Colin and do chores for Mom. Would this be like a real job?"

A smile slides easily over my lips. "Yes, you'll be our official artist. I can't pay much, but I have several projects that you could handle."

I invite her to my first all-hands meeting, and she readily agrees.

Leaning against the porch railing, I watch her walk to her car. We both jump when Peter Pike rushes around the corner, calling, "Wait!"

He carries a large wooden desk against his hip, stained a pretty, daisy yellow that nearly matches her car, and plops it on the gravel drive with a loud clank. "Wait, Marigold," he says again, though there's no way she can go anywhere with a desk blocking her exit. "I, um, made this."

She looks entirely unimpressed.

So, he breathlessly adds on, "For you. I made this for you."

"Just now?" she asks, sounding bothered.

"No. Ages ago. After I upset you at the art show. I didn't mean to upset you. I felt bad."

Her head tilts as she considers him. "What is it?"

"An art desk. Look." He shows her a wooden crank on the side. Turning it, the surface of the desk rises. "You can use it flat or like an easel. The drawers have slots and cubbies for paints, pencils, and brushes. There are clips, see? To pin papers or inspiration pieces to the sides. I stained it yellow. That's your favorite color, right?"

Marigold eyes the gorgeous desk with enviable calm while poor Peter Pike anxiously awaits her verdict.

I am absolutely dying over this, drowning in giddy, feel-good feelings like I'm witnessing a people-version of a sugar rush. I only hope she doesn't mention the trees killed in its construction.

Her eyes cut to me, and I flash her my girliest grin and most encouraging nod.

"I will give you a second chance, Peter Pike," she decides.

His bulky frame deflates in relief. "May I bring this to your house tomorrow?"

"Not before ten."

He nods, side-hipping the desk again, and motions over his shoulder up the lane to his workshop. "Would you like to see my trains?"

She looks toward me again, and I offer a reassuring nod. "They're spectacular, Marigold. You'll like it."

Then, with a brief nod, they stroll up the driveway together, leaving a trail of romantic magic behind them.

CHAPTER TWENTY-FIVE

Grady

I POUND on Marina's door, unable to hide my irritation that it's after midnight, Marigold's still here, and neither bothers answering their phone. Meanwhile, my phone's been pinging for nearly an hour. When the texts started, I'd just finished suturing a pissed-off thoroughbred's eight-inch gash at Adkin's horse farm. The long drive back to Seagrove felt ten times longer, with my phone continuously lighting up from Mom, Dad, and Gil, all worried about Marigold. She's twenty-two; she doesn't have a curfew, and they know she's with Marina. But she's also skittish about nighttime driving and never stays out later than nine. So, perhaps their concerns are valid.

I pound again.

The door swings open, ruffling the silk fabric of her robe. Her *short*, white robe. Her long hair is soaking wet. Bare legs, bare feet, the v-neck dipping dangerously low on her chest. The hard tips of her breasts peeking under her wet hair and damp fabric. Fucking hell.

I can't form words.

"Grady, what's wrong?"

I shut my eyes. "Why are you, um..." I motion to her get-up.

"I was in the shower. What's wrong?"

"Where's Marigold?"

She edges by me, brushing against my shoulder with her damp-ness. "Oh, her car's still here. She's with Peter Pike. Oh, my gosh, I wish you could've seen it. So..."

She launches into a story about a desk and trains that I honestly can't listen to because focusing on her means, well, *focusing on her*. I try locking my attention on her face, but inevitably my eyes drift down—I can't fucking help it. She's wet, soft, and so alluring, like a castle, and I want to explore every room, floor by floor, top to bottom. My hand practically twitches to pull the robe strings that barely hold her together.

"... She probably lost track of time. Get it? Train pun."

She laughs, stirring me from the thoughts I shouldn't be having. What's my mantra again? Something about her age or, shit, I can't remember.

I clear my throat, still diverting my eyes. "She came here for a game night, and you set her up with some dude?"

"No, not some dude. Peter Pike, my landlord. They already knew each other. It was unintentional on my part, but it's so cute, Grady."

Before she launches into an excited explanation about the evening's *cuteness*, I put a shaking hand between us, stopping her. "Why isn't she answering her phone?"

"Don't know." She smirks coyly. "Maybe she's in the shower, too."

"Fuck, Marina!" Both hands go to my head like I might rip it off to rid myself of the image.

She chuckles. "Sorry, couldn't help myself. I'm sure she's fine. I've known Peter forever, and he's completely trustworthy, and it's not like Marigold will tolerate any silly nonsense." She leans against the doorjamb, eyeing me with too much amusement. "I would tell you to relax, but you're *very cute* when you're being brotherly."

"Brotherly." I take a breath, letting my eyes roll over her again. "That's not entirely what I'm feeling right now. Promise me something."

She nibbles her bottom lip, looking pleased at my obvious reac-tion. "Yes, Grady?"

"Never answer the door like this again."

She locks eyes, daring me. "I thought it might be Marigold. Maybe my next place will have the benefit of a peephole. What's the problem, anyway? You've ripped my clothes off and been inside me before, so this should be no big deal, right?"

I gape, images of that day crashing into my thoughts. I made a similar joke *that* day, a lame effort to put her at ease. It takes on a totally different tone now. Her blood on my hands, on the concrete, her pulse faint under my finger. "That's... not funny."

"Oh, Grady, I'm sorry," she gasps, my stern expression turning her amusement to shame instantaneously. She gathers her robe tighter around her and folds her arms over her chest. "I was just trying to lighten the mood."

Still, I stand there, gawking and breathless, like she's punched me in the stomach with the memory. I'm startled by how much it hurts me, how vividly I remember my fears over losing her, her life drifting away from me with every passing second, and how those fears still fucking exist even with her standing whole and healthy right in front of me. *Why am I still afraid of losing her?*

She reaches out, barely touching my arm. "You look exhausted. Come inside. I'll throw something on, and we'll spy on your sister through my back window. It's got a good view of Pete's workshop."

"No." The word erupts with a snap I don't intend. My hand runs over my shorn head, frustration rising. "She's fine. You're fine. And you're right. I'm tired."

I skip any further pleasantries and quick-step to The Beast. She calls for me, but I don't turn, desperate to escape her, though I have a hard time understanding why. I don't *want* to escape her. Maybe *that's* the problem. Hell, I sold my truck yesterday and switched to The Beast permanently just to please her—this isn't a woman I want to avoid.

But I need to.

Soon, I'm through my cabin door, greeted by the dogs.

Moonlight dances across the darkened living room, glowing against the black veneer of my baby grand piano. My fingers twitch to play, but I don't anymore. I have a useless piano, just like Marina has unplayed games.

Well, unplayed until tonight. Maybe there's hope for me, too.

The bench creaks when I sit down. The keys practically glow under the moonlight. The dogs bark and settle around the piano like they're getting comfortable for a performance—strange, considering they've never heard me play it. Blackbeard nudges my side, either begging for attention or encouraging me.

I imagine playing, and thinking of Marina's CD collection in her bedroom, I decide on Norah Jones. The slow, sultry notes alight in my thoughts alongside the words. *Come away with me in the night... Come away with me, and we'll kiss...* My fingers dance over the correct keys but don't fall.

I haven't played since my last good day with Emma.

"Why do you keep the piano then?" Marigold once asked.

"It's a part of me that I can't let go," I answered vaguely. It's the truth, but more than that, I don't want to forget.

In the shower, I wash myself clean of horses, barns, and the night's frustrations, but not Marina. Her red hair, darkened from dampness, her cold skin, the robe clinging to her wet body, I think to purge my thoughts of her, right here and now. It's devastating how much I want her. It'd be easy, letting my imagination take the reins with her fresh in my mind and finding release in the safety of this closed private space.

But I can't do that either. It feels wrong, disrespectful even. I want all of her or nothing, not even imagined pieces she doesn't know I'm taking.

Too much has been taken from her already.

I lie awake in bed, restless, staring at the ceiling, where tree branches shimmy in the moonlight beyond my window.

Marina is okay. She's done with Ashe and the Sullivan monarchy. She's nearly healed. She's got a new job that she's somehow excited about. Her transportation issue has been solved, judging by the truck *with character* parked outside her place. She's even found a new friend in Marigold. She doesn't need me.

And I don't want to need her.

I reinstate my life code and decide to limit my involvement to only what's necessary for the deal with Wade—a good decision that will spare us both. She's too young, too gorgeous, too goddamn sweet for me. She deserves more than the man who wrecked her life.

CHAPTER TWENTY-SIX

TWO DAYS LATER, my determination to stay away is shot to hell. I show up at her all-hands meeting, though I have no good reason to be here. I simply *want* to be.

She looks surprised to see me and stumbles over the words I interrupted, like a record player gone off kilter. Sympathy flashes across her face, but she recovers by directing me to a recently cleaned section of The Canteen. Donuts and a portable carton of coffee sit there, ready for the taking. The others have already armed themselves with her offering. I wave a quiet hand, not wanting to interrupt further.

"Okay, where were we?" She sounds nervous as she refers to her green notebook.

The boys occupy their usual places—Wade and Christie behind the counter, and Roy, belly-out, donut resting atop it, stretched on a stool. Marigold stands off to the right, hugging her sketchpad and shifting on her black Mary Janes. The cigarette smoke may be making her uncomfortable. She's very sensitive about her environment. Lighting, sounds, temperature, movement, and smells. It's a wonder she's inside at all.

But Marina comforts and encourages Marigold, like with the Peter Pike situation and now, with what Marigold describes as a "real job." Watching Marigold do new things after only a few interactions with this charismatic woman fills me with uncharacteristic optimism that one day, she won't need me to back her up on library book fines or drive her to places she doesn't feel comfortable going. A friendship with Marina might be good for her in surprising, strange ways.

The same is true for me.

Marina stands mid-store like she's approaching the counter to make a purchase. She wears faded denim overalls, a t-shirt, a light pink sweater, and a high ponytail. The overalls and ponytail make her look even younger than she is, a needed relief from my last memory of her. She *is* younger, I keep telling myself.

She clears her throat. "The way I see it, to turn this into a profitable business, it all comes down to three golden rules."

"Rules?" Wade belts back with irritation.

"Only three?" Christie asks over top of him.

"Just three," she reiterates. "If we team up and use these three rules to guide our decisions about the G&G, then I'm one hundred percent confident that it'll become a money-maker, a real contender in Seagrove."

Christie claps. "Oh, Marnie, I have chills."

"Rules sound stuffy," Roy complains. "We ain't in elementary school anymore."

Marina's mouth quirks into a half-smile like she expects pushback, even wants it. "Right, but I don't mean rules like raising your hand before speaking. I mean, general practices that will bring in customers."

Roy looks confused. Then, raises his hand. Idiot.

"Oh, what nice manners. Yes, Roy?"

He looks sheepish and unsure. "Um, speaking on behalf of the establishment," he says, motioning to Wade, "I'd like the record to show that we don't like rules."

"You won't like these, either. *At first,*" she says. "But I promise you will once customers start pouring in. And they're easy peasy."

"Just tell us what they are," Wade orders gruffly.

"First, we must be clean."

A silent beat passes.

"Second, we must be family-friendly."

Again, silence as they share bewildered glances.

"And finally, we must have what customers *need.*"

She lets the silence hang there as they wrap their slow brains around her rules like she's waiting for lightbulbs to flicker and come to life on unreliable circuits.

Ever the encourager, Christie is first to say to the others, "Those sound reasonable... easy, too."

"They *sound* easy," Wade protests, "but they won't be."

"What does she mean by family-friendly?" Roy asks the other two, leaning in and whispering as if Marina can't hear.

"I'm thrilled you asked," she pipes in, "because that's where we're starting today. What does it mean to be family-friendly?"

I roll my eyes, folding my arms over my chest. *They* need a lecture on what family-friendly means, but I don't. *What am I doing here?* It's a gorgeous March Saturday, crisp, cloudless, and ushering in Spring. I should be on my dock or boat, wrangling a fat trout for tonight's dinner. I don't need to be here. I need to be alone and not thinking about Marina Ann Strange.

But when she moves to the black curtain marked *Members Only* and rips it from its staples over the doorway with one determined pull, I laugh, almost disrupting her meeting again. The three men gasp in unison, and she stands victorious over her confident decision.

"Is this family-friendly?" She poses the question so sweetly that I can't imagine anyone will argue. She grabs a random title from the tiny closet of makeshift VHS and DVD shelves and reads it aloud. "*Sex & Sexability.*"

Now, she gasps and looks aghast, holding it up to the men— that's not what she expected. "A Jane Austen porno?"

She grabs another and reads the title. "*Pride & Penetration.*"

"I prefer the Busty Brontës Series," Roy says. "*Jane Bare. Trembling Heights.*"

Wade laughs at Marina's astonishment. "We have a discerning clientele."

"The curtain and sign were my idea," Christie defends weakly. "See? I tried to be family-friendly."

Marina takes a cleansing breath. "I appreciate your effort, Christie. But pornography isn't family-friendly. It doesn't belong here."

They exchange unsure glances before she explains, "Imagine a mom stopping on her way home. She's in a rush, tired, but must grab some milk and eggs, or she'll have nothing to fix the kids for breakfast in the morning. She races in, kids in tow, and grabs her items, but with her arms full, given that there are no hand carts or shopping carts anywhere..."

She moves across this section of the store, waving her hands to prove her point, as she shares her dramatic story.

"... she doesn't hold their hands, and they wander off. Where do they wander? Behind the mysterious curtain. Now, she'll use her precious dinner time with the family to explain why some movies are hidden behind a curtain and why kids aren't allowed to see them... More importantly, what have *you* lost in this probable scenario?"

They glance at each other. Roy raises his hand.

"Yes, Roy?"

"Our pride?"

"Our dignity?" Christie tacks on.

"Our patience," Wade mumbles.

"No, you've lost a customer. For life. *For life*, gentleman," she repeats.

And suddenly, I don't care about fishing because this is too entertaining. I barely control my laughter with a hand over my mouth.

"But a customer looking for vintage pornos, on the other hand," Wade tries, sounding defeated.

"Most people wouldn't expect to find that here. There's a valid market for such materials, but not here if we're trying to be a convenience store. Ask yourselves, what do you want the G&G to be?"

"A convenience store," they mumble together.

"The porn has to go," she says, hands on hips.

"She's right," Christie says.

"Fine," Wade barks. "We'll... consider removing it."

"Not *consider* it, Wade," she chirps back. "You *will* remove it."

"You aren't the boss of me, missy. Why should I do anything you say?" he challenges, his eyes dark and narrow and his mustache twitching.

"That's why you hired me, right?"

His eyes cut to me like he might end our deal right then. "Yes, but maybe I like things as they are. A little tidying up, sure. But this? I never agreed to big changes, and why should I make 'em anyway?"

She perches her hands on the counter, making eye contact daringly but maintaining her usual smile. "Because Maureen wouldn't want this for you, Wade."

My heart stops—I can't believe she said it. Neither can anyone else. She promised me she'd turn him into a teddy bear, not a damn, pissed-off, claws-out grizzly.

This is why I need to be here—to regulate them and protect her from their bullshit.

Wade glowers at her, practically bubbling with anger, while the others stare, mouths dropped and eyes wide. He stands, his chair shooting out from behind him and maintaining his glare, like Marina has thrown a shit-brick directly in his face. Her soft smile feels like fuel, feeding his rage.

I *must* intervene. This was my idea. I divulged Wade's history. And suddenly, bringing her into their lives feels like introducing a lit match to a gas spill. This is not good.

But seconds into their stare-down from hell, with Wade seething and her softly smiling, she does the unthinkable. She lays her delicate hand on his fisted one across the counter.

"Tell me something, Wade. What was her favorite color?"

"Um, green," he spits out harshly.

"Apple? Sage? Olive?"

"Shamrock. Her Irish roots and all," he says, slightly softer.

"Perfect, we'll go with green for good luck," Marina decides, nodding to Marigold, who quickly scribbles notes. Then, in the gentlest tone, with her hand still atop his on the counter, she says, "Let's make this place beautiful again. *For her.*"

She tempers her words with an expression that reads *I'm here to help you through your bullshit,* not unlike the ones Maureen would give him *all* the time. It's uncanny, the Maureen memories she stirs.

And unbelievably, grizzly Wade transforms into teddy bear Wade. His eyes go hooded, his jaw slackens, his shoulders release, and he doesn't move his hand away from hers, like she's a lifeline pulling him from a mental prison.

"Okay," he says finally, shifting away and restoring his knocked-over chair.

Christie gasps and waves a hand over his eyes like he might cry. Roy sits up, removes his tattered baseball cap, and seems to say a prayer in reverence.

My eyes fix on her satisfied gleam and knowing smirk—I can't look away. She is effervescent.

A loud honk and the rumble of tires against gravel interrupt the moment. Marina perks up. "Oh, my surprise is here!" she coos, waving for everyone to follow her.

When we file out the front door, we find her directing a pick-up truck pulling a flatbed trailer to the side of the building between it and the swamp. An odd structure is strapped to the low-lying trailer.

Marina introduces the bulky man emerging from the truck as Peter Pike. Marigold lights up when she sees him, her usual expressionless face beaming into an almost-smile. I fielded texts in the family chat all day yesterday about Marigold's late-night date and her new desk, delivered promptly at ten yesterday morning. It's nice putting a face to the guy who seems to be romancing my sister. I have to give him credit. Building a high school crush an art desk after upsetting her, keeping it for years on the chance she might reenter his life, and then presenting it, hulk-style, to her when she happens to visit your tenant and following up that genius move by dazzling her with trains—I don't blame her for being enamored with him.

Based on the Tripp family texts, we all are. Marigold hasn't had many friendships, none that have stuck, anyway. Dating prospects have been an even farther reach—she's never shown interest. Now, even I see the sparks between them. It makes me smile.

Marina bypasses questions about the structure by organizing us to move it into place—an effort she attempts to join, taking one side, and I quickly refute, reminding her that she's still healing. Though big, it's not very heavy. We move it exactly where Marina wants it—butted against a sprawling live oak between the store and the swamp.

It's a half-circle structure with pallets for floors and old doors for walls, some with windows, one with stained glass, and all different paint colors. A glass and wood hodgepodge that somehow works elegantly together. A metal roof finishes the piece, creating an eclectic covered porch.

"What the hell is this?" Wade barks. "Grandma's garden shed?"

"No, your smoking porch," she returns. "Going family-friendly means no more smoking in the store. So, with Pete's help, we devised a pleasant alternative."

She doesn't wait for their reactions but turns to Marigold. "Your first project is to create an employees-only sign, weatherproof and rustic to hang on this. Christie, you're responsible for chairs, environmentally-friendly ashtrays, and twinkle lights."

He claps and bounces in his hot pink clogs. "On it, Marnie!"

Then, she breathes in deeply, eyeing the structure with awe. "It's perfect, Pete."

Wade examines the structure sheepishly. Roy scratches his head. Marigold and Pete talk softly to the side.

I move beside her, nudging her shoulder and admiring her and her efforts at once.

"How in the world did you come up with this?" I ask.

"Oh, with the help of my elaborate Pinterest board and my carpenter neighbor with a shed full of scraps, and a serious interest in seeing Marigold again. It didn't take us long once we figured out the plan. Isn't it cool and weird?"

"You're cool and weird." Her eyes cut to me, making my head swim. "I'm impressed."

"Don't sound so surprised." She laughs.

"Blown away is more accurate," I admit, an uncontrollable rumble stirring in my chest. "This. The way you handled Wade. How you've helped Marigold. You're incredible. Truly."

Her pale cheeks pinken as she shrugs. "Thanks. What can I say?

I'm a strategist. Can't expect them to give me their all without giving them something first."

"Smart."

"I'm surprised you're here today," she says, shuffling on her white sneakers.

"Couldn't miss this. It's okay, right?"

"Of course. Always. Just... could we talk? If you have time?"

Her arms fold over her green notebook, her brow pinching as she awaits my answer.

As if I could say no.

"Wren! Honey, what happened?" Christie's distress pulls everyone's attention to the black-haired teenager behind us. Her arms are folded over her untucked white button-down, and black streams of mascara streak her tear-stained cheeks.

Christie races over to his upset daughter, and she says weakly, "I got fired."

"Oh, honey, you hated that job anyway. Bad energy," Christie consoles.

"She didn't even give me a good reason," Wren sobs, "just that I no longer met expectations."

Christie gasps with offense.

Roy and Wade meander over, serious looks under their ragged facial hair, and Wade says, with a fatherly tone I've long forgotten, "Want us to rough someone up?"

"We've got chainsaws, hungry gators, and alibis," Roy adds, making her laugh.

"No felonies necessary," she mutters tearfully.

Marina wilts with a sigh, mumbling, "Cora," under her breath. She straightens and says, "It's my fault. I hired you at Sunny's. I should've taken you with me when I left. That place is too small for us. We need more character." She waves her arm around before slipping it onto Wren's shoulders. "Come work for the G&G."

She glances at the others, unsurely. Wade looks ready to protest, but Wren's tears soften him like Marina's words earlier.

Marina continues, "We need someone already trained in customer service and register operations. Part-time. Oh, and once we get this place cleaned up, it'll need a spiritual cleansing, too. Can you help?"

Her teary eyes widen. "I'll stock up on sage. We'll need a lot of sage. And green tealight candles, for abundance."

"Perfect."

Once again, I stand in awe of her. That is, until Uncle Wade gives me a pointed look, reminding me of our deal. *How am I going to pay for all this?*

I decide to worry about that later. Christie engages Wren in collecting furnishings for the smoker's porch while Roy and Wade test its stability. Marigold and Peter discuss the best options for her first project.

And Marina takes my arm and guides me to the pier.

CHAPTER TWENTY-SEVEN

Marnie

THE SWAMP IS SURPRISINGLY LOVELY. The morning light hits the still water, reflecting the perfect blue sky. Dragonflies skitter over the surface like *Hungry Hungry Hippos*, snatching up bugs. Cattails and overgrown grasses line the banks, lazily waving hello to the Spanish moss high in the trees overhead. A white heron regally prances along the opposite bank while algae-covered turtles sun on a broken log perched in the shallow water.

I take another breath, deciding this could be *my* spot. The boys have their little place to get away. Why shouldn't I?

Who knew a swamp could be so beautiful?

"I'm sorry about the other night," I say. "At my door... I'm sorry for being insensitive. With my appearance and especially my thoughtless jokes. I selfishly forgot how *that* day was traumatic for you, too."

He shuts his eyes tightly like he's trying to block the image. "What did we say about apologies?"

Warmth spreads from head to toe at the sound of his low, raspy voice—*this* after I promised myself no more naughty thoughts about Grady Tripp.

No frowns. No fears. No tears. No imaginary sexcapades with Grady Tripp.

Tacking on that last rule felt necessary after the other night. I hide a breathy shudder, remembering his intense gaze, that sexy voice telling me never to open the door like that again, and his obvious frustration, seeing me so bare. The what-ifs kept me awake for hours. What if he'd come in? What if he'd lightened up and extended our banter to include *why* I shouldn't open the door that way? What if he'd just kissed me out of my robe like I suspected he wanted to? *He did want to, right?*

It's nice to still have that effect on someone, nice that I haven't been rendered completely sexless and unattractive over this. Nicer still that it's him, slowly restoring my scarred ego, piece by broken piece, with every intense stare.

Still, I *need* the rule. Fantasizing about Grady could easily lead to falling for him, and that's a risk my heart can't afford to take. Moving on to someone else is frightening enough without preexisting obstacles to claw over. His guilt, for one thing. My situation, for another.

This *one thing* will make loving me a challenge, as if it's not hard enough to find someone to love me in the first place. Every chance after, for me, comes with a caveat, a disclosure, and an inevitable question. *Am I enough?*

Easier and less painful than dealing with the inevitable rejection, never asking again. I'm okay being single. Alone has been my vibe for so long that it seems natural. Joining Ashe's family always felt impossible, even when the walk down the aisle was all that stood between me and having a family. Maybe that's my story—Marnie Strange, friend to all, family to none.

Eeesh.

Grady stares me down, waiting.

"Yes, I know what we said. But that was then. This is now. And I need to say I'm sorry."

His veiny, tattooed arms unfurl from his chest and hang limply at his sides. God, when did arms get so sexy?

"I *never* answer my door that way," I go on. "I thought it'd be Marigold, but it was *you*, and something about you and what we went through together makes me, I don't know, feel like we're *beyond* that now. Beyond pleasantries and decorum and normal stuff."

I scoff and wince, knowing I'm not explaining this well. "I'm too comfortable with you, I guess. But more than how I answered, I regret joking about *that* day. In some ways, what you went through was worse. You had to think and act and wait…"

My voice trails off like I've expended my oxygen with the memory. I wonder what that was like for him—the waiting. "…and I'm sorry for making light of what must've been terrifying for you."

"We're beyond it, you're right," he says. "It's like we started a book together but skipped to the tenth chapter."

"More like twentieth," I smirk.

"It *was* terrifying." He glances from me to the stagnant water surrounding us, the herons and ibises pecking along the shores, the cattails swaying in the light breeze. "It's almost worse now because I *know* you. It kills me to think that you could've been lost."

"But I'm not lost. I'm here."

"I'm forever grateful for that. And it means you get a free pass. As many as you want. You have nothing to apologize for. And honestly, I love that we're beyond fucking pleasantries and basics. I hate that shit."

"Me, too." A laugh rolls out, bringing my hand to his strong arm like a magnet. "So, we're good?"

"Always." He drapes his hand over mine and holds it between us, oblivious to how this might play into my fantasy files later. *Marnie, stop.* "Still, I worry about you. What happened hits me every day like a freight train. I don't think it's hit you yet. Not fully."

My brow pinches, but I laugh him off, pulling my hand free from his. "That's because I stay off the tracks, Grady."

"Yeah, that's what I used to do, too. But you can't avoid it forever. It's not healthy."

A scoff takes the place of my usual smile. "Agree to disagree? I'm not avoiding anything. I'm moving on. Kicking ass and taking names." I motion to the new smoking porch, where the guys still arrange their spots while Wren dutifully assists. "What should I be doing, huh? Should I be at home? Throwing darts at a corkboard with Ashe's picture on it? Or crocheting little knit hats for babies I'll never have?"

I cover my mouth with my hand, shocked and immediately regretful that such a thing came out. What is it about this man that crumbles my carefully constructed barriers? My mouth is set to unfiltered gushing whenever he's around.

With a gentle touch, he shifts my hand away from my mouth, easing me closer. "It's okay. There's nothing you can't say to me. Remember what I said to you? I want it branded on your brain."

My thoughts swirl with his words, the ones I know he means. *I'm here, Marina. Whatever you are. Whatever you need. Whenever you're ready to fall apart.*

"A sweet sentiment," I allow, diplomatically. "For sure. But honestly, Grady, minus that one exception you witnessed at the hospital, I don't *do* falling apart. Or neediness, generally. It's just not who I am. I've been alone for over a decade, and, if anyone's counting, years before that, so I'm sorry, but falling apart isn't—"

He steps closer, cutting me off. "You're not alone anymore."

I suck in a gasp along with my leftover words, my entire body alighting with shock over his abruptness and, at the same time, his almost mystical gentleness. His closeness isn't intimidating but tender, reminding me of *that* day and the comfort I took in a stranger holding my hand.

I nod, unable to deny him anything, not with his soul-penetrating stare.

"Good." He says in that gravelly voice of his. If that weren't enough to make my heartbeat thump at exorbitant speeds, he reaches up, fingers grazing my forehead as he tucks a wayward lock of hair behind my ear. My toes curl in my shoes, and my entire body lights up at his touch.

"Anytime for anything still stands, Marina. Always."

The loud clang of a wind chime draws our attention to the bank, where Christie stands awkwardly on a lawn chair to hang the decoration on a tree branch near the smoking shed.

I stumble backward. "Um, wow. An emotional roller coaster ride on the Grady Tripp Express is better than coffee."

He chuckles, stuffing his hands in the pockets of his jeans. "Happy to be of service... and I want to help, so what can I do?"

It surprises us both how quickly my finger wags between us. "Oh, no, Grady. It's your day off. I want you on your dock with your dogs, fishing. Besides, they're like putty in my hands now. I need to see how long I can drive the momentum, and I need you to relax, huh?"

He shuffles on his feet, seeming almost disappointed that I'm not putting him to work. A beat passes as we both take in a hawk diving for something in the brush—a mouse that wriggles free from his beak midair, lucky little guy. The hawk fails to find him again and retreats to his tree branch perch for other opportunities.

"How do you do it?" Before I ask the inevitable follow-up, he goes on, "How do you keep smiling through all the bullshit?"

"I have this little thing I say to myself that helps me through tough times. I've recited it since I was fifteen, and it's the only thing that has stayed with me through it all. Don't you have a mantra or something that guides you?"

He blanches but recovers with, "Don't get involved."

I laugh. "That sounds like you. You aren't practicing it, though."

"Yes, I am, just not with you. Rules don't apply to you. You're my *one* exception."

I swallow the lump lodged in my throat.

"What's yours?" he asks.

"No frowns. No fears. No tears." I decide not to tack on the recent addition of *No Grady sexcapades* for obvious reasons.

He nods lightly, seeming to absorb it. "Those are natural human necessities, Marina. You can't fight them."

"Oh, I can. I do, mostly," I say, heavy with assurance.

"Well, that's dysfunctional, not that it surprises me. You hide behind that charming smile of yours—"

"You think my smile's charming?" I ask, cooing and smiling wider.

He chuckles. "I also called you dysfunctional."

"Well, I try to focus on the positives, Grady," I smirk.

"Seriously, Marina. Frowns, fears, and tears are okay. Necessary, even."

"Not for me." I huff. It's rare for me to feel annoyed, but the niggling sensation grows the longer he dissects me with his ice-cutting eyes. It's like he wants me to fall apart. Would that bring him some strange satisfaction? What good would falling apart do, anyway?

"When you're ready," he says, many heartbeats later. "I promise. I *will* catch you."

"Oh, Grady Tripp, one accident doesn't mean a lifelong commitment."

"I *want* to be here," he shrugs. He steps closer again. "So, forget no frowns, fears, or tears. The next time you're pushing yourself through a mess, just think... Whatever I am, Grady's got me."

I break free of his intense stare, fixating on the water where the green algae and lily pads mix with blue sky reflections. Tears well in my ducts again, like they, too, are begging to satisfy Grady Tripp. *Not today, tears. Not today.*

"Hmm," I chuckle, "mine was catchier. Besides, if that's true, stop asking to *help* out and ask me to *hang* out instead. Marigold had fun with me. You might, too."

The idea transforms him into Grouchy Tripp in a flash. His grimace snuffs out all our earlier sparks like a bucket of ice-cold water. *Ouch.*

"Um, I don't know if—"

"Nevermind. Dumb idea," I say, waving my hand between us. "Now, you've got fish to catch, and I have worker bees to wrangle—"

"No, wait. The other night, you said something about your next place having a peephole. What did you mean? Your *next* place?"

My head tilts in a silent sigh. Since my conversation with Peter Pike about my future tenancy, I've busily pushed that problem out of my mind. I can't think about moving now. I can't.

Smiling, always smiling, I bring a hand to Grady's shoulders, squeezing gently. "There are those impressive shoulders again, trying to carry everything. Relax, Grady."

He shadows me as I leave the pier, stepping over worn boards and dodging mud patches along the swamp bank. Near the store's side, Christie and Roy argue about hanging a pin-up calendar of scantily clad women inside the smoker's porch—a nice diversion from Grady's rejection. I'm officially bothered—he wants to be there for me, but draws the line at hanging out? That's fine—I won't make the mistake of asking again.

Grady veers toward the parking lot without a goodbye, and it's a relief watching him go.

CHAPTER TWENTY-EIGHT

Grady

A MONTH PASSES IN A BLINK. Indecisive March, caught between winter cold and hints of spring, finally gives way to April, with hot days and rain storms. My bad mood settles around me like the growing humidity. Even fishing with the dogs fails to satisfy me.

I wish I'd said yes to hanging out with Marina. I wanted to, but she caught me off guard. *Everything* about her catches me off guard. I caused the impact that started us, but she's crashed into me ever since. Barreling through my walls. Softening my rough edges. Bringing me out of the shadows.

Still, I fumbled the chance, too stuck in my mantra and my fears over spending time with her. *Alone.* The uneasy truth is that I *ache* for her. Feeling this way not only takes me off guard but also unnerves me. Making her think I don't want to hang out was probably for the best—she's fine, and, given her slight tone after it happened, she won't ask again. Perhaps it's my punishment for what happened, an insatiable yearning for a woman I'll never deserve—that's okay, however much it worsens my mood.

Nothing affects her, though. She's been in excellent spirits, as always. The G&G's transformation has been astounding. She posts photos and reels, archiving the before and afters and highlighting unique finds around the store, like the antique Budweiser sign she's since fixed up and displayed. Roy and Christie looked like proud parents, standing in front of it with Buds in their hands. She's also shared the store's history whenever Wade divulges it. Stories about him and Maureen, my grandparents, and even my great-grandparents, the original owners, who traded ten cows for the "worthless swamp" and started the G&G as a produce stand for local farmers—a vibe Marina has vowed to recreate. Marina is rewriting public opinion of the place, humanizing it through stories. I created an Instagram account to follow her daily updates and keep tabs on her without physically lurking, hoping she doesn't figure out *PianoMan* is me. How could she? My avatar is my piano, which she's never seen, and I have zero posts or followers. Her followers keep growing, up by a few hundred since I started paying attention.

She doesn't post the negatives, like finding a den of 'water bugs' under the ice cream freezer or the horrifically dirty bathroom—Marigold tells me about what she calls the unpostables. Marina took care of a dead rat found outside the dumpster and a questionable can of Spam, cracked at the bottom and oozing a bluish mold. The horrors have become a cautionary amusement between them, not to be shared with *other* people.

Good thing I'm not *other* people, according to Marigold.

I always see Marina when I'm there to do tasks for Wade, even though I go at odd hours (the only time I have). I don't seek her out, but she's there, working on projects that have become increasingly more ambitious as she's healed. The last time, I found her on top of a ladder, painting an awkward corner in the store. I spent the rest of the day holding it steady and spotting her, worried she'd fall or need something. Her soft smile assured me she appreciated it.

I don't ask to help—I know what she'll say. Instead, I just appear and make myself useful. This works better for us, putting me in her vicinity without much engagement and giving me an excuse to be near her. I *want* to be near her. I *want* to talk. But truthfully, I'm scared.

I once told a well-known MMA fighter with his own gyms that he was a lazy fucker and an asshole for not taking better care of his dogs —a confrontation that ended with police involvement and him relinquishing his pets. I almost got my ass kicked, but still, I wasn't scared.

Marina scares me. I'd give her anything, everything, even the real me—a frightening prospect since history proves I can't hold a relationship together. Or even deserve to be in one.

Our encounters are always the same.

She smiles widely, and I offer something more muted.

We ask each other if we're okay, and both say we are (though I'm not).

Then, the *hesitation*.

Finally, we return to our prospective work zones, usually after she says something like, "Well, those shelves aren't going to paint themselves," or "Back to the old coffee grinder."

I spend the rest of the day ruminating on our hesitation—that moment between us when more begs to be said, but neither of us gives in. I get back to work thinking, what should I've said? A million answers flood me at once, dredging up her strange words to me that day. *You look like a man with a million thoughts and no one to tell them to.* Now, she's the one I want to tell them to, only I don't.

She doesn't need me and deserves better anyway. Something more. Someone her age, for one thing. Someone to match her brightness and charm, who won't bring her down. I'm not good for her. So, maybe that's why I keep my mouth shut and my thoughts to myself.

But I miss her. Even when she's right in front of me, gleaming with hope and beauty, I miss her.

"What's gotten into your craw lately?" Elena asks as she helps me restock my supplies for farm visits. It's a Thursday, barely seven, and I'm already late for the four farms on my itinerary. "Carmela said you missed Zoe's horse show last weekend. Again."

"So did you."

"I told Carmela that my grandniece and grandnephew can have me for one event a month—that's it—unless she wants to give up our Friday lunches or game nights or something else to free up the schedule. Too many expectations, right? You know that better than anyone, especially now that you're helping Wade, too."

Her raised eyebrow looks challenging, prodding me for more

information about my arrangement. "That's where I was Saturday, not that it's your business."

She chuckles. "I love it when you play cagey with me. But you'd better come up with a good explanation for yourself. Mack knows you've been spending time over there."

"Shit, I asked Mom to keep it quiet."

"It wasn't her. Mack saw some of Marigold's sketches. She's been so excited to work on the new signs and, dang, a billboard! Marnie's giving her such an incredible opportunity."

My eyes cut to hers at the mention of Marina's name, and she grins like that's the reaction she wanted. "Hopefully, Dad will see that, too. I'll talk to him. I should've done it sooner."

"How are things with Marnie, huh?"

"I don't have *things* with Marina."

"Ah, Grady, don't be coy."

"She's fine. I'm fine. Everyone's fine and moving on. You should, too."

"Hm, not everyone is fine." She holds up her phone. "She's getting major flack on her IG account. Have you seen it?"

She's baiting me. "No."

"It started with random comments about the G&G being grubby and gross—very original—and moved into horror stories about the store's lack of cleanliness and creepy employees. Lately, it's about Marnie, too. How she's betrayed Sunny's, yada, yada. It's only the unidentifiable profiles hating on her. If I had to guess, I'd say Cora and her rich friends are targeting her."

"Marina can handle it," I say with stern confidence.

"No doubt. I noticed many unidentifiable profiles following Marnie's account."

My eyes cut to hers again.

She grins. "Like PianoMan."

"Don't you have better things to do than trolling social media and goading me?"

She laughs. "Not really. Wade tells me business has picked up regardless, even without the renovation being complete."

"That's the idea."

"Wade seems happier, too. Never thought I'd live to see the day," she continues, handing me wrapped gauze and extra gloves. "Don't you think this could've happened for a reason, Grady? The universe's way of reuniting the family and bringing you and her together?"

"No, it was a damn accident, not divine intervention. What she lost... It shouldn't have happened."

"Everyone seems better for it, though. Everyone's doing fine, except you."

"Elena, I'm already running behind, and the day hasn't really started yet. Can we just cut to whatever you want to say so I can get out of here?"

"You care about her, but Marigold and Wade say you're quiet and distant around her. Why?"

Because she scares me.

Because she deserves more.

Because if I hold her again, I won't let her go.

Because my guilt is a burden I should carry alone.

"She's too young, too beautiful, and too goddamned cheery for me," I say with my sternest, surliest voice.

"No, she isn't. She's not too *anything* for you. Don't use her age as an excuse—"

"I'm not. I mean, maybe I am. Look, I'll always feel bad about that day, but she needs space. I've done enough for her now, haven't I?"

"Of course, you have. I didn't mean it that way," Elena says. "I just meant... You've connected with this woman, asked her to rely on you, and she has. I only wonder if you could rely on her, too."

I cut her a confused look. "What do you mean?"

"I think she might understand you in ways others can't. Have you told her about Emma? About what happened?"

"No." I scoff. "Why would I?"

"Oh, let's see... it could unburden you and make you feel better. Marnie might understand and help remove that gigantic chip off your shoulder. You might let go of the past. It'd be good for you to talk to someone. She's lovely, and you know you like her. *Like her*, like her. Pick your reason, Grady."

My shoulders slump, and I don't know where to begin, not that I have the time. So, I give her my stock answer. "I'll take it under advisement."

Her eyes roll under her chunky reading glasses. "Grady, go to her. Spend time with her. Give her a try. What harm would it do?"

I groan, flooded with answers.

Still, Elena gets her way—I spend my ten-hour farm rotation thinking about Marina until I'm desperate to see her, desperate to test Elena's theory.

CHAPTER TWENTY-NINE

Marnie

IT'S BEEN A STRANGE MONTH—STRANGE, even for me. Grady's become my stealthy assistant. I get on a ladder, and the next thing I know, he's at the bottom, holding it steady. I try to lift a heavy bag of trash into the dumpster, and suddenly, there he is, grabbing it and tossing it in. Once fully engrossed in painting the storefront window trims, I didn't notice him until he met me in the middle—he'd done half the work without saying a word.

He's there, but he's not *with* me—and it's killing me. Each time it happens, a little hope sparks within me that this may be our chance to build our connection, but then it fizzles out when our awkward engagement comes to nothing. My cats have stopped sleeping in the bed with me at night, for all my restlessness over Tripp Grady Tripp —he truly befuddles me.

Befuddles *and* beguiles me. He has no idea how much I *long* for him—longing that's left me stranded in a strange, unfamiliar place. I loved and enjoyed Ashe, but he never kept me up at night, pining over him, or inspired me to peek around corners to catch glimpses of him. It makes me uneasy how quickly I jump out of bed in the morning, excited to see Grady, only for our disappointing encounters to keep me up at night, wishing and wondering. Is my desire rooted in something real? Or do I want him because he makes it clear I can't have him? It's hard to tell.

I try to engage him, but it's all fluff-talk. Once, we got into a slightly interesting conversation about our favorite chips. He prefers plain, ruffled chips, better for dipping, whereas I'm more of a nacho cheese or sour cream and onion fan. Otherwise, it's crickets.

He won't make plans with me but shows up at my side. He's there but doesn't talk. The man who promised to always catch me avoids real connection with me—not that I *need* catching or should require more from him. Even so, whenever I see Grady, questions dangle between us, begging for takers like baited hooks. He wants to talk to me—that's clear. Why he doesn't is a mystery.

I asked Marigold for insight into her aloof brother, and she shrugged and said, "Shadow man."

"That's it!" I gasped. "He's my shadow."

Perhaps this is just Grady—the man with the soul-penetrating stare who prefers living in the shadows. I bet it's safer there.

I should be relieved that he's pulled back since our pier conversation. His intensity and concern overwhelm me and inspire feelings I shouldn't be having, especially for a man who doesn't want to spend real time with me. I wonder if that'll ever change or if we're cursed the same way *that* day is and always will be for me.

Besides that, he's done so much for me. Spending more time together might reveal my future housing problem, something I don't want him tackling for me. The distance between us seems to alleviate his guilt, allowing him to get on with his life—I desperately want that for him.

So, perhaps it's better to let those words hang there, unsaid. No matter how much I want to be in his arms again.

The G&G's renovation keeps me busy, and so does house hunting. There is absolutely nothing affordable in Seagrove. One possibility is an apartment complex in the next county over, a twenty-mile commute that'll cost me over double what I'm paying now. It's that or one of Wade's trailers. Though that option gets bonus points for location, it's not what I want. They remind me of my transitory life with Mom—unstable, vulnerable in bad storms, and impermanent.

But problems are opportunities in disguise with the right attitude. Something will turn up.

Work at the G&G's been going too well to get down about anything. Thanks to Marigold and Peter, we have new street-side signage—a gorgeous shamrock green *Welcome to the G&G* sign outdoors. We adorned it with lights and hints of pistachio, light orange, and pale yellow, which has become our color palette for the entire project. She's painted similar welcome messages on the clean store windows and glass door. We refinished the concrete floor with funky, hand-painted tiles branching out from our new logo at the main door with hidden shamrocks for Maureen. My before-and-after Instagram posts brought people to see it in person.

They've also shown up to see our other standout upgrades, like:

The fishing rod and net display constructed from old pallets along the corner wall.

The updated, refreshed Canteen, now serving hot dogs, coffee, and fountain drinks (a big hit with the lunch crowd).

The wall of wood crates, painted to match our color palette, puzzled into an eclectic display of canned goods and non-perishable dinner options.

The snacks, candies, and car games aisle, complete with everything kids (and parents) need for a long trip.

The local section, featuring fruits, veggies, and farm products like honey and lavender soaps.

The everything-you-need aisles—must-haves from batteries to laundry detergent to medicines to paper towels, name brand and generic options. No one's forced into five-dollar mac-n-cheese here.

The updated beverage department now sells craft beers along with name-brand ones, local wines, and every conceivable soda, fruit drink, iced tea, milk, and seltzer.

Wren's witches corner, boasting Tarot cards, crystals, teas, sachets, and incense.

A book nook, curated by Wren and Christie, featuring their favorite mass market paperbacks.

Roy's spot, offering antique fishing lures, hubcaps, and metal signs. It adds a unique, homey vibe.

Adhering to our three rules and letting our imaginations fly with the rest has been miraculous. The store is bright, cheery, clean, and family-friendly.

Now, they're working on a billboard—a huge, back and front invitation to the store that'll perch on the corner of Highway 40 and Lakeview Drive, mere yards from the parking lot at Sunny's. We're still working on the exact wordage, but I predict that adventurous families looking for a diversion will bypass Sunny's for the G&G if we play our cards right. All we need is the right incentives. What they will be, I'm still brainstorming.

Regardless, I've charted our course directly into the bloated hull of the Sullivan Cruise Liner.

I don't *really* expect to dent Sunny's success. They've been here for decades. Sunny's will always have us on size, offerings, and location. I only want to rescue the G&G and make it the best it can be. With customers streaming in, our plans are working.

The only downside to our glorious progress is that the one person I want to share it with isn't into sharing anything with me. That's not true for the rest, though.

Wade confided in me about Maureen. That man grieves her every day.

Christie told me about his vicious ex-wife, who belittled and mistreated him until he found the courage to leave. He said he couldn't have done it without Wade and Roy's support. Wade even offered him the trailer for next to nothing to give him and Wren a safe place to go.

I *knew* Wade was a secret softy.

Even Roy divulged his devastation over losing his job as a power lineman to one bad move that left him with a bum hip and a slight limp. The work he loved best was traveling to areas hard hit by storms and restoring their power. It always made him feel like a hero. Now, he feels he has nothing. He'd built his identity around his job, only for it to be taken away.

I relate to that and all of them in strange, beautiful ways. My unlikely associates are becoming my dear friends. They prove, once again, that everyone has a story, stories that should be heard.

I wonder about Grady's story.

CHAPTER THIRTY

Grady

THE DOOR CHIMES MY ARRIVAL, and all eyes turn toward me—I've interrupted something. Marina stands at the counter (now in the center next to The Canteen), holding up a rumpled manila envelope while her other hand is attached to her hip. Wade, Christie, and Roy stand in front of her as if on the receiving end of a lecture. Wade rubs the bridge of his nose. Christie shakes his head, flapping his dangling earrings. Roy looks aghast.

"I stand by it," he says, hands splayed over his protruding belly. "I don't get what the big deal is."

Marina sighs, returning her attention to them. "The big deal is that it's completely and utterly inappropriate."

"What's going on?" I ask, moving in beside her.

"Yeah, let's get Grady's opinion," Roy argues while the other two shake their heads like it's the worst idea ever. "He'll back me up."

Marina smiles weakly, handing me the large envelope. "Roy got me a present."

The puffy envelope is soft. There's a phone number scribbled on it under the name *Bobby*. I lift the flap and pull out the cheap, sateen fabric. Ogling the light green, frilly *thing*, it takes me a minute to realize what it is. The enormous cups give it away.

"What the fucking hell, Roy?" I bark, tossing the lacy, emerald green baby doll nightie at him.

He catches it, holding his hands up submissively. "You, too? Dang it. I thought it was a nice gesture."

"A nice gesture?" I demand, furious. "She's young enough to be your daughter, perv!"

He shrugs. "I didn't mean anything by it. It's her color. Soft and pretty, like her. I thought she'd like it."

"It's sexual harassment, dumbass!"

Marina's hand curls around my bicep, holding me in place. "Relax, Grady. He meant well. He's just being a numpty."

Everyone goes silent, staring at her.

"What the fuck is a numpty?" Wade asks.

"Sorry, it's a British version of a bonehead," she says, shrugging. "Too much PBS."

Christie, Roy, and Wade nod in unison at this new fact, as if she regularly blows their minds this way.

I groan. "How does he *mean well*, gifting you lingerie?" I fume, truly ready to drag his ass behind the store and beat him senseless like I'm a damn teenager, blood pumping with hormones and idiocy. I don't care how macho-dumbass I'm being. Roy thinking about her, Roy imagining her in something like that, Roy imagining her *at all* pisses the reason and sensibility right out of me. My hands fist at my sides.

Still holding my arm, like she knows what I want to do, Marina explains, "He got me this after a discussion we had, the four of us, about how we're all single and what Seagrove's dating scene, or lack thereof, is like."

"Such a nice talk. Affirming and supportive," Christie chimes in. "We told Marnie about the singles night they do at Rebellion and how she should give it a shot. She'd have a much better chance than us old farts."

"I explained that, first of all, none of us need a partner to feel fulfilled or happy," she says. "And that dating is off the table for me."

My eyes cut to hers, but she avoids my gaze.

"You said you'd *never* date again," Christie corrects, his bushy brows perched high on his wrinkled forehead, "which made us all sad."

"Hearing that bummed us the fuck out," Wade says more empathically. "We respect your independence. You don't *need* a man. But swearing off dating sounds like you're giving up rather than deciding you don't want it. And when have you ever given up on anything?"

"*That's* why I did it," Roy jumps in, "to encourage her to get back out there. There's no good reason a fine lady like her should go unattached for long. Got her my cousin's number, too." He taps the envelope I'm still holding. "He's her age, likes a good time, and gets out in a few days."

"Gets out of what?" I ask through gritted teeth.

"Jail. Just some unpaid parking tickets. Nothing violent. Anyway, Marnie could use a rebounder, right? He'd make a fun pizza delivery boy if you know what I mean."

The asshole dares to laugh.

"Roy, best shut up now. You're asking for a beating," Wade says with a huff.

"Why? She's an attractive woman, stuck with us all day. She needs something else in her life, someone to keep her warm at night," he says enthusiastically. "Besides, it's not like you want her, Grady. You've made that—"

"Stop fucking talking," I snap.

Marina's hand falls from my arm, and the room stills. They probably don't see the hurt etched on her face. It disappears when she replants her signature smile and focuses on Roy.

"Roy, I appreciate the kind gesture—you were thinking of me... not *about* me. But the only person you should give a gift like this to is an intimate partner. Not a friend or co-worker."

"We'll have to add it to the rules," Wade chuckles.

"We're tainted by our bachelor ways," Christie says. "It's so good you're here, Marnie."

Her muted smile returns at the compliment. "It's good for me, too. All this change we've gone through together has been tough. But the store looks beautiful, we're a wonderful team, and we learn from each other every day."

They nod in unison—leave it to Marina to turn an outright

offense into a teaching moment. Even my hands unfurl under her calm tone and easy smile.

"Something you fellas have taught me is that we all have a story," she says, "and things we need to let go of, right?"

They nod again.

"Roy's excessive porn habits perhaps, but more than that, his lack of purpose and identity after losing his former career..."

Roy nods and removes his hat reverently.

"... Christie, your ex and all the unkind and untrue words she said to you," she lists off, moving from one to the other, "and Wade, your guilt and grief."

"You have grief, too, Marnie," Christie says softly.

Her voice catches, but she maintains her smile. "Yes, I do."

For a moment, I wonder if she's told them. Their sympathetic looks echo with understanding, but I suppose it could come from any of her losses and doubt she'd reveal something so personal to these... numpties. Still, I feel like I've skipped an entire season of a show I created, and everyone's undergone cathartic changes except for me. Maybe I'm the numpty here.

Roy hands Christie the babydoll negligee. "You want that, Christie?"

"Course, Roy. Gem colors bring out my eyes," he answers. "Right, Marnie?"

"It's because *you're* a gem," she smirks, and everything suddenly feels lighter.

"May I suggest a cleansing ceremony?" Wren emerges from behind the counter like a gothic princess, timing her intervention. I hadn't seen her there, as if her black garb made her blend into the background. "To release our negative energies?"

Marina bounces on her sneakers, bringing my eyes to her tight, worn jeans and green tank top. A broken belt loop dangles as she moves, making me want to tug it and pull her into me, especially after Roy's remark about me not wanting her. What does he know?

"I love, love, love that idea!" she claps. "What if we each wrote down the things we need to let go of, and then... I don't know— something symbolic of letting go?"

"We'll make them into paper boats," she says, "and we'll set them free on the swamp."

"Perfect! Look at you, so creative!" Marina beams. "What do you think, fellas?"

They exchange sheepish looks as if worried about what the others will say if they agree to it first. It's not exactly normal operating procedure for them. They don't even appear to be drinking today.

Wade speaks first. "I, um, well, there are a few things I could write down."

"Yeah, me, too," Roy agrees.

Christie gives his friends a proud grin. "It's a beautiful idea. Let's do it."

Marina grabs a spiral notebook from a nearby shelf and tears out pages, handing one to everyone, including me. I ball up the rumpled manila envelope I'm still holding, ready to throw it away.

She grabs it instead. "I'll hang on to that, thank you very much. Hey, Roy, is Bobby cute?"

"Oh, quite the looker," he nods. "Still has all his own teeth. Not everyone loves the face and neck tatts, but his soulful brown eyes cover a multitude of sins. Know what I mean?"

"Hmm," she smiles dreamily.

I snatch the envelope away. "You will not."

Her brow cocks like she might call him just to spite me. Still, she doesn't retrieve it from the trash can I toss it in. She hands everyone a pen from the case tucked into her green notebook and then brushes by me.

"Let's meet at the pier in an hour," she tells the group. The door chimes as she exits.

I debate following her, but my feet move before my head catches up, and I'm out the door with Elena's words echoing. *Just go to her, Grady.*

She doesn't stop moving until she reaches the end of the old pier, where her shoulders straighten as she inhales the warm spring air. I edge beside her, not knowing what to say, especially since we don't apologize anymore. Fucking Roy. Should I apologize anyway? I never *said* I didn't want her.

But I can't admit I do, either.

Before I say anything, she giggles, hand to mouth, eyes watering, and shoulders scrunched together. Her cheeks redden with her laughter. I gawk at her, dumbfounded, but can't help the smile that crests my mouth.

Playing witness to the three stooges back there *is* funny.

Watching her laugh about it is, too.

Maybe she's right—I need to relax.

She waves a hand over her face, drying her watery eyes. "Those three... they tickle me every day."

"Don't tell them that. They might get the wrong idea and do it for real."

More laughter erupts, sending a nearby cardinal flapping away. "I could barely hold it together back there. I didn't want to make him feel bad. He bought it from Walmart. Said it was either that or a box of condoms, ribbed for *my pleasure.*"

She curls over in giggles like she can't stop. "Wish you could've seen the looks of horror on Wade and Christie's faces."

I buckle with laughter, imagining it.

"Did you see the cup size on that thing? I couldn't fill that with tube socks!" she howls.

"All women are voluptuous porn stars to Roy."

Her giggle is infectious—I haven't laughed this hard since before...

"And his cousin," she cackles. "Gosh, that was the cherry on top."

"Oh, so you *were* just playing with me about calling him? Thank God."

"You know how much I love seeing you get *brotherly*, Grady Tripp."

I groan, my laughter dwindling.

"Or were you jealous of jailbird Bobby?" she goads.

"Well, he *does* have all his teeth and face tatts," I play along. "I'll dig it out of the trash if you're so inclined to call him."

Her smile fades, but only slightly. "Ah, that's okay." She taps her temple. "Already memorized it."

"Fine, call him. Have a good time. Then, imagine Bobby giving Roy all the juicy details of your date. Do you want *those* images in *that* mind?"

She slumps, smirking. "Ah, you just ruined *Bobby* for me."

"Better to ruin him before his next sentence starts, right?" I smile, but it falls fast—*I was jealous.* "I, um, apologize for them, though I know we're not supposed to do that. The world has left them behind, and they've enjoyed watching it go."

"Oh, don't you worry, Grady Tripp. I'm bringing the world to them, with Wren's continued help, of course."

"I don't doubt it, darling." *There's that word again.*

Our chuckling dies into a soft silence that has me thinking, probably too much.

"It's good to laugh," she says with a breath.

"If you're not laughing…" I say, letting my voice trail off like she did at the hospital when she said the same thing. A beat later, I ask, "Never dating again, huh?"

She shrugs.

"You'll get over Ashe," I say after another hesitation.

She grunts. "I *am* over Ashe. Over him. Over Sunny's. Over it. I don't even need to put him on my list. That's not why."

"Then, why?" I turn away from the eerie swamp's full-sky reflection, preferring to see her instead. "Talk to me."

She plops onto the dock, sitting cross-legged with her paper pressed against her notebook in her lap. She tucks her pen behind her ear. I sit across from her the same way, awaiting her explanation, though I already suspect what she will say.

"Truth," I say when she gets quiet. "It's okay."

"Truth is, I don't want to make you feel worse."

"The only way you can do that is by not talking to me."

She scoffs. "That's what you've been doing to me. Why should I be the open book when you slam yours shut every time we're together?"

"I don't *slam* it." I rake a hand over my head. "You're better at being an open book, but I'm trying. Tell me why you've sworn off dating."

She sighs. "Fine. It's not so simple for me anymore. Imagine how nerve-wracking it would be to start with someone new, only to tell him I come with a disclaimer? Then, if I like him, hoping that he'll be okay with it. Then, feeling bad about it, even if he is. Every chance after is tipped against me, tainted, over this *one* thing, over unfair expectations. For families. For pregnant bellies and labor stories, and *oh, he's got your dimple*, or *oh, she's got your hair color mutation*. Ugh. Putting myself out there again would make me feel like a day-old cupcake, sitting on the clearance rack, hoping someone would pity me and take me home. Do I put sans uterus on my dating profile underneath cat lover and board game enthusiast? Do I talk about it on the first date? Wait until the third? Spring my childlessness on him after we have sex or before? How do I bring it up? Would broaching the subject be a red flag for a guy? Would not bringing it up be deceptive? What would it even sound like... *Oh, by the way, before you get any long-term ideas, not that you would—no pressure— you should know that this girl doesn't come with a uterus.* Would *you* want to have that conversation with someone you're dating? That would turn Grouchy Grady off in a second, wouldn't it?"

"No, it wouldn't. Honesty and openness should *never* be a turn-off. You tell him when *you're* ready. Not before. However you choose to say it, *when* you choose to say it, it'll be exactly right. Don't swear off dating out of fear—you have a rule against that. Remember?"

She smiles lightly. "Yes, but it's not *only* fear, Grady." She takes a breath, eyes shifting away from me in a gentle roll. "Funny thing is, I was never sure I wanted kids. When Ashe or Cora talked about it, I thought if it happened, great. If it didn't, great. I would've done it for them, but not for me. I never had much of a childhood and wasn't keen on reliving it by caring for someone else. I should've been upfront about it with Ashe from the start. Even so, my self-worth never centered around future motherhood; it's a shame that my worth to them did."

She holds a wagging finger up between us. "For the record, this isn't me falling apart. This is me having a moment."

"Understood. Have all the moments you want. I get how the Sullivans made you feel, but fuck them. A man worth your time wouldn't care."

"That's the thing, Grady. *I* care. I have to, now." She glances at the swamp, seeming to take an interest in the skittering dragonflies or the sunning turtles. "I'm used to being devalued, and that's okay. Devalued for working in a grocery store, not going to college, not having any family or even many friends. That's all okay. But this... *this* time, I *feel* devalued. That's what I hate. *I. Am. Less.* A future with me means a sacrifice for someone else. How can I ask anyone to give that up for me?"

"The chance to love you forever, to be *yours*, wouldn't be a sacrifice. It'd be a gift, an honor, the best pirate treasure. Truly." I grab her hands across our laps and hold them between us as she chuckles. "Want to know what's better than having a family?"

Her brow scrunches. "I can't think of anything."

"Creating one wherever you go. That's your gift, Marina. One of many. You are beautiful, intelligent, motivated as fuck, and so warm, like a fire on a cold night. I've never met anyone quite like you. Just existing in your periphery makes me a better person. As the surliest asshole in Seagrove, I'd never say any of that unless I meant it. I can't imagine a luckier man than the one who wins your heart."

Her lips curl while her eyes stretch wider than usual. "That's definitely the nicest thing anyone's ever said to me."

"Shit," I breathe out in a smile. "I'm losing my edge."

Her hands tighten around mine, and she whispers, "I won't tell anyone."

She pulls the pen from behind her ear and clicks it into action. She scribbles something on her page and then holds it up to me.

I, Marina Ann Strange, release my fears to the swampy void so that I might open my heart to the one who loves me as I am, not for what he imagines me to be. I let go of limiting expectations and choose limitless possibilities instead. I release those who have held me back for those who push me forward.

She takes the page down as soon as I read it, and her delicate hand curls across it once more. She holds the new addition up, smiling.

I let go of regrets over that day, and I hope Grady does, too. He saved me. Truly.

My eyes find hers as soon as her words come together, and her accepting, even loving expression assures me that she means it—and it does something to me. The man numb to feelings is overcome by them, starting with relief and ending somewhere around humble admiration.

This woman *is* my family.

I don't notice the tears welling until her hand drifts to my cheek to catch one with her thumb.

"It's okay," she says softly.

I drag her notebook to my lap and place my page atop hers. Once again, I think of *that* day, catching her in my arms, two feathers caught in the wind, making the pen move fast across the paper.

I, Grady Macmillan Tripp, release my guilt to the swamp, where it'll find Marina's fears, wrap them up, and pull them into the mud where they belong. Forever.

She nods, reading my words. "I like that."

"Me, too." I start to fold the paper in half, done with the assignment, but she grabs it from my hands.

"Not so fast. You forgot a few things," she tells me with a smile. "And Macmillan?"

"It's a family name. My father's name."

She giggles. "Aw, that's sweet. Can I call you Mac-Attack? Maca-roni? Mac-nificent?"

"Not if you expect me to answer," I grumble.

As she writes on my paper, I watch her—the way her high pony-tail falls to her shoulder as she leans over, the tiny dimple in her cheek as she smirks at what she's doing, hell, even the graceful movement of her fingers and the unique smattering of freckles on the outside of her palm hold my attention. I want to be one of her freckles, forever attached.

Before I register what I'm asking, the words come out. "Come to my place for dinner. Tonight."

She peers up at me, lips spreading further as she considers it. "Oh, to the Fortress of Solitude? How intriguing."

"I mean, if you want," I stutter, "if you don't have like plans... whatever... um, no pressure."

She smiles. "I'd love to." She holds up what she's added to my paper. "It's working already. See?"

I read her new words:

> *I, GMT, also let go of self-imposed overworking and taking responsibility for everyone else, especially at my own expense. I promise to be more careful with myself, relax and have fun, and not be afraid to spend more time with Marina.*

I realize that is what I want, as if her words grant me permission. Grinning, I initial my approval beside her addition.

But as the others join us and the makeshift ceremony ensues, misgivings take over. Everything about her feels completely beyond me—the man who swore off relationships after fate proved I didn't deserve to be in one. I don't deserve her.

And if I get her alone, how the hell will I keep my hands off her?

So, instead of relaxing, I switch into protector mode again, protecting her from me.

CHAPTER THIRTY-ONE

Marnie

FOR ALL ITS CASUAL AWKWARDNESS, the ceremony has the beautiful finality of a funeral. Wren, wearing a long black cape and jeweled everything, including sparkly flecks around her eyes, shares a few monotone words about how decay is needed for growth and letting go of past pains will do the same for us that it does in nature—she's very profound for a seventeen-year-old.

She tells us to speak or not, however our hearts guide us. Then, she releases her boat first after showing us how to fold it. It drifts into the almost stagnant water, finding a little breeze to travel on.

She lights a thick stick of sage, running the smoke clouds over herself, which she does for each of us in turn after we release our boats.

Wade goes next, saying nothing, eyes glassy with tears—he claims allergies, but we all know better. I imagine guilt over Maureen makes his list, but I hope he also includes the grudge with Mack. It'd be such a joy to bring the Tripp family back together.

Christie clears his throat and says, "I'm letting go of insecurities for having a sensitive soul and liking pretty things. My wife, Wren's mom, would say I wasn't 'man enough' for her, and that was long before I wore what I wanted. She also dressed Wren in pink hair bows and frilly dresses, so she didn't know us at all. She could never know us or love us truly, if she refused to *see* us as we are."

He pulls Wren close to his side, and she leans her head against his shoulder.

"Wren and I have been exactly ourselves since she left," he says, "and we're happier for it. So, goodbye, Jessie Dean, and all your hate talk and narrow-minded judgments. I will never again apologize for being myself."

"Neither will I," Wren says, "and that's entirely thanks to you, Dad."

"Love you, Moonbeam." He sets his boat free, his long, floral kimono flapping as he wishes it away. Wren puts her black lace arm over his shoulders before cleansing him with the sage's smoke whisper.

Roy steps into the dock's center. "I have a statement prepared." He sets down the paper plate of chicken wings he brought with him, still holding the drum he's in the middle of eating. BBQ sauce covers his lips and drips into his unkempt, patchy facial hair.

"I deeply regret my actions in buying the babydoll nightie," he says, eyeing me between glances at his paper, "and any discomfort it caused. My heart is bigger than my brain. That said, I'm letting go of certain ideas about women—Wren helped me make a comprehensive list."

He holds up the BBQ-stained page that contains dozens of listed items.

"When I fell off the pole—the electric pole, not the stripper's pole," he goes on, "and had to take disability after being a lineman for twenty-five years, I felt depressed and found comfort in things that weren't good for me. But Marnie's helped me see that I still have a life and a purpose... although that purpose is not to get her laid." He breezes through the chuckling. "I let go of feeling lost over what I've lost."

My heart pitter-patters over his profound statement and how it's what I need to hear, too.

He clears his throat and reads, "*Your absence has gone through me like thread through a needle. Everything I do is stitched with its color.*"

I gasp, taking in the imagery, and feel tears threatening to fall. "Oh, Roy."

"Those aren't my words. A guy named Merwin wrote it. But, you know, Google's a wonderful thing." He sticks the wing in his mouth, roughly folds his boat, and sets it, lopsided and stained, on the water, setting the chicken bones inside. Then, he pushes it away from the dock, where it mingles with the others.

That's how I felt after the accident—lost over what I'd lost and everything shadowed by the absence. My hand goes to my stomach, missing what will never be, and my head falls softly on Grady's shoulder, standing beside me.

His hand circles my waist, pulling me closer. Softly kissing my forehead, he whispers, "Ready?"

We say nothing as we set our boats adrift. Though it's only paper that will soon be saturated and vanish into the murk, sending them off feels freeing and necessary—like these delicate, little objects hold the heavy weights we've all carried for far too long.

The tiny paper boats bobble, causing small ripples in the water underneath them and changing the surface reflection into something more unique. It's lovely in the strangest way. One tear slips out that I quickly brush away, and Grady tugs me closer like he knows what I'm feeling.

I take in the occupants of this rickety swamp dock as we stand in silence. I'm surrounded by people who defy expectations.

Wren, for being a teenager who chooses to be herself over fitting in.

Christie, for raising Wren to be a free spirit, and showing me what a father should be.

Roy, for simply being Roy and for his big heart.

Wade, for giving me a chance at the expense of his comfort and letting me change everything.

Grady, for giving up his solitary life, his time, his everything. For me.

Now, I'm counted among them—The Queen of Lost Causes and Second Chances, spared from an expectant life for one that will be whatever I want it to be.

And Grady Tripp asked me to dinner! At his place! *Eep!* Every time I think about it, I feel butterfly wings in my stomach and tingles everywhere else—all those lovely things I thought were over for me. I'm flushed and flustered with excitement. To be there. To see how he lives. To meet his dogs. To eat his food. To be with him on his dock as the sun goes down on the lake. And maybe...

Nope, I can't think about that now.

His hand brushes against mine as we stand there, watching our little boats teeter. Mine starts to tip, drifting against Grady's. Wren's boat seems magically pulled into the tunnel of bald cypress trees and waving moss. It's so serene, the quiet.

A gator suddenly breaks the surface, snapping its impressive jaws over Roy's boat, taking it and capsizing the others.

I scream, grabbing onto Grady's shoulder. Christie and Roy jump and curse. Even Wren takes a startled step back.

"Holy fuck. Bessie's back," Wade says, completely still and mildly amused. "You frightened us, honey."

"Guess she likes chicken wings," Roy decides.

"You okay?" Grady asks.

I nod, even more flushed. "Yeah, wow, she's a big girl."

"Twelve feet as the day is long," Wade says. "Comes here to have her babies. Ain't nothing like gator watching in the spring."

My brain fires with new ideas as Bessie chomps on the paper-covered chicken wing and disappears into the algae, taking our meager boats with her. "That's it."

"What's what?" Roy asks.

"Our hook to bring in tourists," I say. "Local products, hot dogs, and gator spotting. We'll need signs and a new observation deck with a railing. I'll call Peter Pike. What adventurous family on vacation wouldn't detour a few miles for a chance to see gators? It's perfect."

"They're so misunderstood," Christie nods. "It'd be nice to give them some positive attention."

"Oh, I could give gator talks," Roy offers, "tell 'em stories about playing keep-away with the babies and that time Bessie nearly killed Wade."

He shrugs sheepishly. "We were still getting to know each other then."

"Well, let's keep the near kills on the down low," I say, "but the rest, yes. We'll win the locals with lower prices and our new, family-friendly look. But now, we'll win the tourists, too."

"We could sell gator gear," Roy chimes in, "like little stuffies and toys. Kids love that shit."

"Hell, *you* love that shit," Wade laughs.

"There's a kid in all of us, Wade," Roy says.

I flip my notebook open and start jotting down ideas.

Grady's hand circles my waist again as he whispers in my ear. "I'll leave you to it. See you at six?"

"Maybe sooner because I can't wait," I giggle in return. As he wanders away, the rest turn to me with wide eyes and gaping expressions. I'm not sure who starts cooing first, but they all join in—a teasing chorus. Out of the corner of my eye, I spot Grady hesitating at the sound before heading to The Beast anyway.

"Oh, stop," I tell them, blushing. "It's nothing. Just dinner. We're friends."

"Well then, can we come?" Roy asks.

"I'll bring a Chardonnay," Christie teases.

"I've got the love potion," Wren adds.

"Aw, how sweet, but no," I laugh. "Don't worry. I'll give you all so much homework you'll be too busy to think about me and Grady Tripp."

They groan and disperse quickly, as if worried I might divvy out tasks right then and there.

The day creeps by slowly. I make phone calls, arranging the billboard designs with Marigold, and construction of the gator observation deck with Peter Pike. The boys and I rearrange the cigarettes behind the counter between taking care of a slow trickle of customers, more than usual but still not enough to make up for all I've spent on upgrades. It's a marathon, not a race, I tell myself.

Excited for my date with Grady, I leave earlier than usual, desperate for some me-time. I spend time with the cats, telling them and all my plants about my plans for the evening. I put on music—at first heart-pounding rap to match my excitement, but already too hyped, I soon switch it to something more low-key. The calming sounds of Norah Jones fill the house as I deliberate on my outfit. With four possibilities strewn across my bed, I take a long bath, towel-dry my hair, put on lotion and light perfume, and even paint my nails a soft pink. First dates don't happen very often, at least not for me. Why not make it the celebration it is?

I finally decide on a silky light pink cami with lacy edges, a cute jean skirt, white sneakers, and my fuzzy pink sweater, in case I get chilly. Casual meets sexy. I top it off with a dangly gold chain with a peony charm and little gold hoop earrings. I wear my hair down and wavy and put on a touch more makeup than usual.

I stand at the mirror by the front door and ask the cats how I look. Hershey meows, Triscuit curls around my legs, and Sunkist narrows her eyes like she's annoyed at me for disturbing her cat nap. Even so, I take it all to mean I'm not too shabby.

I take a breath, nerves rising again. I worry this might be another ride on Grady's guilt train, with him leaving me stranded at the end.

But it's Grady. Thinking of how he held my hands at the pier, his lone tear over what I wrote, my heart plays an erratic beat to my thoughts, and the hope that he's finally *seeing me*. Not a victim of his mistake. Not an obligation. But as *his* Marina. Because I long for him to be *my* Grady.

I leave for our date, feeling giddy-hopeful and planning out my moves—an embrace at the door, for starters, with a kiss on his rough cheek. I want Grady Tripp to know that affection is allowed and encouraged. I want him to know that I'm ready for this.

For him.

For everything.

CHAPTER THIRTY-TWO

Grady

OPENING the door to Marina is exhilarating and devastating at once. Fucking hell, she's stunning. Not just her everyday beautiful, either. She's date-ready beautiful. My eyes don't know where to land, taking her in. Glimpses of the smattering of freckles on her bare shoulder, the lovely lines of her collarbone, her brighter-than-usual smile, the way her short skirt grazes her legs, and her big, hopeful eyes gauging my reaction all beckon for more attention.

"I'm early," she says when I don't speak. Then, she leans in for a warm embrace—a move that happens too quickly for me to stop.

Not that I would.

She smells faintly of roses as I breathe her in, her long, wavy hair tickling my nose. My hands drift over her back—the silk of her blouse and the softness of her bare shoulders. She's intoxicating.

"Thanks for having me over," she whispers before kissing my cheek. She lingers in the tiny space between us, meeting my eyes with her easy smile, tempting me to kiss her.

I want to. God, I *want* to kiss her.

That's when it hits me how badly I've ruined this.

After leaving her at the dock, I wandered into an elaborate, confusing labyrinth of misgivings about our date. Asking her to dinner felt as natural as the swamp around us—time alone with Marina was what I wanted. But insecurities battled my desires, convincing me that our age difference, origin story, and her deserving better mattered more and ultimately won out. So, anxious over what might happen between us, I arranged precautions to ensure the answer was *nothing*—self-sabotage at its absolute finest.

Precautions I now deeply regret. She's so excited, alluring, and goddamn hopeful. Now, I'm about to hurt her. *Again.*

The dogs rush up. Harley leads the charge, wagging her stubbed tail, with Hannibal and Blackbeard behind her. Marina coos and drops to her knees to greet them.

"Oh, my goodness!" she laughs, rubbing Hannibal's uneven ears. "Grady, they're perfect."

"Imperfect, actually," I note, glad for the distraction and amused at her willingness to engage them. They can be a lot all at once.

"But, see? That makes them perfect," she laughs as three-legged Blackbeard tries to shimmy into her lap, nearly knocking her over backwards.

"Alright, guys. She's had enough," I say, adding a stern whistle to show I mean it. They disperse enough for me to pull her up, inadvertently bringing her close for a second time. She falls against my chest to get her balance.

"Marina, I messed up." My breath catches on hers between us.

"Messed up?" Her brow pinches with curiosity, but we're interrupted when the dogs go crazy over the sound of another car in my driveway.

She glances through the glass in the door. "It's Marigold. And Gil."

"Yeah, I know. I invited them," I say, deciding to completely own my fuck-up. "I thought it'd be better this way."

Confusion cuts through her smile, followed quickly by sharp disappointment. Her entire demeanor sinks, and she shifts away from me, literally taking two steps back.

"Oh, okay." A strained smile pushes through. "Right, wouldn't want me to get the wrong idea. Silly me. I won't make the same mistake again."

She's out the door before I can argue or launch a defense. She greets Marigold with chipper enthusiasm, waving happily. "My favorite artist of all time! So glad we get to hang out. Gil, nice to see you. Looking handsome, as always."

My brother blushes at the compliment, unsurely eyeing his dark jeans and fitted Zelda t-shirt. I'd asked him to make an effort, although our definition varies. Along with wearing clothes that fit and look nice on him, he even tamed his messy brown hair and wore his dark-framed glasses, highlighting his strong cheekbones and bold blue eyes. He goes in for a hug as she approaches, nestling her to him while eyeing me over her shoulder and smirking, the asshole.

But I deserve it. This was a shit idea.

They file into the house, greeting my rambunctious dogs. Gil hands me a bottle of wine, surely pinched from my parents' collection since he doesn't go to grocery stores.

"How thoughtful, Gil," Marina coos. "Let's crack that baby open. Oh, I brought something, too." She picks up the bag she dropped at the door and holds it up. "It's a game. Tic Tac Trivia. A twist on tic-tac-toe. You can't take a square without correctly answering a question, and all the answers contain x's or o's or their phonetic sounds... If I'd known there'd be four of us, I would've brought a game we could all play at once."

Her eyes cut to mine, but only for a second. She meant for us to play it—just me and her. *Goddamnit!*

"I love Marnie's games," Marigold says, taking the bag from her hands.

"Sounds fun," Gil says, "but won't you know all the answers?"

She laughs, her hand landing comfortably on his arm and squeezing. "Shhh, you weren't supposed to think of that."

"Gil, let's play first," Marigold says. "Marnie plays the winner."

"Sounds good, Marigold," he says, "but wine first, huh, Marnie?"

"Absolutely! Thanks."

He snatches the bottle from my hands, brow cocked challengingly. Marigold takes the game to the coffee table, spills the pieces, and sets it up. Marina's smile falls as soon as they're gone. She pulls the pink sweater she carried onto her bare shoulders, refusing to look at me.

"Let me explain," I say, but she cuts me off with a wave.

"What's to explain?" she asks, fake smiles returning. "You invited me over to set me up with your brother. Two Grady responsibilities handled at once. I get it."

She brushes by me and heads toward the kitchen, her sneakers tapping against my wood floors.

I slump. *Fuck.*

When I asked her to dinner, I wanted her here *for me*. But the more I thought about it, the less it seemed like a good idea. She assuaged my guilt about the accident, yes, but I carry much more than that, and isn't it wrong, dragging her into it? She's all sunshine, and I'm nothing but storm clouds. We don't fit. *Do we?*

Even if we do, fears arose over the idea of us. The last time I dated was in college, and there's been no one since my wife. The idea of loving Marina and then losing her, or, hell, even disappointing her somehow, filled me with apprehension. I don't trust myself to be the guy she needs and deserves.

Since I couldn't handle the pressure, I turned our unofficial 'date' into a get-together instead.

Besides, I wanted to show her that not everyone expects a family. Gil's a good guy. Single. He doesn't want kids. He's her age, and they went to high school together, giving them a starting point. They liked each other then; they could now. And, yes, she might work wonders on his agoraphobia like she does everything else. Perhaps, subconsciously, I was ticking two items off my list of responsibilities —a shit thing to do.

Now, I'm paying for it. The look on her face crushes me. Doubly painful, I'm hit with unexpected jealousy over her hugging him, touching him. I thought seeing her with Gil would be okay.

Wrong. So fucking wrong.

I should kick them out with a firm *'change of plans'* and *'thanks, anyway'* and attempt to salvage the night with Marina. But Marigold hates sudden changes in her plans; it took thirty minutes to convince her to postpone Marina's G&G homework for this instead.

Besides, Marina is pissed—rightly so. And Gil has a rare opportunity to rub my nose in my dumb move, like he did when I called him for this favor.

"You obviously like this woman," he said then. "Why don't you date her?"

Unable to explain my insecurities to my little brother, who has his shit to deal with, I said, "It's dinner. Not a big deal. Would you like a chance or not?"

"Hmm, she's hot, and you're an idiot," he answered. "I'll be there."

Now, as Gil pours the wine and Marigold arranges the game, it feels too late to stop it. I tend to dinner, back and forth to the grill outside—at least they'll get a good meal out of this—while they chat over her game. It must be fun because the room fills with laughter as they play, and she cheers them on.

Waiting for the roasted vegetables to bake, I grab the wine and refill their glasses before getting one for myself. I sit with them in the living room, just as Marigold and Gil's game ends.

He wins. Marigold stifles her disappointment, moving aside for Marina to take her place. She fake-cracks her knuckles over the rustic board, challenging him with a villainous grin.

"Don't worry, Marigold. I'll avenge you," she says.

"Only because she knows all the answers," Gil protests. "I've never met a game maker before. This is really cool."

She shrugs sheepishly. "Thanks."

"You were always creative," Gil says. "I loved your sets for SOM."

"SOM?" I cut in, desperate to be included.

"*The Sound of Music*," he says. "The musical we worked on together in high school. Marnie constructed backgrounds out of recycled bottle tops."

"The hills were alive with Mountain Dew caps," she sings with a giggle.

"One of my favorite things," he hums. "Oh, that and wine corks."

"Yes, it was surprising to discover how many bottles of wine Seagrove goes through in a month," she returns.

"Probably still not enough," he jokes, clinking his glass with hers and making her laugh.

I hate this.

"I must've been away at school. I don't remember seeing that one," I say.

"Yeah, you weren't there. A good thing, probably." His grin falls as his eyes cut to hers across the board. Worry flashes across her face at whatever memory they share, and he recovers with, "I mean, we were behind the scenes."

"Yeah, and everyone's seen SOM," she tacks on weakly.

"You didn't miss anything," he says, assuring me that the opposite is true.

I know to drop it—Marina doesn't want to talk about it. And I don't want to make her more uncomfortable. Or more upset.

"Dinner's almost ready," I say before retreating to the kitchen again. From there, I see Marina mouth the words *thank you* over their game, and he gives her a reassuring smile.

Not only do they have history, they now have a thing between them that I'm not privy to.

I really fucking hate this.

We eat outside on the rugged picnic table that came with the house. Gil carries the bread. Marigold gets the roasted veggies. I deliver the fish straight from the grill to the middle.

There's a slight hesitation to sit, no one knowing where they should be, until Gil plops down and pats the space beside him for Marina to follow. Marigold quickly steals the seat across, leaving me facing Gil, who smirks smugly.

A collective coo (started by Marina) erupts when I peel the aluminum foil apart. A wave of rosemary, lemon, butter, and garlic steam rushes out, and they see the fish inside: two lake trout, freshly caught this afternoon. It's a masterpiece.

"Looks good. Grady's a gourmet when it comes to fish," Gil says, throwing me a bone.

Marina nods. "Impressive. Looks delicious."

"It's always a work in progress," I say, offering her a weak smile. "I tried to get all the bones, but be careful."

I serve her first, transferring what I hope to be the best portion onto her plate. Gil adds the roasted veggies.

"Thanks," she says, glancing from me to him.

The food is surprisingly perfect, considering my anxiety while preparing it. Light conversation ensues, disregarding me and mostly spear-headed by Marina as if she's promised herself not to make this weird for the others.

But soon, silence prevails, and her attention drifts. "So, what's with the piano? Do you play?"

"He plays," Gil answers for me, "or he did. He's really good, too."

"Very talented," Marigold confirms. "You should've seen Luke's talent show—"

"I don't play anymore." I pass the bread, hoping to shut this down.

She hesitates, brow pinched, before meeting my eyes. "Why not?"

"It triggers bad memories," I admit.

"Then, why keep the piano?"

"It's a part of him that he can't let go," Marigold reports.

"And I don't want to forget," I say, not wanting to hold back. She could ask me anything, and I'd tell her the truth if only to tip her favor back in my direction after this fuck up.

"Would you, though?" she asks.

"What? Play?"

"No, forget?"

"No."

"So, really, holding on to the piano and not playing it, is you punishing yourself? Pianos are meant to be played, Grady. Played and enjoyed and shared with people. They should spread joy, not be turned into dust collectors, mocking your pain every day. It's right there, waiting for you, hoping you'll take a chance and try again, and you walk on by it, selfishly ignoring a beautiful opportunity. *This* is why you'll never be happy—you're too damn busy being miserable."

She rises, resting her napkin beside her plate.

"Sorry, guys," she smiles shortly. "Wine makes me too loosey-goosey with words."

"I liked it," Marigold says.

"Me, too," Gil agrees.

I hang my head, not knowing what the fuck to say. Only that she's right. Absolutely right.

And not just about the damn piano.

"Well, y'all keep eating. It's delicious, Grady," she says. "I'm just going to powder my nose."

"Um, it's—" I start to direct her.

"I'll find it," she snaps.

"Wow," Gil says when she disappears into the house. "I'm liking her more and more. Think I still have a chance, or did you fuck it up for both of us?"

"Chance at what?" Marigold asks, face pinched with confusion.

"A chance to be more than friends with Marnie," Gil says.

Marigold looks from him to me. "But you said you were just friends, and you're an old man."

Gil laughs. Marigold's ability to remember everything a person says is endearing, but not always. "Remember how you said you didn't like Peter Pike? Things change."

Her lips pinch as she considers this. Then, she nods. Marigold may not always understand social shit, but she's extremely logical. "Peter Pike is two years and three months older than me. We're all adults. Age differences don't matter."

"Marnie would agree, I think," Gil says. "Grady's the only one who cares."

"I don't care. It's just... I don't want to talk about this anymore." I rise, bumping the table. I grab my plate and hers, as my siblings give me their adult versions of stink eyes.

I go inside, balancing dirty dishes and not expecting to see her. If it were me, I would've bailed the moment another car appeared in the driveway.

She stayed, anyway.

For them or me, I don't know. Maybe both. But after what she said, I'm sure this marks the bitter end to any ideas about us. Why would she want to be with someone she believes prefers misery? And if that's true about me, why would I wreck her with my miserable life?

I pile dishes into the sink, expecting to hear the front door slam and her truck revving in the driveway. But I don't.

I only hear her voice, soft and upset, behind me. "Grady."

CHAPTER THIRTY-THREE

Marnie

"GRADY." My voice sounds weak, annoyed, sad—a mishmash of emotions that I can't seem to hide now that I've had my outburst. *Dang it, Marnie.* I *never* have outbursts. It's just not a Marnie thing to do. Even at *The Sound of Music*, when everyone expected me to lose my cool, I held myself together.

Held *her* together, eventually. I couldn't salvage us, though. Mom left the next day, and I haven't seen her since.

There's nothing to salvage between Grady and me, just feelings I shouldn't have, and he clearly doesn't want.

He turns, leans against the sink, and dries his hands on a dishtowel. "Marina, I'm sorry."

"Me, too," I breathe out weakly. I don't know what I'm doing here. Don't know what I thought might happen between us. I feel foolish. Naive. Sad. Angry. Well, maybe not angry, but anger adjacent.

I probably should've left when I realized what he'd done, but I didn't want to embarrass him or myself in front of Gil and Marigold. Besides, when Gil went in for that unexpected hug, he whispered, "He's freaking out about his feelings for you. Try not to hold it against him."

So I tried not to. Gil's words restored a little hope, and I played along, thinking Grady might come to his senses and want another chance. All I got was Bothered Grady, Grouchy Grady, stubbornly refusing to end this charade, no matter how much Gil pushed the limits.

But the piano pushed me to my limit. I glance at it across the room. Its glossy black exterior shines in the dying sun, and with the lids closed, it reminds me of a coffin. Grady keeps a coffin-like reminder of his bad memories, and I'm his human version of this. He keeps me around to make himself miserable. I'm not his piano. I refuse to become Grady's unloved, unplayed, token of guilt and regret.

I don't want that for him. I don't want it for me, either.

I force a smile. "It was a lovely dinner. Thanks for inviting me. I'm going to head out, though. Best to avoid any more embarrassing outbursts, right?" I chuckle, though nothing is funny.

A beat passes with his face fixed on distress.

"I shouldn't have said that around them," I say. "That was my mistake."

Pause. Nothing.

"Say my goodbyes for me?" I motion to the window. "And tell Marigold to keep the game. She'll get a lot more use out of it than me. Maybe she'd like to play with Peter."

He hesitates again, like a million thoughts might be spinning through his head, and he can't latch on to any of them. He wrings the towel, unfairly drawing my eyes to the muscles tightening in his forearms. *Stop it, Marnie.* The silence lingers like he wants to speak but can't.

"Nothing?" I challenge, shrugging my shoulders. "You can't think of anything to say to me?"

He scrubs a hand over his head. "This isn't what I wanted to happen."

In a warm flood, tears fill my eyes and threaten to spill over. His words force me to zoom out from this awful farce of a "date" to our beginning—he never wanted that to happen, of course, but he never wanted anything that came after, either. Not the responsibility. Not the guilt. Not me.

"Yeah, I got that. Goodbye, Grady."

I don't breathe again until I'm outside, the door slammed shut behind me, and that breath comes with a choking sob.

CHAPTER THIRTY-FOUR

Grady

THE SLAMMING door rattles the house and shakes me to my core. I close my eyes to the aching finality of it. She's not the door-slamming type, but that's how much I've hurt her. In a breath, I race through the living room, but only to see her disappear onto the main road, top-down, her lovely red hair flying behind her.

It's too late. She shouldn't give me another chance anyway. I busy myself in the kitchen, burying my emotions behind tasks.

But when I hear the front door reopen, I rush to meet her, desperate to wrap her in my arms and apologize until she tells me to stop.

Only it's not her. I'm sucker-punched with sharp disappointment.

Mom and Elena stare me down critically until Mom says, "Grady, what's happened?"

"Why are you here?" I demand instead, returning to the kitchen.

"We brought dessert," Mom says, holding a covered casserole dish.

"And wine," Elena offers, holding up a bottle.

"When Marigold said you were having a dinner party, we thought we'd swing by with a sweet treat to end the evening," Mom says, setting her dish on the kitchen island.

I huff. "They told you?"

"Yep, and we couldn't miss this disaster," Elena laughs. "Where's Marnie? Is she onto your ridiculous plan yet?"

"She's gone."

My mom and aunt share a concerned glance before Elena helps herself to wine glasses, and Mom unveils her pineapple cake. "Well, we're here, so you might as well tell us what happened."

Marigold and Gil enter from the porch with the dogs, graciously taking attention away from me.

"Where's Marnie? I want to take her to the pier and put on my best moves," Gil grins.

"Gone," Mom chirps. "Your brother's self-sabotage is complete."

"Don't blame her for leaving after the piano incident," Gil explains everything Marina said and how upset she was.

"She's so right about you, Grady," Mom says.

"Now, she feels like that piano," Elena tacks on.

"Look, the party's over," I decide, holding my hands up to usher them all to the door. "I don't want to talk about it. You all need to go."

"Grady, dessert!" Marigold orders, pointing at Mom's cake. "You can't leave a party without having dessert, remember?"

I sigh with resignation. "Yes, Marigold. You're right. Please, have dessert. But the rest of you—"

"Grady, you're upset." Mom rests her hand on my arm in an attempt to be soothing. "Maybe we can help, huh?"

I press my lips together defiantly. If I can't talk to Marina, I'm certainly not talking to them. They pipe in with advice anyway, barely taking turns with shit like "Stop being afraid of love," and "You shouldn't be alone forever." I hardly listen. Platitudes won't help me scale the walls I've worked so hard to build or wrestle my shame over screwing this up.

But the simple truth might.

"If you like her, you should tell her," Marigold says, her mouth full of cake. "Marnie's upset. You should make her feel better. It's like her games. She wants someone to play with, and she wants it to be you. So, why not play? Don't you *want* to make *her* happy?"

"Yes, Marigold. Of course, I do," I sputter.

"Then, take her some cake," Marigold advises. "It's very good."

"Fine."

Mom prepares a cake slice to-go while Elena initiates a long list of pointers for winning Marina back—not that I listen. I grab my keys and the airtight container and ignore their little pep talks as I race to the door.

It's dark when I pull beside her truck in the driveway. Warm glows emanate from her windows, and her shadow moves across the living room. I grab my apology cake and approach the door. She swings it open before I knock.

She looks surprised, pained, and unsure all at once. Her hair is piled atop her head in a messy bun. Her shoes are off, but she still wears the pink blouse and jean skirt. She twiddles with her necklace.

"Marina, I'm a fucking numpty."

Laughs bubble through her distress like sunshine through a cloud. "You *are* a numpty."

I shrug lightly. "I wanted it to be the two of us, but overthinking got the better of me. I thought I might be doing you a favor, easing you back into dating with someone I know is a good guy."

She leans against the doorjamb, arms folded across her pink blouse, and blows a lock of hair out of her eyes. "*You're* a good guy."

"I didn't think you'd want me. Or, at least, didn't think you should."

"Damn it, Grady. You don't get to decide that. I don't want another Tripp or anyone else. I want *you*. Just tell me—what is it about me? Am I too young? Too broken? Too much of a bad reminder? Truth. What's holding you back?"

I take a breath, if only to gather strength to say it. "I'm falling hard and fast, and it's making me dizzy. Nothing makes sense. How can I curse the day I hurt you and be grateful for it at the same time? How could you even want me after everything? You are so loving, so forgiving, and so beautifully, unequivocally, perfectly *you*. Marina, you're everything I want, exactly as you are—and that scares the hell out of me. I'm sorry for that shitshow. Sorry for pulling away. Sorry that I let you think for a second that you aren't enough for me. You are more than enough. You're *everything* to me. Truly."

She takes me in, tilts her head to one side, and nibbles her bottom lip. Meanwhile, my heart rams in my chest, waiting for her to say something. She doesn't smile, and finally delivering the words I've wanted to say doesn't feel like enough.

"I brought you dessert, if that helps," I say, offering her the container.

She takes it, setting it on a side table next to her. "It doesn't hurt."

"Give me another chance. A real date tomorrow night, just you and me—I promise."

Her brow pinches as she glances from the porch floorboards back to me. "You're falling for me?"

"Darling, how could I not be?" I breathe out in a sigh. "You had me at *eep*, and a hundred times after that. You had me the second you fell into my arms."

She laughs, her eyes rolling to fight back the tears I see welling in them. "Kiss me, then, you numpty."

Relief sweeps me as I close the distance between us, but I don't kiss her yet. My hands tangle with hers before my fingers drift up her arms slowly, softly, and then trace her collarbone across her shoulders.

Her breathing quickens as my thumbs roll over her cheeks and my fingers circle her neck. Maybe I'm overthinking, wanting to savor this. But her hands rise to my forearms, and she explores me with touches, too. My forehead rests against hers, taking her in until we're breathless and desperate.

She smiles, and I smile back, and my lips land on hers like that. Smiling.

Soft and sweet eases into intense in a breath—her lips are a delicate comfort and driving force at once. She plays me like a game that she knows exactly how to win. And I'm happy to surrender. A light bite on my bottom lip has me melting into her, and when her tongue playfully finds mine, I moan over how good it feels.

Her hands drift over my chest, tugging my shirt to pull me closer. My hands wrap her up, tightening us together, feeling all her glorious curves pressed against me.

It's not just a kiss. It's the kiss to end all others. The last first kiss.

She pushes me against the opposite doorjamb, taking over and making us laugh at her unrestrained aggression. I fucking love it. She's beautifully confident and unhindered. I expected sweet and amenable, not to be turned inside out by how unbelievably sexy this is. She moans against my lips and whispers my name like a prayer.

"Falling even faster now," I say.

"I'll catch you," she promises, and I believe her. All my insecurities and fears melt away in the warmth of her arms and the strength of her promise. I have no doubts anymore.

She must think the same when she says, "Want to come in?"

I rest my forehead against hers, and I ache to say yes. "If I do, I won't leave."

She smirks. "I know."

I groan, considering it. "I want you so fucking bad but... Say yes to tomorrow night and no to me right now."

"Yes. And why?" Her brow cocks in suspicion—the same reaction she had when she learned about my unplayed piano.

"This isn't me ignoring a beautiful opportunity, Marina. This is me savoring the hell out of it. Take me inside with you, and I won't hold back. I will worship you until there's nothing left."

A breathless sigh escapes her. "Why would I say no to that?"

"Because I don't want it to be the nightcap to my fuck-up. You are the best thing that's ever happened to me. You deserve more. Let me make this right," I tell her, however much my body protests against saying it. "Or take me inside. Either way, I win. Your choice."

She chews her bottom lip, scrutinizing me with her dreamy eyes. Slowly, she eases away from me. "Better make our date good, Tripp Grady Tripp. No freak-outs allowed."

"Aye, Captain. How early can I pick you up?"

"For dinner?"

"For whatever I plan. How early?"

Her lips curl like she enjoys the mystery. "Um, three?"

"I'll be here at three."

"I'll be ready."

"Enjoy your dessert, Marina."

"Already have... oh, wait, you mean the cake. Right," she grins. "Oh, I will."

I lean close for a quick kiss before saying, "Good night."

"Good night, Grady."

I ache, leaving her. I love her like this. Her flushed cheeks, swollen lips, dewy skin, and giddy smile make me desperate to make her happy. Starting with the perfect date.

CHAPTER THIRTY-FIVE
Marnie

ENDING our evening at the door after those knee-weakening, toe-curling kisses took nearly every drop of my fierce fortitude.

Almost as bad as waiting ALL DAY for our date!

I try distracting myself with work, errands, cats, plants, game-making, *anything*. But any momentary relief veers sharply into Grady territory, turning me into a lovestruck and utterly useless pile of goo lost in imagined sexcapades. *Whew*. It's a wonder I didn't retract my refusal and put his *anytime for any reason* promise to the test.

But he's right—we *should* savor it. Besides, I spent years with a man who took whatever he could get from me. Last night, once again, proves Grady is refreshingly, adorably different.

Also different... Grady's kiss. I've never been kissed like that—a weird realization because one would think that, by and large, all kisses are created relatively equal. Lips plus touching equal nerve endings properly engaged, and temperatures rising. But his kiss brought on a raging inferno. His delicious intensity, pulsing through him and onto me, created a blazing ecosystem between us. Hot, wet, lush, and sweetly contained, just for me. A greenhouse effect. A Grady effect.

I get hot just thinking about it.

So, it's no surprise that when he arrives at three o'clock on the dot, I'm out of the door and into his arms before he has a chance to knock. He laughs as he reciprocates, wrapping his big arms around me, lifting me, and easing me inside. He slams the door shut behind us while I ravish him with wild kisses.

"I've been dying to see you," he breathes between my lips.

"Not as much as me," I giggle, finding my feet again. "I can't wait to savor Romantic Grady on this date. Where are we going?"

"I forget," he says, making me laugh. He tugs a bag of cat treats from the inside pocket of his jacket. "In lieu of flowers."

Giggling, I shake the bag, and the cats twirl between our legs. We fill them up on treats and pets until Grady rises, reaching out to help me up.

"You look amazing," he says, eyeing my olive green dress—a vintage score with a deep V-neck and cute little buttons down the front. I call it friendly casual.

"So do you," I say, grabbing my purse and jacket from the kitchen table. His dark gray jeans and black jacket are offset by an olive green t-shirt that almost matches my dress. We are adorably date-ready.

Ten miles into our excursion, Grady's phone chimes repeatedly.

He removes it from his inner pocket and mumbles a curse. "I have to make a call."

"Okay."

During the short conversation, Grady mostly listens. When he hangs up, he drops the phone on the seat between us and runs a hand over his head.

"Dad needs me at the farm. His horse, Buck Rogers, got spooked and rammed against a shovel hanging on the wall. He's got a gaping wound. I'm sorry."

"It's okay."

"I'll drive you home. Can we resume this later?"

"No, take me with you. Maybe I can help."

"Marina, my job isn't pleasant," he says, fisting the steering wheel. "You don't want to see that."

"I can handle it. I want to stay with you."

He looks surprised. "Okay. But I won't fault you if you stay in the truck."

At Tripp Family Farm, he bypasses the house for the dirt road leading to the stables. The property is expansive, stretching out on the horizon like an ocean. A nondescript white building serves as the dairy, and the muddy lot is surrounded by outbuildings, tractors, and trucks of every variety. Beyond that is a gorgeous red barn with a peaked roof.

"Wait. I'll come around for you," he says after he parks.

He meets me at the passenger side, holding rubber boots. He shifts me in my seat so my legs hang over the side, a rough but sweet move, especially the way his eyes stay locked on mine. With a featherlike touch, he runs his fingers down the back of my bare leg to my shoe, slipping it off. My breath hitches at the warmth spreading across my core. He does the same with the other leg, making me want to close them around him and yank him toward me.

His fingers drift over my feet as he smiles at me. "Don't want you to get dirty."

Flushed and bothered in the best way, I grin. "Just have dirty thoughts, huh?"

He chuckles. "That's a bonus." He slips me into the rubber boots like I'm Cinderella trying on the glass slipper, and rubber boots have never felt sexier.

In the back of The Beast, he unlocks a metal box containing his bags and supplies. He sheds his jacket and shoes, pulling on overalls and rubber boots.

His dad meets us at the door. "Hey, Marnie. Sorry to interrupt your date."

"It's okay, Mack. A vet must what a vet must," I say, making Grady smirk.

Mack leads us to a wide stall where a ginormous black horse wriggles against his tethers and neighs disconcertingly. Blood stains the hay beneath his left side, where a crescent gash on his rump oozes steadily. I stand with Mack on the other side of the half door while Grady moves into the stall, assessing the wound.

"Yeah, that's a bad one," he says. "What spooked him?"

"A squirrel," Mack laughs, and turns to me. "For large creatures, horses are surprisingly skittish."

Grady snaps on gloves and gives the horse an injection. He

arranges his tools, cleans the wound, and deftly sutures the gash—quick to action, just like *that* day. The blood stirs unpleasant memories but gratitude, too. We got through it together.

"You okay?" He says, catching my gaze from the other side of Buck Rogers.

"Yeah, good."

The horse meanders closer to the entry, nosing in our direction.

"Can I pet him?" I ask.

"Of course," Mack says, rubbing the creature's long nose.

"I've never been around horses." I gently run my fingers over his velvety nose. "He's sweet."

"So, I hear you've been changing my brother's life," Mack says.

"Turning it upside down is probably more accurate," I say.

"No, I've only heard good things. 'Bout time he got his act together."

"Well, it's hard to imagine his pain, losing his love, especially like that," I say gently. "Fixing the place up has been his tribute to her. You should come by and see it sometime."

Mack huffs. "He won't want to see me."

"I think he would. He wants to reconcile. He just doesn't know how. He asks about you and Carmela, you know."

Mack's eyes snap to mine. "He does?"

"All the time, when he knows I've seen you or if Marigold's around."

"Well, wonders never cease," he breathes.

"Your family is a wonder," I chuckle. "I love all of you, even the outliers with their rough edges and bad reputations. You're all teddy bears."

"We're a motley bunch, for sure. I'm not sure about teddy bears, though," Mack laughs.

Grady soon finishes his work, gives his father instructions for Buck Rogers' care, and then smiles when he says, "I'll send you the bill—I'm charging double for interrupting my date."

"In that case, put it on my tab, son. Thanks for taking care of Buck. Y'all have a nice time."

Our date resumes with little time lost. He refuses to tell me where we're going, but I'm excited to solve the mystery. In downtown Wilmington, Grady parks on a quaint street of eclectic shops and takes me to the Game Café, a cute and cozy coffee shop with games at every table.

"Oh, my gosh, Grady," I beam as we scan the options. "This is… so ME!"

"Yep, how about chess?" He motions to an empty table for two by the front window.

My shoulders slump. "You won't believe this, but that's the *one* game I don't know how to play."

He's shocked. "What? You call yourself a keen strategist and don't know how to play chess?"

I groan. "I could've learned, I guess. Wanted to. But it seems like such a beautiful, intimate game. It felt wrong learning it on YouTube."

"It's much better learning with a partner." His hand slips in mine and pulls me to the table. "Play with me, Marina?"

"Oh, Grady, I love it when you talk dirty to me."

He laughs and blushes—score for Marnie!

We order fancy coffees and chocolate treats, and he teaches me, sweetly and patiently, how to play the game of all games. I get giddy and clap whenever I make a smart move and melt into my chair when I don't.

I'm an expert by our third round, determined to beat him.

But then he says, "Tell me about *The Sound of Music*."

Grady

"WHAT?" she asks, smile gone.

"*The Sound of Music*. What happened at that play?"

Her head tilts as she examines the board, clearly bothered. "Your family hasn't told you?"

"No, I didn't ask. I'd rather find out from you. I mean, if you don't mind talking about it."

She leans back, scrutinizing me with her soft blue eyes and debating it. Maybe I shouldn't have brought it up. I don't want anything to ruin this date.

"It feels important." I lean forward, locking in her stare. "I want to *know* you. Better than I know myself. Your loves. Your hurts. All of it. I want to be the one who *truly* knows you. More than anything. Starting with *The Sound of Music*."

Her apprehension melts under my gaze. "Fine, if you promise to tell me about the piano."

I hide an internal cringe but nod. "Fair enough."

"*The Sound of Music* was the first school activity I ever tried to do," she says with a weak smile. "It was just me and my mom. We moved frequently, always searching for Mom's version of the perfect place to call home. Seagrove came closest. We were here a year, longer than we'd ever stayed anywhere. She's a hairstylist and had a great job at Mel's—they were good friends. Still are, I think."

She moves her rook—a bad choice. But I say nothing, fixing my eyes on her as she tells her story.

"I'd just gotten the job at Sunny's. I remember Cora saying, '*Welcome to the family,*' when she hired me." Her smile returns, but only for a moment. "Things were the best they'd ever been."

She sits up, twiddling her fingers as she tries to talk, nerves growing as her memories pain her.

"Mom taught me games. That's what we'd do when money was short—it was *always* short. She taught me to read and do math through games. She was a good mom. I loved her. But she struggled."

"With what?" I make a quick, throwaway move.

"Bipolar disorder. She called it upsies and downsies. I didn't understand it growing up. She'd bounce off the walls one minute, excited to take me on some wonderful adventure. Then, she'd crash. Spend days, weeks, in bed. It was... day to day, I never knew what mom I'd get."

"Fuck, that must've been hard. How did you handle that?"

She shrugs lightly. "I made the best of it."

"How? You were just a kid."

"Kids adapt, don't they? I adapted to whatever she was and learned to care for myself. It wasn't that bad. I had freedoms most kids didn't. She taught me to be creative and independent. When she was up, she was so fun."

"But when she was down?"

She lets out a resigned sigh and refocuses on the game like she'd rather forget the rest and certainly doesn't want to discuss it. Her brow scrunches in contemplation, but she's lost the game already and can't figure out what to do.

So, I lean forward, swiping the chessboard with a hard forearm. The pieces clatter to the floor, and surely people look. But I fixate on her and reach for her hands across the empty board.

Her hands find mine but hesitantly. "How romantic," she says.

"I forfeit. Finish your story. Tell me about when she was down."

"It was like she wasn't there at all," she says in a breath. "She spent nine days in bed once, only getting up to go to the bathroom. Nine days, barely eating. Nine days, no shower. Nine days, no groceries or money coming in. That was the worst time. I was... twelve."

My hands tighten over hers. I'm heartbroken for her. "You must've been... terrified."

She gasps, looking up at me, and admits in a whisper, "All the time."

"Did she ever seek treatment?"

"Yes, on and off. Mel helped her find a good therapist, and she got on medication. It helped. That's why we stayed put in Seagrove."

I recall what Mom said about Marina bargaining for extra pills.

"But she'd forget to take them," she continues with a wry smirk. "Or she'd *think* she took it, but we couldn't be sure. Or she'd lose them. She'd miss appointments. And not pick up her refills. When she felt better, she didn't think she needed them."

"Even though she felt better *because* of them," I breathe out.

"Exactly. We tried to make Seagrove work, but then, *The Sound of Music*. I didn't tell her. It was the first thing I'd kept from my mother. I stayed after school every day, designing gorgeous sets and, I don't know, having fun. People were kind to me, like Gil. They loved my work. I was *seen*. So, I made excuses, trying to keep her out of it. A week before the performance, she became depressed, and I was actually... *glad*. I wanted her pain to last, for her to be stuck in bed so that I could get through it without her blowing it up. I wanted something *for me*. It was selfish and wrong—"

"No, it wasn't."

"Yeah, it was, and it backfired. She found out," she says, her beautiful face tainted with disgust at herself. "She showed up during *Alleluia*, off her meds and self-medicating. She came onstage, shouting, '*Where's my daughter? Where's Marnie?*' No one knew what to do. She wasn't herself. She made this huge scene, talking about how great I was and how, if she'd known, she would've been here, too. Helping. *Proper momming*, she called it. She melted into tears and apologies on stage. It took me twenty minutes to talk her down—a performance everyone got to see. Finally, I took her home."

"Marina, that's... I'm so sorry. You never should've been in that position."

She shrugs. "I was okay in that position until then."

"You were fifteen."

"I was all she had," she answers softly. "She was all I had."

I squeeze her hands a little tighter, running my thumbs along hers.

She forces a smile. "The next day, I went to school, and people *spoke* to me. I didn't want them to feel sorry for me, but it felt like a bridge, you know, to finally being in a place that might understand me, somewhere I might make friends. Everyone was so kind. They asked how I was and said I saved the performance. All I did was talk her down and take her home, but their appreciation and understanding felt nice. I didn't feel alone anymore."

She shifts in her chair, bringing it closer. "So, when I came home that day and found Mom loading the car with our stuff, I just... I fell apart, Grady."

"So, it does happen?"

"Rarely," she chuckles. "But yes. She wanted to move, to wipe the slate clean for the next town. That's what always happened. She'd go through a bad breakup or job situation, and we'd leave just as I started feeling comfortable. I hated it." She leans back.

"What happened?"

"I told her I wasn't going. She could stay with me and get better or leave and fend for herself. She threatened to take me anyway. I was fifteen, after all, and didn't have a say. I told her if she tried to force me, I'd tell social services about her myself. Her illness mortified her, one reason she struggled to manage it. I said I'd be better off without her. She agreed, so she left."

I nod, knowing it must've been difficult to say. Hard to hear, too. My biggest concerns at fifteen were having time for video games and making the varsity team in baseball. She had to survive—I can't imagine her life.

"Didn't people know you were alone?"

She shrugs lightly. "After *The Sound of Music*, I think people understood. Mr. Pike, Peter's grandfather, knew. He looked after me and probably assuaged any worries about me from the community. I had a job, good grades, and never made trouble—I kept my head down, paid the bills, and never gave anyone a reason to be concerned. If someone asked about her, I'd say she was on a trip or visiting relatives. I finally started saying that she'd become an airline attendant. It didn't take long for people to stop asking."

"What about your mom? She's never reached out or returned?"

She scoffs. "No. She's sent cards over the years, always from a different place. Mel must talk to her. She sent a card for the wedding."

"What'd it say?"

"I didn't open it. I haven't opened any of them."

"Why not?"

"I suppose it's wrong not to. I spent the first year expecting she'd see it my way and come back full of love and apologies. That didn't happen. Holidays, birthdays, nothing. So, when the first card came about two years later, I put it in a box, too angry to read it. I've done the same with the rest."

"Even though they *might* be filled with love and apologies?"

"After two years of silence, it was my one act of teenage rebellion. I'm not angry anymore, but then, it felt too late. I liked my peaceful, drama-free existence. It suited me. Then, there was me and Ashe, and I feared she'd show up like a tornado, spinning out of control and ruin it." She laughs weakly. "The irony, huh?"

She takes a breath, forcing a smile. "So, that's me, Grady. The world's biggest hypocrite."

"Hypocrite? How?"

"For wanting to belong to a family but turning mine away," she says.

"She left you no choice. She should've fought harder for you. This isn't your fault."

"Eh, she once told me that having a Valentine's birthday meant I was cursed to be alone. She was right."

"No, she wasn't."

Her hands tighten on mine. "She *left* on Valentine's Day. You can't tell me there's nothing to it."

"It's a shitty coincidence. Bad things have happened, yes. But you deserve all the love in the world, and you'll have it because you're not alone anymore. So, please, tell me you aren't buying that bullshit."

She smirks slyly. "Ask me next Valentine's Day."

"Fine. I will."

The server interrupts, asking if we need help picking up the game pieces. Feeling slightly bad, I gather the scattered plastic pieces from around our table and put the game back together. "Sorry, we're fine."

"Want to play again?" she asks.

"Yes, but not here." I rise from my seat and extend my hand to her. "Come with me."

CHAPTER THIRTY-SEVEN

Marnie

HE TAKES me to the Riverwalk just in time for sunset, the orangey bands of sunlight blanketing the sky and making everything shimmer—the ripples on the Cape Fear river, the reflections off of cars heading over the bridge, even his eyes look amber in the light. He wraps me up from behind, snuggling me against him while we watch the sun's descent, saying nothing. I love the silence. I've learned this about him over the last month when he's appeared at my side, helping—with Grady, I don't have to talk. I don't have to engage or make people comfortable or keep conversations going like I used to do with the Sullivans.

With him, I can just be.

After what I've shared with him, watching the sunset is the perfect chaser.

He's the first to know that story from my perspective, the first to ask, and having shared it, I feel lighter. But also sad.

The Tripp family rotates around each other exactly as they are. Helping when needed, supporting when necessary, and loving, always.

Vague memories of what that felt like surface beneath the struggles. Mom and I were like that once. But we lost that beautiful rotation. We went lopsided until collapsing altogether. I used to push her out of my thoughts and stuff her cards in a box in anger. Now, regret compounds in the emptiness she left behind, and I feel like I've let her down.

I need to read her letters. I *will* read them. Just not tonight.

Once the sun fades and darkness takes over, Grady takes me to Cape Fear Games, a social club and store, where he insists on getting a fancy chess set and anything else I want.

"It'll be the first thing that's *ours*," he explains, motioning to the chessboards. "Something we play for decades during rainy days and hurricanes."

I almost purr over his cozy idea. "That sounds lovely."

If Grady believes in us like that, so should I.

We agree on an elegant wood set with hand-carved pieces and felt bottoms. He takes our selection to the counter while I browse the aisles. But soon, I give up on buying anything else. A shared chess set is definitely enough for me.

I find him at the counter, talking with the employees.

"Oh, yeah, my girlfriend's incredibly talented," he says to them, making my breath hitch on the nervous lump in my throat. "Her games are so fun and inventive. How would she go about getting them into a store like this?"

"She could reach out to the big game companies like Hasbro, but nowadays, she should get the game some attention first. Post reels of people playing her games on TikTok or YouTube and see the response. Many of the games we sell were funded by KickStarter campaigns. She should look into that, too. We do open gameplay on the weekends. She's welcome to bring her games here for beta testing."

"Thanks. That'd be great," Grady says as the man hands him a card.

"Have any questions, give me a call," he says.

"What're you up to?" I ask behind him.

He slides the card into his pocket, shrugging. "Nothing. See anything else?"

"So many things! But, no. I want to become a chess queen first."

He pulls out his wallet and hands over his credit card. "Just this, then."

Once in The Beast again, I smile at Grady. "Did you call me your girlfriend back there?"

He twists in my direction, grinning. "Did I?"

I feign upset. "And what's with telling them my secret hobby?"

He smiles, lazily draping his hand over the steering wheel. "I think it's more than a hobby. Why not see if something can come of it, huh? Besides, I like bragging about my girlfriend."

I turn toward the window, hiding my enormously cheesy grin and blushing cheeks. "And just yesterday, you tried fixing me up with your brother."

"Fuck, I'll never live that down. Will I?"

"No, probably not."

"I suppose that's fair." He shrugs, grip tightening on the wheel, revealing all those glorious veins in his forearms. *Cool it, Marnie.*

"So, where's my boyfriend taking me now?"

"Dinner. Luke's holding a table at Rebellion."

"Nice, and since we have a little drive ahead, would it be a good time to tell me about the piano?" I say. "I haven't forgotten."

He flinches, bringing both hands to the wheel like he means to strangle it. "It's not that I don't want to tell you. It'll be difficult for you to hear."

I twist in my seatbelt, bringing my leg up between us and giving him my full attention. "Now, you know more about me than anyone. Let me know you."

He takes a breath and launches into his story. "I met Emma in vet school. We were good for each other, very compatible. We became vets together, got married, and started a practice in Charlotte—that's where she wanted to live. She adored the city, its nightlife, and her friends. It was busy, hectic. We were content with each other. I wouldn't say happy, but certainly not unhappy."

His hands wring the steering wheel again as he fixates on the road ahead. "She got pregnant. Our world switched from mediocre to incredible all at once. We were happy again, overjoyed, in love. We couldn't wait."

He hesitates. Unease grows in my stomach, making me almost

queasy. I had no idea where his piano story would take us, but I wouldn't have guessed this.

"Grandma taught me how to play the piano when I was a kid. Then, I took lessons all through high school. There are exceptionally dorky pics of me playing for the chorus in the yearbook."

I smile. "I'll definitely have to see those."

"When I imagined being a dad, playing the piano together was what I pictured. Emma went on runs to baby stores. I bought the piano, and every night, as Emma's belly grew, I'd play for them. It was the happiest we'd ever been."

"We lost the baby at six months." His voice cracks. "She stopped kicking. Stopped moving. Her heart stopped beating. No one could tell us why. She just stopped. We lost her and lost each other, too."

Tears well in my eyes, and I don't stop them. Some things need tears, like a salve on a wound.

"I shut Emma out after that, consumed myself with work. When she filed for divorce, I was grateful. I wasn't there for her, not that we were right to begin with—I see that now. We were pieces that fit off-kilter, and we spent years forcing them to fit anyway. I came home, hating myself. For letting Emma down. For failing my marriage. For losing her."

"Did you name her?" I ask, and he glances at me for the first time since his story began.

"You're crying?"

"Of course, I'm crying. It's devastating."

"Sara," he says, his voice soft and weak. "After my grandmother."

Tears flow down my cheeks in streams, his story breaking through the dam and all my backup defenses. "Grady, please. Pull over. Anywhere."

"You okay?"

"I'm just... having a moment."

He pulls into a church parking lot, empty and illuminated, and screeches to a stop, catty-corner to the lines. We get out and meet in front of The Beast.

"I'm so sorry for you, for Emma, for Sara," I say through sloppy sobs that make me feel ten years old. Only, I can't help it. "After the accident, I felt wrong for grieving. How can you miss something you never had? Or never felt sure you wanted? Still, my heart was broken over what could never be. But you *had* Sara. Felt her kick and grow, and bought things for her, and had visions of her childhood. I can't imagine what you went through. Or how it still hurts."

Tears slip from his eyes as he steps closer to me. My hands go to his rough cheeks while his circle my waist, grabbing onto me like he needs the support.

"But this is why you fought so hard for me, why you were there, time and time again, making sure I was okay. Why you needed to see me fall apart; *you* needed to fall apart, and you didn't."

"I went on like nothing had happened," he confesses, eyes brimming with fresh tears. "When I saw you doing the same thing..."

"I fell apart at the hospital when it felt safe. With you there, I could. But not usually. That's why I have my policy, Grady. No one wants to see my frowns, fears, and tears. *Alone* has always felt safest for me."

"That's not true anymore."

"I know." I grab his collar, pulling him closer. "I felt it *that* day, and every time since. Maybe that's what we needed—to feel safe enough with someone to fall apart."

He nods against me, sinking into my shoulder. "Thank you," he breathes into my hair. "For so long, I've pushed it away like it never happened. Crammed my pain under bullshit and anger. You've got me feeling things again. Hell, it's freeing just saying her name. Sara."

"Sara," I smile through our tears. "Who would've loved animals and been a pianist."

He laughs. "Sara, who would've been sweet and talkative and would've told bad jokes, like her old man."

A sobbing giggle sputters out of me. "Sara, she would've had your eyes and been just as stubborn."

"Sara, who would've been in the chess club and never would've been allowed to date," he tacks on with a smirk.

"You would've been a great father," I say. "You still could be."

"Marina." He takes my damp face in his strong hands, locking eyes with me. "I don't need or want kids. Not unless you do. *If you ever do*, we'll find a way and love them all the same."

The lump returns to my throat. "You make it sound like... this is it. You and me."

He shrugs, pulling away and wiping leftover tears. "Isn't it?"

Too surprised and overrun with emotions, I can't answer, only stare. Dumbfounded.

He rolls his eyes sheepishly. "I know. Says the guy who tried to fix you up with his brother yesterday. I don't care. Everything's different now."

A warm, worrying feeling blossoms inside me, hearing him say that. I feel like our relationship has traveled light years in hours, and it's been sad, beautiful, and tragic all at once. What he says is true—everything's different.

"You and me. Together. *This* is where we belong." He's stern and sudden, locking on to my hesitation like he's reading my mind. His eyes drift over my face, measuring me, and I feel our belonging like a sore muscle, finally getting relief. I *belong* with him.

He seals his words with a kiss, and I'm already breathless. Breathless and scared and hopeful. Loving and delighting in him like I've never done with anyone before. I want it to be true so badly, but believing in happily-ever-afters counters everything I've ever known.

I smile when he pulls away and rests his forehead on mine. He strokes my cheek with the backs of his fingers, and I don't think I've ever felt so loved.

"I promised you dinner," he says. "Think we can pull ourselves together?"

"I hope so. I'm starving," I chuckle.

CHAPTER THIRTY-EIGHT

Grady

AT THE RESTAURANT, Luke seats us near the front window —a corner away from the crowd at the bar but still front and center to the place. We can see the foot traffic outside, the lights twinkling from the courtyard, and the stage, where instruments sit listlessly, waiting for action to come later this evening.

Even so, this place is alive, and, for the first time in ages, I don't mind being here. It feels right to smile, talk, and be with her here, where anyone can see us.

Of course, as soon as that thought clicks in my mind, the universe shits all over it. The door swings open, and the host says, "Sullivan, party of four."

We glance up simultaneously to see Cora, Wes, Ashe, and some bouncy blonde in a low-cut top stroll in. She hangs on his arm, two-handed, like a leech, not that he minds the attention. I meet Marina's eyes, and she smiles, returning to the menu like she's completely unaffected.

I hope that's true.

Cora notices us and, taking in the nearly full restaurant, sees that the crowd notices too—the Sullivans, Marina, and me in the same place. Smugly, she strolls over, and the others hover behind her, unsurely.

"Marnie," she coos, "how nice to see you."

"Nice to see you, too. Hey, Ashe, Elise, Wes." She offers them a chipper wave and her usual bright smile.

Before anyone can respond, Cora cuts in. "Hear you're cashiering at the G&G. My, what an interesting choice."

"I'm managing, not cashiering, and giving the place a makeover. It looks amazing. You should all come and see it sometime."

Cora scoffs. "With all the horror stories I've heard? No, thanks. Most people wouldn't set foot in it, but I'm glad you found something that suits you. I'm just surprised it's trailers, cigarettes, old men, and a swamp."

Her entourage looks confused by her antagonism, especially Ashe. He tugs on his mom's sleeve like a child. "Our table's ready."

"Definitely better than the funeral home you tried hiding me in," Marina adds. "Or moving, like you wanted."

Wes and Ashe turn toward Cora, surprised.

Marina takes a deep breath, grinning. "The G&G's rustic, broken, homey, and beautifully genuine. There, I'm valued *exactly* as I am and credited for what I do. That has made all the difference. I wouldn't change a thing."

Cora offers a satisfied humph before tapping her fingernail on the table. "Really? Not even the fact that Guilt-Trip-Tripp here is funding this awful experiment? You know he pays your salary, right?"

She points to me, and Marina freezes.

Cora chuckles while Wes moves beside her. "Honey, the table."

She waves him off. "Oh, dearest. You didn't know? You should've taken my advice about relocating. It would've saved you so much trouble. You still could. Plenty of towns need cashiers. You finally cashed our check. I bet you're grateful for that Sunny's severance now, huh?"

Her dark eyes cut to me when she says it, and there's that *us and them* mentality again. Fucking Cora. I'm bombarded with anger and questions. *Cora tried to get Marina to leave? Severance? She could've left? And she stayed, anyway?*

"Mom!" Ashe protests. "That's enough."

"Ashe, it's okay. Marnie needs to know—everyone else does,"

Cora coos. "She should be let in on the G&G joke. I'm doing what's best for her."

"It'd be *best* for you to carry your ass away from this fucking table. Now." I keep my voice down but say it sternly, ready to bull-doze them out of here if need be.

Cora laughs, putting her hands up defensively. "You really should've let us sue him, Marnie. I only speak the truth."

"Truth, huh?" Steeling herself with a deep breath and her forced smile, Marina locks eyes with Cora. "It's a *family* business. He's a Tripp. They're *all* funding me. That's the truth."

"It's a farce, regardless."

"No, it's competition," Marina quips confidently. "This little engagement reminds me of that time you got defensive when one of our best vendors threatened to leave—Cora the Conquerer came out in full force. You have no reason to antagonize me now, unless..."

Marina giggles, slapping her hand on the table.

"... Oh, my goodness! I see right through you. You're worried."

"Ridiculous!"

"No, you are. Look at your little forehead lines," Marina coos. "Has the G&G dented your profits already?"

Cora gapes, silent for once. Wes and Ashe share a bothered look. Holy shit, Marina's right.

Marina shrugs and shakes her head. "No wonder you still want me to skedaddle out of town. Well, sorry-not-sorry. I'm staying. Now that that's settled, I suggest going to your table because you're making your guest uncomfortable, and, you know, *optics*."

The word breaks out of Marina like a trapped animal, pissed and hungry. Fuck, even I have chills. Cora shudders, taking in the room again and stepping away.

Then, Marina says, casually glancing from Cora to Ashe, "I write my own narrative now. I wish you'd do the same."

Ashe looks puzzled before he drapes an arm over his mom's shoulder and pulls her away.

"Have a nice dinner," Marina tacks on like a champ. "Oh, and Elise, good to see you. Hope you're enjoying that promotion."

The bouncy blonde isn't so happy as she moves away from the table.

"Damn, that was some badass pirate shit," I tell her.

She grins. "It's hard not to scream and jump up and down, knowing that the G&G is making them nervous. Can you believe it?"

"You can do anything. Of course, I believe it."

She blushes and tuts, staring at her menu. "I trained Elise at the same time as Wren. Now, she has my old job, a different title, of course, and my old boyfriend. Creepy."

I don't know what to say—that Cora's dropped my secret and Marina isn't storming out of here should mean it's okay. Cora tried to use it against us and failed.

But her smile wanes.

I breathe out a heavy sigh. "Are you mad? Is this you not letting them break you?"

Her eyes bounce up to mine. "I don't break. I bend. They don't have that kind of power anymore, regardless. Wade, Roy, and Christie, bless their souls, can't keep a secret to save their lives, especially not with me. They let that bomb drop weeks ago. I already knew."

"If you knew, then why did you stay?"

Her shoulders slump as she drops the menu and stares at me like I should know. "You needed me to be okay. I stayed for *you*."

My mouth drops, bringing with it what's left of my barriers. She saved me. All this time, I thought I was the hero—helping her, protecting her, giving her chances. But the Queen of Lost Causes and Second Chances rescued *me*.

"I don't know what to say. But I think I'm in love with you."

She smirks, her eyes perked but fixed on her menu. "Well, let me know when you're sure."

"I can't believe you aren't mad at me."

"You'd do anything for me. How can I be mad?" She meets my eyes, smiles, and returns to her menu. "I'm peeved at Cora—the nerve of her, huh? Wade will have to afford me if he wants to keep me. I never cashed his or, um, *your* checks. I shouldn't have let it go on for as long as I did, but I was having so much fun, and you seemed less shadowy," she giggles, using Marigold's term. "Things must change, though ... But that's a problem for tomorrow. Don't you think?"

"Tomorrow, definitely." I smile, relaxing into her more than I thought possible. This woman unraveled me even before I let her—how is that possible?

It doesn't matter. I don't care. That she's unraveled me means I'm free to wrap myself completely around her.

"You were right. I dodged a bullet. Marrying into that family would've been a disaster." She scoffs, shaking her head. "It's more proof that I never belonged with him. I always knew it, too. In the back of my mind. I never relaxed with him or told him things. Never felt I could fully trust him. Ha, I even doubled up on protection."

"With Ashe?" I say, a little surprised at the subject.

She nods. "With him. With the two boyfriends I had before him. I refused to be my mother's daughter."

A beat passes before she meets my eyes again. "What about you?"

"Me?" It slowly dawns on me—the conversation we're having.

"Any partners since Emma?"

"No. And only a few before her. I was always safe."

She nods, smiling softly. "Good. Then we don't have to be. If that's okay with you."

"Um, okay. That's—good thinking. I'm good with that."

She giggles as I stumble over my words. She stands and moves to my side of the table, slipping her arm over my shoulder. She drops a quick kiss on my forehead and says, "Relax, Grady. Order me a fun drink and a burger. I'll be back."

Then, she heads toward the bathrooms in the rear of the restaurant, leaving me with my imagination. I can't wait to get her alone.

Luke comes over, notepad in hand, and I give him our order. Over his shoulder, I spot the Sullivan's table. Ashe and Cora exchange words, occasionally glancing our way, while the blonde and Wes look more uncomfortable than usual.

Still irritated with them and overrun with affection for Marina, I tell him, "I want to do the thing."

"*The* thing?" he gawks, blue eyes going wide. He braces himself against the table, showcasing his muscled arms covered in tattoos, some of which we got together. "Seriously?"

"Can we?"

He glances around the restaurant, scraping his hand down his impressive beard. "Fuck yes."

He whistles loud enough for all eyes to meet his. He snaps his fingers at the guy behind the bar. "Jake, *the* thing. Now."

The glass Jake holds falls to the floor, shattering. When he realizes it's happening, he rushes to the stage, taking his place on the drums, nearly knocking them over in his excitement to get there. *The Thing* has become somewhat of a legend around here since high school, especially among fellow musicians.

I stand, stretching and cracking my knuckles as Luke and I confer, remembering our *thing* with surprising accuracy. High school was the last time we did it successfully. We tried reprising it for Luke's wedding last year, but we were too drunk to take it seriously—that's the last time I touched keys.

Luke flips the white towel from his shoulder, tossing it to the bar.

"You lead. We'll follow," he says, leading me to the stage.

"Yep."

"Same start?"

"Slight diversion. But yep."

"You good?" He eyes me before we take our positions. "You sure?"

My crooked smile grows. "Never been better."

Jake cracks his sticks together. Luke strums his guitar. And I start to play.

CHAPTER THIRTY-NINE

Marnie

WHEN I EMERGE from the bathroom hallway, I find our table empty. Glancing around the darkened, busy restaurant, I see faces drawn to the stage and hear instruments tinkering. I search for Grady as I shift into my seat and nearly fall out of it when I find him.

On stage.

Smiling.

At me.

From behind the piano.

His raspy voice hums through the microphone perched near his face. "So, you're about to hear a mash-up set that my brother Luke and I performed for my high school talent show."

"Did you win?" an audience member shouts.

Grady chuckles, "Ah, no. But we did it a second time at *his* talent show. Didn't win then, either, but that's okay. The violin rules high school talent shows—if you're wondering."

Laughs.

"Tonight is my first date with Marina Ann Strange... Marnie, as you know her," he announces amid clapping and cooing. "You might also be aware that a few months ago she..."

He pauses, playing a familiar chord on the piano, before singing, *"She had a bad day,"* from the Daniel Powter song of the same name. *"She had a bad day."*

Everyone laughs and claps because my 'bad day' is well-known in these parts.

"But I want her to know that... *here comes the sun*," he sings, "*and I say, it's alright...*"

More laughs and cheers at the familiar Beatles song before Luke's guitar riff fades, and Grady speaks again. "Marina, you said to let you know when I'm sure... *I'm sure*... This is for you. Thanks for saying yes."

My heart leaps from my chest and does fifty somersaults as I stumble, rising from my chair. His hands dance over the keys, moving me closer on weak knees. The familiar notes tickle my heart. "Romeo and Juliet" by Dire Straits, a sweet oldie that I'd know anywhere since the CD sits in my AM collection at home.

I am awestruck—Grady Tripp can sing!

"*You and me, babe... how 'bout it?*" he croons, low and husky, looking straight at me. Luke's guitar picks up the riff, but I can't take my eyes off Grady and the sly smirk planted on his face. He's so proud, so comfortable, so sweetly happy. "*Juliet...*"

Can someone overdose on romance? If so, I might be in serious trouble. I bounce on my feet, giddy with it. Hyper on it. Desperate for him.

A crowd gathers around the stage, moving tables aside, especially as the song picks up its pace. But I stand just below him, devouring him, aching for him.

I've never felt more loved or special. Not only that, I've never felt so worthy of feeling loved and special, either. He makes me *want* to be seen, heard, regarded, valued, loved, and admired, revered and feared, pirate-like—all I've missed in my *before* life. *This is after.* My happily ever? I don't know. But certainly, with the wreckage cleared and finding each other through the losses, he's the closest I'll get to one.

"*I love you like the stars above, love you til I die... Juliet,*" he sings, and I melt. "*You and me, babe. How 'bout it?*"

As I get bumped by the people dancing next to me, I glance toward Ashe's table, where he and Cora engage in a heated discussion, rendering them too busy to notice. Or they're trying hard not to. It doesn't matter. I meant what I said to Grady—they no longer have power over me. I feel free to be me. Free to love Grady. Free to be loved by him, too.

As the song trails to its gentle end, Grady switches seamlessly into the mellow bounce of Blackstreet's "No Diggity." Grady laughs sheepishly as the audience recognizes it.

"It was high school," he shrugs.

Luke takes over the vocals, and the audience chimes in for the chorus. *I like the way you work it. No diggity.* I giggle like a middle schooler at a Taylor Swift concert, especially when Grady's eyes find mine when he sings, *"She's a perfect ten."*

Everyone laughs while I blush. The crowd coos and cheers as they dance.

As that song ends, Grady switches to Tupac's "Changes." Luke is surprisingly deft at rapping—his voice pairs perfectly with Grady's elaborate piano work.

And the crowd goes wild for it—it's no longer a restaurant but a concert. *"That's just the way it is... Things will never be the same."*

"Excuse me!" Cora's irritated voice again draws my attention as she pushes through the crowd with her party behind her. They're leaving—their table sits empty, their drinks abandoned.

My smile widens, shifting my eyes back to Grady.

The song changes again, slowly. "Last one before the real band takes over," he says. "Come here, Marina."

I hesitate, but the crowd pushes me up there, cheering me on as I go. He takes my hand, pulling me around the instruments until I'm beside him. From this vantage point, I spot Wade, Christie, and Roy at the bar's end, beaming at us and cheering louder than anyone.

"Help me get her to say yes to a second date, huh?" he grins, instigating the crowd as he starts playing "Iris" by the Goo Goo Dolls. I match his slow swaying beside him, my arm drifting naturally around his waist.

His fingers bang the keys. The crowd dances, lifting their drinks. It's a celebration.

The song switches midway, transitioning perfectly into "Slide."

I wanna wake up where you are... I won't say anything at all... So, why don't you slide?

His words fade, and the song transitions again into "Better Days" —a Goo Goo Dolls compilation that somehow makes sense though they're three different songs.

'Cause tonight's the night the world begins again.

The words hit home as I stand beside the man I want to Super glue to my side for the rest of eternity. Tonight feels like a new start, a new world, a better us now that we've let each other in.

Thunderous applause and raucous cheers bring the song to a close, but it grows even louder when he wraps me up in a wild kiss.

"Looks like a yes to me!" someone yells, rousing the crowd to cheer again.

When our lips part, we're laughing.

"Is it a yes?" he asks breathlessly.

"God, yes! A million times, yes! That was... wow, Grady... Maybe I'm in love with you, too."

He laughs. "Let me know when you're sure."

Tugging me with him, he shakes the drummer's hand, followed by Luke's, and we all descend the stage as the regular band takes their places, looking a bit worried about topping Grady's act.

Townspeople shake our hands, hug our necks, and pat our backs as we drift slowly through the remaining crowd. All smiles and joy. My drama with the Sullivans is long forgotten now.

So is Grouchy Tripp. He maneuvers us through, smiling and chatting like the friendly man I know he truly is. He even gives Wade and his friends warm embraces.

"Now, I get why you were so mad about that nightie," Roy quips.

We don't bother arguing but circle through the group to our table. The energy is so palpable that it's hard to settle again. We're flushed, giddy, and happy, and I'm ready to throw myself at him for the volcanic eruption of love spilling out of me.

Dinner arrives and vanishes quickly. I doubt I've ever eaten so fast, risking heartburn for my burning heart. I don't even finish it, though it's delicious, but toss my napkin on the plate as soon as he seems done.

He runs a hand over his short hair and gives me a questioning look. "That's all I've got planned. How do you feel? What do you want to do? Anything? I could take you home if you're tired. Or not. I'm open."

He almost sounds nervous, prompting my coyest smile. I lean closer across the table.

"Grady Tripp, I swear, if you don't get me out of here pronto, I might give this crowd a show they *shouldn't* see. Please don't make me wait any longer to get you all to myself."

I tack on a little whine while nibbling my bottom lip, which has him laughing and blushing simultaneously.

"Yes, darling." He motions for the check.

Inside The Beast, I slide into the middle of the bench seat and buckle in beside him. "Another benefit of an old car, right?"

He grins. "Absolutely."

"Let's go to yours, okay?" I ask.

"Do we need to run by your place? Check on the cats?"

"Nope. Wren is cat-sitting tonight. *All* night."

His handsome grin widens. "Ah, my amazing girlfriend, the strategist. Good plan."

"I like thinking ahead. Thanks for today. Best. Date. Ever. And the music! I'm so incredibly proud of you. How did it feel?"

"Natural. Better than I thought it would," he says, "I should be thanking you. No more missing out on beautiful opportunities. Pianos should be played, right?"

"Right." I snuggle against his arm, and he gently kisses my forehead.

"There's one more song I want to play for you tonight if that's okay."

I inhale sharply—he's going to play *the* piano? "Time to shift bad memories into better ones?"

"For both of us," he says, his right hand drifting to my leg and squeezing lightly.

The cool night air hits me sharply at his house when I exit The Beast, forcing me into my sweater. Tall, Longleaf Pines wave in the breeze overhead, and Carolina barn owls hoot in the distance. It's darker than I'm used to here, where streetlights don't reach. It feels so beautifully peaceful.

He leads me into a dimly lit and quiet house.

"Where are the dogs?"

He grins wryly. "Marigold is dog-sitting at the farm. *All* night."

A laugh rumbles from me. "My sexy boyfriend, the strategist."

He leans in for a soft kiss that electrifies me. "I only wanted to think about us. Make yourself at home."

I kick off my shoes by the door and drop my bag on the couch. He dumps his keys and wallet in a basket by the door. He starts a fire in the fireplace that crackles and pops and mesmerizes me. After a few sips of wine, we relinquish our glasses to the coffee table. Then, he takes my hand and leads me to the piano.

CHAPTER FORTY

Grady

SHE EASES beside me on the piano bench—two beauties I've denied myself together in the same place. She slips one hand behind me and flashes her sweet smile that encourages me to go on. With a deep breath, I close my eyes and think of Sara, for once letting the memories come, knowing it's time to let them go. Trading what *could've been* for what *is* makes room for the beautiful future that still could be.

That's what I want—a future with Marina.

When I finally lift the key lid, it's like releasing my paper boat and everything that should've made the page.

I don't sing, preferring quiet. I stroke the keys softly, and Norah Jones's "Come Away With Me" comes to life under my fingertips. I'm rusty and nervous at first. Tears blur my vision, thinking of times I played *this* piano. Memories slip through me onto the ivory keys and fade behind the slow, soulful notes, easing my guilt away with them.

I breathe. Straighten my back. And the song emerges like a gift, assuring me that it's okay to move on. To smile. To play.

To love again. Marina nestles to my side like she was always meant to fit there, and I feel like an ass for ever saying she was too-anything for me. She's only perfect.

I don't know when I stop playing or if I even finish the song. But drained of all those bad feelings, I lean against the keys, head low, and relax.

Truly relax.

Soon, Marina stands and shifts my left arm. I push the bench back, and she moves between my legs and the piano, her ass lightly grazing the keys. Her pink lips curl into a soft smile as she looks down at me. I'm struck by how beautiful and understanding she is. This couldn't have happened without her. The orange glow from the fireplace flecks her eyes like fireworks, and her gorgeous red hair trails down her shoulders like ribbons. She's my celebration. My heart's song.

I latch onto her by her hips, dragging her closer. My ear presses against her stomach, hearing the gentle thump of her heartbeat underneath. Her fingers slide around my neck and shoulders, accepting me fully. I caress her lower back, her hips, her ass, bringing her as close as possible like this.

But soon, she drags back, bumping the keys again. My gaze draws up as she starts unbuttoning her dress, opening herself up to me a few inches at a time. She smiles and nods when I find the bottom-most button and undo it, racing upwards to meet her.

Her dress falls open. Her hands drift to her sides as I explore her. Pink lace on pale, speckled skin, satin-soft and flushed warm, she's glowing and hopeful and sexy as fuck.

Her scars catch my gaze, and I trace them with my fingertips. The surgical incisions are barely there, just ghosts etched into her skin. The knife wound is darker, more jagged, and longer—a forever scar. The deeper scars within, I only imagine. My lips follow my fingers, kissing the wounds, tugging her into me, tears in my eyes once again. Loving her, kissing her pain away like I've longed to do all along.

Part of me wants to whisper *I'm sorry* one last time. Sorry for how I hurt you. Sorry for what I took from you. Sorry for what will never be.

But she doesn't need it. Neither do I. We are *exactly* as we should be. No more. No less. Just us. And that is enough.

My hands graze the edges of her pink panties, unabashedly discovering her. I steal a glance at her daring expression. Her eyes meet mine, and she nods again. I lock my fingers around the lace and rid her of them completely. The sweetest moan escapes her. I push her against the keys, instigating a clanging cacophony, before peppering her with delicate kisses. Her inner thighs. Her lower stomach. Then, the triangle between her legs. And when she whispers my name in a moan, I take her... desperately... fully... achingly in my mouth.

Her legs spread, hitting random keys, but the sound doesn't distract me from my feast. She perches one leg against the piano bench and wraps the other around my shoulder. I take my time, tasting, teasing, and then devouring her with my tongue. Her hands slip, banging the keys on her sides and creating a strangely beautiful background to this, her sweet undoing.

"Grady, please," she breathes out as she gets close.

My fingers push into her gently. Her breath hitches in a low moan. Then, she comes, convulsing deliciously against my fingers. I drink her up, relishing it. My dick aches against my jeans like it's never been this hard before—fuck, maybe it hasn't—but I'm patient. I want to take my time with her. Go slow and easy until I can't anymore.

Her legs return to the floor like she's melting off the piano. She fists my shirt at the neck, bringing me to her. "Kiss me, Grady."

She doesn't have to ask twice. Her kiss enflames every tight and throbbing muscle in my body with its sweet intensity. Her lips are strong, and her tongue playful as she taunts mine. Her hand slides down my chest to the bulge in my jeans, making me groan and bite her neck.

She laughs and utters breathlessly, "You are terribly overdressed."

"A problem easily remedied," I return, my tongue slipping behind her ear. "Want to move upstairs?"

Her eyes go wide, and she nibbles her bottom lip. "To your bedroom? For more? Absolutely, yes!"

A laugh catches in my throat, and she launches into a full-on giggle when I scoop her into my arms, whisk her through the living room, and carry her up the stairs. I lay her on the bed, but she doesn't stay there.

"Oh, Grady, this is..." She rushes to the sliding glass doors of the upper deck overlooking the backyard and lake. Moonlight highlights her as it does the water below. Even at night, it is a gorgeous view, but my eyes are fixed on her. She lingers at the doors, taking it all in, still wearing her dress, open like a robe.

She's the first woman I've had here. I already know she'll be the last, too. My last love. I move behind her, easing the dress off her shoulders and unclasping her bra. Everything falls to the floor. She twists in my arms but does nothing to shield herself from me.

Open. Lovely. Mine. All fucking mine. A truth I'll honor and take joy in every day for the rest of our lives. She smiles like she reads my mind and concurs with every thought. I want to explore her breasts with my mouth, play dot to dot on every freckle, and memorize every curve. But there's time, and tonight, I want to give her something I doubt she's had before.

I corner her against the glass, my hand perched over her shoulder and lean in. "How do you want me? What would you like?"

Surprise alights on her face, but then her brow pinches like she doesn't know how to answer. "Um, downstairs was nice."

"*That* was me saying thank you. *This* is the start of us." I edge closer and run my finger down her bare breast. "How do you want to play, Marina?"

Her mouth falls open in a giddy smile, blushing. "Truth?"

"Truth."

Her lips curl, matching my gaze like a predator ready to pounce. She presses her naked body into my clothed one, busily undoing me. My shirt lands in the clothes heap, followed quickly by my jeans and socks. Her eyes wander over my chest, her fingers drifting like feathers across my skin.

Then, she drops to her knees, bathed in moonlight and smirking like she's already won. She maneuvers me out of my underwear like she means to...

"Fucking hell, Marina," I sigh as my boxer briefs fall to the floor.

"Just a taste."

She kisses the head, sliding her tongue over it, and then slips me into her mouth, soft and slow, taking enough of me to make me groan, almost destroyed by it, especially when she reaches for my hand and gently places it against her cheek. She wants me to guide her, feel her doing this, to enjoy her fully, and to know I have her trust. In all my years, I've never felt anything more intimate. Or been so turned on with each tongue stroke.

I can't take it long, and I don't want our game to hit pause over this. Not tonight. I bring her back up to me, stroking her cheeks and pushing her hair away from her shoulders.

She smiles. "I like this game. Your turn."

"You're going to come again before you're ready for me. Get on the bed."

She obeys, shifting further onto the bed on her back. "Oh, Grady, I don't think you could possibly make me come again," she jokes, with a coy smirk that assures me she wants me to try.

She laughs when I crawl after her, stopping to kiss her feet, her legs, and her thighs. Then, I climb between her legs to continue my kisses up her stomach, her breasts, and the crook of her neck. I intend to kiss every inch of her, to worship her, tonight and every night after.

It doesn't take long until she's writhing with release again.

Whimpering, she tugs on my shoulders. "My turn. I need you in me."

I obey, positioning myself just right so that she feels me inside and against her at the same time. She moans at my sudden thrust. I groan over how damn wet and warm and tight she is. Just like with her mouth, I won't last long.

"My turn," I say, nearly fucking breathless. I shift her into my lap so she's straddling me and curse at how deep I get this way. Her back arches as she grinds against me. She drapes her arms across my shoulders, bringing me closer. We kiss as she rides me. I stroke her hair, and she rests her forehead on mine. Her soft smile captivates me, assuring me that this is as unbelievably good for her as it is for me. My hand drifts to her clit, bringing her with me as the beautiful pressure nears its end. Tangled like this, two feathers caught in the wind, we build and come together. Music. Magic. Pain. Sadness. True love. This is it. Always.

She stills, resting against me with my head on her chest, heartbeat racing underneath. "Three to one, I win," she chuckles lightly.

I laugh. "You have a distinct advantage, but I'll let you have it. The next round? We'll see."

Her giggle is infectious, and, damn, I don't giggle. But here I am, unraveling with her once again.

"I love you." The words jump from her like she can't contain them. Her brow pinches uncertainly as they escape. She shuts down her unease with, "I'm sure."

My mouth quirks into a smile, taking her in, kissing her lips, and squeezing her closer. "Then, I get the prize, after all." Her coy grin fills me with immense satisfaction. "I love you, too."

Her eyes dance over my face, flecked with moonlight and dilated with delight. My fingertips skip slowly down her back.

"I want to stay the night, sleep with you, wake up next to you," she whispers, nuzzling me. "Be here, like this, for as long as we can."

Her voice catches with sadness, creating the list like she thinks our time will run out.

I cup her cheeks, locking eyes with her. "*This* is us now. Stay tonight. Every night. Bring the cats. Move in. Or I'll be at yours with the dogs. I don't care. It doesn't matter where we are as long as we're together. *This* is home." I motion between us, and moonlight catches the gleam in her eyes.

She laughs, letting a tear slip. "We're Brady-Bunching our pets now?"

"Whatever it takes. I mean it. We are family. I'll say it as often as you need to hear it. Understood?"

She nods, holding back tears that make me hope she believes it.

"I've never been happier, Grady. Never." Her words are barely a whisper and sound sad.

Hearing her say that should please me, but it doesn't. For her, happiness is a mirage, a gorgeous, dream-like oasis in the desert that vanishes as soon as she gets close, and she believes this will disappear, too.

I'll prove otherwise.

CHAPTER FORTY-ONE

Grady

WE DON'T SLEEP MUCH, but it's still the most restful night I've had in years. My arms are empty when I wake, and the bed feels cold. I jerk up, rubbing my eyes to take in the room. She's gone.

I find her on the dock, a throw blanket caped around her naked body, staring at the lake as the sun rises. A misty fog lingers, waiting for the sun to burn it away. Orange bands peek through the towering pine trees, spotlighting the water in pieces, bringing color to the grayness.

That's what she's done for me—brought color to my grayness.

My arms lock around her, and she leans into me. I kiss her exposed shoulder. "You disappeared on me. I should've been clear—I wanted to wake up to you, too."

"Sorry. I wanted to see."

"Wake me, next time."

"Imagine waking up to this every day," she sighs. Since I *do* wake up to it every day, it seems like she's talking more to herself. "It's beautiful. I see why people pay big bucks to live here."

She takes a deep breath, twisting in my arms and smiling wide when she faces me. "Good morning." A soft kiss bookends her greeting. She wraps her blanket around me, crushing her naked body against me. Our kiss deepens in a breath, and damn if I don't want to take her right then and there. Against a dock post. In my deck chair.

On the pier itself. Hell, even in the water. I don't care. I belong to her now.

Like she's read my mind, her hand slips over my pajama pants, gripping me. The blanket falls off one shoulder, exposing her breast. And she smiles over my sharp inhale, seeing her like this. We are raw from kissing. Raw from fucking. Yet, I want her again, desperately, like we haven't spent the last eight hours this way.

She agrees without a word when she lets the blanket fall to her feet.

Naked Marina, drenched in morning sun. Achingly beautiful.

A protective pang rips through me, scanning our surroundings. I don't want anyone to see her. She is for me. But it's a quiet nook of the lakefront. It's early, and the mist acts like a shield. I hope.

She backs against a post, and I follow, devouring her lips, her neck, as she wraps her legs around me. She moans full-on when I push inside, scaring birds into flight nearby, which makes her laugh. I love that she's having fun with me. That she wants me like this. That dock-fucking might become a thing for us, like playing chess and impromptu *things* at Rebellion.

I want us to have so many things.

After, we shower. She lets me braid her hair, a much sexier activity than the first time I did it. We fix breakfast. Over coffee on the back porch, we make plans. It's Sunday. Barring any emergencies, we're both off. She wants to play chess and learn how to fish.

I'm in heaven.

Her ringing phone breaks our peaceful moment. She rushes inside, searching for it in her bag.

"Wren?" she answers. "Everything—"

In the heavy pause, her demeanor changes, light to dark, in a cold second.

"What?" Her voice trembles before she swallows a lump in her throat and seems to return to herself. "Yes, I'm sorry, Wren. I hate that you're in that position. I'll be there in five minutes."

She ends the call and calmly reports, "There's a woman at my door claiming to be my mother. Wren doesn't know what to do."

It's impossible to gauge her reaction—she's stoic like her shields went up at the word *mother*.

"It's okay." I grab my keys and offer a weak smile. "Let's go. Whatever happens, I've got you."

I don't know if she hears me because she's already pulling on her sweater and reaching for her bag. I follow her outside. In The Beast, she says nothing, even when I prompt her, only stares out the window and fidgets with her fingers.

The Beast squeaks to a stop behind an old, red Honda Pilot, packed to the brim with stuff, even on the luggage rack. Wren leans against the front door, closed behind her, like a sentry at a castle. A woman in her late forties with flaming red hair stands on the porch steps, unquestionably Marina's mother.

She brightens when we pull in, a smile that is all too familiar, and she quick-steps to greet us. Marina's breath hitches beside me, and she's out of the truck before I put it in park.

They embrace, and it lingers.

I shouldn't be surprised. Marina is the most understanding and forgiving person I've ever met. When she told me about her mom, it was clear how much she missed her.

Her mom seems to have missed her, too. She runs her bright fingernails down her daughter's arms, beaming over how beautiful she is. Marina fiddles with her mom's hair, lined with gold streaks to make it look like flames.

"Mom, this is Grady Tripp," Marina says, pulling her toward me. "My boyfriend."

"Hey, I'm Leonie." She shakes my hand. "Good to meet you. Oh, I remember the Tripps from the salon."

"Nice to meet you, Leonie."

She perks up. "Hey, if you two get married, you'll be the Strange-Tripps."

Marina and I glance at each other, mouths open at the obvious thing neither of us thought about, while Leonie cackles delightedly.

"Um, that's... we're only dating, Mom," Marina says awkwardly, and I try not to take offense at the word *only*.

"Are you here long?" I ask, hoping light conversation will bring us some answers.

"Um, well—"

Thumps running down the porch stairs draw our attention. A little girl with bright red hair and freckles scurries up and takes Leonie's side unsurely. I imagine Marina must've looked just like her at that age.

"She has cats, Mom," the girl says, "and games and lots of plants."

"Wren let her in to use the bathroom," Leonie explains. "It was a long drive."

Marina gasps beside me. "Who is this?"

Leonie wags her finger at Marina. "You didn't read my letters, huh? That's okay." Her hands go up submissively. "I don't blame you. I was in a bad way back then, and, anyway, water under the bridge, I hope. This is your sister, Matilda. Everyone calls her Tilly."

The little girl sticks her hand toward Marina. "Nice to meet you. I've always wanted to know you."

Marina drops to her knees, bare against the gravel. She shakes the girl's hand, ogling her with wide eyes. It's hard to tell if she wants to laugh or scream.

Tilly laughs at her sister's attention. "Mom, I think the cats got her tongue."

Leonie chuckles. "No, honey. She's just surprised, that's all."

No fucking shit, surprised.

"It's nice to meet you, Tilly," Marina finally says, her usual smile barely there. "Hope you like cats, plants, and games."

"Oh, yes. Never had a cat before, but I think I like them."

Leonie gives Tilly a nudge. "Tell them about yourself."

"I'm seven, but I read middle-school books. I'm in second grade," she peers up at her mom, "Mom says I might go to school here."

"Honey, go grab your Switch, huh? Let the grown-ups talk," Leonie says. Tilly shrugs and obeys.

Leonie laughs once she's on the porch, game console in hand. "It's all video games these days. Glad you weren't into that when you were little, Marnie."

"Mom, what're you doing here?" she asks flatly.

Leonie's eyes drift to mine like she wants me to go. I stand firm, folding my arms over my chest and raising my brow to urge her to answer the fucking question.

"Mel told me what happened with the wedding and the accident," she says. "I thought you might need me."

"*That's* when you thought I needed you? That was months ago."

Leonie rolls her eyes, waving her hand toward her other daughter. "Well, you know how it is. We were in Arizona. I had to... figure things out before I moved us across the country."

"Moved?" Marina shoots back. "You're moving here?"

"Thought we'd give it a shot if you're okay with it," she says, glancing my way again. "Maybe we could talk about this privately?"

"He stays."

"Okay." She huffs. "Marnie, I'm so much better now. I'm on meds and in therapy. My doctor and I meet virtually, so it doesn't matter where I am. I haven't had an episode in over a year. After Tilly, I got my act together. I told you all about it in the letters."

Marina stiffens beside me. After Tilly, she got her shit together? Why not before? Why not *for* Marina?

"I'm glad you're doing well, Mom," Marina sighs. "It's all I ever wanted for you. But I don't know what you want from me."

"I wanted to know that you're okay," she answers.

"I'm okay."

"I want you to know your sister and for her to know you. I want us to be a family again. I've told her about you, all our old stories."

"*All* our stories?" Marina demands.

"Well, no. She's seven. But all the good ones."

Marina shifts on her feet, folding her arms. I unfold mine, slipping an arm around her.

"Look, I know this is a lot. I probably should've had Mel give you a heads up that we were coming," Leonie says. "Why don't we just go inside and talk? I'll make some coffee. Breakfast, too. How about cinnamon pancakes? Oh, you used to love those. We're starving. Tilly and I can tell you all our adventures. Bring Mr. Beefcake here, too. Then, we can figure things out from there. Okay?"

Now, I stiffen. She wants to fix breakfast and serve guests like she's already moved in and made herself at home. And I'm the outsider?

"Do you have money? Some place else to go?" I interject, going for gentle but failing.

Her eyes cut to me like I have no business asking the question as if she hasn't just barged in on *our* family.

"That's a bit insulting," she huffs, cutting her eyes to Marina. "He's a little old for you, huh, Marnie?"

"Answer him, please."

"Yes, I have money." She rolls her sky-blue eyes. "I *always* find a place to go. We Strange girls know how to survive and thrive. Right, Marnie?"

Marina's eyes catch mine, her smile gone. The easy afterglow of our incredible night together vanishes into sad resignation, like she expected this. As if the universe routinely whacks her down the second things go well. She looks completely lost.

Lost over what she lost.

"Did you even *keep* my letters?" her mom asks, disappointed. "Was I *really* that bad?"

"You *left* her." I scoff—this woman is another version of fucking Cora, all judgments and manipulations. "It was your job to be her mother, not her job to bother with your shit apologies. Don't put this on her."

Her hands go up in a wall. "Alright, beefcake. No need to get upset. I'm fully aware of the million and one ways I let Marnie down. That's why I'm here—to make up for it. But that's between us. We're family."

"My name is *Grady*. Stop throwing the word *family* around like you know what it means. *Family* would've been by her side the day she was hurt. *Family* never would have left her in the first place."

She winces and shuffles backward, and I immediately regret my harshness for Marina's sake, especially when her hand goes to my arm to stifle me.

"Grady," Marina breathes out, "please. Mom, give us a minute."

Leonie wanders over to Tilly and sits beside her on the porch steps.

"Look, I'm sorry." My hand rakes over my head. "I don't mean to be a jerk, but please don't be nice to her. She'll move in and take over. You should say no."

"Would you? Would you say no, Grady?"

No, of course, I wouldn't. I don't even say no when I should. I hang my head, bothered. "Fine. I'll play nice."

"Good." I move toward the house, but Marina drops her hand onto my chest, stopping me. "Um, could you take Wren home? I'll, um, reach out later. Catch a few fish for me, eh?"

"Wait, what? You want me to leave?"

"I should handle this alone," she says.

"I disagree. She'll take advantage. She already is. You aren't responsible for her."

"That's a bit hypocritical. Don't you think?"

My shoulders slump in a frustrated sigh.

"Please give me time to assess this situation. She'll be more open without someone else around."

"More open to manipulate you," I counter. "Let me be your buffer."

"I don't need a buffer. I can handle her. Trust me, please."

"Marina, it's not that I don't trust you. This is fucked up. I'm worried about you."

"I know," she smiles weakly. "Me, too. I'm overrun with big feelings and don't know where to land. Should I be angry at her? Sad that I've missed seven years with my sister? Judgy and pissed that she keeps having kids when she couldn't even finish her job with me? Tell me, Grady. How am I supposed to be?"

"I don't know. Cautious, for one thing. Not *nice*." My hands run up and down her arms—none of those options sound like her. "What do you *want* to be, Marina? How do you want to feel?"

"Happy." She chokes on a sigh. "I'm in love. I'm strong and free; nothing she can do will break me, even if she tries. I might have a chance at a family again." She falls into my arms, landing exactly where she belongs. "I'm just having a moment, Grady."

"Just? This feels like more than a moment. But take as many as you need."

Still latched on, she peers up at me, her bright blues even brighter somehow. "I love you. But I'm asking you, politely, to back the hell off. You said I could do that, remember?"

"Marina," I breathe, ready to argue.

But she presses her head to my chest. "I refused her once. I can't do it again." Her words muffle against my shirt. "She's my mom. I have a *sister*. Please, Grady."

I fucking hate this. I don't trust Leonie not to bulldoze through Marina's life and break her heart again. I also know Marina's too good-hearted to stop her. Her pushing me out feels even worse.

But she wants me to go, and I can't refuse her anything.

"Fine, but here's what's going to happen. Come to my place for dinner tonight. All of you. I promise to behave, make it nice. It'll help us get to know each other."

Her soft smile makes me feel slightly better. "Okay, that's a good idea."

I leave after a lingering kiss that I don't want to end.

Marnie

MOM CUTS MY HAIR. An hour into our visit, she says, "You have wicked dead ends, sweetie. Let me take care of that for you," and, perhaps needing her attention, I can't resist. She gets her kit from the car. We scoot a chair out from the kitchen table, and she makes the sunlight flicker when she flips out her signature leopard-print cape. It's just like the old days.

She fingers Grady's braid loose, fanning my locks and scrutinizing them. "So, what happened to the Sullivan you were supposed to marry?"

"We didn't work out." It's an obvious answer, but it spills out. "Ashe couldn't handle hard times well."

"Huh, better you found that out before you walked down the aisle." She unsheathes her expensive tools, arranging her combs and scissors on the table. "What have I always said? Men can't be trusted. They never do what they say they'll do."

"That's not always true," I say gently. "Grady's not like that. If you stick around, you'll see."

Old Mom would've jumped into a whirlwind defense of her long-held beliefs about men, highlighting proof, particularly centered around my deadbeat father. I barely remember him. As a teenager, I wanted to argue against her, to ask why, then, did we know so many happy couples in Seagrove, men who loved their wives and stayed.

Why did that rule seem to apply *only* to her? And why did she keep finding men if she truly believed it?

But often, I didn't have the energy to argue, not that she would've heard me. When Mom got ideas in her head, she rarely, if ever, shifted them. So, I kept quiet, managing our household peace like it was my job—school, chores, and keeping Mom calm.

She moves to the front of the chair, eyeing me. "Always so pretty, Marnie. You've only gotten prettier, you know?"

A weak smile pushes out, though it makes me feel awkward. "Thanks."

She kneels before me, straightening the cape and resting her hands on my knees. "I'm so sorry, Marnie. I should've said it then, *that* night. But I was so ashamed. I knew I didn't deserve your forgiveness, even if you gave it to me. Finding out about the play and that you couldn't tell me about it—which I understand now, but I couldn't take it then. I induced a manic episode with pills and booze, creating the perfect storm that rained all over you. You didn't deserve what I put you through... not that night. Not all the years before. It was unfair, you managing my condition while I just went wherever it took me. God—I'm sorry. I never gave you a chance to be a kid."

She shuts her eyes to the tears springing in them. *Mom cries?*

"I never should've left," she goes on, "Never should've run from you and what I caused. I never wanted to be without you. I knew you'd be okay—you were always okay. I also knew that I needed to be okay without you—"

I bolt from my seat, the chair scraping out from under me. "You're my mother. How could you ever think I'd be okay without you? I was fifteen."

Mom steps back, nodding as tears spit from her eyes. "You're right."

I scoff and decide not to be nice. "I don't want to hear I'm right. I *know* I'm right. I want you to explain *how* you could do that to me. How you could leave me. How you could wake up every morning after and decide not to come back again."

I keep my voice low for Tilly, sleeping on the couch nearby, but inside, I'm screaming the words. My arms fold over the cape, awaiting her answer.

Her arms wave off her hips as she shakes her head. "I *hated* myself, Marnie. That day and every day after for what I did to you. I convinced myself you were better off without me, and I was too cowardly to set anything right. Mel kept tabs on you. I wrote the letters, hoping for another chance, but you didn't answer. I assumed you didn't want me back, and I didn't blame you after the burden I'd been. When I finally got my disorder under control, I decided it was too late."

Too late. My arms fall to my sides—that's how I felt about her when her letters came. "But you kept sending the letters."

"I never lost hope," she cries, taking a small step forward. "Send me away tonight, and I'll still send them. I'll always send them, just in case."

"Why now? *Why?*"

"Mel told me about the accident. I thought that if there were ever a time you might let me back into your life, it'd be when yours had gone so wrong. Not that I wanted it to go wrong... It's just... I hoped you'd *need* me—and that's selfish, I know, and dumb because you're so much stronger than me. Maybe it sounds crazy, but I *felt* that you needed me."

I nod weakly. *That* day replays in my head, a montage of all the times I wanted her there. "I did need you."

"I'm here, now."

"I can't forgive you, Mom."

She swipes her wet cheeks with her fingers. "I understand."

"I might, though. Someday."

A smile breaks through her distress. "That's good enough for me."

"But here's what's going to happen," I say, stealing Grady's words. "You can stay here temporarily, but you must find your own place if you plan to stay."

"Of course."

"I want time with Tilly—just me and her."

"Absolutely."

"If your disorder gets out of control again—if I *tell you* it's out of control—you must promise me..." I swallow the lump in my throat and almost can't say the words, but I need her to know how serious I am. "...you'll stay and get help and entrust Tilly to me."

With a deep breath, she nods. "Yes, Marnie. I will. I promise."

I look for signs of deception, some hint that she's only saying what I want to hear. But I don't find any. Instead, she looks relieved.

"Okay," I say after a short silence, repositioning the chair. I take my place again. "Please, cut my hair, Mom."

She wipes her cheeks. "It'd be my pleasure."

"I'm sorry I didn't read your letters," I offer as she brushes my long locks.

"Eh, I get it. Why settle for Hallmark when you deserved a mother? Hope you saved them, though. I put money in those when I could."

I scoff-laugh, rolling my eyes. "I had no idea. Well, reading them now will be like a treasure hunt."

She takes a deep breath. "Thanks, sweetheart. I don't deserve a second chance, but I'm grateful for it."

I melt, nibbling my bottom lip and hoping she means it. She seems different than I remember, and even if she isn't, I can't miss a chance to have a family again. "That's good, Mom, because I'm the queen of second chances."

"Don't you worry about a thing. I'll find Tilly and me a place. It's not like we can all fit here for long."

"I won't have it much longer, anyway. Mercy Pike's replacing me with her sister, Charity."

"Geez, I bet Charity's as generous as a rabid raccoon if Mercy's any indication." Mom laughs, rolling her eyes. "I'll find a place for all three of us if you want. Or help you find your own place. I'm not here to intrude, Marnie. I have money, and Mel's offered me a job. I promise, you won't need to take care of us. But Tilly needs a family. She needs her big sister. Maybe you need us, too."

I smile as she continues her work. Grady fills the emptiness of my losses and loneliness, but Mom's words cover the small gaps, spreading warmth and joy all through me. Maybe I shouldn't trust her. Maybe this is only temporary until the next "better place" she races to find. But for now, in this kitchen, with the sun streaming in, her fingers running through my hair, and a sister snoozing on my couch surrounded by happy cats, it's a chance I'm willing to take.

"I know a place you could go," I say, thinking of the beautiful swamp and my band of misfits. "You can stay here until we get things sorted."

"Thanks, honey." She fluffs my long, wavy locks. "So, what're we thinking? Just a trim? Long layers? A new look?"

"Um, long layers would be nice."

"So, let's play salon like we used to," she says. "Tell me all the *hot goss* like my clients do."

I giggle. It was a game we played when I was little, and I didn't want to get my haircut. She'd sit me down and tell me outlandish stories from the salon, using funny voices. "What do you want to know?"

"Mel tells me you aren't at Sunny's anymore. What happened there?"

I start talking, like she's switched my lever from a trickle to a waterfall just by being here. I tell her everything—my relationship with Ashe and the Sullivans, the accident, and all that's happened like a news broadcast. She listens. She gasps. When I tell her I can't have children, she stops her work and swallows me in a massive embrace.

"It's not a problem. It's an opportunity," she says. "The world is full of people to love and good work for you to do. You will have a full, wonderful life without them or, if you want them, there's no such thing as *can't*. Not for Marnie Strange."

"Thanks, Mom. That makes me feel better," I say because it's true.

"A man worth your time will love you for who you are, not what you can give him," she adds, waving her scissors. "Dang, those rotten Sullivans."

"Grady loves me like that."

"You really like this guy?" When I nod, a warm smile emerges under her fiery hair. "Then, so do I. I promise I won't be snippy next time. He's just looking out for you. I respect that."

"He's invited us for dinner tonight."

"Lovely! I can't wait to get to know him," she says, spritzing my hair with water. "I hope you're completely yourself with him... and him with you."

"Being yourself is the key to true happiness... and true love."

"That's been my problem, I think. Your father, Tilly's, they never really knew me. I hid behind my ravishing smile and beautiful hair," she laughs. "Not anymore. If I ever date again, it'll be *all me*, on my terms, open and honest. Course, that'll scare most of 'em away."

Tilly wanders into the kitchen, rubbing her tired eyes. "Oh, no, haircuts?"

"Yep, you're next," Mom says. "We have to look our best for dinner tonight. Everyone used to be crazy over those Tripps. I get it. He's *so* handsome."

"Mom!" Tilly and I groan together, which makes us giggle. Having an ally with Mom might be nice.

CHAPTER FORTY-THREE

Grady

I NEARLY REPEAT the mistake I made with our first dinner date—inviting the whole family over as camouflage. I don't, but I considered it. It's easier to avoid conflict when hosting a crowd. The noise alone might drive out my anxieties. I don't like that Leonie's here, don't trust her, and know that, chances are, Marina will be hurt in the end.

But my misgivings aren't shared. It's all smiles and warmth when they pour into my house. Marina leads, giving me a quick hug. Then, her mom does the same, thanking me for having them over. And Tilly, not to be left out, latches onto my waist before yelling, "Dogs!" and rushing to play with them.

They've brought wine and dessert—a chocolate dream cake from Saddletree Farm and Café, which they promise was worth the half-hour drive.

"Especially with the top down in that cute truck of hers—a truck with a name. Beauty is a beaut," Leonie adds, taking everything to the kitchen.

I seize the opportunity for a quiet moment with Marina and tug her close. "Everything okay? Has she asked for money? Are you letting them stay at your place?"

"Relax, Grady. I think it'll be alright."

"Really?"

"She's different. Better."

"What about you? How are *you* with them here?"

She smiles. "Well, it was shocking, but I felt good after we talked. Don't worry. I wasn't *nice*."

"Good. You shouldn't be."

She leans up and gives me a short kiss. "We've come to an understanding. She apologized and wants a second chance."

"Yeah, but for how long?"

Marina shrugs. "I don't know. Does it matter?"

I nod, glancing at Tilly rolling around the floor with the dogs. Maybe it doesn't. Marina knows to take her joys when she can get them. That's a lesson I need to learn, too. To not always think in what-ifs, worries, and obligations. It's enough to be here and now with the woman I love and basking in the hope of second chances.

"It takes as long as it takes, right?" she smirks. "Let's show her what family really means, huh?"

My hardened heart liquifies and swirls around her. "I love you so much. Anything you say becomes my new mission."

She laughs. "Oh, with great power comes great responsibility. I'll have to be careful not to take advantage."

"No, please. Take advantage," I grin.

The evening passes pleasantly. Leonie and Tilly regale us with stories about their travels and experiences over wine, soda, and make-your-own pizzas off the grill. They're charming, outgoing, and funny, just like Marina. And easy to like.

Marina could be right that things are different. I hope she is.

Still, when Marina and Tilly go inside to get everyone's dessert, I lean forward, locking eyes with Leonie across the table. "I love your daughter. Her happiness is my own. I'll protect her fiercely. I won't let her be manipulated or mistreated—she's just gone through that, and it won't happen again. Stay and behave, and you'll earn my respect, even love. Don't, and your second chance will be your last with her. Understood?"

She blanches but recovers in a breath, offering a soft smile. "Yes, Grady. Understood and appreciated. You're intense and don't mince words. I like that. You care for her. I like that, too. I can't fault you for having doubts about me. But I love her, too. I'm fiercely determined to win my daughter back, and you better not stand in the way. Is *that* understood?"

Her brow cocks, and her lips curl, and I can't help but warm to her. Not only did she match my intensity, but she also seems sincere. Hell, I'm even rooting for her.

I hold my wine glass up, and she grabs her diet soda, meeting me in the middle. "To Marina, then."

"To Marnie." She takes a healthy sip. "Let's get another thing clear. Is it love or guilt driving your intentions with her?"

I scrub my slackened jaw over the surprise question, and that Marina must've opened up to her. "Love, obviously."

"Is it obvious?" Her narrowed eyes focus on me. She flicks her fingernails like sweeping a bug out of the air before pointing at me. "I don't want my daughter heartbroken *again* when you feel like you've paid your penance and decide you want kids the ol' fashioned way after all."

I scoff. "Mothering on her behalf already? You've got some nerve."

"Told you. I'm in. For good. What about you, Grady Tripp?"

I lean forward with my sternest glare. "All that I have, all that I am, is hers. Now. Forever. I love her. Never question that again."

Her eyes widen, and her hands go up submissively. "Gosh, I felt that in my bones. I guess time will prove it for both of us, then. Huh?"

Marina and Tilly arrive, arms full of plates, and the subject drops. Leonie has won my respect, somewhat, and bothered me at once. I adore Marina—that won't go away. But I wonder if she has doubts like her Mom. I wonder if she trusts it yet, if she has faith in me. In us.

My mission isn't just to show Leonie what family means, but to assure Marina that's what this is.

"Your boyfriend was just telling me how crazy he is about you, Marnie," Leonie coos. "He's a sweetheart. Any other single Tripps I should know about?"

"Mom!" Marina and Tilly snap at once.

"What? We're here. Might as well see what Seagrove has to offer, right?" she laughs.

Marina settles beside me, her hand squeezing my thigh under the table. "How about we explore other amenities first? Like housing? The library?"

"The school!" Tilly chimes in.

The chocolate cake melts in my mouth—definitely worth the drive. But even sweeter is Marina's hand locking with mine under the table.

CHAPTER FORTY-FOUR

Marnie

ACCOMMODATING three people and three cats in my small place is a challenge—I don't know how Mom and I did it. Of course, I didn't have a room devoted to game-making or a living room full of cat towers back then. But, we make do.

Tilly is a curious bundle of adorable excitement. She raves about Grady's place, the dogs, the cats, my truck, and even my place. She happily takes on chores like watering the plants, feeding the cats, and helping with dishes like she's desperate for a normal home life.

I remember how that felt. I also remember how lonely a nomadic life was—I don't want that for Mom or Tilly if I can help it. They stayed at their last place for three years—a new record for Mom. So, maybe there's hope that they'll find a permanent home here, especially with a support system.

Soon, when tapped out on self-assigned chores, Tilly crashes. I give her and Mom my bed—it makes more sense. And when the house is quiet and my guests completely taken care of, I let Mom know that I'm heading to Grady's for "a game of chess."

"Is that what you kids are calling it these days?" She laughs before kissing my cheek. "See you in the morning."

The night air whips through my hair on the short drive to Grady's, making me cold, but I like it. I want Grady to warm me. The last twelve hours have been an emotional flood, overrunning me with love and excitement, but also fears and misgivings—I am mentally spent. Through it all, I've latched on to how I *want* to feel, as Grady said, and trusted my feelings to lead me as they should go. And the overwhelming feeling now is how desperate I am to get back to him.

Every part of me aches for him.

I've got no complaints about my previous sex life. I've had very capable, enjoyable partners. But I didn't realize what was missing, how much *more* sex could be with someone like Grady Tripp.

A strong connection magnifies everything. Touches feel electric. Kisses feel intoxicating. Everything is more intense, deeper, and breathtaking.

I knew sex. I didn't know sex like this. And that's not simply because I've moved from an emotional baby pool to the vast and tumultuous deep end. It's because of him.

Grady makes loving me an art, an act of worship, his magnum opus. I have *never* been loved like this. I feel it pulsing through his veins and charging my core. His intensity invigorates me. Frees me. He makes me more myself than I've ever been.

That's what I need tonight—to be myself with him.

It's nearly eleven when I pull in next to The Beast, moon high and lights low. Tomorrow's a work day. I bet he's sleeping. Sitting in the driver's seat, twisting the steering wheel in my hands, I second-guess myself. A sigh putters out of me—I never told him I was coming. Never even hinted. It's been such an overwhelming day. Should I be here?

But then, I remember what he said. *Anytime for any reason.* I exit Beauty anyway.

The porch light blinks as I approach, and I find a note on the door.

Marina,

It's open. Meet me on the upper deck.

Grady

I choke on a gasp, snatch the note off the door, and go inside. It's dark. The dogs sleep peacefully around the fireplace, barely noticing me. I lock the door behind me, kick off my shoes, and follow the light glowing from upstairs. I traipse through his quiet bedroom to the sliding glass doors.

The deck is aglow with white lights over the railings and soft lanterns tucked in corners. A thick pile of blankets and pillows occupies the wide flooring. A table in the corner holds wine and snacks, and soft music plays from somewhere I can't see. Grady leans against the deck railing, facing me with a soft smile.

It all comes over me at once. Remnants of my lonely, scared, and difficult childhood butt up against the joy of Mom's return. *I have a sister!* And a sweet second chance at a family I thought I'd lost and didn't know I had. Hope battles leftover resentment and anger—yes, I had it tough, but I'm stronger for it.

Even so, I ache for thinking I wasn't enough. For all the time and energy I spent being the go-to girl for the Sullivans. For fooling myself into false love and what would've been a fake family.

Now that I know what family truly feels like, fear edges in. Letting Mom back in means I could lose her again. Lose Tilly. I'm devastated for the seven years I've missed with her already. I ache for lost time, and time I don't want to lose as a big sister. Even being a big sister strikes fear into me. All this fear and regret compound into relief, too, thanks to him.

He holds his arms open to me. An emotional tidal wave hits me, so overcome with feelings that I can barely reach him. I fall apart. He catches me. Once in his arms, I break down, crying.

Crying!

Bawling into his shoulder, the strength of our connection strikes me. He knew I'd show up, knew I needed him, and did all this for me.

"This is me falling apart," I blubber, reminded of that night in the hospital when he held my hand, and feeling grateful that we're beyond that now.

"I know, darling," he says, holding me tighter. "Is everything okay with your mom and Tilly?"

I nod against him. "Better than okay. It's... lovely. And frightening."

"I have a good feeling about it, though. Don't you?"

"Yes, but I needed us. I came here for sex, but then, seeing that note and you, it all caught up with me at once."

He laughs. "You get the prize for holding it together this long."

"I'm a smidge overwhelmed," I confess.

He nods. "Rightly so. Tell me what's upset you."

My shoulders bounce in an I-don't-know. "All of it. None of it. It's all too much. She apologized to me... in tears, Grady. I want to believe her, but how can I?"

"It's a risk. She'll have to earn your trust again. It'll take time. The longer she's here, the more you'll relax into it."

"And Tilly. Oh, my God, Tilly. She's an adorable bundle of sweetness and smarts. It kills me that I've lost so much time with her, but at the same time, I'm scared to death. I don't know how to be a big sister."

"Yes, you do," Grady laughs. "You already are a big sister. Look what you've done for Marigold and Wren. They adore you, and you've done all you can to help and encourage them. That's what it's all about—loving and supporting them."

I wipe my tears, thinking of my sweet friends. "You're right. I'm good at loving and supporting people I care about."

He chuckles. "See? It's easy. It'll be even easier with Tilly because you know exactly what her life has been like."

I take a breath. "Yeah, I do."

He leads me over to the cushy space he's created. "Get comfortable and have some wine. The more you talk, the less overwhelmed you'll feel."

Sinking into the blankets and pillows, I feel nested—warm and protected. He hands me a glass of wine, and, between sips, I tell him everything, from Mom's sweet apology to my un-niceness to my housing problem.

"Move in with me," he says with zero hesitation. "I want you to, anyway."

"Do you always ask women to move in after only *one* date?" I joke.

"Never. You will always be the exception," he says, making me swoon.

I match his intense stare with my own, considering it. Saying *yes* goes against my hard-earned independence and good common sense. It feels too soon.

But Grady's my exception, too. If he isn't my soulmate, then soulmates don't exist.

"I'll think about it," I finally say.

His lips curl into a sexy smile. "Fair enough. Think about it. Think hard, though."

I laugh. "I will."

"Perhaps a preview of what that'd be like will get a *yes* out of you," he says, making me giggle as he moves closer.

"It couldn't hurt," I say.

He moves our wine glasses aside and scoots toward me on his knees. I expect him to meet me where I am, lying on the blankets and pillows and ravishing me with kisses. Instead, he holds out his hand.

"Come here, Marina."

He reaches out for me, and I meet him there. He brushes my fingers with his lips. "I love holding your hand."

He pecks each finger before kissing my palm and then my wrist. His touches are soft and delicate, yet my heart rate kicks into a wild flurry. He takes my other hand and does the same, his touch almost featherlike.

"These hands that create games and carry notebooks and rescue things," he whispers, his voice raspy.

A breathless giggle escapes.

"Rescued me." He sets my arms around his neck, his fingers dancing down them. Goosebumps break out over his soft touch and the night air.

"I love these arms that steer the ship across the high seas," he grins, and I laugh. "I love them most when they're around me."

I want to speak, but I'm breathless and captivated by him. His fingertips skate over my neck and collarbone and then down the front of my dress. He finds the hem and lifts it over my head.

His hand falls over my raging heart. "I love this heart... that always makes room for everyone."

He leans down and kisses my chest, his lips lingering there. "I love that it has the most room for me."

His hands slide around my back, unclasping my bra. He tugs it away and eyes me lovingly.

"I love this body. Every freckle. Every scar. Every beautiful curve," he says, his fingers traveling over my breasts before cupping them. His thumbs drag over my nipples, making me moan. I swear my heart might ram out of my chest—loving every second of his attention but desperate for him to give me more.

More, Grady. More. I almost whimper.

His hands slide under my panties, yanking me closer by my ass. I cry out again, and he smiles.

"I love every moan," he whispers, his breath hitting my lips, "when you're breathless, when you come."

I tug on his shirt, nearly ripping it as I yank it off him. My hands tremble, undoing his pants.

"I love the desperate way you love me."

"I am desperate, Grady," I manage.

He smiles with soft satisfaction while I die for him. My hands race over his bare chest, but he grabs them, holding them still.

"I love that when you fall apart, it's only with me," he says, his voice almost stern.

He turns me around, pressing me to him with an arm wrapped over my breasts. With the other hand, he tugs my hair to one side, kissing my bare shoulder. I lean against him, head tilting toward the night sky. He twists my long locks in his hand like a rope he's winding. I love the pressure of him holding me like that, keeping me positioned exactly how he wants me.

With a hand on my back, he bends me forward on all fours, still holding my hair. My back arches to accommodate him. He yanks my underwear down in one tug. Then, his fingers claw gently down my back.

"I love you, Marina. Forever in my heart. Forever in my bed—if I have my way," he says, one hand holding my hair and the other rubbing my ass. "Tell me you love me."

"I fucking love you, Grady," comes my breathy reply. "Please."

I hear him chuckle behind me—I don't cuss often. Then, he rams himself inside me, one beautiful, aching, forceful thrust that makes me cry out and beg him for more.

"Damn, Marina," he groans. He takes me again, slowly. Savoring it. Exploring me.

His pace soon quickens, and I think he's getting close.

But then, he brings me to him, pulling my back against his chest and ravishing my neck. His dick stills inside me as he holds me in his lap. His hand slips around to my front, finding my clit. I relax, savoring his touch, as he whispers, "You first."

I grind against him as he rubs me. "Let's go together," I challenge.

"You first," he demands, "then together."

I give in, his stern voice enough to send me over the edge. He braces me against him, still inside me, as I tremble and fall apart all over again.

"Good," he breathes against my ear. "I love making you come."

Then, he maneuvers me to the bedding and massages my thighs as he hovers over me. Climbing between my legs, he kisses me, desperate, tongue-laced, intense kisses that fire every atom in my body at once. Reenergized by it, I push him onto his back and climb on top.

"I love making *you* come," I say, shifting my hips and forcing him deep inside me. He watches me, moving up and down him, nibbling his bottom lip. I smile, loving his eyes on me. He grabs my hips, pulling and pushing with my rhythm.

Soon, his eyes roll back, and he mutters, "FUCK, Marina."

"Say you love me again," I demand sweetly.

"I fucking love you," he grunts.

I go deeper, making him moan, and grind myself against him, wanting every inch of him I can get. "Now, show me."

His grip tightens, and his face contorts at my command, and I feel him spill inside me. His heat, his pulsing dick, bring me to my breaking point again, and I convulse with aching, intense, beautiful pleasure.

He holds me there, watching, and his hand rests over my heart like he wants to bring us down together. My hand falls atop his as I slow my breathing.

He groans. "Fucking hell, Marina," he breathes out. "How does it keep getting better?"

I chuckle and collapse beside him. "I don't know. But I'm okay with it."

He leans over, kissing my shoulder and then my lips. "Pretty good argument for moving in, huh?"

An owl hoots in the trees high above us. His smile matches mine at the sound. We're outside, surrounded by trees, darkness, and soft lights, and nothing could be more perfect.

"The pros list is pretty long and impressive," I admit, "but I need to think about it."

A slight twinge of disappointment flashes, though he says, "Of course."

I curl closer, kissing his chest and shoulder. "Grady, I've never felt so loved. That's enough, right? For tonight?"

He scoff-smiles. "It's enough tonight or any night. This is all I want. You and me, together."

I nod, grateful and in a perpetual blush over everything that's happened. "Should we go inside? Go to bed?"

He shakes his head. "Hell, no. You and me, under the stars."

"Won't we get cold?"

"Darling, I'll keep you warm. I promise."

I believe him. And I get my wish—naked Marnie in a Tripp Grady Tripp nest.

CHAPTER FORTY-FIVE

Marnie

MONDAY MORNING AT THE G&G, I'm met with a bewildering surprise. It's not even eight when I pull up, ready to organize my thoughts for our 10 o'clock all-hands meeting. But despite the early hour, I find not one but all three of my misfits—Wade, Christie, and Roy—already at work and dressed up.

"You fellas look... nice. What's all this?" I ask, approaching the counter and eyeing their new looks.

Christie's long gray hair is swept up into a high man-bun, neat and tidy. He's freshly shaven, wearing lip gloss, and donning his mother's emerald earrings, which I already know, he only brings out on special occasions. He's in a silky Bermuda shirt, jeans, and Birkenstocks rather than his usual clogs.

Wade's improvements are more subtle. His trimmed beard matches his tucked-in plaid button-down and combed-back hair.

Roy has undergone a total makeover. His jeans, dirty t-shirts, and falling-apart sneakers have been replaced with what I call 80s biker couture. His black leather pants, which look entirely uncomfortable, match his jacket, and both are adorned with silver chains and doodads. He wears motorcycle boots, a band t-shirt, tucked in, and has buzzed off the remains of his hair. He's almost completely bald. He gnaws on a toothpick in his mouth, and I fear he might choke on it.

"What's wrong, Marnie? It's not okay for us to make an effort?" Roy huffs.

"It's wonderful to see you make an effort," I chime in, "but I only wonder, why? Not for our meeting, surely."

They glance at each other uncertainly.

"Well, my clean-up is just a coincidence. But they heard your mom's in town, didn't they?" Wade says, looking sheepish.

"What?" I demand, aghast. "You aim to try flirty business with my mom?"

"We only want to look nice, in case she comes by. That's all," Christie says.

"*I'm* trying flirty business," Roy corrects. "Grady won't mind me getting your mom a nightie. She doesn't work here, so it's not inappropriate. See? I remember the rules." He taps his forehead proudly.

"It's still inappropriate." I groan. "*Et tu*, Christie?"

"I *always* make an effort, Marnie," he reminds me. "She's your *mom*. You're getting a second chance with her. I wanted to look nice, so she feels comfortable with us."

"She ain't gonna feel comfortable with our freaking Hells Angel over here," Wade quips, turning to Roy. "You damn numpty."

"I thought a redheaded hair stylist might like flair," Roy defends. "It gives me an edge."

"The only edge you'll see is the one she pushes you over," Wade chuckles. "Marnie, I apologize on their behalf. It was a dumb idea. Not our first. Won't be our last."

I huff out a sigh, holding back my laughter. I take a quick picture of them and text it to Grady with the caption: *The fellas found out Mom is in town.*

He texts back a minute later. *Fuckheads. I'll swing by at lunch. I don't want to miss that shitshow.*

A warm smile emerges. I hoped he might join us to tour Wade's available trailers. I have time at my little cottage, but Mom and Tilly need something sooner.

Now, I stare down my three friends, still shaking my head over their brazen efforts. "Well, gentlemen, maybe it's your lucky day.

Mom's dropping by at lunch. She wants to see what's available to rent." I hold a finger up and put on my best stern face. "But the last time a guy flirted with her in a way she didn't like, he ended up with a broken penis."

"What? That's not a thing," Roy argues, jolting up in his chair.

"I've heard of it," Christie nods solemnly. "Male gymnasts get it when they fall wrong on the pommel horse."

"That's right," I agree, though I'm clueless, and Mom's not violent. But they don't need to know that. "He had to go to the hospital. Ice and heat for weeks."

"Dang, what'd he say to her?" Roy asks, wide-eyed.

"Don't know, but I wouldn't want to find out the hard way."

They wince simultaneously. I hide my inner smile—I doubt they will risk flirting now.

"Wade, can we talk?" I wave my notebook toward the office nook I created in a large closet in the backroom. He nods, shifting between his friends as they heckle him.

"Uh, oh, that sounds like trouble," Christie coos.

"Like being called to the principal's office," Roy laughs. "Best cover your penis, Wade. The apple might not fall far from the tree."

They laugh as we disappear behind The Canteen.

The "office" is a shelf nailed into the wall with a small desk lamp and a pen holder. It isn't glamorous, but it's the best I could do since I reclaimed most of the backroom for the selling floor. He sits in a repurposed lawn chair, and I take the desk stool.

"It's time to renegotiate. You're dealing only with *me* now, not Grady. I want him out of it."

I expect an argument, but Wade leans up. "I'm listening."

I flip my green notebook open and run through the numbers again. "Business has increased drastically, but so has our spending. Our billboard will be up soon. Peter Pike is starting on our gator observation deck today, and we still have more to do before our Memorial Day Extravaganza. The bottom line is, I work for you, and you can't afford me."

"I'll fire Roy."

"No, you won't," I scoff. "We need everyone for our grand reopening. We have a month until then. Pay me whatever the budget allows. Hopefully, we'll increase sales to afford me permanently. If not, the Extravaganza will be my last hurrah at the G&G."

His shoulders slump, and he purses his lips like his brain is working overtime to devise a solution. But I already know there isn't one. If not for the Sullivans' severance, I wouldn't have been able to stay this long. I tug my previous paychecks free from the binder and hand them over. "Please, return Grady's money and free him from whatever obligations he promised to get me this job."

"Fine, but I'm keeping his shares," Wade says, accepting the checks. "I deserve majority ownership of this place, and he's one less kid I have to pay out profits to. Besides, I did him a favor."

"Grady gave up his shares for me?"

"Yep."

I swoon. *Ah, Grady.* "Well, that's between you two. At the all-hands meeting, we'll brainstorm more ways to get customers in here, so let's brew a fresh pot of coffee, huh?"

The brainstorming goes surprisingly well. Making an effort with his clothes inspires Roy with better ideas, like offering a G&G delivery service.

"You said to think about what our customers need," he explains. "The pizza guy's on this road a dozen times a day. Why not get your eggs and beer delivered, too? That's something Sunny's doesn't have."

Marigold offers the design for our new billboard, going up later this week, featuring groceries, grub, and gators—it's her best work yet. Even better, it'll go up near Sunny's parking lot. Travelers won't miss it, and, for once, they'll have a choice.

Grady arrives around the same time as Mom and Tilly, and they funnel into our meeting together. They meet Marigold, Peter, and Wren before rounding to the boys. Christie trips over his Birkenstocks, rising to greet her. Roy looks a bit more guarded, his hand hovering in front of his crotch awkwardly as I introduce him, and he barely speaks, as if afraid the wrong thing might come out. Good.

Mom is quite lovely, with her fiery hair, full curves, and bright personality, and Wade must think so too. Their handshake lingers between them, and we're all surprised by the gentleness in his voice when he says, "We love Marnie and hope you find a home here with us too. You and Tilly."

He then offers Tilly his hand for a high-five. Tilly giggles, slapping it and saying, "You're a funny bunny."

Wade straightens at this and hesitantly glances at his friends, as if worried they might start referring to him this way. "Better than being a grumpy Gus, I suppose." He scratches his head, mussing his combed hair.

A bubbly laugh erupts from my sister, filling the room. Grady and I share an amused grin.

"How sweet," Mom coos. "I appreciate it, Wade. Once I'm settled, I'll give you all free haircuts to say thanks."

All three men run their hands over their heads sheepishly.

Leaving the rest to run the store, Wade takes us to The Marshes to tour the trailers available to rent. A wide dirt road leads into the woods, flanked by trailers on each side, starting with Wade, Roy, and Christie's. Though somewhat dated, the homes are clean and well-maintained. An older couple waves at us from their screened-in front porch. Children Tilly's age wobble on bikes up and down the lane. A family hangs wet beach towels on clotheslines as we pass. It's a cozy, homey place tucked in and tidy.

Wade has a two and a three-bedroom to rent, but Mom's quick to take the larger home.

"In case you ever need a place, Marnie," she says, "and if you don't, it'll make a lovely craft room for Tilly and me. I make my own jewelry these days." Her pink fingernails dance over a chunky beaded necklace in greens and pinks, matching her army green pants and delicate pink blouse. Mom has always been thrift-store chic.

It's an adorable home, white with blue shutters and a screened porch ready for plants. It has a small side garden where Tilly wants to plant wildflowers to bring butterflies. Mom hands over the security deposit and first month's rent, cash from a hot pink, zippered make-up pouch she's always used to collect her tip money.

"Welcome to The Marshes," Wade says, shaking her hand again.

While they discuss the place and make move-in arrangements, Grady pulls me to the pier for a little us-time before he returns to the clinic. Bessie loiters nearby, gently hovering over the water amid the green muck, eyeing us suspiciously. Last week, Wade spotted her egg den on the other side of the swamp. Soon, gator babies will fill the swampy nursery, just in time for our new decking.

"Will you move in with them?" Grady asks, tucking his hands into the pockets of his scrubs. "I mean, I get it since you just got them back. I mean, hopefully, they'll stay. You know what's best, and I support you. But I'm here, too. I'd love to live with you. We could have last night every night. So, my offer still stands, regardless."

A giggle slips out of me over his obvious nervousness, and I blush over memories of last night. Waking under the hovering trees, the air cold but warm against him felt heavenly. He *really* wants me to live with him. Already. His strong and sudden commitment to me is such a weird feeling. A good feeling, though, that I'm enjoying with caution. Who doesn't long to feel this wanted?

He steps closer, slipping his hands around my waist and nuzzling my forehead. "*You and me, babe... how 'bout it?*" he hums, making me giggle again.

Then, he sways softly in a gentle dance before dipping me. "I promise music and chess every night."

"Oh, Grady Tripp, I like the sound of it. What else will you promise me?"

"Homemade meals, coffee every morning, free animal care, and unlimited cat treats, of course."

"Of course, but sometimes a girl likes flowers."

"Oh, I'll get you flowers. And braid your hair," he says, snuggling against me. "And let you have the remote."

I laugh. "You won't mind my obsession with PBS and British TV?"

"Nope. I encourage it, especially if it wins us words like *numpty*. As long as you're okay with me, old-man drifting off to sleep watching nature shows."

"Heck, no. I love it. Oh, Grady, we're going to be the boringest couple ever," I beam, leaning in for a kiss. "I can't wait."

"Is that a *yes* then?" he asks, kissing me again.

All the romantic wheels turning in my head come to a sudden, squealing stop. "Um, it's a maybe?"

His eyes squint, considering me. "Did I forget to mention all the amazing sex you could possibly want?"

"Oh, I know," I chuckle. "It's not that."

"Tell me. What is it?" When I hesitate, he adds, "Truth."

"Truth is, I have a month before I need to move, a month until I'll probably be out of a job again," I say, shoulders deflating. "I don't want to rush. What if my next job is an hour away?"

"Then, you'll commute," he says sternly. "Or we'll move somewhere else together."

"It's not just that. Leaving that cottage scares me."

"What? Why?"

"It's my home, Grady. That place has been my saving grace for a decade. First, it comforted me after Mom left. Then, it let me be myself, building me up when there was no one else to do it. After *that* day, it was my safety net, my healing place. When I started at the G&G, all I had to do was look around my little place, and all I'd built to feel I could do anything. It's hard, letting it go. Not because I don't want to live with you. I'd pick living with you over Mom, of course. It's just because... I don't want to be without it. *Yet.*"

I fear I sound ridiculous, putting so much sentimental value in a tiny house. But for better or worse, it's how I feel. That long chapter of my life is over—I *must* leave. But is it wrong to extend the epilogue until the last possible minute?

He sighs. "I understand. Take all the time you need."

"Really?"

"Of course, but here's what I think we should do." He latches onto me again. "Whenever you stay the night, bring something of yours over. And whenever I stay the night with you, I'll take something when I leave. Seeing your things a little at a time at my place might help ease you into the idea."

I almost tear up over how sweet and understanding he is. "Kiss me."

He takes my face in his hands and gives me the kind of kiss that makes me want to take him somewhere—*anywhere*—right this instant.

"We'll start tonight," I say, breathlessly. "I'll come over for chess."

His coy grin widens. "Yeah, chess. Perfect."

CHAPTER FORTY-SIX

Grady

A MONTH EARNS me twelve potted plants, her PM CD collection (but not her boom box, oddly), six pieces of wall art (now lining my mantelpiece), three of her favorite coffee mugs, two sets of pajamas, and all of her board games (I took one each time I stayed). Staying at hers has helped me better understand how hard it is for her to leave. Her place is cozy, safe, and unequivocally her from its rescued décor, lively plants, and eclectic everything.

But it also represents her lonely past, and it's time to move on—a message I tenderly keep pushing. Last week, with my encouragement, she moved all three cats in (one at a time to ensure gentle transitions). Hershey's still unsure about the dogs, but Sunkist and Triscuit love curling up against Blackbeard's belly for their many catnaps. And Blackbeard, the least pirate-y dog ever, adores the attention. Merging our lives has gone incredibly well, though awfully slowly.

Now, we're one week away from Memorial Day weekend, the fate of her job, and her move-out date. And for the first time since I've known her, Marina is stressed.

Not about her Mom. Leonie and Tilly moved into the double-wide at The Marshes the same week she handed the payment to Wade. We barely had to lift a finger to move her in. Wade, Christie, and Roy did most of the heavy labor, even helping her score extra furniture. Whether any of them scored romantic points with her remains to be seen.

Leonie has made commendable efforts to reconnect with Marina. From shopping trips to long park walks, Leonie is always ready to spend time with her girls. Marina says she doesn't just have her mom back; she has the mom she's always wanted. Tilly has easily warmed up to her big sister, as I knew she would. Marina has spent a lot of one-on-one time getting to know her, and Tilly adores the attention.

She's not stressed about the G&G, either. Business has steadily picked up. Roy's delivery idea has paid off; he's on the road more than he's at the store now. The old pier has been replaced with a wider one with a railing and bench seats for gator observation. The billboards are up. The Canteen is fully operational. And locals are loving it. Marina posts progress on Instagram daily, quadrupling her followers. Wade complained recently that he barely has time for smoke breaks anymore—that's how busy it is.

If it's enough to afford Marina going forward, that's another story.

I don't think Marina is stressed about us, either. We are as happy and desperate for each other as we were that first night, with zero signs of change.

But that's the problem, I think. *Change.* Everything fell apart the last time she was on the cusp of leaving her place, and the family she thought she could count on abandoned her. If I can show her that's not happening this time, she'll relax into our new living situation once and for all.

So, tonight, I have a plan.

She doesn't arrive with the boxes I hoped for but a single blanket —the quilt of many colors off her bed. "It's my *only* family heirloom," she explains, hardly setting it down.

"No, it isn't. What about our chessboard?"

She smirks. "You know what I mean."

"Anything else? In the truck?"

"Nope. Sorry." She looks anguished, like this was all she could do.

"That's okay. This quilt is special to you, so that's a big step."

She smiles, relieved. "It is! We could put it on the end of your bed."

"*Our* bed. Good idea."

She slumps again. "*Our* bed. I'm such a... flibbertigibbet."

"There's that British TV talking again," I laugh. "It's okay. Be as flibberty as you want."

She curls into me. I kiss the top of her head and hold her close to me. She's had many moments lately—that's how I know she's stressed.

"Thank you, Grady," she breathes, staring at me. "I love you."

"Love you, too. We'll get there. But tonight, we're going out."

"We are?"

"Yep, I want you to stop worrying about moving or the G&G or any of it. Tonight's about fun."

She perks up. "Fun? Oh, Grady. That's what I need. Is this... am I dressed okay?"

She twirls in her little summer dress, pink and soft, that moves with her. She's worn more dresses lately, light, pretty things I can easily slip my hands under.

"You're perfect."

"Where are we going?" she asks as I grab my keys and wallet from the table by the door.

"It's a surprise, but trust me, you'll love it."

She takes a deep breath and pushes out her usual smile. She rests her hand on her quilt, draped easily over the couch, and grabs her bag. "Okay."

She says nothing when we pull into the driveway at Tripp Farm. We're late, but I texted Mom and Elena with clear instructions to start without us. Marina doesn't ask questions when we park in the crowded lot, nor does she note the familiar cars.

But at the door, she yanks me to the side. Under the soft porch light, she fidgets with her hands, looking nervous. "Grady, tell me this isn't a proposal."

"It's not a proposal."

She looks confused. "Mom's here. Your family. Is that Wade's truck? Are you sure?"

"Marina, tonight is not that night. Promise."

Her tension abates in a breath.

"Not that I wouldn't marry you," I tack on, suddenly nervous. "I would. I will. Someday. If that's what you want."

"And not that I wouldn't say yes, in a second, it's just—"

"Too much right now. I get it."

"Exactly. I don't need to be Strange-Tripp, not yet. I just need to be Strange. With you."

My lips curl, holding her there. "That's all I want, too."

"Thank you, Grady... and just for the record, whatever it is, I love it."

I chuckle. "How can you love it before you even see it?"

Her hands slide over my chest, and she grins coyly. "Because you always know what I need."

I kiss her then. Hard and soft at once. I have to.

"Yeah, and don't you forget it," I say before pushing the door open and leading her inside.

Family game night greets us in a wave of light, movement, and laughter—every game station bustles with excitement. An unprecedented six tables have been arranged to accommodate the extra people, and each game is in full swing. Taylor Swift's "Ready For It" plays through the TV, and nearly everyone sings along during the chorus. Everyone is here. Peter Pike plays next to Marigold. Ivy, Marina's nurse from the accident, wedges between Gil and Wren at another table—she visited the clinic last week with her new puppy, Buster, so I invited her. Wade stands sheepishly with my father at the bar, both sets of arms folded but talking nonetheless. Christie and Roy sit on either side of Leonie. Tilly plays with Zoe, Zach, Tamsyn and Colin. Luke and Willow play against Elena and Jim. Mom scurries about, refilling drinks and checking the cameras on the phones perched at each table.

"Eep, Grady! Those are my games!" Marina gasps beside me, grabbing onto my arm. "They're playing my games! *Tickety-Boo! Tic Tac Trivia! Milk & Eggs! Scaredy Cats!* Gosh, even *Zombie Grocery Store* and *Play Together, Stay Together*—that one needs work. How'd you— why'd you—Grady!"

"Games should be played, right? What says family better than a board game?"

Her hand goes to her mouth, probably to stifle more *eeps*. The soft glint of tears in her eyes tells me I've done a good thing.

"What's with the phones?" she asks.

"Gil's going to post our gameplay on YouTube and TikTok. He wants to start a Kickstarter campaign, like he did for Marigold's comics—she'll be able to self-publish them soon. So, who knows? Something might come from it if people enjoy them as much as our family does."

"Do you really think they're that good?"

I wave toward the crowd. "This is proof, isn't it?"

"Marnie, you're here!" Mom pipes up, gaining the room's attention. "Your games are wonderful."

The room claps and cheers in wild approval.

"Come, take over as Games Master," Mom says, waving her into the room.

Marina peels out of her jean jacket, a giddy look on her face, and moves into the rambunctious group. She rounds the room with side hugs and game tips. I make my way to the bar area for a beer.

"Dad."

"Grady."

"Wade."

"Grady."

"Everything good?" I twist the cap off a bottle from the cooler beside them and take a swig.

They nod in unison. It's not the first time Wade and Dad have connected this month. With Marina's encouragement, Dad stopped by the G&G. Though it was awkward at first, Wade gave Dad a tour of the new store, and they bonded over the beauty of the perfect hot dog from The Canteen.

The following week, Wade visited the farm and gave Dad a hand with feeding—a good thing since I'd been called away for an emergency and couldn't be there to help myself. They ended that visit with a couple of beers and a tentative handshake.

As far as I know, they haven't said a word about what tore them apart in the first place. Maybe neither remembers. Or maybe it's better to forget. For the stoic males of the Tripp family, their reconciliation is as good as it gets.

At intermission, the family eats their fill of tacos, laughing over what is now known as "The Battle of the Terrible British Accents," brought on by *Tickety-Boo*. We've never had a more fun or boisterous family game night, which says a lot since we tend to get rowdy over them.

I no longer view family events as obligations I'd rather avoid but for what they are—chances to be together. I may have shown Marina what a real family can be, but she's taught me to appreciate and enjoy it.

This is family. Celebrating, being together, and loving each other over all obstacles.

"If I could have your attention." Wade's deep, raspy voice cuts through a lull in the laughter and conversation.

All eyes across the living room turn in his direction. He still stands near the bar, beer in hand, and my father stands tall beside him.

"Thank you to Carmela and Mack for hosting." He tips his beer toward them.

"Here, here," everyone sings along.

"Thanks for including us ol' coots in the festivities," he says, gaining some laughs.

"Here, here," shout Christie and Roy.

"Marnie, thanks for the entertainment. These games are something special, just like you," he says, amid claps and chatter.

"Best games ever!" coo the kids.

"So much fun," says Elena, tipping her wine glass.

Marina beams beside me, slipping her hand into mine as the crowd cheers her.

Wade clears his throat again. "I ain't done."

The room quiets.

Wade's bushy brows pinch as he struggles with words. Dad lays an encouraging hand on his back, urging him on.

"I'm not one to give speeches," he says. "But I'm not one to back down when something needs to be said, either. Marnie, you're a miracle. You haven't just revitalized the G&G. You've turned us around—Christie, Roy, and me—and given us purpose again. You've brought me and Mack back together. Grady's no longer an asshole. And hell, Roy's taking regular showers now."

Laughter.

"The day we met... that was a hard day. But you crashing into our lives was the best thing that ever happened to us. I ain't a father, but I'd be damn proud to call you my daughter."

"Ah, Wade," she mumbles beside me, tears flooding her eyes.

"Nope, don't get mushy on me yet," he says, wiping his tears. "I ain't done."

The room quiets.

"Next week's Memorial Day Extravaganza is meant to determine whether or not the store can afford you going forward. But the truth is, Marnie, you're better than us now. You got the store where it needs to be. You don't belong behind the counter serving hot dogs or cleaning bathrooms, whether I can afford you or not."

She gapes beside me. "You're firing me?"

"Hell, no. Don't be a numpty," he returns with his angry glare. "There will *always* be a place for you at the G&G, even if I have to fire Roy and Christie and hand over my salary to make it happen. You never have to worry about having a job. But you deserve *more* than a job, Marnie. As your boss, I want to keep you forever. But as your... friend, I want you to pursue something better."

"What's better than the G&G?" she asks.

"How 'bout helping other hurtin' businesses?" His hand goes up submissively like he expects she might be upset over his idea. "I got a friend in Burgaw who owns a gas station laundromat combo that's been in tough times for a while. I bragged about everything you've been doing for me, and he threatened to steal you away. But, of course, I told him he couldn't steal family. Anyway, it got me thinking. So, I called him and asked how much he'd be willing to pay to get you to come in and give him an overhaul."

Wade smirks, shoving his hands in his pockets. "He gave me a number—a dang good number—and I told him to raise it twenty percent. I think you'll be pleased. Expect his call Monday morning."

"Ah, Marnie Strange, Business Consultant," Leonie says. "I can see the business cards now."

"She'll save your business and brighten your day," cheers Mom, adding the tagline.

"I like Marnie Strange, Business Hero, personally," Ivy claps. "This is fun."

"I ain't done," Wade spits, bringing all eyes back to him. "One last thing."

He clears his throat and takes a breath, fighting back rarely seen emotion.

"Just so we're clear—you aren't leaving the G&G. You're moving up to part-owner."

She gasps, hand going to her mouth.

"That's right. I'm giving you shares in the G&G and The Marshes. Grady's ten percent, which he gave me to hire you in the first place, and ten percent more from me. I own forty, you twenty, and the rest ten. You will always be my partner at the G&G, always be our family, and that'll keep you coming back to make sure we're following the rules."

Our whole family busts into wild applause over his generosity.

With her eyes full of tears, Marina rushes into Wade's arms for a warm, surprise embrace that makes him teary, too.

"Thank you, Wade. Thank you," is all she manages to say, but it's enough.

Wade holds his beer high and says loudly, "To Marnie!"

"To Marnie!" the group returns, toasting and cheering.

"Now, I'm done," Wade announces. "Let the games resume."

Activity continues in a flurry of gameplay and congratulations. Leonie wraps Marina up in a tight hug, saying, "You deserve it." Others follow suit, a train of well-wishers and unabashed support.

But soon, when everyone's attention diverts back to games and snacks, I look for her and can't find her. I try the kitchen, the bathrooms, and even the bedrooms, thinking she might have needed some quiet. Nothing.

Catching sight of Leonie at the *Tickety-Boo* table, she points toward the front door, motioning for me to go outside.

I find Marina in The Beast, lying on a blanket on the truck bed. I climb in beside her, and she scoots over to make room. We stare up into the inky night speckled with stars—they are innumerable and delicate, tiny flecks of wonder, like each could hold another love story, and ours twinkles right back at them. Lying with her, relaxing under the massive universe, fills me with gratitude for my universe —her.

Many gentle moments pass. Her hand slips into mine.

"I'm going to be a business consultant," she says softly.

"Yes."

"I'm a business *owner*."

"Yes," I chuckle.

"I have a big, beautiful family."

"Yes."

She rolls over me, sitting up and straddling me. She nestles close, grinding against me through the thin fabric of her panties while my hands drift easily up her skirt. "I have you."

"Always."

She leans down, taking my bottom lip between hers for a tugging kiss. "Here's what's going to happen," she smirks. "Tomorrow morning, we'll move me in, once and for all, and then, we'll spend the next forty-eight hours with *our* pets, on *our* dock, in *our* kitchen, in *our* bed, at *our* place."

"Good, glad to hear you say it. I added you to the deed once the cats moved in. I knew you wouldn't be far behind. It *is* our place, Marina."

She gasps. "Grady, you didn't have to—"

"Darling, I wanted to. I need you to know it's our home, our little nest."

She giggles while her eyes well with tears.

I give her a quick kiss. "You're always telling me to relax. Well, this is me, asking you to relax into us."

"Okay." Her lips press into mine with renewed desperation as she bites my lip playfully and tugs at my shirt. I smile against her, thinking we might add Beast-fucking to our impressive rotation. My hands close in against her thighs, and my thumb drifts lazily over the triangle patch of her panties. She moans at the touch.

"Think anyone would notice if we're gone for a while?" she asks when she breaks for air.

"Fuck 'em."

She laughs. Then, we take each other right there, under the stars.

CHAPTER FORTY-SEVEN

Marnie

THE FOLLOWING THURSDAY, the team and I work on last minute tasks to prepare for G&G's Memorial Day Extravaganza. Peter and Marigold hang outdoor lights along the railing of our freshly stained gator observation deck. Roy posts the necessary signs, warning customers not to "feed, fondle, or otherwise fuck with" the gators—his description, not mine. The sign reads more professionally than that. Christie hangs colorful banners over our new picnic and dining area, stretching from the "smoking" porch to the side of the store. Wren runs the store (busy for lunch) while Wade gives Mom, Tilly, Elena, and Carmela a register and canteen tutorial—they've all agreed to help with our upcoming weekend.

I check in deliveries—the beer guys, the soda guys, the local farmers and artisans here to restock for what's expected to be G&G's biggest weekend ever.

The billboards are up and causing buzz. The mayor has agreed to kick off our festivities tomorrow at noon. We've booked a band and installed a life-size chess board and an extra-large *Jenga* set, adding more fun—I couldn't plan an Extravaganza without games and music. The newspaper gave us a full-page spread. And my Instagram's been on fire this week. The event promises to be a huge success.

Today's already busy, with locals coming by to enjoy the store before the big rush.

Even so, the last person I expect to see today (or any day) is Ashe.

I don't see him initially—just Wade, Christie, and Roy quickstepping in my direction from the dock like Bessie might be sneaking up on me for an afternoon snack. Wade fumbles with his phone, walking while talking.

I turn from my conversation with Alice Harvey, our soaps, candles, and teas vendor, to see what's gotten them so serious, and there's Ashe.

He pulls off his aviator sunglasses, looking dapper in his dark blue pants, striped button-down, and silky blue tie. His curly blonde hair is tamed with product, and somehow matches his cocky smirk.

I turn to Alice. "Hey, how about a fountain drink, on me? I need a minute."

Despite her obvious curiosity, she obeys. The boys move in behind me, pinning me in the middle.

Ashe opens his mouth to speak, but Wade cuts him off. "Sullivans aren't welcome here."

"Wade, that's not true. Everyone's welcome here." I retort, though I understand his disdain. Cora's launched her own campaign against us with Sunny's Beach Party—a week-long celebration highlighting forty-seven years in Seagrove. There's everything from live music in the gazebo to free samples and door prizes. They're advertising the best prices I've ever seen from them, almost on par with Food Lion. On top of that, our health inspector mysteriously kept delaying giving us the all-clear—it took weeks to get him to check out our Canteen. Some suspect his delay was Cora's doing.

Still, I smile widely at Ashe, trying to set a better tone. "Sorry, Ashe, he doesn't mean that."

"Yeah, I do."

"I'm not here to cause trouble," Ashe says, "just to talk to Marnie."

"Maybe Marnie doesn't want to talk to you," Roy blasts back, zipzipping the electric screwdriver he's holding like a gun.

I take a cleansing breath, pushing my notebook and clipboard at Wade. "Guys, it's fine."

Wade, Christie, and Roy exchange bothered glances until Wade leans in, "We've got chainsaws, hungry gators, and alibis."

"Yeah, we're watching you," Christie chimes in, his red finger-nails pointing at his eyes and then at Ashe.

"Dudes, back off. I come in peace," Ashe tries, half-laughing at their efforts. "Please, Marnie. Five minutes."

I step away from my protectors with a stern look, telling them not to follow. They should know by now that I can take care of myself, however sweet their intentions. Peter and Marigold finish their work on the lights and head toward the store. I direct Ashe toward the dock for privacy.

Ashe glances at the swamp but doesn't seem interested in the swaying moss, the sunlight prism through the trees, or even Bessie, lingering in the green water nearby. Her eggs have hatched, and her babies scurry over her head like they're playing tag. Few things are as strangely cute as that.

When he hesitates, I think to switch into old Marnie and help him along with pleasantries and guiding questions. But why should I do anything for the man who told me to get out of *his* store? My arms fold over my chest, and I plaster on a polite smile. "Well, what do you want, Ashe?"

"Granddad sent me. He's pissed."

My brow crinkles, trying to understand. Cora's Dad, Bill Biggums, founded Sunny's and would often pop by for white-gloved inspections after handing it over to Cora. I found his visits fun—he never found a speck of dust on my watch—but he stressed Cora out every time. Being handed a legacy as incredible as Sunny's would be overwhelming and stressful, I suppose.

"Pissed about what?" I ask.

"What he's calling The Great Sullivan Cock-Up," he groans. "He sent me here on behalf of Sunny's to apologize."

"To me? And he sent *you*? I'm surprised Cora didn't step in and do it for you."

He nods, shuffling on his feet and looking extremely uncomfortable. "I deserve that. After what happened at the restaurant, what you said, yeah, I realized I owe you an apology. *Many* apologies."

The new decking must've fallen into a black hole, swirling us into oblivion, because I am flabbergasted. Dumbstruck. Confused.

"I'm sorry for how I treated you, Marnie. It was shocking at the time, having everything ripped out from under us. I've always looked up to Mom and how she handles the business, trusted her to tell me what to do," he says. "So, when she said go, I went. When she said your notebook belonged to Sunny's, I believed her. I didn't fight for us when she said I should end things. I couldn't even do it myself. I fucked up everything."

He glances everywhere but at me as if struggling with every word. I don't think he's ever said so many things without inserting a laugh or joke. "I appreciate that, Ashe. Granddad must be furious."

A smile cuts through his anguish. "Livid. He's come out of retirement."

"What?" I gasp. "Isn't he like... almost eighty?"

Ashe nods. "Yep, but he's made Mom take a step back from operations at Seagrove. We've had to cut staff. The new store manager is terrible. Granddad's worried that a damn convenience store might put Seagrove's Sunny's out of business. Our profits are down twenty percent, and that's before your grand re-opening."

I gasp so sharply that I choke on a bug. "Twenty? Seriously?"

"I'll deny that outside of this conversation," he says. "But yes. We're hoping things'll pick up with the tourists, but for now, the locals prefer you."

I do a shameless happy dance on the dock—I can't help it.

"Don't get too excited. The beach store is doing great, and Grandad's tasked me to revitalize the Seagrove branch. We won't be down long."

I grin widely. "As part owner of the G&G and soon-to-be business consultant, I look forward to the competition."

He smirks. "Yeah, I heard about that... This might help."

He pulls out his phone, swipes the screen, and shows me a picture. It's the front wall of the beach store, where the managers are listed with their pictures under the beach mural and bold *Welcome to Sunny's!*

Beside Sunny's Store Manager portrait is a picture of me next to the words *Store Designer & Concept Creator.*

"Eep!" I gush, my wide eyes going from his to the picture and back again. "I can't believe it! Are *you* responsible for this?"

With a sheepish shrug, he says, "What you said at Rebellion about getting credit for your ideas and being valued as you are. That's on us, too. I'm sorry."

"You should be, but it's on me, too—I should've insisted. But thanks, Ashe. That means a lot."

"Least we could do." He shrugs, smiling in a way I once loved. Only now it feels fake. My eyes narrow as his apology ping-pongs in my head, and my defenses rise—I *know* the Sullivans, and they're never generous without a reason.

"You want something," I decide finally. "What is it?"

He rolls his eyes, clearly irritated, but he swallows it. "Come back to Sunny's," he says, looking nervous again. "I promise, you won't be devalued again."

My mouth drops, but then I remember the bugs and close it again. It's like I have a brain freeze, though I haven't eaten anything cold. "Come back to Sunny's?"

"Granddad wants you to manage the Seagrove store. Full benefits. Full control. Profit sharing. He said he'd move Mom's office elsewhere. He's offering six figures, Marnie. You'd make as much as me, more if you haggle."

"That's bold, considering what your family's put me through. What makes you think I'd want that?"

"Just consider it. He wants you to join him for dinner at the club to discuss it. A future with Sunny's would be easier and more lucrative than resurrecting places *like this.*"

My brow cocks at his tone change. I glance around at the gorgeous swamp, the alligator nursery, and my three protectors watching from the smoking porch. Wade now has a shovel to heighten his intimidation factor. I chuckle at them and take in the old store with warm admiration.

"Places like this have character," I say, smiling. "Tell Bill thanks, but no thanks, and good luck to you both. I predict a dreary summer ahead for Sunny's."

"Yeah, told 'em it'd be a long shot," he says with a small shrug. "Thanks for hearing me out, though."

"Oh, my pleasure." I stick my hand out for him to shake, but he yanks me to him instead.

"It's really good to see you," he says near my ear. A show for the boys or just typical Sullivan entitlement—I don't know. But I push him away, having none of it.

Behind him, The Beast tears around the corner and whips into the parking lot.

"Oh, hells bells. They called Grady," I say.

Grady exits The Beast, slamming the door, eyes locked on us. He's in his scrubs, and I suspect some poor puppy or kitten has been left with Aunt Elena mid-examination at Wade's urgent call. He beelines toward us, eyes narrowed and fists tight.

"Tell me something," Ashe says, seemingly unworried about my angry boyfriend. "Does he make you happy? Truly happy?"

A wide grin stretches over my face with the question, sweeping me into a memory of just this morning, when Grady woke me with coffee and said, "Here or outside?" just as he's done every morning since I moved in. I'll never know why I dragged my feet over moving in with Grady. Fear, I guess. Or maybe I was just too set in my lonely ways. Whatever the case, I have settled into our place in no time. Like this morning, when, to answer his question, I said, "Here *and* outside?" just as I had every morning. He took his cue, putting the coffee aside and climbing into bed with me for our *other* wake-up tradition. Then, our shower. Then, fresh coffee on the porch or at the dock. Already, we have this beautiful routine that's easy and entirely us. He's where I belong, a truth I'm assured of every time I see him.

Even when he's in jealous, protective, grouchy mode.

"I couldn't be happier," I say, almost dreamily.

Ashe meets Grady at the foot of the deck and extends his hand. The men shake, though Grady looks suspicious. Then, Ashe turns to me with a coy smile. "Glad for you, Marnie. Hope I never need a business consultant, but if I do, you'll be the only one I call."

"I'll be waiting," I chuckle.

He leaves then, brushing by Grady carelessly as he approaches me. I greet him with a big smile and a soft embrace. "Everything's fine. Relax, Grady."

"What the fuck did that mean? Why would he call you?"

"We did it, Grady. We rammed our pirate ship right into them, and now, they're sinking," I say, beaming. "Sunny's is *sinking*. Cora's already gone down with the ship."

I rattle off my explanation, wide-eyed and animated with excitement. Justification, validation, true comeuppance—these are precious rarities in real life, and I can't help but do another victory dance as I explain it all to Grady. I hit him with terms like *twenty percent* and *Store Designer and Concept Creator*, which I will, of course, be adding to my new business cards.

"He offered me the store manager job. Six-figures! And I turned him down. Do you know how badass I feel right now?"

He laughs. "As you should. As you deserve."

"So, see?" I give him a playful slap on his arm. "You left that poor Chihuahua on the exam table for nothing."

He looks sheepish. "It was a beagle, actually."

"Did you really think I couldn't handle Ashe myself?" I turn to my three dads, still watching from the smoking porch, and repeat the question to them.

Christie shrugs. Roy scratches his head. Wade leans his shovel against the side of the shed, defeated.

"Go back to work, you numpties!" I order, shooing them along.

"Okay, you made your point," Grady says when my attention returns to him. "I overreacted." He slips his hands around me. "Sorry."

"Well, maybe don't be at Wade's beck and call next time. I can handle myself."

"Don't I know it?" He leans into me, lips coiled coyly. "Congratulations, Captain."

After a tongue-laced kiss, I relax against him. "Well, thanks, and it's not such a bad thing, your surprise visit. Jealous rage is sexy on you."

He laughs. "You're sexy on me. Have I told you lately how proud of you I am?"

"Um, no, actually." I tap my chin thoughtfully. "I don't think so."

He nuzzles my nose with his, leaning closer. "I'm so incredibly proud of you. You are the baddest badass I know. I fucking love sailing the high seas with you."

Laughter fills the small space between us. "Oh, my. I can't wait for home."

He slaps my ass and gives me another short kiss. "Me, neither. Don't be late."

Then, he leaves me for the poor beagle needing his attention.

The Extravaganza goes off without a hitch, well, except for the long lines and parking—we had to think on our feet to alleviate those issues. We invited extra vendors to set up their wares outside, creating a farmer's market. Peter sold four rocking chairs and got two orders from customers wanting a "door porch" for their backyards. Marigold sold six swamp landscapes and dozens of handmade cards and postcards—she's embraced the swamp theme. We sold out of hot dogs twice, leaving us scrambling to get more from our distributors—a good problem to have. The G&G profited more in one weekend than Wade's entire last year.

And, with a promise to continue the farmer's market on weekends and all of our extra amenities for traveling families a huge hit, we expect our numbers to keep rising all summer. *Suck it, Sunny's.*

We end the weekend's events with fireworks Sunday night. Locals come out in droves carrying picnic blankets and lawn chairs. The lot is full, and the store is busy.

Grady finds me, wrapping his arms around my waist as the professionals I've hired ready their display. I lean into him, tired but exhilarated. "You're chilly," he says, rubbing my arms. "Want me to grab you a hoodie from The Beast?"

I almost say yes. But looking around at the full, happy crowd, and seeing everyone doing such a great job at handling the event, I'm overrun with deep satisfaction. My work here is done. I don't want the hoodie. I want to go home.

So, I twist in his arms, catching the soft blue of his eyes in the twinkle lights overhead. "Let's sneak out of here, okay?"

"Definitely." He takes my hand, pulling me gently through the masses and behind the building. We climb into The Beast and go home.

We watch the fireworks from our dock, curled under a blanket to keep the evening chill off, and see most of the show just over the tree line. I text Wade, letting him know I left early and congratulating him on the store's success. He answers:

It's so perfect that my eyes fill with tears.

I'm okay with tears these days. It's like Grady once said. Frowns, fears, and tears are human necessities. Someone to share them all with is another. Grady is and always will be that person for me. He holds my hand across the armrests of our chairs, butted next to each other, twiddling with my fingers and warming me while fireworks reflect in his eyes. It's a strange, beautiful moment, knowing nothing is missing.

"Keep staring at me like that, and we won't finish the show," he says, keeping his eyes on the fireworks overhead.

I giggle. "Fireworks, eh. Who needs them?"

Then, he pulls me into his arms for our own fireworks.

Epilogue

Valentine's Day, Next Year.

GRADY

IT'S BARELY 5 A.M., still dark, and an early-morning chill beckons me back to sleep. I roll to my side with a bothered sigh— Marina's not here. As scheduled, my alarm sounds as I rise from our bed and flip on the bedside lamp. I intended to get up before her. But a late emergency call kept me out, and she's been relentlessly busy with work lately.

We've shared our home for nine months. We've brilliantly navigated the major holidays, her mom's first (and so far only) semi-episode, Tilly's flu (which she generously shared with the rest of the family), a break-in at the G&G (Uncle Jim's still investigating), Roy's eccentric new girlfriend (yes, he has a girlfriend), and Sunkist's impacted hairball. Marina's taken it all in stride with her signature bounce and optimism. Hell, even with the flu and a raging fever, I could barely keep her in bed—she wanted to be up, working on her next game or filling her next store revitalization plan notebook. Still, even being sick and stuck at home together was fun.

But *fun* has faded behind forced smiles lately. I suspect I know why, but she's not saying. She denies there's anything wrong at all.

I know her best, though. I know she gets nervous whenever she's scheduled to meet a new client. I know she can't handle scary movies. *At all.* I know she obsesses over her plants and even talks to them. She doesn't know I know that, but I overheard her one day— adorable. I know strong storms freak her out, and British TV mellows her. I know she prefers showering with me rather than without me, and often can't sleep if I'm not beside her. I know she loves our life together. She's brought beauty and energy to my minimalist cabin— it's almost greener inside than it is outside now. Sitting on our dock or back porch together is her favorite thing to do. And she's taken quite a shine to Blackbeard (he follows her around the house like he's in love with her). He'll even jump between us on the couch and lay his head in her lap—commandeering my spot beside her is the most pirate-y thing he's ever done. I know that despite her sunshine persona, Marina's a surprising introvert. She craves time to herself, and, especially, time with me.

Lately, though, she's practiced avoidance, reminding me of myself before her. She claims that it's a tough client keeping her distracted.

I know better.

At Christmas, my brother Colin announced that he and Tamsyn were expecting their third child. A month later, at our family game night, Luke's wife, Willow, said they were pregnant, too. Both times came the inevitable well-meaning but insensitive backlash.

"You're next, Marnie!"

"Can't wait to plan your baby shower."

"You'll get your turn!"

"You'll make such a great mom."

I was about to tell them to fuck off, but she stopped me. "Wouldn't that be something?" has become her typical response.

I tried talking to her afterward, and she said it didn't bother her. But I doubt that's true. Not because either of us needs a child to feel complete—we don't. But it's the expectation that's frustrating. An expectation that surely puts stress on her shoulders and, at least, makes her uncomfortable in situations like that. What is she supposed to do? Ruin everyone's celebration with the truth?

Nah. Marina's too kind for that.

More than that, though, I wonder if those awful feelings of inadequacy embedded by society and reinforced by the Sullivans have snaked their way back into her head. Does she feel like something's missing? I remember (vaguely) what it was like to be in my twenties. You think you can do anything, and most of the time, it's true. A story that diverges from the typical plot lines might feel like less of a story, even though it isn't, especially when everyone around you follows the same formula.

I need to know how she feels about our next chapters.

And today's her birthday. Valentine's Day. The anniversary of the day her mom left her. And one year ago today, *that* day. She believes this day is cursed, and it's my first opportunity to prove her wrong.

She leans over the kitchen table, notebook and supplies spread. Her long red hair is piled into a messy ponytail on her head. Coffee wafts in the air, and the warm glow of a desk lamp heightens the coffee-shop vibe. Hershey perches on the table, as if reading over her work. Sunkist swirls around her legs. The dogs sleep around the fireplace, Triscuit curled into Blackbeard's belly.

Quietly, I slip behind her, melding myself to her soft curves and kissing her neck. She breathes in sharply before relaxing, and I can feel her smiling without seeing it.

"Good morning," she says.

"I missed you in bed."

"I couldn't sleep."

She twists in my arms, and her coffee lips melt against mine. Her arms dangle over my shoulders, pulling me closer. I don't care how many times I see her smile or she holds me close, loving Marina Ann Strange will always be my absolute favorite thing.

"Happy birth—"

Her hand covers my lips, holding them shut. Her forehead presses against mine. "Don't say it," she whispers. "Please, don't say it."

My brow cocks in a question. "Happy Val—"

She presses harder, keeping my words in.

I gently tug her hand away. "The universe knows what day it is."

"Yes, but let's not remind her," she whispers. "Please, Grady."

I kiss her hand. "Happy just another day, then."

She breathes out a relieved sigh. "Thanks, you too. No more talking about it."

"I'll make more coffee," I say. "Here or outside."

"Outside," she says, returning to her work.

Over coffee on the back porch, she tells me about her newest client. She's had a dozen since the G&G, and all have thrived under Marina's consultancy. *North Carolina Magazine* called her "the angel of mom-and-pop businesses." Now, she has a waitlist of potential clients across this half of North Carolina—she's even raised her fees. Twice.

The projects she's most excited about are the unusual ones. Soon, she'll work on transforming The Curiosity Museum downtown—a rundown, campy place that she said gave her the creeps as soon as she walked inside. Marina calls it "her strangest case yet." It's a unique challenge, and the guy who inherited it is a history teacher and single dad, so she's only charging half her usual fees. I love that she's successful enough to be selective about her projects and the people she wants to help.

"How about I fix us breakfast," I say once our coffees are empty and the conversation wanes. "And then, let's play chess."

She gives me a coy look, her red brow cocked on her freckled forehead. "Are you sure your ego can handle it?"

I laugh. I rarely win, and if I manage to pull it off, it's only by distracting her. Not that I care about winning. Beneath that gorgeous red hair and disarming smile is a keen strategist. I only hope she never gets bored playing with me.

"How else will I get better?"

She giggles. "In that case, yes. I'll make a fire."

We enact our plan. The cabin is soon warm and cozy with the fireplace crackling and bacon smells in the air. We eat, then take our places around the game—cats and dogs curling up beside us.

Over our third round, I lock eyes with her across the board as she contemplates her next move. It's the closest I've come to beating her, and I can tell she's grown worried by the way she nibbles her lip.

"Today should be a celebration, Marina."

"A celebration of how many times I beat you at chess?"

"You know what I mean."

She sighs, annoyed. "I don't want to talk about today. Quit distracting me."

"Then, let's talk hypotheticals. *If* we celebrated, what do you worry might happen?"

"If," she groans. "Anything could happen, Grady."

"Have you ever had a good one?"

"A good *today*? Um... a few when I was young."

"What were they like?"

She leans back, folding her arms over her chest. "Mom took me to the North Carolina Zoo once. She gave me a cute pink button with BDAY GIRL written on it, so all day people said... well, you know. Another time, she gave me her grandmother's quilt as a present."

"The one on our bed?"

"Yep. I love that quilt."

"So, the day isn't always unlucky?" I reason.

She rolls her eyes. "Grady, can't we just have a quiet Saturday?"

"Aren't we?" I challenge. "But to be clear, am I *never* allowed to celebrate my wife on the *one day* that's just about her and us?"

She smirks and scoffs. "I'm not your wife."

"To me, you are. I'd marry you today if you'd let me. No big fuss. Just you and me in our backyard with the rings I bought."

Her brow quirks. "You bought rings?"

"Simple, beautiful wedding bands. Bought them in August, after that weekend at that B&B on Oak Island."

Just bringing up that amazing trip makes her blush and smile.

"I rescued them from an antique store," I add, making her gasp with delight. "I have them whenever you're ready, *if* you're ever ready. Wearing a ring that tells the world we belong to each other would be nice."

Her lip tucks into the other one as she considers this. "I don't know whether to be angry that you did that without me or happy that you still want to marry me."

"Still?"

Her shoulders slump, and her eyes fix on the game. She makes a move, but not a good one. Her eyes roll when she takes her hand off the pawn—she knows it. "You must really want to win, playing the marriage card." She whispers *marriage* like the universe might strike her down for saying it.

"You're the prize I'm after. What'd you mean by *still?*"

She hesitates, giving me an annoyed, urging look to remind me that it's my turn.

"Marina, truth."

Her shoulders bounce in a weak shrug, and her smile vanishes behind uncertainty. "Fine, the truth, but only if you tell me the truth, too. Colin and Tamsyn. Now, Luke and Willow. Your brothers are building families. Does that make you... sad?"

I blanche at the question. "Me? No. Why would it? I've built my family, too."

She slumps. "You've seemed different lately."

"Only because I'm worried about you. Does all this baby talk make *you* sad?"

"Sad for you because I can't give you that," she says, "and sad because everyone thinks it's possible for us. It feels dishonest not to say something, but I don't want to throw a wet blanket over their baby parties. You know?"

"I do know. But Marina, I have everything I need. I get to be with the most brilliant and sexy woman I've ever met. Not only that, I get to be *myself* with the most brilliant and sexy woman I've ever met. Every day with you is a gift. I don't need anything else."

Her eyes water with tears—though I'd never call her a crier, she's become freer with tears since we've been together.

"Unless *you* need something else," I add. "Do you feel like something's missing from our lives?"

"God, no. Are you kidding?" she guffaws. "I'm Tilly's big sister—that's a full-time job right there, making up for lost time with her and Mom. Marigold and I are besties. I'm quickly becoming everyone's favorite pseudo-auntie and sort of sister-in-law. Plus, with the boys at the G&G, I'm overflowing with family. Nothing's missing for me. I am *completely* happy." She swipes the pieces over, giving up on the game. "I only hope that you are."

I smirk at the toppled pieces. "How romantic. Of course, I'm happy. It's funny—we were both just worried about each other."

"I'm glad it was *just* that." She crawls in my direction, weaving through cats and dogs, and edges into my lap, straddling me. "We should talk more. Next time, I'll be upfront with my worries."

"Good. Me, too." I give her a short kiss, wrapping my arms around her. "You know, you don't have to be *pseudo* or *sort of* anything."

She sighs. "I thought you said you didn't need anything else."

"I don't. But I *want* to call you my wife. I *want* to wear rings so the world knows it. I *want* this day to be a celebration. On this day, the universe brought you into the world and, twenty-five years later, brought you forever into mine. Why shouldn't we celebrate it?"

MARNIE

"You're right," I say, breathless and spinning over his words. *He wants to marry me?* After Colin and Tamsyn's Christmas miracle and Luke and Willow's 'accident,' I thought for sure Grady was having baby yearnings. His doting attention upticked significantly, but at the same time, he grew quieter.

Like he felt sorry for me.

Sorry for us.

Sorry for himself.

Sure, I let my curse-minded brain take over at that point. It's hard not to think everything will fall apart when we've had it so, so good. That's been the story of my life.

But that's not our story.

The intense way he stares into my eyes—so loving and familiar —his beautiful words, tender touches, and this lovely home we've created together shore up my belief in something stronger than any supposed curse. True love.

And that love for him swells so intensely just then that I'd do anything he wants.

He's right. Maybe my perspective is cursed rather than the day itself. Yes, one year ago, I nearly died, and part of me did. Everything I thought I wanted was wrecked by chance, and it was the worst day for us both.

But it was also the day we found each other. It was the day I finally belonged to a family after all (though not the family I expected), because he became mine. He fought for me. He comforted me. We bonded together.

"I'm right?" he says, eyeing my lips like he wants to give into them again.

"We should celebrate."

His smile curls up his cheek. "Good."

"We should get married."

His face lights up. "Really? You'll marry me?"

"Yes, darling," I smirk.

"Today?" he asks.

"Today or any day," I say with a kiss.

"Today?" he asks again, with a serious, raspy voice.

My brow shoots up my forehead. "Are *you* saying that can be arranged?"

"You don't even have to leave the house," he grins.

"Eep! You planned it? Arranged it?"

"Just in case."

I melt into his tender kisses.

"Say yes, Marina. Please be my wife."

"Yes, Grady. Absolutely, yes."

The wedding comes to me. Within hours, our cabin fills with our friends and family. Everyone arrives with a contribution—it's a potluck wedding—and nothing is what one would expect.

But that's been us from the beginning.

Mack, Christie, Roy, and Wade bring hay bales and blankets, creating picnic-style seating in the backyard. Elena, Carmela, and Mom provide a buffet-style meal on the back porch, featuring smoked meats and all their best desserts. Peter delivers a replica of the G&G's smoking porch, only with windows overlooking the lake, for our altar. Wren decorates it with gauzy tulle, twinkle lights, and hanging crystals that create prisms in the sunlight. Marigold provides a comic-book-style wedding program that tells the story of Shadow Man and his sunshiny nemesis, Fire-Bright. Luke and Gil team up as deejays. Alice Harvey brings lavender bouquets and arrangements, and my new bestie, Ivy, acts as our official photographer. They set up games as table centerpieces for the reception and put little bowties on the dogs and cats.

Tamsyn and Willow bring a gorgeous a-line, sweetheart, corset dress, off-white and covered in embroidered wildflowers. Mom says it flatters my figure while still making me look like a princess. That's how I feel, too, like I've walked off the page of some fairy tale. But more than that, I stare in the long mirror of our bedroom, surrounded by my favorite women, and I feel confident and empowered.

Mom does my hair, expertly knotting it into an intricate, romantic braided updo with flowers intertwined. Mel does my nails and make-up—she's definitely less of a bulldog now that her best friend is back in her life. Carmela takes care of my *something old* and *something borrowed* by lending me a delicate gold bracelet with multi-colored gems.

Not that I need the tradition, but a little extra luck wouldn't hurt.

Soon, I'm ready.

I couldn't have planned a better wedding. It's more perfect that I didn't for all its delightful surprises. It's everything I love in the place I love. With none of the stress of a traditional wedding—I'm not the go-to girl; I'm the cherished bride. Fussed over. Loved.

Music plays. Wade walks me down the aisle behind Tilly, our flower girl. Christie acts as our officiant. Mack is Grady's best man, and Marigold stands beside me as my maid of honor. Surrounded by our big, beautiful family, I meet the man who changed my story forever on the lake's edge, ready to pledge my love to him *officially*.

With watering eyes, Wade kisses my cheek before moving aside for Grady. He smiles, and I giggle. I can't help it, especially as he wraps his hands around my waist and pulls me close.

His forehead drifts against mine. "My beautiful Marina."

"My handsome Grady."

"Thanks for meeting me here."

I smile sheepishly. "You know I'll meet you anywhere. Thanks for making it easy."

His brow kinks. "Do you like it?"

"I love it." The words escape in a breathless moan, nearly making me tear up, especially at his worried expression when asking the question. "It's truly perfect."

Grady's smile widens, melting my heart into gooey bits at how in love with him I am. Whenever I think, *"Geez, Marnie, in love much?"* my heart answers by falling even more, as if love is this infinitely expanding universe that I'll never stop falling into.

"Shall we begin?" Christie chimes in softly, looking somewhat nervous but sweetly official in his 1950s veiled hat and elegant kimono.

"Okay?" Grady asks me.

"Okay."

We face Christie but keep our arms wrapped around each other. Christie smiles and relaxes into his sweet words about cherishing love and each other and being grateful for every second. I lean my head on Grady's shoulder, and he kisses my forehead.

A small wooden box holds our rings. He shows me both together, wedged into their velvet casing. His is a simple gold band, thick and gently engraved with intertwining leaves, reminding me of the trees around the swamp. Mine is more delicate, rose and yellow gold, interlaced with leaves and gems—one main diamond, many smaller ones, and the rest multicolored.

"Ruby for your hair," he says as he slips it on my finger. "Sapphire for your eyes. Emerald for luck."

I laugh. "It matches my dress."

"I knew it belonged to you the second I saw it," he tells me.

I smile, sliding his ring onto his finger. "Strong and dependable, just like you. I love you, Tripp Grady Tripp."

He laughs. "I love you, Mrs. Marina Tripp."

"Mrs. Strange-Tripp," I correct with a shrug. "I'm embracing the combo. It's been a strange trip, after all."

We kiss, gentle and sweet at first, but it turns into more when he lifts me, crushing me against him and laughing as he swings me around. Our family laughs with us.

Our reception lasts hours with dancing, eating, and, yes, even game-playing. Gorgeous bursts of happiness follow the main one.

Grady and Luke doing *The Thing* with Christie as honorary drummer (who knew?).

Marigold confessing that she hopes Peter asks her to marry him soon.

The late arrival of Marty Tripp—Grady's globe-trotting-for-the-good-of-mankind younger brother.

Lena, Ben, Ruthie, and her friend Adam, arriving from Saddletree Farm and Bakery Café with the most decadent dream cake ever—shaped like a pirate ship, of course.

Mom, telling me that Wade asked her on a date, and she wanted my blessing before saying yes.

Gil, hitting it off very well with Ivy.

And finally, a breakthrough.

"They say things happen in threes," Elena says, casually motioning toward Tamsyn and Willow before giving me and Grady a not-so-subtle wink.

Carmela chuckles. "Wouldn't it be wonderful for the cousins to be in the same class at school?"

"A triple baby shower," Tamsyn coos, rubbing her slightly extended belly.

"Hell, yes," Colin chimes in. "One big party instead of three sounds great to me."

"Enough with the baby pressure," Mom says, eyes cutting in my direction. "It's their wedding day."

"Amen to that!" Mack says.

"Not everyone wants to jump on the baby bandwagon, anyway," Mom says awkwardly.

Elena and Carmela look bothered before Elena says, "Better sooner than later. Marnie's young, but Grady's no spring chicken."

Carmela says, "Can't help the baby talk. It's in the air."

"It is, but not for me." The words slip out nicely, but suddenly. I glance at Grady uneasily as all eyes fall on me. His sexy side smile encourages me that it's okay. "Grady and I have decided not to have children."

"What?" Carmela asks over Elena, who says nearly the same thing.

Smiling, always smiling, I take in my large, beautiful family, knowing it's time. "I'm unable, but even if I could, we wouldn't. We love it for the rest of you, but it's not for us. We're completely happy, exactly as we are."

"And being the coolest aunt and uncle your kids have, no offense to the rest of you," Grady laughs.

"Here, here!" Luke cheers, holding up his glass, and the rest join in. The party resumes with barely a ripple and a future that feels even more hopeful.

GRADY

It's late. The house is finally quiet, the guests gone. Marina and I sit on the back porch, transfixed by the moonlight shimmering across the lake. We're tired but elated, unable to let the night end. She sits on the railing, her back perched against a column. Her dress drapes over the side like a curtain, and her pale skin glows in the moonlight. I twist my wedding band around my finger, grateful and happy.

"It was the perfect day," she says, almost dreamily. "Perfect, Grady. Thank you."

"It's not over yet."

She turns toward me, brow cocked and lips curling into a smile. I know that smile—she's thinking sex. "Just so you know, I'm sleeping in this dress and never taking it off."

I laugh. "Oh, you'll take it off. I'll make sure. But that's not what I mean."

Her head tilts, eyeing me in that skeptical way of hers, like right before I make a move in chess. "Whatever do you mean, then, husband?"

Her giggle feels like magic in my chest. I love hearing her call me husband. "I have a gift for you."

She gapes, her eyes going wide. "This entire day has been a gift for me—"

"For us."

"Grady, you've done too much already."

"I could never do enough for you. And it's not just our wedding day." I reach behind my chair for the wrapped gift behind it. She takes the floral-wrapped rectangle, eyeing it with giddy curiosity before ripping it open.

She runs her fingers over the leather notebook, smiling as she reads the words, "Travel journal" on the front. "It's beautiful."

"Look inside."

The pages flip in her hands until she lands on the first page, where I've handwritten our itinerary for our trip to England.

She gasps, her eyes flipping from me to the extensive list.

"Best practice that terrible British accent of yours, darling," I tell her as she laughs.

"Righty-oh! I'm chuffed, Grady! We're going to England?"

"Two weeks of castles, pubs, cozy villages, and riding the Tube. Whatever you want. Oh, and we're meeting with the game company that's buying *Tickety-Boo*."

"Eep!" She slides off the railing and hops into my lap, kissing me all over my face. "I love it! I can't wait. When are we leaving?"

"Tuesday. I checked your calendar—it'll be fine."

"Oh, I know it will be! I'll make sure. That gives me two full days to pack and—"

I kiss her lips to stop her talking. "Tomorrow. Let's worry about it tomorrow."

"Not worried. Just excited," she corrects, nibbling my bottom lip, "but you're right. You're welcome to get me out of my dress now."

"Yes, wife. I'd love to."

Join my subscribers for FREE BONUS CONTENT and read Marnie & Grady's extra epilogue. Enjoy more laughs with Roy and Christie. Plus, discover Marnie's "strangest case yet" with a sneak peek into my next romance, *Venus Love Trap*, featuring Vee & Henry's story, coming Fall 2025.

jessicasherry.com/bonus-content

From the Author

I didn't know Marnie and Grady's story would be about defying expectations. The story evolved from a simple question: What if a bride gets into a car accident on her wedding day? Then, these beautiful, unique characters kept popping up in my imagination, fully formed like they've always been there, waiting. Marnie, Grady, and their ensemble cast, in one way or another, struggled with what they were "supposed to be" until ultimately finding where they belonged.

That's been me on my writing journey, too. It's taken me decades to grow into my writing and gain confidence in publishing. My underdog characters belong to an underdog writer. But with each book, we get better, and, hopefully, defy the expectation that indie books somehow fall short or don't belong on your bookshelves.

That work isn't done alone. So many wonderful, intelligent, amazing, and talented people have joined me on this journey to bring you *Every Chance After.*

Thanks to Sam of Ink and Laurel for this absolutely breathtaking cover. I still find myself staring at it.

Thanks to Bree, my lovely PA, for helping me stay organized and spreading the word out about my underdog books.

Thanks to my incredible ARC team for reading, reviewing, and promoting my work—I have the best team (I'm not biased).

Special thanks go to my insightful beta readers for commenting, correcting, encouraging, and making me laugh. Mai, Liz, Alexanna, Marcella, Amber, Gina, Nati, Stephanie, and Kristina—I'm still swooning over you!

I'm endlessly grateful for my invincible alpha readers—Tabitha and Julie—who gave me crucial first notes on the story and supported and encouraged me while writing it. And to Jenny, who not only acted as an alpha reader but also professionally edited multiple drafts and stayed up into the wee hours checking my commas and googling strange things on my behalf (broken penis aftercare). Thanks to all my alphas for the free therapy and advice and for making me so happy to have such amazing friends!

Last but never least, my unending thanks go to my husband and publishing partner, Joe, who routinely motivates, inspires, and makes me laugh. Thanks for doing everything that stresses me out, making dinner when I'm lost in a scene, being my number one alpha reader, and taking me on bookish excursions, like book signings, to help me believe that "This will be you someday."

And, thank you, readers, for taking a chance on this indie author!

Big Hugs,

Jessica Sherry

instagram.com/authorjessicasherry

tiktok.com/@authorjessicasherry

Also by Jessica Sherry

YES NO MAYBE

THE SADDLETREE SERIES

ONE THING BETTER

EVERY GOOD THING

THE DELILAH DUFFY MYSTERY SERIES

SEA-DEVIL

LUNA-SEA

SEA-CROSSED

PYRA-SEA

ODD-A-SEA

COMPLETE BOXSET